In 2015 Lin Treadgold returned ⌐ '
in the Netherlands. She gave up h
to be with her husband and his
industry. Now retired, they live in
Jack Russell dog, Dylan.

Since writing her first book in   ⌐,
which was nominated for the RNA ͺ ͺ ͺ ͺ ͺ ͺsayon Award, Lin has
spent her time refurbishing her new home and writing a further two
novels. *The Tanglewood Affair* is her second book. She is presently
researching her third one, centred around World War II and the
war letters her father wrote during his time in a prisoner of war
camp in Italy.

Lin is the group organiser for the Romantic Novelists'
Association, Exeter Chapter, and enjoys art, photography, and
wildlife. After sailing around the world in her youth, she has
acquired plenty of life experiences to assist with her future novels.

For more information about the author and her work visit
www.itslinhere.wordpress.com

Also by the author
Goodbye Henrietta Street

The Tanglewood Affair

LIN TREADGOLD

SilverWood

Published in 2018 by SilverWood Books

SilverWood Books Ltd
14 Small Street, Bristol, BS1 1DE, United Kingdom
www.silverwoodbooks.co.uk

ISBN 978-1-78132-784-5 (paperback)
ISBN 978-1-78132-785-2 (ebook)

British Library Cataloguing in Publication Data
A CIP catalogue record for this book is available from the British Library

Page design and typesetting by SilverWood Books
Printed on responsibly sourced paper

To Ros
and our mutual friend Nicholas

Ode to a Horse in Foal

I recall the late summer nights,
the horses beside us in the stable.
Dirk, his head resting on the door
breathing steam against the twilight air.
The dingy tack room and used tea bags,
stewed again until dawn.
There, you and I sat dreaming.
The leather polish and delicious new mown hay,
flaring our nostrils as we kissed.
And Jonni with his smile, patted Merry,
'Come on old girl. We aren't going to leave you.'

Chapter One

July 1966 – Devon

Mary Hannings couldn't swim. Since the age of ten, the helpless terror of watching her sister drown had kept her away from the swimming pool. Sunday by the lake on the Tanglewood Estate had always been a tradition, but her thoughts of the past made it difficult to be near the water. As long as she kept close to the man she married twenty-five years ago, she knew she'd be fine.

"Gus?" said Mary. "Why are we here?" She gripped his arm as he opened the iron gate to the jetty and gestured for her to go through first. With Gus by her side, she'd felt more confident, but when he'd tried to persuade her to go swimming she couldn't do it and vowed that lessons were out of the question.

"See, the water is reflecting on your pale skin," he said. "You should get out in the sun. You could at least try to look a bit more glamorous, darling. Tie your hair back, you know, wear makeup."

Cosmetics were too false, she thought. She preferred to look natural, unlike cousin Connie, who plastered Max Factor Pan Stick all over her face.

"I thought you loved me enough without." She was reluctant to start another argument on such a lovely day.

In recent months the increased tension between them had escalated and Gus needed to straighten things out. Something had driven him to it and why had he become this other person?

Gus ignored her comment. "We need to talk. Come on, it's fine, you're getting better at this," he said.

Her pale blue eyes met his. "Anyway, I've got a little something for you since we started your therapy. You're doing well." He smiled to reassure her. If he timed it right, she would have an 'accident' and his deception would never be discovered.

A bottle of the best Scotch should do the trick. He prayed she wouldn't make too much noise and her end would be swift. If someone saw him he would pretend she'd fallen and he'd tried to save her. His head was full of his past, present, and future and visions of the dead and dying he'd seen in the last war invaded his mind. The German soldier he had strangled, the woman he'd had to shoot to put her out of her dreadful misery and pain, her dead child in her arms. One more step and it would be over. Richard had said there was to be no remorse, just do it. Today would be no different.

Avoca House stood on the outskirts of Allanfield. An imposing building with tall turrets and a winding driveway leading to enormous iron gates. A black Labrador lay asleep on the granite porch. Lady Mary Hannings gazed out of the dining room window at the far-reaching garden with lawns, trees, and pathways lined with flowers. It made her think about her late father; she knew how much he loved the garden. She planned to take leave whilst Gus was away on a business trip. She'd been thinking about it for a long time. Maybe take a holiday by herself in the sun to give her time to consider what she should do about Richard. Perhaps her late father's house in southern France would be wonderful.

A few days before, her younger brother, Richard, had brought a couple of young girls home. It was their presence and what they were doing that concerned her. It wasn't the white robes they wore and the chanting, but the silly laughter and the pleasurable moaning that made her feel sick. Avoca House was large enough to be a hideout for this kind of behaviour. She gave a deep sigh. She never wanted to be part of the Pagan followers, even though Gus had told her his initiation had been a success. She had scoffed when he walked from room to room in his robes like a priest, wearing a red biretta on his head, and chanting some inharmonious lament. He looked and sounded hideous. How could he believe in all that stuff?

"Mary, dear," he protested. "Being part of the priesthood is paramount to my position in life, my success in society."

She knew well it was a cover-up, an excuse for Richard's endless string of women. It was always hard to prove that Gus was involved, although at times it seemed obvious, but never absolute. He'd always been generous, but something had changed him and she couldn't pinpoint his odd behaviour. Of late, he seemed weaker and followed Richard around like a dog.

Her brother always selected the girls from his group of hippy friends, the 'beautiful people' he called them. The ceremonies were part of his plan to convert them to the ways of Paganism. He could be very persuasive and the young followers were gullible believers. His obsessive study of hypnotism gave her concern. He'd wanted to try it out on her, but she refused. It was all false and only for two reasons—money and sex. How could Richard behave in this way? He'd had a good upbringing, everything he'd ever wanted and now he had a responsible position at the house. He needed a woman in his life to keep him on the straight and narrow, but not like this. Mary shook her head in disbelief. With his good looks and demanding character, he'd always managed to get his own way. She gave a mental sigh. But Gus…always a follower and never a leader, she thought. He'd spent hours gazing into the fire or sitting on the bench in the garden, watching the fountain. He said it confirmed his understanding of the world and the bad times he'd served as a solider, and he often remarked that the earth spoke to him. Mary never understood what he meant. He could no longer be a true Christian and preferred to worship the natural world. On those evenings when he conducted his 'sessions', Mary hid away in her study to paint her watercolours. She preferred to sign the pictures under the pseudonym of Conor Perkins. In that respect, she remained anonymous, which suited her. Yes, she was sure Gus was depressed, but she felt powerless to do anything for him. There was no one out there who could help; a man of his status couldn't be seen as weak.

That evening Gus arrived late. He walked through the great hall, his melancholy building with every step. The inglenook fireplace had a less-than-enthusiastic glow in the hearth. He didn't go straight to bed but lounged on the sofa with a gin and tonic in his hand. He judged the women he'd had at The Lodge. Julie was the best, aged eighteen, or so she said. She was prepared to experiment. And blonde Petra, who called herself 'Hairbell', was sweet and lovely, always trying to please him—she seemed to understand his dilemma. He couldn't stop now; he and Richard had gone too far with their deception, but it was becoming too much. He had to prove his manhood. Erectile dysfunction was no joke to a man of his age. He needed something really exciting to improve his sex life and the girls had boosted his ego, but it was not enough. Mary wasn't exactly…attractive anymore. She did nothing to turn him on. The 'virtual virgin Mary' as he called her. The fertility clinic had told him there would be no children and worst of all he felt he had failed in his job as a husband. He wished close friends would stop feeling sorry for him, telling him he would have made a great father. It made him feel sick at the thought of what might have been. He had failed Mary and the Hannings legacy. Why was he so inadequate at everything he did? He scolded himself at his stupidity and Mary's impatience wasn't helping the situation. She'd talked about adoption and each time he'd refused; he'd wanted his own heir to the Hannings estate.

It wouldn't be long before she knew the whole truth about the rituals and the gambling, and go to the police. As a middle-aged man, his future was melting before him. It seemed he'd taken too many liberties with Avoca House. Something had to be done.

*

A few days later, Richard Millington drove to the house and dashed across to the marbled porch out of the pouring rain. Inside, he caught a glimpse of himself in the mirror and took a comb out of his jacket to tidy his thick brown hair. Barrington, the butler, took his coat and left for the cloakroom.

"We have to talk," he said, short of breath. "The press have got hold of young Marianne Schofield. I have seen to it that she doesn't say anything."

Gus turned to Richard with relief and a warning. "This is a serious matter. We can't keep fobbing these kids off with expensive gifts. Someone will find out and I don't want to be around when they do."

"What about Mary? What will you do about her?"

"She won't say anything either. I'll make sure she doesn't," said Gus.

"I think you have to get away from here and take her with you. You know what I mean?" He spoke in a too-quiet voice. "I think she knows more than you realise."

"She's your bloody sister, for god's sake." Gus reminded him.

"We must keep the priesthood moving forward, but I'm thinking of changing our situation to help keep the movement alive—make it more believable. We need to earn some quick dosh."

When Mary had suggested Gus was depressed, he was having none of 'that stuff', as he put it. He had to find a way to mend his finances. Damn it! He never wanted to be a lord; he and his father were always at loggerheads, he didn't deserve all this wealth, and the house cost a fortune to maintain.

"What do you mean?" Gus stared at his own feet and then gave a quizzical gaze at his brother-in-law whilst waiting for an answer.

"I have this friend who mentors young couples, wanting to marry. I recently took part in one of the rituals. He's also one of our suppliers. We could do that, you know." He paused and then proceeded to explain. "First they must be initiated into the society and we give them a series of tests. Make sure they are prepared to

11

'bare all', so to speak. We can use Avoca House as a handfasting venue and invoke our existing members as high priests. They are the ones that will pay us, don't you see? Just as it was in ancient history. We could do the handfastings here and earn something from it."

"Hell, Richard, yes I know about the ancient rites but never thought..." He paused to reflect. The handfastings would help a lot with costs and perhaps it wasn't such a bad idea if Richard could pull it off. His mind was now racked with confusion; he'd already made his own plans. Richard had convinced him that now was the right time to do something about Mary. She would get in the way. A divorce would do the trick. Adultery, something solid, he thought. She knew too much, he was sure, and she would talk. He had to let Richard do his handfastings and...oh, bloody hell, if only he could disappear and never come back. He was now living too close to the edge of a very high precipice.

"Yes, why not? Make them believe it's all part of the rituals. These little bastards are just the right age to take it all in for the offer of a large cash prize." He grinned.

"Too dangerous,. You're mad." He knew fine well about Richard's taste in teenage girls.

"Too late. We're both in this now. We need cash to buy a stack of 'shit' for the party. The next shipment is coming from Belgium very soon. As far as I'm concerned, there is one person too many in this little group of ours. Get my drift?" Richard shrugged his shoulders. He gestured toward the ceiling where Mary resided and turned to face Gus with a stern look on his face. "There's nothing between you two now, admit it. Listen to me, Gus. Look at me. You have to do this. You have to listen to me, understand? There's nothing between you and Mary anymore. Nothing. You have to do what must be done."

Gus seemed to go into a trance. He calmly agreed and walked away. He was now firmly under Richard's influence.

Richard smiled to himself. All this would soon be his. Gus was easy to manipulate. It was only Mary who would stand in the way.

*

Two weeks later and certain that something was amiss, Mary listened at the dining room door. Richard had invited a young couple home and provided them with an impressive lunch with the best wine, showing them around the grand house to impress. He'd befriended them at a pub in town. The west country was a great place to pick up hippies wanting to earn easy cash for LSD. Mary heard Richard say to the man, "How are you fixed for the Pagan rights? You heard my sermon about it, yes? You are still up for it then?"

The girl chimed in. "It all sounds very daring, doesn't it?"

"Well, if we get paid, then fine. We could have a great honeymoon," said the man.

"Of course," said Richard. "You are also doing this for the pagan gods who want to see you both set up for life together."

The young girl gave a small laugh.

Richard tested the young man standing in front of him.

"Show me what you've got, my son, and I'll make you an offer."

Mary kept listening outside the door as everything went quiet. Her insides pounded with shock at what she heard. This was not the brother she grew up with. Had she misheard him? She listened again and heard Richard complimenting the young man about his manhood. She almost burst through the door with disgust, but thought better of it. Surely, it wasn't real.

"Okay, young lady, they're lovely child-bearing hips you got there and you have all the right credentials." He looked across at the young girl. "I bet, young Stuart here, is very proud of you. We'll sort some dates for the initiation and the mentoring. I'll offer you five grand for the wedding rituals. What do you think? Will it be enough to set you up with a new house?" He gave them an exaggerated warm smile.

"Wow, man," they chorused together. "More than enough." said the young girl.

"However, you have to comply with the rules, though. We're a secret society and although the Rites will be conducted away from the main guests at the wedding, you will have to take the oath and sign a document of consent. You're to tell no one, understand? Absolutely no one. The ancient gods will be proud of you." Richard laid his hands on their heads. "Bless you my children," he smiled.

Mary tip-toed away from the door, with a hand clasped over her mouth. Did Gus know about all this? When he got home she had to confront him. What should she do? Call the police and tell them her brother was a sex maniac? She felt her heart torn out. What would her mother have said? Too shocking to say the least. She had to confront Gus with her discovery.

As the days progressed, Gus had been away and the following morning, Mary sat at breakfast. "Gus, dear, I'm worried about Richard," she said.

Gus snapped. "Not again, please, Mary. It's got nothing to do with you."

"This is serious, Gus, it's about Richard's plan to conduct handfastings here at the house. There was a couple here yesterday and from what I heard, he wasn't planning any ordinary wedding."

Gus looked hard into her eyes. "I *said*, Mary, *this* has nothing to do with you. *Okay?*" He stood and made his way to the great hall. His anger scared her; he never used to talk to her like that.

When Mary saw him carrying a small suitcase on the way to the car, she chased after him. "Where are you going?"

"On a small business trip this evening. I'll be back soon."

"What, *again?* You've only just got home."

"I'll see you before I go. Perhaps we can take a walk. I have things I want to discuss with you." He brushed his dark hair from his eyes. Very soon, he would grow a beard and style his hair longer, like the hippies.

"Gus, what's gone wrong between us? We used to be so close and now I hardly ever see you. You've changed. What the hell's going on?"

"Let's leave it 'til this afternoon okay? I've got something nice to show you. I bought you a present." He tried to sound thoughtful and kind.

Despite her misgivings about her brother, she felt, at least, Gus still had some good points. But had she misunderstood Richard's conversation? No, she knew what she'd heard and it wasn't a conversation she ever imagined could be real.

Gus drove in the direction of Tanglewood Farm so he and Mary could take a walk before he left. In his head were Richard's words, '*You have to do something about Mary*'. He wore driving gloves, and a Harris tweed flat cap. It was early Spring and the breeze flapped his open Barbour jacket as they walked together around the lake.

It was the perfect day for a murder, he thought. '*You have to do this.*' His cousin, Connie, and her band of followers were not at home until the evening to milk the cows. They were far enough away that day for anyone to hear Mary's cry for help. With luck, it would be a few days before she was discovered. Richard had arranged it all and would tell the police she had planned a holiday. The staff knew about it, so there was no reason for doubt. He hoped to make it look like an accident and the police would think he disappeared in case he got blamed. Richard would explain it all; how he was weak and suffered with depression.

Connie was aware of the cult, but she never complained. Richard always made sure she said nothing. Connie's past was precious to her and Richard knew everything. He would tell her husband all about her and elaborate on the truth if she said one word.

Gus' head rang with Richard's words. '*You have to do this; do you hear me?*' He opened the gate to the small jetty and took a bottle from his inside pocket. "Here, something for you, dear. A special malt I got in Scotland. I bought it for you last week for your hunting flask. I know how you love a tipple on your ride. Have a taste. It's very good. Go on try it."

"That's kind of you, Gus. Thank you, dear." She gave him a kiss on the cheek then took a sip. Gus kept his gloves on. "Mm, it's very… very um…earthy tasting, isn't it? A good malt I would say."

Gus laughed and offered her a tot. After a while he urged her to try some more until she felt light headed. He pretended to drink his, but didn't swallow it. He needed a clear head for his plan. "Anyway, I have surprise for you. I got Anita to pack your suitcase. We are going away on a short holiday. I think we both need a break."

"Oh…where are we going?"

"I'm taking you on a surprise trip. You'll soon see."

The small wooden pier led toward the centre of the lake and she gave a tentative glance at the fish swimming beneath, but walked on holding the railings until they reached the end with Gus by her side. He kept her talking as they strolled along the pier, but time was not on his side; someone was waiting for him.

She turned quizzically to toward him. "Let's turn around now and go back," she said, losing her confidence at standing on edge of the pier so close to the water. "I'd like to know where you're taking me."

Gus took his chance to trip her up with his foot. He gave her a small push. "Whoops, sorry." A part of him wishing it didn't have to be this way. She fell into the deepest part of the lake. "This is your trip," he called. "Now you can learn to swim." He heard her splashing and calling for him to rescue her, then gave a last glance, and quickly turned away.

Out of shock from the cold water and light-headed from the whisky, she sank beneath the dark brown lake. He felt a torn kind of remorse, but for reasons he didn't understand, he was compelled to do it; something was driving him on. No one would ever know what had really happened. With Richard's help the plan was all in place and it wouldn't be long before the police had their verdict of death by drowning; they would conclude she drank too much and Richard would confirm it. It would look as if she had committed suicide or fallen into the lake whilst under the influence of alcohol. Even if they concluded it was murder they would never find him.

Gus drove his car as far away from Avoca House as soon as possible. He planned to abandon it near a roadside café. Barrington's instructions were to pick him up and drive him to the coast. He must get away, far away, before they discovered Mary floating in the lake. Richard vowed never to tell anyone, on the proviso that he could manage Avoca House as a business. Two years before, the contract he'd signed with his brother-in-law to become the estate manager would make Richard a wealthy caretaker until the house was sold once Gus was pronounced missing presumed dead or in the worst-case scenario, if Gus' plans were rumbled. By that time, Gus would be far away in a hot country never to be seen again. No more business trips and no more Lord Augustus Hannings; he'd find a new name and a new identity. The only person he would miss would be Connie's daughter, young Rosie. He'd spent a lot of time with her when Mary took care of the child. If only he'd had kids of his own, things might have been different. Rosie was special to him; she was like his own daughter after her father left. It had been his fault that his wife couldn't have children; he couldn't stand the humility of it all.

A yacht from Plymouth awaited him and under cover of darkness they landed on the beach in Oostende. Life would never be the same, he thought. New passport, false name he would forget shaving for a while. Thank god for Hugh Miles and Clive Barrington. They owed him this from the war time for saving their lives at Dunkirk. After he returned from the war, the army didn't seem to care anymore. There had been nothing on the news about Mary's death. He hoped they hadn't found her yet.

He walked along the beach until he met Miles, who piloted a small plane bound for Lisbon airport. On arrival at a private airfield they shook hands and parted. He was now Marcus Dawson. Occupation: Farmer, Nova Lisboa, Angola.

Chapter Two

Jess – Spring 1976

I had been here many times, but today my senses flowed with anxiety. As much as I needed the job, would my life be different if I reinvented myself?

After a four-month absence, it was time to get back to work. I arranged to meet with agency boss, Verity Cresswell. My appointment led me to her new office in Middlesbrough, and as the lift reached the third floor, I hoped that by the end of the morning I still had the will to work again, especially after my father had just passed away a few months before. My ever-increasing curiosity and zest for life had kept me in a positive light, but it was my confidence that needed repairing. I had to get away from all the misery of a cold northern winter and losing my dad. Living at home had depressed me and besides, my sister Anna was more than capable of taking care of Mum.

It was one of those mornings where I wished I had stayed in bed. I hadn't expected Verity to provide a life changing opportunity, but it seemed that my phone call had her hell-bent on sending me somewhere with a bit of a challenge. She'd always been helpful to me and I trusted her to come up with something worthwhile. However, her intentions for my next assignment had me feeling nervous again. For my own good, it seemed she wanted to send me on a long working holiday and there was a certain obligation not to disappoint her.

"Fill out this form for me, please. Would you mind?"

I bent over the desk to complete the details *Name: Jessica Stamp—Age 29* and circled the word 'single'. Only my address had changed since Tim and I split up. I signed and dated the form: 12 April 1976.

"Okay, this is what I'd like you to do. I've found you a PA job down south, with a Ford franchise. You've done this before, so I know it would be perfect for you. We have a parent company down there, and I spoke with my colleague, Pauline Acton. She said the position is urgent and she wants someone to fill the vacancy after Easter. I was on the phone to them about another contract and Pauline mentioned this job. I thought about you."

"So where is this place?"

"Not far from the seaside resort of Lyme Regis and outside of Axminster on the Devon border. I *know* it's a long way from home, but I took a chance on this one. I'm sure you'll love it," she enthused. "The coast and countryside are wonderful. In view of your circumstances, it might be good for you to get away." She smiled and turned to a magazine on her desk. "Here, you may want to look at this."

From a copy of *The Lady*, she handed me a pen-circled advert.

"I was reading through the ads yesterday with you in mind. This house sounds like the perfect place to gather your thoughts. Why not give it a try? You never know it might change your life." She gave a quiet laugh.

My eyes skimmed the words. *Room for Rent. 14th-century farmhouse, close to Lyme Regis. Suitable for single professional person. £15pw.*

"Oh my, that sounds lovely. I'll phone them. I need this and, you're right, why not?"

Nothing ventured…as my dear dad used to say.

A few days later I drove four hundred miles to the south-west of England in pursuit of a new life.

I opened the car window for a blast of fresh air, much to the annoyance of my route map which flapped in the breeze. On passing the sign for Lyme Regis it seemed that the April showers had turned the grass greener overnight. Why was I doing all this? Was it for Dad? My split from Tim? Or purely for selfish little me? Give it time, I thought, give it time.

Mid-afternoon and the shimmering azure sea rolled back and forth along the shore. My eyes traced a young couple strolling arm-in-arm on the beach. Their dogs barked and yapped as they bounded along the water's edge, which made me smile.

I stopped outside Blue Horizons guesthouse to take in the salt air. The view from the small front garden overlooked the sea and seemed a thousand miles from my usual seaside haunts on the North-East coast. The sea was bluer, for a start. The window boxes, full of spring flowers, provided the much-needed colour in my life. The sign on the bell said *push* and the owner answered the door. She escorted me inside and we climbed the winding staircase to the next floor.

"I thought you'd like a room with a view. Breakfast is from 7.30 in the morning. We serve full English, but there's a menu as well."

"Thanks." She closed the door behind her. All I needed now was a lie down and a spot of shut eye.

I set the clock and took a nap for what seemed like ten minutes until the alarm told me otherwise and, with some confusion, I awoke, to the sound of herring gulls calling over the bay.

My appointment with the owner of the house, the one in the advert, was in less than an hour. There wasn't much time between now and Tuesday to find somewhere to live, so I snatched the car keys from the table. The journey was a twenty-minute drive between the guest house and Tanglewood Farm and I didn't want to be late.

The road to Tanglewood led me through a tunnel of beech and oak woodland and a row of whitewashed thatched cottages nestled in neat gardens. Virginia creeper and clematis clung to the walls—

a world away from my usual jobs in industrial Middlesbrough. Had the eagerness to come here overtaken my common sense? I felt the guilt at leaving Mum and Anna behind, but all this was new and naturally there were deep concerns, especially when I didn't know anyone. I felt my brain would burst if I didn't stop doubting myself.

The recent weather forecast claimed we were due a hot summer. I imagined wearing a bikini top and shorts, drinking cola, and listening to the sound of disco music playing on the promenade. My senses picked up the imaginary sickly aroma of candyfloss mingling with onions in hot dogs along the sea shore, but Lyme Regis didn't seem to fit that description. From what I'd seen it was a cosy seaside place with bobbing boats, cafes, pubs and ice creams and lots of people window shopping on the hilly street.

At the end of the small lane off the main road, the tarmac had run out of tar and the 'mac' became 'muddy access'. I stopped the car to open a five-bar gate. It groaned when I pushed it toward the other side.

I drove on and glimpsed through an opening in the trees. There stood an impressive house, built of timber, tiles, and red brick. I gazed in awe of the mediaeval architecture. A lofty double chimney stood tall in the middle of a sagging roof and the mullion windows reflected the trees. I hadn't expected *this*. It looked rustic and perfect but after further scrutiny—not so perfect. The gutter sagged and a lick of paint was required here and there. I had driven through the most delightful countryside in England, tall and gracious trees, woodlands, grasslands, and coastal pastures, and now this…a charming place on the edge of a wood, a retreat. It was the kind of home you always dreamed of and knew you could never afford.

Only the sound of happy magpies and the clunk of my car door echoed over the parkland. I couldn't help but stare. I wanted to share all this with Mum and Anna, but the sudden realisation I was alone pulled me back to reality.

I became aware of my own footsteps crunching over the stony pathway. The tangled ivy on the wall at the front of the house hid a solid oak door, but there didn't seem to be a bell to press. After knocking and waiting, no one answered. A quick sneak around the back led me to an open door, so I pushed it wider to listen.

"Hello, is anyone there? Hell-o." I stood, waiting. Waiting for the sound of footsteps that never materialised.

A blackbird flew onto the garden wall and gave a loud alarm call. On the ground rested a pair of gardening gloves, palms crossed in an offering. A knife and a tool for scraping out the weeds between the paving slabs lay beside the gloves. Whoever had been gardening must have abandoned the job, and everything felt too 'Marie Celeste'. A patch of ground for growing herbs lay nearby, each herb labelled with a wooden stake. The magpies chattered again or were they laughing?

I trudged back to the car and folded the map only to discover a forgotten Marathon on the brink of meltdown in the glove compartment. The temptation was too great. How much longer would I have to wait before anyone came? After checking my watch, I walked back to the gate. Yes, Tanglewood Farm on the nameplate, for sure. So, Mrs Dijkman, where—are—you? She'd told me on the phone her surname was Dutch. She seemed talkative and, after making the appointment, why hadn't she turned up? Travelling all this way had been difficult enough for one day. My life was about to change and I didn't expect to be let down before I'd been given the chance.

Forty minutes later and with a spot of sunbathing into the bargain, Mrs D had let me down. My reflection in the wing mirror showed chocolate on my lips, so I used the tissue in my pocket.

I'd waited long enough. The time had come for me to return to Lyme Regis and with a heavy sigh I realised that things weren't going according to plan. It was best to phone her later. There could be a feasible excuse. Sure, it was disappointing, but as I drove toward the gate, I stopped to listen and heard the sound of an engine. In the distance, a woman came toward me driving a battered green Land Rover, which bounced over the holes in the track. She gave a smile, and we both leaned out of our respective windows. Why had she kept me waiting?

"Hello, dear. Sorry I'm late—got held up with the shopping and traffic in Axminster—dreadful." She shook her head. "There was an accident. It was good of you to wait. You'll want to view the room, I assume—you must be Jessica?"

I took a breath and felt like hugging myself with relief at her arrival.

"Yes, that's right." If I hadn't been Jessica, how would she have coped with her embarrassment? I thought.

"What a lovely name, dear. I'm Connie Dijkman."

I admired the way she spoke. Like the Queen.

The clouds parted to reveal the warm sun, which caused her to squint down her long nose and through obvious false eyelashes.

"Follow me up to the house and I'll show you the room." She beamed as if I was the only person she'd seen all day. Connie's long greying hair blew around her face in wisps. I visualised her as a young girl with sleek black hair falling over her shoulders. Her thin face was stretched by the comb at the back of her head which was probably a way of disguising her wrinkles. She wore red lipstick and pencilled-in eyebrows, reminiscent of an ageing, but still attractive, film star; a meld of Greta Garbo and Gypsy Rose Lee. I couldn't help admire her theatrical personality and reckoned she must have been in her mid-fifties.

"Thanks. I'll turn the car around," I said, but doubted she heard me above the diesel roar of the Land Rover. As I turned the car on the grass, the ground was wet and getting stuck in the mud was not going to make my day. Ahead, Connie removed her shopping as I pulled up at the entrance to the house. She placed a large hat, braided with flowers, on her head and tied it with a long trailing silk scarf under her chin. As she opened the back door of the Land Rover, she revealed a cross-Alsatian dog, asleep on a blanket. His ear was torn, and his rib cage, rising, falling, with laboured breath. Connie scuffed her way toward the house with a slight stoop whilst carrying her heavy shopping bags. I glanced at her green wellies. A hole in the side of the boot accommodated a large bunion on her toe. Her denim midi-skirt flapped as the tops of her boots hit the hem. "Come on, Alvin, let's go," she called. The reluctant animal slid from his resting place.

Connie didn't wait for me as she trudged over the loose stones. The rear door of the Land Rover was still open and the equipment in the back caught my eye in the place where the dog had been sitting. Blankets, shears, spades, and boxes of farm tools filled the vehicle.

I followed the sound of her gravel-trodden footsteps with the dog panting at her heels and caught up behind her.

"Come on, Alvin, old thing, get in the house. Come in, dear, come in. I'm sorry you had to wait so long for me. Would you like some tea?"

She gave a weary sigh as she placed her bags inside the door. If she hadn't walked so far ahead, I would have offered to carry them for her.

I followed her into the kitchen and noted bunches of drying herbs and flowers, hung on string and tied to the oak beams above me. A coal-fired cooking range stood inside the inglenook fireplace with a brass coalscuttle on the stone floor. A stockpile of *Horse and Hound* magazines lay in one corner and fresh daffodils stood in an undersized vase. The kitchen wasn't pristine and well kept, but quaint with washed-up pans on the wooden drainer. I took in the charm of the old place; it seemed very homely and welcoming. Connie removed her hat and placed it on a barstool.

I sat in silence whilst she poured water into the teapot from the simmering kettle on the stove. She searched for cups and saucers in the cupboards and set the tray. It seemed they were her best Royal Worcester. I smiled to myself. My grandmother used to have an identical set.

"Milk, dear? It's from the goat."

She poured the milk into her cup then paused waiting for me to answer.

"No, thanks." I had once tasted goat's milk and didn't like it.

"My grandparents had a farm when I was a teenager. It was more of a smallholding. They had their share of dramas when they were out on the moor. It was never a good situation in the winter, especially with the sheep, they often got snowed in."

Connie smiled as if she well understood the dilemma.

My eyes searched the room as Connie busied herself. The overwhelming feelings of 'something that couldn't be explained' hovered over me, but there was nothing to worry about, so why did I feel this way? I suppose I wasn't used to such wealth and history surrounding me after living in a modern three-up two-down for most of my life.

I was naturally curious about Connie, and glanced at her left hand for signs of a Mr Dijkman, but she wore no rings.

She darted me a smile as we sipped our tea. "How was the journey? You must have set out very early this morning."

"Yes, 5am. It was fine, but I'm used to driving…" I stifled a yawn, "…often working up north in Newcastle."

I mentioned Yorkshire, the Dales, and the Moors and she listened as I explained about my new temping job at the garage.

"I want to gain as many life experiences as I can. It's only now that I've started branching out in my life and going further afield. I promised my father I wouldn't hang around and do nothing. I am a free bird right now, no ties. I hope this position at the garage may be a stepping stone for me."

"Jolly good idea, so that's why you've come this far. I understand. It's the university of life when you travel," she enthused. "As a child, I lived on the Isle of Skye. Daddy always had his colleagues for dinner at weekends and we used to dance the Gay Gordons around the entrance hall; I loved it. He was very musical and played the bagpipes as well as the piano."

I stifled another yawn, although her story seemed interesting.

"...my sister and I, we had a nanny and a governess; we never went to a private school until we were older. I went to Roedean School in Sussex. It was all home education in those days and we both found it hard to adjust when it was time to leave for the mainland. We were far away from our parents." Connie supped her tea with a distant expression. "I hardly saw my mother, she always seemed to push us on to Nanny Ferguson who was rather strict with our upbringing."

I began to relax but wished I could get on with seeing the room. For a moment, I wanted to close my eyes, it had been a long day.

"...then the war came—everything changed. It flipped our lives like a tossed coin." She paused for a moment before she took another sip of tea. "I suppose we were rather isolated on Skye... but we had fun. We used to go riding over the glens and each had a pony of our own. From my bedroom window we had the most wonderful views of the Cuillin Mountains."

"It sounds lovely," I replied wishing to hear more, but tiredness called me back to reality. I tried to bring Connie around to the subject of the room.

"Tell me about this house, it must be teeming with history." I referred to the 14th century bit in the advert.

"Yes, that's true. The house has been in my family for the last four generations. My husband was an artist, and also an art dealer, but we've been divorced many years. I would like to have changed my name, but never got around to it." She turned her gaze to the floor.

"Oh—I see." I said, not *really* seeing her point.

"Theo, my ex, lives in Holland and Rosie, my daughter, doesn't see her father anymore." She gave a sigh and raised a hand of dismissal.

I knew there was something missing and it seemed I was right.

"You see, Theo was from an aristocratic Dutch family, a very successful art dealer. He also inherited his father's estate. It was my mother's idea we should get to know each other after…I mean, that was after the war. We were in London for a while. My father had three houses; one in the city, this one, and the one on Skye. Theo left Tanglewood when Rosie was younger and returned to his own country and we divorced. He kind of drifted away from us. You know, Jess, I try to enjoy myself, otherwise if I don't, someone else will surely come and take it away." She moved her head and sighed, almost defiant of her past. "My heart is with the animals, the nature and the land." At last she paused for breath. "I hope you will come and stay with us. It's a lovely place to live."

I realised perhaps we both had something in common. "Yes, it sounds as though you've had an interesting life. I agree, it *is* lovely. I am into nature, too and I love animals. I've only just arrived, so I look forward to exploring more of it. To hear you talk about your life in that way makes me realise there are lots of other things to see and do and I should get on and do it," I exclaimed.

Connie nodded and raised her cup in agreement. "You have age on your side, my dear, and if you love animals you have come to the right place."

I had only been there half an hour and already Connie had provided me with her life story. I couldn't stop her, but it was interesting to know something of the family background. I sipped my tea, not wishing to appear impolite. Lapsang Souchong wasn't my taste in tea at all, I thought.

Connie, at last, changed the subject. "We should go upstairs now." She checked the clock on the wall. "'The Household Cavalry' will be back in an hour, so we have time to chat. Sorry I was late. I hope the room is what you're looking for."

Household Cavalry? "There are others living here?" I asked.

"Oh yes, Rosie, of course…" Connie counted on her fingers, "…then Jonni, Hans…and Ewan, who has lots of chickens." She smiled. "On the other part of the estate, there's a young couple who rent a cottage. You'll not be short of company here, that's for sure."

"Are they *all* your family, Connie?"

"Oh, my dear, heavens no, they work on the farm. Jonni is the herdsman, Hans does the machinery and manual labour, Ewan was studying philosophy until recently but, sadly, he gave up…" Connie paused for a moment and seemed despairing. "…and Rosie runs the stables with him. I never invited them all here," she laughed. "They turned up one day and kind of stayed when we needed the help. You don't have to do any of that though. You told me you have a job at Parson's garage. I know Mark, the director, he's quite a character."

We left the kitchen and stepped into a hallway. A red wall-to-wall carpet lined the floor. My attention was drawn to the tracks of the upright vacuum cleaner; someone had made a token job of hoovering the dog hairs.

I followed Connie up the narrow staircase; the oak treads creaked as I grabbed the marine rope functioning as a handrail. "Watch how you go, dear," she announced. "The stairs are very steep. It's a Grade II listed, so we can't do much to modernise it—that dreadful double glazing isn't allowed on these windows. It would spoil the look of the house."

I felt my leg muscles tense as we climbed the creaking staircase. We reached the top where the red carpet continued, leading the way into a bathroom. Why would we want to walk through the bathroom first? Beyond, another door led to the bedroom. Connie explained how to put the small metal stick on a chain in the hole to stop the latch from opening. "Don't worry no one else uses this bathroom, it will be for you only," she announced.

Glad to hear it, I thought.

With the faint odour of fresh paint, it seemed obvious the room had been decorated. Chintz material hung from a central point on the ceiling to all four corners, as if we stood under a canvas of flowers, reminding me of my old dolls' house. In the centre of the room, against the wall, stood a double bed draped with a bedspread complementing the décor. A bit too flowery for my taste, but I reckoned I could live with it. On the walls, my eyes fixed on the portraits. A label under each picture confirmed they were lords and dukes from the past. I admired this spacious room with a green velvet chaise-longue in the far corner. Someone had plumped the faded green and yellow cushions. The antique furniture and historical pictures led me back to the story of her family background. I opted instead to enquire about the rent.

"So…how much did you say you charge for the room?"

"It's £15 per week. We share the cost of electricity. It's a very cold house in winter and the central heating isn't that good. It's a big house and probably not what you are used to. Will that work for you, my dear?"

"Yes, I think so—and when do you want the rent?"

"Is weekly and in cash okay?" replied Connie. "I think it may be easier for both of us."

I paused to think. Why did she need to rent out the room, especially as she seemed to be so wealthy? Maybe that was the reason she had wealth because of her ability to keep her affairs in order. I would find out soon enough, no doubt.

"Ok, I'll take it."

With all these folks living here, I hoped to enjoy myself again. At least, I wouldn't be lonely and if it didn't work out, it would give me a few weeks' grace to find somewhere else to live.

"When would you like to move in?" she asked, stroking back her wispy hair.

"Tomorrow? I mean, it's Good Friday and it'll give me a chance to settle down. I start work on Tuesday after the bank holiday."

"Of course, my dear, it sounds wonderful. I love having young people around me. I'll get the bed made up."

"Oh, don't worry, Connie, my own bedding is in the car."

"Oh, okay—if you're sure…" She smiled.

We returned to the stairs, and I followed her. Next to the bath-room was another room; someone moved around inside. Ahead, the long corridor led to where I assumed Connie resided.

As we entered the hall, she guided me into the oak-beamed

lounge where another enormous inglenook fireplace dominated the room and cold wood ash lay in the hearth. Two large sofas covered by throw-over blankets stood either side of the fireplace and on the walls hung portraits of gentry. Connie ushered me to the kitchen where I sensed heavy footsteps.

"Oh hello, Rosie darling, glad you're back. I'd like you to meet Jessica, she's come to view the room." Connie picked up her handbag from the worktop and clutched it close to her. Rosie gave me a welcoming smile. Her light-brown hair hung down her back in a long single plait. Between her lips was a thin self-rolled cigarette; she sucked in her cheeks to keep it alight. She wore jodhpurs and on her feet a pair of black Dutch-style clogs, which tapped over the hollow tiles as she walked. "Hello, Jessica. Are you coming to live with us?"

"Yes, I've accepted your mum's offer and made arrangements to move in tomorrow…and please, call me Jess." I didn't really want to sound formal.

"I hope you know what you're letting yourself in for, we're one big family." Rosie gave a broad smile.

I liked her personality, but her comment jolted me. Was I going to fit in here?

"I'm afraid things are probably not what you're used to, but give it time, we all mean well, don't we, Mum?" Rosie gave her mother a knowing look.

The phone rang and Connie strode into the hall to answer it.

"Tanglewood Farm. Hello. Oh, it's you, Jonni. What's happened? You're where? Okay, I'll be down soon."

"Do you like horses?" Rosie poured orange juice into a glass. "We own the riding school along the lane behind the house."

My ears pricked with interest. "Yes, sure. My sister and I used to ride, but that was when we were teenagers."

"Well, I think you'll discover our lifestyle is somewhat basic and unconventional but I suppose we make up for it in other ways. If you like riding, we can provide you with a horse any time you wish."

Rosie clogged her way across the kitchen floor and plucked a bread knife from the drawer. She carved a doorstep slice of brown bread and pushed it into the toaster. I watched as she peeled a banana, then reached for a jar of peanut butter from the cupboard. When the toast popped, she mixed the ingredients together in a mash to spread on her toast.

Connie shuffled her feet over the floor. Only then did I notice she wore pink fluffy slippers as she hurried to put the shopping into the cupboards. Her calm demeanour seemed to have changed after the phone call. "Sorry, ladies, I'll have to dash; I must go and meet the vet. That was Jonni on the phone; a difficult birth, he's called the vet in."

Rosie rolled her eyes as daughters do when their mother is doing something embarrassing. "See you later," Connie called as she collected her shawl.

I glanced again at Rosie. It was hard to tell her age. Around twenty-two or three? Her weathered cheeks and sweet smile gave the impression she had an older face on young shoulders. Connie waved as she hurriedly left. "Bye, Jessica. See you tomorrow afternoon—is that okay?"

"Yes, fine. Thanks, Connie, for everything." I had visions of her in those pink slippers, scrambling to pull a calf from the back end of a cow. I didn't get the chance to tell her she was still wearing them, but who was I to say? I wanted to giggle.

"Mum," Rosie called, "bring some butter please when you go into the village, we're running out, the shop closes at seven on Fridays."

Connie had already closed the latch on the door and walked briskly past the kitchen window on her way to the cowshed.

"I hope she heard me." Rosie raised her eyebrows. "Sometimes I despair," she announced, shaking her head.

Perhaps the mild discord was supposed to let me see how it was around here.

"What's the routine, is there much to do in the evenings?" I asked.

"Not really. We have the local pub and a restaurant up the road, but we make our own entertainment and I'm getting married soon. We're having a pagan wedding."

"Congratulations. I hope you have a wonderful day." I wasn't sure what it entailed, this pagan wedding.

"The ceremony will be held in the park, here at the farm, with lots of people. You can join in if you're still here. Ewan and I, we're learning the pagan rituals—although…" Rosie swallowed her words, "…it's a busy time, but Ewan wants this to be a special day for both of us."

She gave a very deep sigh, and it struck me that something bothered her. *Pagan wedding, eh?* I tried to imagine her in a wedding gown and mingling with the posh guests, but for the moment, nothing came to mind.

I took the car keys from my shoulder bag and my eyes fixed briefly upon Rosie's finger; she had a piece of string knotted around it. I could only assume that due to working at the stables, she didn't want to spoil her engagement ring.

"I must go now. I've loads to think about before I come over tomorrow; I've had a very long journey. I'll see you soon."

My skin prickled as I opened the back door and into the fresh air. I wasn't sure whether to laugh or be afraid of myself. At least, if things didn't turn out, I had the option to leave. I could be living with the Addams family for what it was worth, but as I stood outside, I felt a belonging to this lovely scenery and the sounds of the countryside; perhaps my apprehension was unfounded.

I returned to the car and drove back to Lyme Regis and my view of the sea. There were moments like these when I wish my dad were here. He was always my protector. As I drove toward the coast, thoughts of our family life came to mind. The days we had spent in Scarborough sitting on the beach, eating our ice creams, and Anna harping on about wanting to build a huge sandcastle. Family life had meant so much to us all. I suppose I missed all that with Tim. I had made a huge mistake in the last five years and my concern was that I was about to make another one.

I turned off the main road toward Lyme Regis and, on opening the window, the sea air wafted through the car. With thoughts of childhood days, I remembered to phone Mum; her voice would be a comfort.

On arrival, I found the phone at the bottom of the stairs in a sort of broom cupboard with a glass window on the door. The words, *Guest Telephone*, were transferred on the glass. I dialled the number and Mum answered.

"Hi, Mum. How are you? I got here, although it was a long journey."

"I was worried about you, pet—all that driving. How are you? Tired I assume?"

I knew she hadn't been so depressed in the last few weeks. She was learning to cope without Dad; it had all been a shocking and difficult experience. He was too young to die at fifty-nine. We loved him a lot and he was always very supportive of 'his girls'.

"Fine. Yes, Tanglewood is lovely. It's an old farmhouse with lots of interesting people; I don't think I'll be lonely." My voice must have sounded cheerful and positive as Mum responded likewise.

"Oh good. How exciting. Glad it's working out for you, love."

We chatted further about the journey and my meeting in town on Tuesday with the agency boss in Axminster. I heard voices in the background, and then Anna spoke.

"Hi, Sis. Yes, we're doing fine; are you? I'm pleased we managed to sort everything before you left. How was the journey – did it take you long? Was the Viva okay?"

"Just under eight hours. I'm shattered, but I took a couple of breaks along the way and listened to the radio. The car was fine. The roads were very good, with the new motorways. How do you feel about me being away for eight months, eh?"

"I sometimes wish I had your confidence. Now you're not here, I get all Mum's attention. I'm not sure if it's a good thing or bad."

She giggled. "We'll see you soon, but you're such a long way from us. We'll miss you. Mum wants you to be happy, that's all. Maybe we can meet somewhere for a couple of days, eh? We could come on the train to London."

I felt Anna's urgency in case she couldn't finish her conversation before the pips sounded. She always flitted through her words trying to cram every last breath into her phone call in case she missed something. This was so typical of Anna.

"That's a good idea. Anyway," I said, "if you need to talk, call me—okay?" I was comforted by her voice. There had rarely been sibling rivalry between us over the years. Her cheerful personality always gave me confidence. She was not only my sister, but my best friend too.

Before the call ended, I gave Anna the Axminster STD code and phone number for Tanglewood.

"Come back and see us soon, Jess, and phone as much as you can, okay?"

"Will do. Take care of yourselves. I won't forget Mum's birthday. Bye, Mum," I called. She took the receiver from Anna.

"Bye, Jess love, and don't worry. Let us know how you get on."

The pips cut in and as much as I wanted to put more money into the box, I would have had to scramble around my purse to find enough change.

Mum had sounded more cheerful in recent weeks. Anna and I did our best to keep her occupied. Our parents always pushed us forward in life, which had been a good thing, but I consoled myself with the fact that leaving home was the right thing to do. Having two of us fussing over Mum, at this time, was not ideal anymore. It was only a matter of time now to get used to being on my own.

Chapter Three

The first week of a new life. I was doing my best to stay calm, but the challenge was beginning to show. I tried to smile but it wasn't working yet.

I gazed from the window toward The Cobb where the many coloured fishing vessels were protected by the curved harbour wall. There were beach huts painted in striking pink, blue, and yellow in a neat line along the promenade. On the way into town I'd seen elegant Regency villas with bow windows and bull's-eye glass. I checked my watch, time to leave.

Returning to the car, I drove down the hill and took a last look at the town before moving on. I noted the bank, and a bakery where the pungent aroma of baking bread and pasties wafted across the road. It was time to draw myself away.

After turning off the main road toward Five Acres Lane I felt a sense of anticipation. What did Tanglewood hold for me?

A curtain, waving in the breeze, attracted my attention to the open window of my new room. In the distance, a man with a dog walked along the edge of the grassy meadow. I stopped the car and opened the door, but decided to wait and say hello. The grey-and-white Border Collie had seen me first and came running toward me; she lay at my feet in a submissive pose. As the man came closer, our eyes met, and he smiled. His soft voice, under rustling trees, made me listen hard to his words.

"She likes you, her name is Ruby Tuesday—Rubes for short.

I'm a fan of the singer Melanie Safka…and the Rolling Stones."

He spoke with an educated voice and I felt we had known each other for longer than a fleeting moment. I knelt to pat Ruby and she licked my face.

"I can tell you like dogs," he said with a smile.

"Yes, we used to have a dog; she died when I was twenty-one." A dog would have been a comfort to Mum when Anna was at work, I thought.

He towered above me as I stood and our eyes met. I guessed he was in his early thirties, I wasn't sure, as his face seemed weather-beaten. Unruly curls bubbled from under the brim of his leather hat, and his dark green jumper, a little worse for wear, was daubed in unmentionable stains; pieces of straw were tangled with the knitting. There was something very welcoming about him and I couldn't explain. His gaze followed me as if studying my face as he spoke.

"You must be Jessica?"

"Yes, that's me, and you are?"

"Jonni Holbrook, I'm the herdsman at Tanglewood."

His handshake was firm and warm and I felt a twinge of pleasure.

"Ah yes, Connie mentioned you."

So, this is the famous Jonni. Mm…

"I hope what she told you was all good." He grinned.

"I think Ruby is lovely, perhaps I can take her for a walk sometime."

"Well she is a farm dog and isn't keen to go walking on the lead. Like all dogs she can be a bit naughty at times."

I laughed at his comment and stroked Ruby again.

"Please, call me Jess. Your dad says you're a naughty girl, but I don't believe him." I looked Ruby in the eyes and gave her a gentle pat on her back.

"Connie told me to expect you. I'm afraid she's not at home just now. I'm supposed to be looking out for you; I hope I wasn't too late."

"No—not at all. I'm pleased to meet you."

"Do you need help with your luggage?"

"Funnily enough, I was about to ask for some help." I grinned. "Would you mind? It's quite a climb up there, isn't it?"

He kept smiling at me and I am sure I must have blushed. I was aware of how my thoughts were easily distracted. He seemed familiar and I realised, with that hairstyle and blue eyes of his, how much he looked like the singer David Essex.

"Here, let me help you carry *that* one." He pointed to the largest of the suitcases.

We climbed the steep stairs, and the time had come to apologise. "Sorry about the weight, I brought a lot of stuff."

"That's okay, Jess, always glad to help. You know, it's a great place here, I'm sure you'll enjoy your time on the farm. If you need anything, come to me, won't you? Connie always puts me in charge of the guests, although I can't think why." He puckered his brow. "You'll find the way we do things here is probably not what you're used to, but I am glad to help. Connie keeps ungodly hours—I'm afraid you won't see much of her."

He placed the suitcase on the wooden floor and puffed out his cheeks.

"Any more to come?" he asked.

We did two more trips up the stairs. I felt I had imposed on his goodwill long enough.

"Do I give you a tip now?" I teased.

He thought about it and laughed through his words. "Another time, eh?"

I gazed at my luggage and allowed myself a mental sigh.

"Thanks a lot for your help. I met Rosie yesterday. She warned me that life on the farm won't be what I'm used to."

"I'm sure you'll be fine. I can show you the cows and sheep but to be honest, it's not very entertaining, and we don't get a lot of free time. Connie always has a job ready and waiting." He rolled his eyes and frowned.

I gazed around the room with ideas on how I could re-arrange the furniture. I felt Connie wouldn't mind. After all, this was now my room for the duration.

"You look after the cows, eh? Interesting job, is it?"

"I do my best although…" he paused "…it's the winter that gets rough, but we keep the cows indoors, so it's not too bad. Connie is very keen on animal welfare; it's one of her attributes."

"Have you any hobbies?" I asked, for the want of making conversation.

"Hobbies? No, I don't go out much. It's a very quiet village and only the pub to rely on. There's Axminster and Lyme Regis, of course. But I'm glad you came to stay. It may help to liven up the place and it'll be someone different to talk to."

"I'm going to be working at the Ford garage near Axminster."

"Yes, I heard. I know the manager, *vaguely*. Connie also knows him, but she's friends with everyone around here; the couple at the corner shop, the guy from the local garage, the vet, the butcher, the baker and probably the candlestick maker." He raised his eyebrows to wait for my response.

"Oh, really?"

"Any more stuff left in the car?" he asked.

"No, I think I've got it all now, thanks."

"I'm going downstairs to put the kettle on. Would you like some tea, Jess?"

"I thought you'd never ask." I grinned but scolded myself; perhaps I had been too forward.

Jonni laughed. "You've got a sense of humour, too—we could do with some more of that around here as well."

I loved the support and kindness Jonni had shown and the way he'd listened intently to my chatty conversation. I relaxed, and with a sigh of relief, followed him downstairs. He showed me around the kitchen and told me which cupboards I should use to store my own food.

"And the fridge is over here." He pointed to an old oversized American-style fridge in the far corner of the room. "And here's the tea caddy. Look…in my cupboard here, I've got Tetley tea, not that China stuff Connie uses, so if you run out, delve in and help yourself." He paused for a moment. "Your accent…I would say…you're from Yorkshire?"

"Spot on."

"Have you been this way before?" he asked.

"No…except, thinking about it, I remember having a holiday with my parents a long time ago, we went to Durdle Door. I must have been about five, and my sister was two. Dad carried her in his arms."

Jonni smiled as he put the kettle on the stove.

"Mum says I complained all the way, because my 'kiddie' legs wouldn't take me over the cliff path." I had this clear vision of happy holidays, rucksacks, and picnics.

With the conversation blooming, Jonni handed me a cup of tea, but it all seemed to fall apart as Rosie strode through the door as if her life depended on it.

"Bloody Darcy's gone lame again. Why do we always have these fuckin' problems?" She clomped her way across the hollow tiles and sat with a thud in an old armchair in the conservatory. "Oops. Sorry, Jess, I didn't see you there. Hi."

I supped my tea, not sure what to say. Hearing Rosie's brash language had jarred me a little. I think I was beginning to comprehend what Rosie meant by unconventional living and this was a farm after all; these things didn't seem to be an issue around here. I didn't expect it to come from Rosie.

"What's the matter this time?" Jonni sighed through his question.

"I jumped him over a low log and he took a tumble. Mum'll go crackers. That lump on his chest has got worse as well."

"I'll come down in half an hour…Oh, heck. Here's Hans and Ewan in the Land Rover. I can't think why, but I promised Hans I would help him repair the tractor." Jonni gave another sigh. "By the way, Hans is a bit of a difficult character, you'll have to ignore his moods, I'm afraid. Connie tells me he's had a strange life."

"He's usually okay with me." Rosie shrugged her shoulders.

Jonni hurried his words. "I'll come down to the stables soon, okay?"

He turned to me again. "Sorry, Jess, I'll have to go. It's a busy place at the moment; there's lots to do at lambing time and the work never stops."

I smiled at his dedication but couldn't help but notice Rosie's glum expression.

As quiet as the house had been before my arrival, a sudden spurt of rallying now filled the air. No wonder Connie named them 'The Household Cavalry'.

A moment later, a blond-haired man stormed into the room, his hair tied in a short pony tail. He wore denim jeans and an old red cable-knit jumper with a roll collar.

His tanned skin and accent made me realise he wasn't English. I waited for introductions. Nothing happened.

"I need a coffee," he said with a sigh. "I'm as dry as a drover's dog."

I smiled at the way he spoke. Australian? Rosie gave him a sharp sideways glance and I sensed a reluctance for introductions. Eventually she spoke. "Ewan, meet Jess."

"Hi Jess, come to shack up with The Cavalry, have you?" he replied in a gravelled voice.

"Yes, I've…just arrived."

Rosie turned to him, exhaling the smoke from her self-rolled tobacco. "Darcy's gone lame." Her face tensed as she spoke.

"Yes, I know, I've been down the stables to see how he was getting on and I don't want to talk about it now. The whole bloody thing annoys me. I tell you, that horse has cost Connie thousands and the lump on his chest is back again. We can't go on like this. Something has to give." Ewan cracked his knuckles on the worktop harder than he meant to. "Awch." He sucked the back of his hand.

"Ewan, listen." Rosie expressed. "I'm not telling Mum. Jonni's going to see if we can fix him ourselves; we did last time. It's my fault for jumping him too soon."

Ewan turned away. I gathered he didn't want to say any more in front of me.

"More tea, Jess?" Jonni cleared his throat. He was doing his best to change the topic.

"No, thanks." I smiled.

Jonni checked Rosie's expression. "Don't worry, Rosie, we'll sort it out, okay?"

I felt uncomfortable, as if I shouldn't be there. Perhaps I ought to leave them and go upstairs, but Jonni spoke first.

"I must go now, see you later, Jess, and thanks for the chat. Great to meet you." His chair scraped against the rough slate tiles as he made his way toward the kitchen door into the yard. I glimpsed the back of his head as he passed by the window. Out of all the people I had met so far, Jonni seemed to be the most approachable.

I must have stared for a while at the chair where he'd sat and wasn't paying attention when a tall, dark-haired man strode into the kitchen with the same urgency as Ewan. His chequered shirt, shoulder-length hair and wild black beard gave the impression of a rugged lumberjack. He left before I could say hello.

Rosie turned to me. "That's Hansi or Hans. You won't get much out of him; he's not one of the world's great conversationalists."

Rosie rolled the cigarette paper between her fingers then licked along the edge. She leaned on the work surface, flicked her lighter, and blew smoke into the void.

"How many horses do you have, Rosie?"

"Fifteen in total and two bays from friends in the village, who rent a stable from us." She took a deep thoughtful draw on her rollie.

"It's been ages since I've ridden a horse. With working and so on, I don't get much time for those things anymore."

"Maybe we can ride together when you get settled in."

"That would be lovely." I paused a moment. "I suppose I'd better unpack my stuff."

41

"D'ye need any help?" Rosie offered. "It's just…I have to go down to the stables to sort out Darcy's leg, but we can chat when I come back."

"No, it'll be fine, I'll manage." I smiled some thanks, knowing how busy she seemed. I had loads to do anyway but it was good to take a break. There was something about Rosie which disturbed me. I liked her but she seemed so…vulnerable and naïve.

Rosie left the room and the latch clicked as she pulled the kitchen door behind her. From the bustle of family life, I was once again, alone.

From the bedroom window, I gazed at the Land Rover standing in the yard; Jonni and Hans leaned on the bonnet. Their posture didn't appear friendly and I felt like a fly on the wall in their lives.

Ewan led Darcy up the path and encouraged the horse 'to take it easy'. He checked the horse's gait and shook his head at something that didn't please him, before going back to the stables. Wisps of his untied hair flew around his face. I stood, staring below me, as he disappeared from view. Jonni moved around the Land Rover to get a spade out of the rear door. As I closed the window, he must have heard me. He looked up and waved. It was his friendly smile that made me feel welcome, and I had to admit that his good looks stirred something within me. I had only known him for less than a day and already had the confidence he was going to be a good friend, someone I could rely on to show me the way of things around the farm.

On the opposite wall in my room hung an old picture. The nameplate on the gold frame read: *The First Lord Hannings after a painting by Sir John Fowlds, 1687*. Perhaps there was a family connection. I gazed at the other pictures. On the adjacent wall was another painting, *Lisbet and Lily*, a picture of two young girls adorned in white dresses with pink ribbons flowing around their waists and a handsome stallion behind them. It was a pretty portrait. I searched for a date but nothing told me who they were or the name of the artist, only the letters TD on the bottom right. Oh, yes of course, Connie's ex—Theo Dijkman? She had mentioned him being an artist. It was very good. Another painting, above my bed, showed an attractive scene of Tanglewood by Conor Perkins. It was more contemporary than the other pictures, but a delightful portrait of the house. I stared for some time thinking of the people who would have lived here in the 14th century, those who had smoothed their hands over the wattle and daub and oak beams, and the ones who had slept in this room. Would the ghosts of the past still be here? I looked out from the opposing window and gazed into the yard below. The open-hand gloves and the knife had been tidied away, and the weeds between the cracks were gone. Things were not so 'Marie Celeste' after all.

With everything unpacked, it was time to begin my new life. I re-arranged the faded cushions and thought about what I needed to make the room my own. Perhaps an eiderdown or one of those new continental quilts I had seen in the shops and, of course, a kettle and I'd always wanted a coffee maker. The money Dad left me would make it homelier.

I had brought with me a photo of Mum and Dad and my sister. It would help to keep a sense of the family and I placed it on the windowsill. I gazed at the photo and found it hard to believe that so much sadness had fallen on us in the last few months and any lost thoughts of him came back into view. He had no reason to have a heart attack: he didn't smoke or drink too much, so why? I asked myself that question so many times. In my head, he was still with us, although there had been a few weeks when it was hard to 'see' him. I know I was grieving for my loss, but he and Mum had been the perfect couple and it all seemed so cruel that I would never be able to speak to him again.

Tuesday didn't seem so far away when it was time to check in at Monks Agency. I had to collect the information to start work that morning. In the meantime, I had the whole weekend free, with time to explore.

As I entered the communal kitchen, I glanced at the tall figure standing there at the worktop; it was Hans. He was spreading unsalted Lurpak straight from the silver packaging onto a pile of brown bread. An open tin of salmon and a few cucumber slices lay on a plate.

"Hi, I'm Jess; I'm renting the room here."

He stared right through me. "Hello," he said and declined to shake hands. He tucked the black wavy strands of hair behind his ear with greasy fingers. He didn't smile nor did he offer to make further conversation. I tried to be sociable and opened up to him.

"It's a lovely old place. I never thought I'd live in a house like this."

"Ver did you come from?" His low gruff voice seemed cold and unwelcoming and I assumed his accent was German.

"Yorkshire—and I hear you are from…is it Switzerland?"

"I suppose Connie told you that. Don't believe everything she tells you, she exaggerates a lot." He sneered as he spoke which sent a shiver down my spine.

"Ok, thanks for the warning." I smiled, but Hans didn't, and continued to stare through me with every sentence. *What was the point?* If he was going to greet me as though I had fallen into a pile of dog poo, then how was I supposed to respond?

He buttered another sandwich and placed it in a box. I wondered about those dirty hands and what nasty germs lurked between his blackened fingernails. I sensed I was in the way and he seemed far too busy to be bothered to make conversation, but I had been warned.

Hans was the last person on my mind, but I hoped I could cope with his distant scorn. Perhaps I should take a walk, get some fresh air, and explore the estate. With a feeling of disappointment, I dashed upstairs to slip into my trainers and took time out to enjoy myself. I headed toward the milking shed where I assumed Jonni worked, but I knew he wasn't there and I didn't want him to think I had sought him out to do another job for me.

An old cottage stood on the estate. The ivy clung to the gable and the garden walls wrapped around the building had fallen into disrepair. I fantasised about what I would do to make the cottage my own if I lived here. Chintz curtains, a climbing rose, and a hammock between the two oak trees. I sensed it was going to take a lot of money to even start a project like that.

A view through a window revealed a young girl with long auburn hair drying the pots on the drainer. The peace and tranquillity, the beauty of spring, and the birds singing, provided me with a sense of gratitude for being alive. I walked on for a while when thoughts of Tim came into my head. Did he think of doing the washing up—*ever*? Our relationship had become a job rather than something special. Oh yes, we'd seen happy times in the first two years but conversations about marriage seemed brushed away. His mother often despaired of him and the same with me, too. He became lazy and it was more than I could take. I am a career person, not his servant.

"I need more security," I'd argued with him on that day. "Honestly, Tim, there's nothing left of 'us'. I have to get away to give me a chance to think about what I really want in life."

"You're running away from it all, Jess."

"No, you're wrong. You just don't get it do you?"

I couldn't deal with both situations after Dad died. I never returned to the flat after I left. I still had the key and finalised the relationship by posting it in an envelope through the door.

Later, Mum had her opinions, too. "I like Tim, but I can't help feeling you could do better, love. Don't waste your life on a man you don't really love. You're a pretty lass, you'll be fine. I'm proud of you. It can't have been easy."

I'd already packed my bags in anticipation of an argument and despite a heavy heart, I knew it was the right thing to do.

That same night Mum, Anna and I went to the hospital to discover Dad fighting his last breath; I almost died with him. Tim's argument became a distant memory. All this fuzziness in my head made me want to suck in my breath and run to the nearest dark corner and hide. Tim came to the funeral and I tried to be pleasant, but that day I had so many things going on I didn't want to be part of anyone or anything. We parted on a sad note, and he never contacted me again. If I stopped feeling guilty about everything that had happened, my life would change. It was as if all this was happening to someone else.

The sudden mooing of cows in the field brought me back to reality. Was this Jonni's herd in the field? I leaned over a gate to find Friesian cows behind the hedge, munching on sweet green grass in the meadow. I smiled. Jonni had been so helpful so why hadn't Tim behaved like that instead of me having to play the surrogate mother? I scolded myself again. *Stop it, Jess, no more Tim, okay?*

I walked back to find the stables behind Tanglewood. I also found Rosie. She was working in the yard with her friend who introduced herself as Val; her horse's name was Briony. Val and Rosie seemed good friends and I hoped I would be accepted into their fold. I began to feel at home with the familiar odour of horses and polished leather. Rosie introduced me to the horses. Merry, who was in foal, due in a couple of months, and Dirk, a brown-and-white beast with feathery hooves. There were six horses in the stable that day. Apparently, Jonni had been down to help with Darcy and I saw the horse with his leg bandaged and purple antiseptic on his chest. His head rested on the stall and his eyes were half closed; I felt his pain.

After my visit to the stables, I walked along a small footpath into the woods and about a quarter of a mile away and came across a lake. The surrounding woodland and the clear water reflected the trees and blue sky and the echo of coot and a couple of mallards drifted over the water. By the side of the lake stood a bench and a sign, *No trespassing. By Order of Tanglewood Estate.* As I now lived here, perhaps I wasn't really trespassing. In the warm sun, I walked around the perimeter of the lake and could hear water dripping into the pool from the stream. There was a small tumbled down wooden pier stretching to the centre of the lake. It was boarded up with a rusty notice that said DANGER. The lake seemed very dark and deep.

On the far side, I watched a heron land, stepping forward on the final approach to the water's edge and folding back its wings. It stood there motionless for a while as it darted for a fish. I stood still and watched it gaze at its own reflection in the clear pool.

With the chance for free riding and mingling with horses again, I would be in my element. It was only Hans who seemed unfriendly, but if I kept out of his way, he shouldn't be a problem. One thing did cross my mind—I'd turned twenty-nine and needed a spot of nightlife and some new friends. Jonni had mentioned the lack of things to do and with the house being on the edge of a village it was hardly a place to interact with city folk. Perhaps Axminster would hold more activities and maybe Jonni or Rosie would be able to suggest something. With a new life ahead of me, the situation at Tanglewood was certainly a place to do a lot of thinking. I gazed across the lake and wondered if it were possible to swim there. It seemed deep enough. I put my hand in the water but it was cold and changed my mind about swimming. I turned back on myself and decided this was a desolate kind of place. I was beginning to feel tired and so I returned to the farm.

Chapter Four

I called Mum again. Connie said she didn't mind me making private calls, as long as I put the money in the honesty box in the hall.

"That's okay, Jess," she said. She gave me a small hug in the same way as Mum would have done. "I know you've only just arrived here but I hope you'll stay with us. You remind me so much of my time as a young girl when I was struggling to find a way in life. If being here helps you recover from your sad loss, then I hope it works for you. If there's anything you need, ask me or Jonni. He's very good at looking after the guests."

I felt assured seeing that Connie had an affectionate side to her. She gave me a smile and went on her way. I dialled my home number.

Mum was delighted. It was a quick birthday call to let her know I'd moved into Tanglewood.

"Happy birthday, Mum. Did you get the card?"

"It was lovely, yes, and thanks for the present. What a pretty scarf. I love blue."

The day before I left home, I gave Mum's present to Anna. I didn't think it necessary to post it.

I explained more about the farm and the people who lived there. I also told Mum how it would take time to settle in, but so far so good.

The conversation was shorter than the last one and she seemed to understand my situation. A pang of homesickness came over me and a tear fell down my cheek. With all our problems at home, I hadn't had a chance to think how I really felt. It wasn't long, through her usual chatty self, before she restored my confidence.

*

After a quiet Easter weekend and Saturday shopping in Axminster, Tuesday dawned and I arose early. My grey trouser suit with a pale pink blouse seemed appropriate. I always liked to dress well for business at work, but why did I feel so nervous?

I parked near Castle Street. Monk's was tucked away on a side road and after a short walk, I stepped inside the office door and introduced myself to the receptionist.

"Would you like a coffee?" she asked. "I'll tell Pauline you're here, take a seat."

"Thank you."

I watched as she lifted the receiver on the phone to announce my arrival. It was like visiting Verity all over again. She had only just placed the coffee on the desk when the call came through.

"You can go along now, it's the door on your left. Take your coffee with you, if you wish."

"Okay, thanks."

On reaching the office, the name on the door read *Pauline Acton*. I gave a gentle knock.

"Come in."

"Jessica Stamp. Good morning." I placed my cup on the desk and we shook hands.

"Pauline," she smiled and sat down.

She wore silver earrings that peeked out from her short brown hair. The smart navy skirt and white blouse suited her professional demeanour; a matching jacket hung on her chair.

"You come to us well recommended, Jessica. I think Mark Parson needs support. He's a busy man—and as you know his secretary is on extended leave so he'll be glad to see you. I only wanted to meet you this morning and update you on the work and complete our registration form."

"Oh—okay. Call me Jess, by the way, everyone else does."

"Did you manage to find a place to stay?"

"I checked in yesterday." When I mentioned Tanglewood her

lips formed a thin line, and she nodded almost with deliberation which made me wonder if she knew something I didn't.

"I'll make a call…" she picked up the receiver, "and tell Mark Parson you're on your way."

I caught the sound of a scratchy voice on the other end of the phone and sipped my coffee.

"Good morning, Mark, it's Pauline from Monks agency. I've got Jess Stamp here; she'll be with you in about half an hour. Yes, that's fine, Mark. Yes, I will. Have a good day. Bye."

Pauline returned her attention to me. "It's great to meet you, Jess. Seeing you're on your own, you'll need to look out for yourself, so take things slowly, and if you want to talk about any aspect of the job let me know. Laura, in reception, will ask you to sign all the usual paperwork before you leave. Have you registered with a doctor and dentist yet?"

"I only arrived on Thursday and with Easter at the weekend, these things will have to wait their turn, I suppose."

She smiled, "Well…we have the surgery next door here, and it's easy enough. We like our temps to be registered in case of an emergency at work." She looked down at a checklist. "I gather you have a clean driving licence. I mean, working at the garage they will need you to drive. Mark is keen to ensure everything is in order."

"Oh yes, I see—no parking fines or speeding," I remarked with ease.

"That's good then," she replied. "It looks like you're ready to go. You look very smart, all ready for a new job. Well done."

"I'm used to working with the big bosses on Teesside. I think skirts are a bit of a temptation, I like wearing trousers for work."

Pauline laughed. "Yes, I know what you mean. I think you'll find Mark to be a temptation, he's very good looking, but married I think." She gave me a knowing grin. "Enjoy yourself and if you need to call me, I am here most of the time. Good luck."

I took a last sip of coffee and made my way to reception.

*

The journey to work took only ten minutes. On the forecourt stood a line of the latest models of Ford Cortina, awaiting customer inspection. I wish I could have afforded one and wasn't sure how much longer the Viva would last. 'Lottie', as Dad affectionately called her, was eighteen years old with a recent overhaul and a lot of mileage on the clock.

On arrival, I greeted a mechanic in overalls.

"Can I help you?" he said.

"I'm here to see Mark Parson. I'm Jess Stamp."

Mark Parson opened the partitioned glass door of the reception and strode forward to shake hands.

"Welcome, Jess, glad you were able to come. Call me Mark by the way. Pauline Acton tells me you've travelled down from Yorkshire to help us out, that's a long way to come for a temping job, but I was rather in need of someone to start immediately and the agency said you were available."

"Yes, I'm looking forward to spending the summer down here. It's such a pretty area from what I've seen so far. It's a kind of working holiday. I wanted a change that's all."

Did I lie? Perhaps I only paraphrased what Verity said when I last saw her.

Mark guided me to his office. "Take a seat," he offered.

Pauline had been right. He was very good looking with dark brown hair, combed neat. His tweed suit was very 'Countryman', and a pink bow tie protruded from under his chin. He bore a goatee beard against his tanned face as if he'd just come back from Majorca, or some other faraway place. We made the usual pleasantries and he seemed friendly enough. I hoped our working relationship would be as positive.

On the desk stood a wire basket marked *Pending*. Next to the Olivetti typewriter, a stack of letters was ready for posting with several more invoices on top of the typewriter. I assumed someone had been working late most evenings.

"I'll be quite honest with you: I need a PA and I hope you can stay with us for as long as it takes. Tina, my full-timer, had her baby four weeks ago, but her child is ill. Tina is very good at her job and I wanted to keep her position open. We're a kind of family business here. She is my niece. I had a temp for a few weeks before she left us, but the young lady wasn't able to continue."

"I'm glad to help." Not many people would keep a position open that long, I thought.

"We're very busy with the Easter sales. How do you feel about being with us for a while? It's general stuff you'll need to do. Filing and organising appointments for me. They told me you had experience of sales and I can't afford to let my clients down. I did explain to the agency; did they tell you?"

I nodded. "That's fine by me, Mark. Yes, they told me it may be a longer contract and, of course, I'd love to help. I've worked with some of the big bosses from the oil companies and shipping lines on Teesside so I don't have a problem with organisation and I'm also used to pressure and working on my own initiative." I hoped he could sense my eagerness to get started and with his slow smile, I took it he was impressed.

"I have to admit I'm finding it difficult to juggle home life without assistance at the office. Anything you can do to make things easier for me would be great."

I agreed to make myself as useful as possible.

I guessed at Mark's age. He seemed early forties, with eyes that beckoned, *'Come here pet, and sit on my knee whilst you drink your coffee. Shut the door, no, lock it, and we'll talk'*. However, ten minutes into the conversation, I sensed the pink bow tie was probably hiding his shy personality. His colour sense seemed hideous, perhaps enough to put customers off investing in a car, although I'd probably misjudged him.

"We need someone to help keep the clients happy. I hope you make good coffee," he gave a wide smile.

I looked around the bright, modern office. A lava lamp stood on a coffee table in the corner of the room with a small orange sofa beside it. A Ford calendar hung on the wall. I smiled; at least I didn't have to spend my days looking at a 'page three girl'. The invoices I could post later and I needed to check with Mark for the whereabouts of the nearest post office. There was a Dictaphone on my desk. My last boss had the annoying habit of leaving cryptic messages on his machine for me to decipher; I hoped Mark wasn't going to do the same. I was capable of writing my own simple letters for the boss to sign. With sensible organising and good communication, things would improve. I wanted to impress for the next assignment and my CV.

It was five o'clock when I saw Mark walking toward me and jangling a set of keys.

"Jess, is that your Viva out there?" he beamed.

I sat up straighter.

"We always give our staff a car to run around in. I thought you might like one of our new Ford Fiestas. I mean seeing you are staying with us for a while and you have a clean licence."

I felt my jaw drop. *Another car?*

"Oh…Wow. That's amazing; I don't know what to say. The Viva belonged to my dad; he passed away before Christmas last year."

"Oh, I'm sorry to hear that, was it sudden?"

"Yes, Mum found him slumped on the floor in the bedroom. It was a dreadful shock. He was in hospital for a few days when his condition deteriorated."

There was a moment's pause in the conversation.

"I know how that feels; I had a similar situation a couple of years ago so I know what you mean. Are you down here on your own?"

"Well, for a while at least. Mum is doing relatively fine and my younger sister is taking care of her."

"I don't wish to appear insensitive, but in view of this being your dad's car, would you mind having one of ours as well for work? There's a logo on the side of the vehicle, its company policy that we give the admin staff a car, temporary or otherwise. You may as well be part of the team on your first day; I want you to feel welcome." He smiled.

"Thanks, Mark, that's really kind of you. I don't know what to say." I thought I'd won a prize in a competition. Blooming heck, a new car. I had only been at the garage less than a day. Amazing. I couldn't have asked for more. I tried to think what on earth I should do with Dad's Viva and a Ford Fiesta as well. I could hardly say no. So, let me get this right: a brand new car, PA to the boss at the local Ford garage, and my own room in the country at this quirky place called Tanglewood. So far, my time here had been full of surprises.

"George will fix you up with the documents."

I glanced at George through the office partition. He wore a grey suit and navy tie and was probably about the same age as me. He leaned against a car, reading a newspaper and as I made my way to the showroom floor, he looked up.

"Hello, Jess, I'm George. Sorry, I haven't been in most of the day. I've been doing test drives for customers. We sold two cars, so I'm feeling pleased with myself."

"Oh, well done. Did you need me to sign anything for the Fiesta?"

"We can do the admin for the car in the morning when you come in to work." He smiled. "You can take it home after the week-end."

"Thanks so much, that's amazing. I really didn't expect a car with the job."

"Oh, that's Mark for you. He's a good businessman."

I checked on the whereabouts of the post office and concluded I would get on fine with Mark; it was important I impressed him. After all, if I was to stay here for the rest of the year, I could see his point about the car, but I wondered how was I going to get it back to Tanglewood. Perhaps if I asked Jonni's advice, he might be able to help.

Chapter Five

I managed to finish the invoices before closing time and drove down to the post office.

When I got home, I changed out of my work clothes and made a macaroni cheese. I was about to close my knife and fork together when Jonni arrived with the dog; he held a lamb in his arms.

"I've just fed this little one." He lifted the lamb toward me. "Would you like to hold her?" He grinned. "She was born two days ago. Sadly, her mother died."

I pushed my plate aside and opened my arms. "Aw, how sad."

"Here you are then." He smiled.

It made no attempt to struggle, and wanted to sleep; I stroked the warm curly fleece and the lamb's eyes closed. Jonni removed his parka jacket to sit beside me. I shot a quick glance and he seemed to be watching me. I cared for the lamb as if I were holding a child. I felt my stomach flip; it was those caring eyes of his.

"How was your day, Jess, and the new job?" he asked as he patted Ruby. She licked her lips and rested her jaw on his knee.

"Odd," I replied. "They gave me a car to run about in, a brand-new Ford Fiesta."

"Bloody hell, Jess, you must have impressed them." Jonni grinned and gently pushed my arm in play. "See, I knew you would be fine."

"Well…Mark told me it's company policy. But right now, I have a dilemma. I've got two cars; how do I get them both back here?"

"Oh right, lucky you, eh? Look…I'll drive one back for

you if you like, let me know in good time and we'll make some arrangements. Is the Viva insured for me as well?"

"Yes, the insurance is fully comp for any driver but I don't wish to inconvenience you, I know how busy you are."

The lamb's eyes opened and bleated as I placed it on the floor near Ruby's bed and like a mother dog. She licked its face.

Jonni's expression changed. He glanced out of the window.

"Is everyone out the house right now?" he asked.

"Yes, I think so, just me here as far as I know."

Jonni leaned forward and rested his hands on the table. "Jess, there's something I should explain before The Cavalry gets back, seeing as you're here for a while."

Why did I feel uneasy at this point?

"I don't want to alarm you, but you may need to turn a blind eye around here. It's all a bit awkward. I mean, you coming all this way here from Yorkshire an' all that, and not knowing anyone. It's only fair to give you an idea of how it is around the farm, so you don't get any uncomfortable surprises."

I felt my limbs stiffen and leaned in to his words.

"You mean Hans?"

"Well…yes and no. You see, Connie lives an odd lifestyle. I've since learned to be like the three monkeys: see all, hear all…"

"And say nowt, eh?" I chorused with a smile.

"Exactly."

"So what kind of things do you mean?"

"Well…it's like this, see. Connie belongs to a kind of religious society and she has…'friends', who come to the house for their meetings."

"Ah, I see, you mean they are…what d'ye call them? Er… Quakers?"

"No, no, nothing like that, but it's not what you will be used to. To be honest with you, I don't ask about it. I have no idea what it's about. Connie can be very deep at times. As I mentioned before, come to me if you need to ask anything. Also, sometime back, so the story goes, a relative of Connie's, they found his wife drowned in the lake, the one near the house. She couldn't swim."

I sucked in a breath. "My god, I went for a walk down there."

"You're bound to hear rumours. It all happened before I came to live here. The lake is very deep. They don't talk about it, but the strange thing was—her husband disappeared and they never found his body. I don't want you to worry about what you might hear from locals in the village. There is always a lot of speculation locally. The main thing is, you have somewhere pleasant to stay and I know you'll enjoy your time with us. I'll make sure you do." He gave a mischievous smile. "No, I mean it; it's great to have you around."

I felt sure he meant every word and gave a sigh of relief, but continued to wonder about his story.

"Well, thanks, Jonni, I appreciate your concerns. So, what's unusual? Perhaps I shouldn't ask. As long as there are no ghosts walking the floor at night, I'm not too worried."

"Ha! There's probably plenty of *ghosts* in this old house." He smiled and gave me a sideways glance. "There's a rumour that the Roundheads used to hold secret meetings here in the time of Oliver Cromwell. Connie tells me there is a priest hole under the stairs."

"Really?" I raised my voice.

"Yes, really."

"Gosh, all this history, eh?"

"Once you get to know us…" he stopped to listen for a moment, "…you'll be fine. It's so you don't worry, that's all."

"And what about Hans? Why is he here?"

"Hans? Oh, he's a lost cause I'm afraid. I often wonder why he's here too. I keep out of his way and so should you."

"Oh, I'm not worried. It's nothing to do with me, I only rent the room. Only I did wonder. He is a strange one, isn't he?"

I heard Rosie coming along the path in her clogs. As she walked into the kitchen, her eyes filled with tears.

"Darcy's leg's getting worse. I've had to get the vet out again.

I don't know how I'm going to pay for it," she wailed.

Why was Rosie so short of money? Didn't they jointly have a business account for the farm? Wasn't her horse insured?

"Mum will go crackers. I tell you, Jonni, it's just not fair."

Jonni stood to comfort her and gave her a friendly squeeze.

"Come on, girl, we'll get through this, we always do," he assured her.

"I can't do this on my own," Rosie cried and sniffed into the sleeve of her jacket, leaving a silver trail. "Ewan has to understand. Oops. Sorry, Jess, I didn't mean for you to be involved here. How was your new job?" she asked with a sob in her voice.

"Fine thanks." I gave a sympathetic smile. I didn't feel now was the appropriate time to elaborate further on the subject of the new car and the boss with the bow tie.

Rosie took the tobacco tin out of her pocket and made a rollie. She flicked her thumb over the lighter, inhaling and blowing smoke to the yellowing ceiling.

I stroked Ruby for the want of something to do with my redundant hands and a sense of 'I shouldn't be here' left me feeling awkward.

"I'll make us a coffee and then I must go to my room." I found the mugs and filled the kettle.

"I'll talk to you later, eh?" Jonni wrinkled his nose.

I agreed. He didn't wish to say any more with Rosie in the room.

"I hope you manage to sort this out soon, Rosie. I know how upsetting it must be. See you tomorrow for the car swap, Jonni, thanks."

I felt Jonni's agitation but left him to comfort Rosie as there wasn't anything more I could do. Rosie blew breath across the top of her hot mug and after a few minutes I took mine upstairs.

The new car—I loved it. The knobs and dials were more modern than I was used to. At the office Mark seemed pleased with my attempt to make sense of the office backlog. I brewed the coffee, organised a new filing system, and made appointments for him to attend various events in London. I was on a roll and I wished I could work here for longer than he needed me; it was easy work in comparison to the jobs I'd had up north.

"Mark will be back soon, he's with a client. Would you like a coffee, Mr Pinkerton?"

"I'll have a tea, please. How long have you worked here?"

"A few days. I'm filling in for Tina who's had a baby."

"I know Tina, she's been with Mark for some time, hasn't she?"

"I believe so."

I left him with his tea until Mark returned.

I sat at my desk gazing out of the window. Mark had asked me to work one Saturday in every month. I didn't feel it would be a problem. At least I could begin to organise my life.

He told me that Tina had offered to come in and help me get into the swing of things.

Later that day, Tina did call by and I learned her baby son was doing well and he would have an operation soon.

"It's been a time of mixed emotions," she explained.

I gave a concerned smile for her sadness.

"I can't help blame myself in a way for all this. Damian has other problems as well. I took some pills they gave me in the early days of pregnancy, I'm sure it had something to do with it."

"Don't listen too hard to the media. Not everything you hear is true. There are things I should have said and done before I came here, but it was not to be."

With tact, I steered the subject away; I had no experience of babies. Still, she reminded me how fragile life can be. She knew her job well and told me how glad she felt that Mark had found someone he could rely on.

Later, Mark left for home and Tina said goodbye and hoped to see me again soon. She seemed to have resigned herself to the inevitable. I admired her bravery. Perhaps I should follow her example and make the best from my grief. Her problems were far worse than mine and I wished her well.

I was thinking of going home early, when a man stopped by to look at cars. As George was out and no one else was around, I felt obliged to introduce him to the various models at a price he could afford. I showed him around and arranged a test drive. One of the mechanics offered to go with him and I phoned Mark at home as he'd asked me to inform him of what I was doing until I got a hang of the job. He was delighted that I'd taken the initiative.

"Of course, Jess, that's wonderful. Make sure you tell him about the new finance deal we discussed this afternoon. Well done, see you tomorrow."

When everyone left, I closed the office door and returned to the farm. On the way home Jonni came into my thoughts. I wondered if he had a woman in his life who he kept hidden away. I didn't like to ask in case he thought I was prying and gave him the wrong impression.

My thoughts turned to his earlier conversation. Who was this relative he'd mentioned? I scolded myself. All this gossip had absolutely nothing to do with me. I would heed what Jonni said. Whatever had happened in the house, stayed in the house. Still, I couldn't help my own curiosity.

I stepped through the open back door to discover Hans sitting on the kitchen stool reading a newspaper. He blew smoke from his cigarette into the room.

"Hi, Hans," I said.

"Bloody horse got it in the head today. That effin' stupid vet. I gave him a piece of my mind I did." His nostrils flared like the horses as he spoke.

I soon realised Hans was stoned. He reeled, slurring his speech. His evil face under the black beard said 'murder'; I hoped I wasn't the victim. He leered at me.

"Oh heck, you mean Rosie's horse, the one with the…?"

Hans put his head to one side looking at me, no—staring at me, in a most unnerving way. His face distorted; I could tell he was about to burst forth with some abhorrent comment.

"Listen, girl, I could have you instead if you like," he slurred.

"What?"

"You heard," he sneered.

He stood and I moved toward the Aga. I spotted the poker in the hearth in case I needed it. If I reached for the kettle, the boiling water would deter him. My thoughts travelled at lightning speed. I turned away from him, my heart missing a beat.

I felt his breath on my neck and grabbed the brass poker. "You see this? Back off Hans, I've done nothing to you." I raised my arms in case he got too close. "Now, get lost and leave me alone. I am not for sale."

He stepped back and sneered at me. "Bitch."

"What *is* your problem, Hans?"

He grabbed my arm, not listening to a word I'd said. "Yeah, and in future you stay out of my way—do you hear?"

He released me. The look in his eyes said 'kill' and I wasn't going to stick around to find I was the victim. I dropped the poker and ran upstairs. In his present state I doubted he could have done anything more serious. Who was this monster of a man? I didn't come here to be insulted. The idiot. Was he always so stoned? He obviously had dreadful issues—one hell of a disturbed man. This was not the result of any encouragement I had given him. What should I do about it? My eyes filled with tears, until I heard the conversation below. I recognised the voices of Jonni and Ewan and listened at the bedroom door.

"Back off," Hans shouted. "Fuckin' leave me alone, will you? It's not my bloody fault the friggin' horse had to be shot."

Ah, so that was it! I happened to fall into the middle of a farmhouse crisis. I had entered the room at exactly the wrong time and got the brunt of the anger. Still, there was no need for him to take it out on me. I ought to mention it to Jonni but my thoughts were interrupted by Ewan's gravelled voice.

"Listen, mate, git yourself outta here, I don't want Rosie to know yet. I'll tell her, she'll only blame herself for this. It's too traumatic for her."

As usual, Jonni tried to calm the situation. "Look, we've got Jess in the house now; we don't want to put her off living here, do we?"

"She'll need to get used to more than that." I heard Hans storm out of the room like a child whose lollipop had been taken away. He banged the kitchen door so hard that the house shook.

It was good of Jonni to stick up for me. He always seemed to hold the flag for everyone; I began to feel sorry for him. Hans was surely an embarrassment to the family, so why was he here and in this dreadful state of mind? No one seemed to know much about him.

But what about Rosie? I thought. Her horse had died and she was about to learn the bad news. I felt my own shock, too, having seen Darcy only yesterday. I knew of his restless pain. I tried not to think too much about it. My heart pounded and then I heard a woman's voice. Connie always seemed to spring up from nowhere.

"What's going on? Oh dear, dear, dear," I heard her say. "This is dreadful, why didn't you tell me sooner?"

"It had to be done," Jonni said. "We called out the vet in an emergency and Rosie was in town, we couldn't tell her. The infection spread up his leg, he was in agony and then he went down, he was very ill, Connie. We couldn't let the horse suffer—I mean he was twenty years old, he's had a good life."

I felt unnerved by Jonni's comments. I didn't know much about horse ailments, but why did they leave it so long? Something didn't seem right; I hoped they hadn't neglected the animal.

"Hm…my own horse was thirty-five when he died," Connie replied. She left the room to climb the stairs. It was as if she was trying to find someone else to blame. I opened the door as she reached top. "Are you okay, Connie? It's so sad, isn't it?"

"Yes dear, it is and sorry you had to hear all that, sometimes it makes me feel so guilty that perhaps we should have done something sooner."

From everything I'd heard, it was Connie who didn't have the money to pay for the horse's treatment. Who was really running these riding stables, Connie or Rosie? Or both?

"I hope Rosie will get over it soon." I suggested.

Connie smiled and walked down her corridor. "Thanks, Jess, you are very kind, dear."

It was like the proverbial ships passing in the night. A quick snatch of conversation here and there and no longer the chatty Connie I had met on my first visit. She was either out the house or spending time in her room. I had really wanted to get to know her better, but at this rate it wasn't going to happen.

Outside my bedroom window I watched Hans heading down the path at a defiant pace and turned away not wishing to look at his mean features any longer.

As sudden as the row had flared, the cooing of wood pigeons in the trees calmed the air. Two hours passed before I could bring myself to socialise. At least I had a place of retreat when things weren't going right. *Bloody Hans.* I took a deep breath and opened a page in my book. Perhaps in a small way my anger was hasty; they had lost a much-loved horse. Hans was stoned and angry with the vet. Even so, to use threats and insults, and come on to me in that way, was shocking. *The idiot!* It seemed obvious I was going to have to learn to be stronger now.

Chapter Six

I thought I could hear the sound of sobbing coming from the kitchen. As I ventured down the creaky stairs Rosie was sat with her head resting on her hands and a soggy tissue gripped between her fingers.

"Oh, Rosie, I'm so sorry. I'm afraid I got on the wrong side of Hans and he blurted the sad news."

"It's all my fault," she sobbed.

"No, surely, it's not your fault at all, Rosie. Do you want to talk? From what I hear Darcy's leg wouldn't have got any better, the infection was serious and wasn't it a tumour on his chest?"

Rosie nodded, sniffed, and carried on sniffing, so I made a cup of tea for which she seemed grateful and put my arm around her. "Come on," I encouraged. "Losing an animal is such a difficult thing."

I suppose I knew how she felt, it wasn't so long ago since I had those feelings of human loss.

"I'm glad you came here, Jess. I need a new friend." In a world of her own, she turned her head away from me and stared out of the window.

I smiled. "Come on, drink your tea."

We sat together and I kept silent for a moment to allow her to calm down. I had been down this road before with Anna and I knew it was best to be there for her. I had nothing more to say.

Jonni had left his coat hung over the chair, and my thoughts led me to wonder what kind of guy he was and what had brought him here. He had become my ally and had only my welfare at heart. Earlier, we'd arranged to drop me off at work after the weekend and for him to bring the Viva back to the farm. I knew Jonni's car wasn't roadworthy and couldn't allow my car to sit on the drive; it wouldn't do the battery any good. Perhaps he should borrow it.

Rosie jolted me out of my thoughts. "I'm pleased you like riding – it's been my life since I was a child." She blew her nose into the snotty tissue. I put my hand into my pocket and gave her a fresh one. "Thanks," she sniffed. "Darcy was like my childhood best friend and it's like…I've lost a part of me."

My own feelings of grief returned and I gave a heavy nod. "At least he's no longer in pain," I offered.

Rosie blew her nose again and changed the subject. "Anyway, I hope you'll like it here. Mum needs the money right now. Let's say financially, things are not good. She has lived a lavish lifestyle and she can't seem to stop. To Mum it's like living in Buckingham Palace and having to survive on chip butties. She just doesn't understand."

"Oh, I did wonder," I sympathised. Her words gave me cause for concern. Any romantic notions of life at Tanglewood began to change, and in a weak moment Rosie had spilled what it was like to be one of the Household Cavalry. From what I'd seen of Connie, so far, there was no doubt she was somewhat eccentric, but Rosie's comments made me view her in a different light. Which one of them was bending the truth? Two sides to every story, I thought.

She sobbed again. "I've had Darcy a long time—I'm going to miss him. He was part of me. Mum couldn't afford to get him fixed last time and the income I get from the riding school is hardly enough to go around for the other horses. Darcy suffered all kinds of problems recently and we ran out of money. Mum takes in all the waifs and strays, so they can help generate income. She has no business sense at all." She gave a deep sigh.

"Oh dear, I wasn't aware of that," I replied.

"There are people who come and go and help on the farm, but they're squatters and that's about it. I kept telling her, Ewan and

I should run the farm, but she won't listen. She says I don't have the experience yet. It's so frustrating."

"Oh, Rosie, I'm sorry. It's such a lovely old place and a pity this is happening."

"I know, but don't tell Mum I said that, will you? You see, she has another source of income. She gets paid for the work she does. I don't discuss these things with her and if it wasn't for her work, we would have to give up this old house. Mum believes that all creations are sacred and this is why she loves the farm with the animals and the land. In a way she doesn't live in the real world. When Ewan and I get married we can prove to her that she isn't getting any younger, I'm sure we could do a better job and let her get on with the things she likes best. I've no idea how she's managing, she doesn't tell me anything these days. She can be very secretive."

I considered what Rosie meant by 'another source of income' but I didn't feel comfortable in asking her to clarify. I tried to show her I understood her difficulties, but, of course, I didn't fully appreciate all of them. I couldn't imagine Connie doing housework to subsidise her. What was she doing?

"I don't have any real friends around here." Rosie looked at me with deep sadness in her expression. "Only Val and her mum and you guys. The stable girls come and go and we never see them more than a few times a month. They are volunteers and not close friends. Jonni is very good to me and Ewan, of course. We all tend to stick together as best we can. Ewan goes to his..."

Then she stopped talking, clamping her hand across her mouth and sniffing at the same time.

I wanted to tell her how much I cared and to be there for her, the same as I am always there for my sister, but it wasn't easy; I had been through it all myself. The fear of taking a step backwards made me stop to think before saying something I might regret. I decided that one small step forward would be okay.

"Well, I thought we were already friends, Rosie. I don't know anyone down here, either."

"That's kind of you, Jess, thanks." She sniffed again. "Though you aren't going to be around very long, are you?"

"Well, that depends on many things, the job and so on. Anyway, you've got Ewan to take care of you." I sensed her loneliness, which didn't surprise me from the things I'd seen so far.

She sighed again and left a small gap in our conversation.

"Yeah, but…" Her clogs hung from her feet as she sat on the tall stool and she fiddled with the string around her ring finger.

"What is it, Rosie?" I softened my tone to comfort her.

"It's the wedding ceremony, I'm not sure. I mean, I love Ewan, he is very caring despite his odd nature at times, and…Mum can't afford it. We don't need a lavish wedding and we don't have that kind of money to throw around. He wanted to study at university, but things are not right for him just now. His mother was very strict and he's mixed up about himself after she abandoned him. It's complicated." She gave a deep sigh as she tried to make sense of her thoughts. "I'm trying to help him move on."

I was about to reply when the back door opened. Connie had arrived home with an armful of shopping.

"Hello, dears. I bought a new blouse on the market stall," she announced with delight. "It didn't cost a fortune: two new pounds, that was all." She seemed to ignore her daughter's distress.

She opened the plastic bag and placed a pretty pink blouse on the worktop.

"It's lovely Connie…but Rosie isn't feeling too good," I said.

I still didn't understand what Rosie was trying to tell me. I'd just helped my own mum put her life back together, and anyway it wasn't up to me to get too involved with the Dijkman family.

"Are you all right, darling?" Connie asked as Rosie sat moping.

"Darcy was everything to me." Rosie cried. "If we'd had the funds to get it right the first time he would still be here. They'd operated on him too many times."

Connie looked down, unable to meet our eyes. "I have to go upstairs, dear," she announced and walked out of the kitchen. "I'll be down soon," she called from the hall.

Why didn't Connie give Rosie any sympathy? Things didn't seem right between mother and daughter and her actions left me speechless.

As Rosie sat licking the edge of a rollie, I could tell she was trying not to cry. I wanted to say something more meaningful, but the words wouldn't come.

"Is there anything I can do, Rosie?"

"No, you just arrived here, Jess. Don't worry. It's another one of our usual crises; we're used to it these days. I expect we'll get over it, like we always do. But thanks." She sniffed. "I'm sorry to lean on you like that."

"No, Rosie, it's fine, I understand and it's good to talk. Stay positive as best you can. I lost my father recently, so I know those feelings only too well." I had to leave before I burst into tears. "Rosie, sorry, but I must get changed. Will you be all right?"

She sniffed again and nodded. "It's okay, Jess, I'll be fine, honest I will."

Chapter Seven

I had become more acquainted with The Cavalry. Hans refused to talk and only spoke when he needed something.

I took a walk along the track to the parkland to scout around and see who was also living within the confines of the Tanglewood estate. I passed along the edge of the lake and watched the ducks swimming on the opposite bank. Was it a suicide or a murder? How dreadful that someone had lost their life here. I couldn't imagine it in such a tranquil place, but there again it was probably the ideal place to commit suicide in such a quiet spot. It certainly put me off any notions of swimming there.

Under the spring sky two aeroplanes crossed vapour trails. I bumped into Ewan. Quite literally. I was too busy looking at the clouds whilst shading my eyes from the sun.

"Watcha gal," he said with a smile.

"Oh, Ewan sorry, how are you doing?"

"Okay, got to finish this job though. I'm making a new hen house."

"Well done. By the way, tell me about this wedding of yours, when's the date? I forgot to ask Rosie."

Of course, I knew the date, Rosie had mentioned it. I wanted Ewan to make conversation with me now we were alone for the first time.

"Ah ya...well yes, er...end of August, I think. Will you be there?" he asked. "Connie said she will send out the invites when she's ready."

"Of course, I will. It'll be lovely to see you both married in the park—how romantic. Thanks for asking me."

He paused for a moment. "It's not a conventional wedding, Jess, I'm afraid...how can I say this? A special wedding, you *know*? Where we celebrate with flowers and *garlands*? And well...look sorry, I haven't got time to stop right now, the chooks need their food."

"Sounds lovely and every wedding is special." I reminded myself that I was supposed to be open-minded.

"Oh, yes, it is. See you later." Ewan raised his hand.

I dreaded to think who or what could turn up next.

I returned to work after the weekend and updated Mark on the appointments. During the half-hour meeting, we discussed sales, and he asked me if I could help George with the test drives. "Business is 'hotting up', just like the weather," he said. "You know, you impress me," he added.

"How come?" I asked, bemused.

"When you first came here, it was wrong of me I know, but I assumed you were the usual 'run of the mill' standard temp. You're a very supportive PA and your organisational skills are tip top. I was delighted when you stepped in for me the other week, and you helped instigate a sale on a car, great work, Jess. Mr Jarvis bought the car, he said you were most professional. I'll give you a small bonus for that, thank you."

"Oh, thanks a lot. I did work for a short while in sales and management and I often used to show customers around a caravan showroom. It was nothing really. I'm glad I was of help to you." I smiled at his offer of a bonus.

"Where do you think you are going with this travelling secretary lifestyle of yours? It's been a while since I was this pampered at work, so I'd like to take you out for lunch as a thank you."

Aware that I was frowning, I soon smiled again at the mention of lunch although for many reasons, maybe I should have kept the frown. Mark was more than ten years my senior, and despite his

70

explanation for the lunch, his motives concerned me, but this was my natural concern against all older men, especially a boss who was in his forties and good looking.

"Where do you plan on going?" I asked.

"The Fox and Hounds up the road, they do a good rump steak."

I checked the diary and having caught up on much of the work, my mind said I should go. Life on the farm had been lonely at the weekend. I hadn't seen much of Jonni and I missed our chats together. He was my back-up for a sense of normality.

"Okay, lunch would be good and thanks for the compliment. The farm is a bit out in the sticks and it'll be good to socialise for a change."

"Well, Connie Dijkman's place isn't exactly…should I say…"

"Buzzing with entertainment?" I offered. "Still, it's not too bad. In some ways it *is* rather entertaining to be looking down on their daily lives. I love the peace and atmosphere of the old house. It gives me chance to read a good book and ponder my future."

Mark seemed thoughtful. "One o'clock okay?"

"Fine, see you then." I nodded as Mark's attention was caught by George on the showroom floor.

Before I left the office, I tidied my hair and wore lipstick. We arrived at quarter past one in separate cars and sat looking through the menu at the Fox and Hounds Inn. Mark bought the drinks and sat opposite me on a small stool. I suddenly felt rather self-conscious, and I think Mark sensed my insecurities as he gave me an assuring smile.

I was still studying the menu to avoid catching his eye as the waitress came to take our order. We thanked her and Mark opened the conversation.

"What do you know about Connie Dijkman?" he enquired.

"Not a lot, I have to admit. I only live there, a bed to sleep on you may say. It's a lovely place, except a bit run down for someone who is supposed to be wealthy."

"Look, Jess, be careful. Connie is a lovely lady, but I feel she has been lured into…shall I say…well she seems easily led, that's all, so I'm told—and I know this sounds ridiculous, but they say she is a white witch." Mark blinked.

"Connie? No. What a load of rubbish." I laughed, not knowing a thing about witchcraft in any shape or form. Perhaps I shouldn't have laughed.

"Well I thought so, too, but folklore and gossip around here are rife."

"So, I'm led to believe."

We sat in silence for a few moments observing the habits of the customers in the pub and I tried not to react to his statement. The waitress cleared the tables and clinked the beer glasses together as she placed them on her tray. My eyes followed her I was getting hungry at the delicious aroma of food which kept wafting from the kitchen.

Mark turned to me. "So, why are you really here, Jess? I mean sometimes I get the feeling you're running away from something. I wanted to ask you what *really* brings you way down south? I mean you don't seem to have any ties to this area. I'm curious that's all. Tell me off if I'm getting to be a nosey parker." He laughed.

I pulled back, not sure what to say, did my feelings show *that* much?

"Yes, you are being nosey, but I don't mind." I gave him a broad smile. "Well, I'm not running away. I enjoy travelling, life is full of new things to be learned and when my father died…" I gazed at the waitress again, "…we had the saddest Christmas and New Year; I'm just getting over it."

"Steak?" asked the waitress.

"Here," said Mark.

I smiled 'thanks' as she served my fish and chips.

"I'm sorry." He looked away, perhaps wishing he hadn't asked. "Do you have a partner, boyfriend?"

Oh, oh…what was coming next? I attempted to smile my way out of his question.

"I used to but I got tired of picking up his socks and underwear and pandering to him; that's not me at all. A relationship should be well balanced, don't you think?"

Mark agreed.

"I understand," said Mark. "But you weren't married, were you?"

I now had the deepest suspicions about his questions.

"Oh no, we just lived together hoping that a wedding would be on the cards someday. But I couldn't see it coming, so gave up on the idea." Why did he want to know all this stuff? I hoped he was only making conversation and nothing more.

"But yes, I agree with you, marriage *should* be all about sharing." He looked away from me and I detected a note of regret when he said, "I'm sorry to hear it didn't work out." He leaned in toward me. "Take care of yourself. You're a good worker, Jess—don't get left behind. I'm sure the right person is waiting for you."

I began to feel odd. Mark had dived too many times into my personal space. Was he trying to get closer to me? Surely not. He glanced at his watch.

Within the last few weeks all I'd heard were warnings to look out for myself. First, Pauline at the agency, then Jonni, and Mark, who lived a few miles away. Connie, it seemed, had made a name for herself. Was I reading too much into all this?

A few minutes later we left the restaurant, as the invoices were calling me back. We agreed to meet at the office.

Chapter Eight

At five o'clock I closed the office door and left Mark to lock up.

"Thanks for the lunch, Mark. See you in the morning," I called. "Glad you had a successful meeting this afternoon." I smiled and made my way to the car.

I had only been polite, talking about work and Connie Dijkman at lunch. I'd asked him about his family, but all he said was, "Ah well, another story for another time"—conversation closed.

As I turned the bend on Five Acres Lane and drew up outside the house, I noticed Jonni getting out of the Viva.

"Hi, Jonni, how's the car? Glad you're using it."

"Thanks, Jess, it's fine. It was good of you to let me borrow it. I've just been into town. At least it keeps the battery topped up and lets me have my freedom again. It means a lot to me."

"Well, seeing as it's you," I replied with a grin.

"Okay thanks, and you're still sure you don't mind?"

I nodded in approval. "I have to admit that I *am* attached to it, but it's getting old and like your Triumph Herald, it's becoming a bit costly to repair. I'm surprised I made it all the way down to Axminster, to be honest."

"Your dad kept it in good condition though, it should last a while yet. I'm grateful for your help. Look, erm…do you fancy going to the pub for a drink tonight?"

"You're asking me out?" I asked. "That's the second date today, I must be getting popular. I've been out with the boss for lunch."

"If you want to call it that," he replied with a grin. "I got paid today." He made the last comment as though he was eternally grateful for his wages.

"Okay. I'll see you back here and we can go in the *posh* car. Say…at seven?" I checked my watch—quarter to six. Ruby Tuesday came bounding toward him. She rolled on her back in her usual submissive pose and Jonni patted her.

He called back to me. "Thanks for brushing Rubes yesterday, Jess, she looked lovely. She's never been this pampered before."

"Oh, it was something to do at the weekend and she loved it." I paused for a moment "Okay, seven then. See you at the car."

We parted and as I went to my room I caught a glimpse of Connie parading down her private corridor in a long white nightie to visit her bathroom. What was she doing dressed like that at six in the evening? Had she been in bed all day and only just got up? I don't think she saw me as she walked barefoot in her long ghost-like attire looking like a character from a Brian Rix theatrical farce. Perhaps she was ill, I thought.

"Hello, Connie, how are you?"

"Yes dear, fine, fine."

I shrugged my shoulders as she disappeared into the bathroom and I reached for the latch on my door.

I knew Jonni's intentions were honourable. Perhaps I had been kidding myself about him, thinking I wouldn't be able to trust another relationship. In one of my 'moments' I realised it would be foolish of me to get involved with someone who had no job and lived on a hippy commune. How did that sound? 'Hello, Mum, I've got a new boyfriend, he doesn't have a real job, he milks the cows on the farm and only gets paid when the boss has some money in the bank.' I had to find out more about Jonni. He was a really nice guy, but…*come on, Jess it's only a friendly date, don't get carried away.*

I changed into my jeans and t-shirt and came downstairs. Rosie put tea in the pot and we sat together discussing her day.

"It's been very hot today, hasn't it? They say we're due a heatwave." I recalled.

"I have to be careful with the horses in this weather. They need to be kept cool," she said.

"Has your mum been ill?"

"No, I don't think so, why?"

"I saw her in her nightie."

"Oh, that's normal for Mum. She goes to bed around four thirty in the morning and spends all day there. She's a night owl, I'm afraid. That's why we don't see much of her in the week except on market day when she sometimes helps Jonni with the sheep."

I wasn't sure what to say. What a strange routine; she must hardly see the light of day. I couldn't get my head around her lifestyle at all.

The room fell silent, as if our mutual interests were cut in midstream. I had often felt Rosie's personality wanted to spring out in front of her, but she seemed afraid that life was about to bite her back.

"I'm going to the pub tonight. Jonni asked me if I'd like to come along."

"*Jonni's* going out tonight?" she asked.

"Yes. Doesn't he usually?"

"Well no, he's become a bit of a recluse of late. You must be in his favour, Jess, well done. He's a good bloke. He kind of keeps us all in line." She laughed.

"He's got my car now, it's made a difference to him. Maybe at the weekend we can all go out—that would be great."

She thanked me but didn't confirm she and Ewan would like to come along as well.

Jonni stood by the Fiesta waiting for me. He wore a fashionable shirt, and had brushed his hair into a smart style. He looked well-turned-out for a change. A dab of sweet smelling man-stuff wafted over the roof of the car. With his dark brown corduroy jacket, slung over his shoulder I had never seen him looking so good. Our eyes met and he gave a slow smile; I felt the need to say something.

"You look great, Jonni, I've never seen you in your posh clothes. I got used to you being the herdsman, in jeans and overalls."

"You don't look so bad yourself," he flirted. "Come on, let's sneak away before Connie grabs me to do yet another job."

I heard him sigh.

I started the engine, turned the car around on the drive, and we set out for the local pub.

"So, how come Connie stays in bed all day? She is a strange one, isn't she?"

He looked out of the car window as I spoke.

"So, how come…" I asked again in case he didn't hear me properly the first time.

Jonni held back. "I'll explain all when we get there."

"Oh."

Why did I have to wait until we got to the pub? Instead, he made general conversation about the warm weather and the lovely scenery. Perhaps there was another motive to his invitation.

As we arrived in the pub car park, I moved into a parking space and switched off the engine. He turned to me.

"Wait, Jess, don't go inside yet. I have a reason for asking you out this evening. I think it's best we get away from Tanglewood and then we can talk, without The Cavalry listening."

My chest tightened. He had tried to tell me before, but there was always someone interrupting.

Jonni put his arm around the back of my seat. I could almost feel his breath on my face. "It's about Rosie's wedding," he said.

I butted in and wished I hadn't. "Yes, Ewan told me all about it. They're having garlands and flowers and it's a handfasting thing. Don't worry, I know about it."

"Well…it's more than that. I'm not sure, but there's something very odd going on and it's got me worried."

"From what I've seen so far, nothing surprises me."

77

Jonni smiled at my comment and our eyes met. "You see, it's like this. You know I'm worried about my future here. Well, Connie goes out every night and doesn't come back until late. She tells me she has a night job, but somehow, I don't believe her. She earns money, but only enough to keep the farm going and enough to pay me— ha, sometimes—and the rest of The Cavalry. She often hosts lavish parties and invites wealthy people to these 'meetings' of hers. I'm not sure exactly where she goes in the early hours. I wish that woman would get her priorities in order." He shook his head in frustration. "One evening, very late, I followed her and this guy picked her up in a Bentley. I've no idea who he was, or where he took her, but to me, the whole thing didn't feel right."

"Maybe she has a new fella in her life?" I suggested.

"No, Jess, I don't think so. She comes home completely exhausted and often high as a kite."

"She's probably shagging the local aristocracy and getting paid for it," I joked, wishing I hadn't.

"Exactly," Jonni exclaimed with widened eyes.

"Huh? That was a thoughtless joke, sorry."

"She's involved in something sinister, that's for sure. Connie is so naïve at times and has no sense of responsibility. She tells me she's saving up for Rosie's wedding. Although she appears, to some, as a fairly astute business person, she just isn't. Full stop."

This was not the Connie I thought I knew, although Rosie had hinted about her mother's impulsive ways.

"Worst still, I fear that Hans is involved in this, too." Jonni sighed. "Have you seen his new motorbike? Where the hell did he get the cash to buy a BMW? It must have cost him at least a couple of thousand pounds." He paused for thought. "D'ye know, Jess, I reckon Connie gave him the money to buy it. She is too kind and trusting and I fear Hans is taking advantage of her."

It was then I got my chance to talk about Hans. "Can I ask you something, Jonni?" My heart began to race.

"Sure, go ahead."

"Well, as we are discussing Hans, I wanted you to know he threatened me the other week. I've not had the chance to talk about it until now. It's really upset me."

"Mm? What kind of threats?" He took a deep breath and I was beginning to wish I hadn't told him.

"I was hoping you wouldn't ask me that, it's a bit embarrassing." I wasn't sure how to word it, so I took the polite option. "He made more than a suggestive pass at me. If I'd been there any longer it could have been much worse." I hesitated to say more. "I find him very intimidating. I had to defend myself."

His jaw dropped. "Jess, oh my god, I'm so sorry. Bloody Hans. I'm afraid you're going to have to keep out of his way. Don't go near him. He's a selfish bastard. Connie tells me he has the most awful problems and we're supposed to understand him. I mean, we're the ones who are supposed to feel sorry for him, but how can we when he behaves like a spoilt child? Try not to talk to him and I suggest you stick with me, Jess, okay? I'll look after you. This is dreadful. Is there anything you want me to do about it?"

I smiled at the thought of being 'looked after' by Jonni. With each passing day I felt myself pushed closer to him and I didn't mind one bit.

"I wish I could report him, but it's going to cause an uproar, isn't it? If I go to the police, for example."

"Oh no, don't do that, erm…yes you're right, it could cause more problems than we are prepared for and the police wouldn't take any notice anyway, it's your word against his."

"But why does Hans not like me? I've done nothing wrong."

"I'm sorry, Jess, it seems you unwittingly got in his way. As I've said before, he's like that with all of us. Tell me if he goes too far and I'll have words with Connie." He sighed. "I'm afraid it's not you, Jess, it's Hans, and he's a very troubled guy. I don't know the full story of why he is here but it seems the whole world gets under his skin and he explodes and doesn't care about other people. Connie tells me there's a soft side to him, but I've yet to see it. There's some odd reason he is here at Tanglewood and I've never been able to fathom it out. Connie says he doesn't mean to be such a bully. Yes, she tends to take in all the waifs and strays. She once told me the farm has been a way to overcome her anxiety by working with the animals. She likes to think of herself as a saviour and I suspect she knows more about Hans than we do. Don't take it too personally, it's shocking when he's so verbally abusive but you should be okay. 'Sticks and stones'—you know what I mean?"

I nodded although inside me I was reeling with frustration. "Thanks, I wondered how I am supposed to deal with it, that's all. He's hardly ever around, it won't be hard to steer away from him. I'm at work most of the time. I wish I understood why he's living here. So...back to Rosie's wedding."

Jonni paused. "Connie's desperate to give those two a special wedding. She always had control over Rosie until Ewan came on the scene and things changed. Connie listens to Ewan, I have no idea why. Even the wedding; she's tried hard to get Rosie to go with her and choose a wedding outfit. I also know Connie is saving up. I think she keeps money in the house, she doesn't bank it. The problem is, I fear Rosie and Ewan are involved in this, too. I don't want you to be shocked when you attend the ceremony. Rosie invited you, yes?"

I nodded.

"Okay well, I wouldn't think it's something you've experienced before." He turned down one corner of his mouth.

I felt as though time itself was running out for Jonni, he had to explain before anyone else got to me first. "What do you mean?" I asked.

"Because...well it's difficult for me to explain but...some of the guests will be quite well-to-do, all money people."

"So?" I frowned.

I felt his reluctance as he took a deep breath before speaking. "Well, see. Ewan tried to explain it to me. During the ceremony, we are the 'outer guests'. Those close to Rosie and Ewan, the close friends, will make a circle in the inner ring. They join hands, and we don't see the bride and groom. I wasn't asked to be one of them, and I'm glad. Promise me you won't laugh when I tell you this?"

"I'll try not to."

"Well, the thing is, Rosie and Ewan are hidden from view in the centre of the circle. It is rumoured in ancient times that the bride and groom used to consummate the marriage in the inner circle surrounded by the twelve elders of matrimony. In my opinion it's a farce and not like any handfasting I've ever heard of. This is why I am concerned, it doesn't fit. Sometimes I think somebody is having me on. I expect someone to spring out and say, 'Smile, you're on Candid Camera', but no, it's quite a serious affair apparently. They are bonding with ancient tradition and there is a rumour that they will consummate the marriage, on that day, surrounded by the elders; like Adam and Eve, you know…"

"Oh my god, will they be naked? And when you said *consummate* the marriage they don't…" I lowered my voice for this bit, "actually 'do it' in public, do they? I had no idea things were going to be that intense. Do we have to run around naked as well?" I asked with an attempt at light sarcasm. It seemed out of character for Rosie as I knew her. I saw Jonni flinch at my comment before he gave a nervous smile.

"No, Jess, of course not, but we have to keep an open mind and I don't think we need worry. I doubt if it's going to happen."

"I suppose this is what you meant by Connie's cult friends? The whole thing sounds a bit, well…you know, ridiculous. What do we do?" I asked.

"Oh, take each day as it comes, Jess. When the ceremony is over, the reception will be the same as any other wedding. I don't want to get involved with other people's fantasies. My life is under my control and that works for me."

"Are you in control? It doesn't seem that way when Connie fails to pay your wages every week. I mean how do you manage?"

He shrugged his shoulders. "I just do. I've had enough problems of my own."

"Are *you* another of Connie's strays?"

"Hell, I hope not. At first, I only wanted a job to tide me over, to give me time to think about my future, but I kind of stayed longer than I intended. Connie relies on me for the cows. For now, though, I like to keep a low profile and I want to enjoy what I have. I mean being here with you this evening is great, Jess; you're so easy to talk to. But I'm concerned about Rosie. I feel certain she is torn between marrying Ewan and losing him because of the things they may ask her to do at the wedding. I hope she can deal with it, she's a good person. I really don't know. I daren't say anything to her in case I say the wrong thing."

"Of course. I understand but…"

"Everyone at the farm has problems that need sorting, and with time, I hope they will see the light and move on. Perhaps I might do the same. I suppose we mustn't judge the Dijkmans by what they do. If Rosie and Ewan want a pagan wedding, then so be it. I mean, we happily mix Christianity and paganism in our love for Father Christmas. Paganism tends to overlap with Christianity in many ways. Therefore, whether they have a church wedding or one in the privacy of their own hallowed ground that's up to them. So perhaps we should smile and accept what we see."

"But don't you have to go to a church or registry office to have a wedding?"

"This is a pagan handfasting. You can do what you wish on your own ground. I suggest if you're really interested you can check it out at the library."

"But if it goes beyond our boundaries, then what do you do?"

"We'll have to deal with it, but I doubt if it will go that far. You have your job, I have mine and we can get on with our lives. We mustn't get too involved."

"Anyway…how do *you* know all this?"

"Ewan—he tells me all kinds of weird stuff. I think he's the one that's not in control of his own actions—it's almost as though someone is pulling his strings. I worry about him at times. He's changed a lot in recent months. Sorry, I didn't mean to burden you. Don't worry, Jess, I will look out for you, I promise. You're an outsider and everyone respects you on the farm."

I fingered the necklace I was wearing.

"I hope so, Jonni, thanks." I smiled. In other words, he was telling me to stay out of it.

I couldn't imagine what this wedding would be like. Despite having to deal with Hans, it was good to have Jonni around me and I supposed he was right: 'say nothing'. His strength of mind gave me courage. Only one comment concerned me—what had Jonni done to change his life? I hoped he would explain further.

"Wait." I frowned. "I wanted to ask you. You know this Lord Hannings mystery, the one who disappeared and his wife drowned? Isn't he a descendant of the person in the picture in my bedroom? He has to be a relative of Connie, don't you think?"

"Yes, but nothing was proven. I mean they could *both* have been murdered for all we know, except it wasn't Hannings that was found in the lake. Someone else could be to blame. I heard he was involved in all kinds of illicit goings on—drugs, gambling—anyway that's all in the past."

"I see." All this information was too much for me. I needed a drink and I suspected Jonni did as well. "Come on, let's go and have a 'bevy', all this is making me thirsty. We can't sit in the car park all night."

As I locked the car door, Jonni stood behind me. We made our way toward the bar and sat in a quiet corner of the room. He asked me what I would like to drink.

"Cider please—thanks."

"I'm pleased you came to the farm. Ewan isn't exactly a mate, he's just a kid really, and Hans is so unpredictable, I can't stand him. He's been in trouble with the law in Austria as far as I know."

Then I saw him lose eye contact and bite his lip.

"What?" I asked and frowned.

"Oh, nothing. No, it hasn't been easy living here."

I gazed at his far away expression. "Why doesn't that surprise me about Hans?" I said.

Jonni turned and put his hand on mine and gave it a friendly squeeze. "Don't worry. I want to say thanks for being so understanding."

Somehow, I didn't mind Jonni being close to me. I knew instinctively whatever he had or hadn't done in his life, it couldn't have been anything violent. As for Hans, I knew where I stood. Regarding the wedding, I was having grave doubts about attending; but poor Rosie, perhaps she was being forced into some kind of arranged marriage. My mind seemed to be running riot again. I know most people have problems or some kind or another, but in this household, nothing seemed to fit as being 'normal'. I suppose the same could be said for me right now.

"Tell me, how long have you been at Tanglewood?" I asked.

"Four years gone March."

"What on earth brought you here?"

"I could ask you the same question, but I'm not sure now is the right time to tell you my answer. It might take all night," he smiled.

"You told me all those other things in the car, so I don't see yet another part of the puzzle could possibly be more shocking than what you told me."

"I think I'll leave that one for later, if you don't mind—come on, Jess, drink up."

"Did you go to university when you left school?"

"Well, sort of, but I want to start afresh now."

I sighed, thinking *come on Jonni you can't leave me in the air.* "Okay, I get the message." The conversation paused for a moment. "Sorry, I didn't to mean to pry."

Jonni leaned forward. "You know, Jess, it's good to have someone I can talk with, away from the madding crowd, you might say. It can get lonely at times."

"I know what you mean."

"I do my best," he replied with a smile. "Having you here

makes it more bearable." He looked away from me then turned back with a smile.

"What?"

"Oh, nothing. You're looking lovely tonight, Jess." He took a deep breath and a gulp of his beer.

"Thanks." I was so engrossed in our previous conversation I didn't fully appreciate his compliment.

I sipped my cider, determined to confirm what Jonni had told me earlier, it was all so farcical. "This pagan ceremony, Ewan and Rosie surely won't go all the way, will they?"

Jonni smiled. "Well…from what I know and have read in the books, I think *tradition* demands they do."

"You're joking!" I almost choked on my drink. "Come on, Jonni, tell me you *are* joking." I felt my eyes widen.

"Well no, actually. I am only saying it is a possibility. Ewan seems to be into 'natural life' stuff these days, whatever that means. He tells me all living things are 'holy' and he has this ecological vision. That's what I mean about Christianity crossing with paganism. I don't think Ewan understands in which direction he is going. He doesn't see anything wrong with wanting to go back to nature and ancient times and—to quote him, 'it's the way of things and I should learn to accept it.' He also said, the act of having sex was perfectly natural, so why shouldn't they have a natural marriage and prove their seed will live on in the pagan way. I know something of paganism. I read about it in my studies and what he describes to me I think is total rubbish. Something isn't quite right. I know it."

I allowed my jaw to drop. "Ridiculous. Why should they need to prove it, for god's sake? It's voyeurism, pornographic, surely? Awful. Ewan and Rosie won't be expected to do all that stuff—no, come on, Jonni, that's absurd. Do they realise what they have got themselves into?"

"I'm not sure. I don't know if Rosie understands what's in store at the wedding ceremony."

"Oh heck, doesn't she have a mind of her own anymore?"

"You see Connie's 'society' members are not what they seem. What they are doing is clandestine or whatever you want to call it. Connie never mentions anything about her nights out with her posh friends or why she stays up so late. It doesn't make sense to me. I can't afford to play a part in their little games. I feel Connie, in her naivety, is allowing it to happen. Unwittingly, she is exploiting Rosie. You will be okay because I haven't told you anything, as far as they are concerned; act normal. I only wanted to protect you 'cos... you're bound to think it's a bit weird." He shrugged.

By now, I did know something. I looked at Jonni and our eyes met.

"I don't want to put you off living at Tanglewood, Jess, I hope you'll stay on with us."

"Well, if I can be allowed to get on with my life, then I am sure it will be okay, don't you? I pay the rent and that works for me. Maybe you can come down to the beach with me one weekend and we can have some fun and time away from the farm."

"Yes. I'd love to. You're right, but there's always the cows to be milked and I can't just leave them."

"There's a new Job Centre opened in town, have you tried there yet?"

"No." he shook his head.

"Perhaps it's something you might like to think about."

One question nagged at me and I had to ask. "So...why do you feel the need to protect me?" I glanced at my feet.

"I suppose it's because you're not eccentric like the rest of us here." He beamed.

"I'm glad to hear it." I pushed his arm in play.

I checked my watch. "Oh gosh, we must get going. I want to get a bite to eat before bedtime. I think we ought to be driving back to the house." I stood to put on my jacket and Jonni helped me. As he gestured for me to go first through the door, we had a moment of adoration as a man walked into the pub with a Jack Russell puppy in his arms. It was almost dark as I unlocked the car doors.

"Jess, don't worry, things will turn out fine. I've enjoyed my time with you this evening. It's a big relief to be able to offload. I hope you didn't mind. Maybe we can go to the pub again, but I'll talk with you soon. The trouble is, I need to keep my head above water and this probably isn't the right place to do it these days. I hope you understand."

What did he mean? Perhaps I should ask him, but before I could, he butted into my thoughts.

"Have you seen the other guys at the at the old tumbledown cottage on the parkland? They help us when we need them. Connie takes in anyone she can pay 'on the cheap' to do the work. She feels sorry for everyone she meets. In a way she has a heart of gold, but it gets her into trouble every time."

"Oh, I see. No, I've not met any of them, although I think I've seen Fergal's girlfriend."

It started to make some kind of sense, although *sense* was not the optimal word. Connie was broke, she belonged to a kind of religious society, and probably got paid for some covert job—who knows? I assumed it was to pay for a lavish wedding and the upkeep of her farm. What the hell was she doing and where did Lord Hannings fit into her life? It was so confusing, but did it matter? In any case I'd arranged to meet Mum and Anna soon. The last phone call, Anna told me she had a new boyfriend. There were better things to consider than the affairs of Tanglewood. Hunger was beginning to call and I needed to raid the fridge before bedtime, a bowl of cereal would be nice.

That night I dreamt the police broke into the house. They asked me if I knew Connie Dijkman. I repeatedly denied it, "No, no I don't know her, I don't, leave me alone," my voice growing shriller each time. I awoke the next morning to the sound of the rooster crowing three times. Was I in denial, too? All this talk of Christianity and Paganism was getting too much. Could this be a warning?

Chapter Nine

I arrived home early one evening to discover Connie preparing for guests. The plates, knives, and forks were set to a measured degree. I gathered it was something she learned from her life in Scotland. An enormous decorative pheasant made of silver served as a centrepiece for the buffet table. Very elegant indeed, and very 'over the top' perhaps. In the kitchen, a large salmon lay on a plate and it seemed she had been busy preparing canapés and vol-au-vents during the afternoon. Finely chopped coleslaw and green salad lay in bowls drizzled with salad dressing. The smell of delicious food overwhelmed me. I had no idea Connie was such a good organiser and cook.

"Oh, hi, Connie. I see you're expecting guests."

"Yes, it's one of my meetings and my turn to do the food."

"Looks like you've been busy all afternoon whilst I was at work."

"Well, Harold helps me in these circumstances. He's our local butcher and extremely clever with the meat. Did you see the hog roast?"

"Ah, that's what I can smell, eh? I saw smoke coming from the side of the house but I assumed Ewan was having one of his barbecues," I laughed.

I began to wonder who was paying for all this; I was not invited. Hans sidled into the kitchen and glared at me. "Sorry, you're not going to the party, Jess," he said with sarcasm in his tone.

I ignored him and looked to Connie instead. "I'm going out tonight," I lied. "I hope you have a nice time."

I went to my room, mainly to keep out of Hans' way, and got changed from my day clothes into a pair of jeans. I decided to take a walk. I wondered why Connie kept the party to herself. Okay, I was not entitled to be there, but if the event was going on until the small hours then perhaps a polite warning would have been helpful and I could have bought a pair of ear plugs. Instead, I took a walk on my own and met Rosie coming from the stables.

"I see your mum is expecting guests."

"Oh yes, I never go to those events. I don't like the people who attend, they're all a bit er…" she lifted her hand, "flash, for my liking. Sometimes she invites the local hunt to gather here. I can't stand it, all that lot in their hoity-toity gear. I never understand how she likes animals and yet she lets the local hounds trample over our land and rip the foxes to pieces. It seems so contradictory to me. I used to go fox hunting but not anymore. She gets paid for it, I suppose. It's all about bloody money these days."

Rosie turned away from me for a moment.

I wanted to ask her why her mother had these parties; she was financially broke, how could she afford it? But I couldn't go that far.

"What're you doing tonight?" she asked.

"Oh, I'll take my book and go and read somewhere, perhaps visit Jonni at the dairy or something."

"Good idea, best to stay out of the way when Mum has one of her do's."

I detected a note of exasperation in her voice and nodded, showing I understood what she meant. I supposed I didn't really understand.

"See you later then." I walked on with a book under my arm. A stroll down to the dairy would do me good and the chance that I would catch up with Jonni finishing the milking. It would be fun to meet the cows.

I had hardly left the driveway, when a stream of posh cars came down the lane. I stepped back to keep the gate open and watched them drive toward the house. The women passengers were dressed to kill; I could see what Rosie meant. The drivers waved a 'thanks' at me as I held the gate.

I walked up the lane and rested for a while to sit on a log. I didn't wish to disturb Jonni whilst he was busy. After reading my book for about ten minutes, the sound of cattle came clattering along the road. Ruby appeared; she was herding the cows back from the milking parlour. At first, she was alone, then I recognised Jonni's hat above the hedgerow and he appeared around a bend in the road. I smiled to myself. One of the cows turned back on herself and challenged Ruby. Jonni stepped in with his stick and moved the animal in the right direction.

"Hey oop our lass," Jonni mimicked my Yorkshire accent. "Stand back we're coming through. Anyway, what are you doing all the way up here?" He beamed.

I mentioned the party. "It's good to get some peace and quiet after a busy day at work. I'm just reading my book."

"Oh yes, of course. You'll find those people only come for a couple of hours and then they kind of disappear somewhere else; for such a lavish party it's a bit short and sweet."

"Oh, I see, so it's not an all-nighter then?"

"Come on, get a bloody move on, animals." He waved his stick again. "Nah, just a gathering of folks for a meeting—all well-fixed people with nothing better to do. Connie has the meetings about three times a year. Move on, girls, keep pace." I saw Ruby nipping and tucking between the herd.

"You okay then?" he called above the noise.

"Yeah fine, I wanted to get an early night tonight." I raised my voice. "What time do you think I should go back?"

"They're usually gone by ten. I think they go to the Millingtons' big mansion afterwards."

"Millingtons? Who are they?"

"It's someone Connie knows. They have parties up there, too. Maybe I'll see you later. I'm coming back shortly, dumping Ruby, and then I have to visit someone in the pub about the animal feed—he's a local guy, so I won't be long. I sometimes go for a drink with him."

"Oh okay, I'll see you later then." He opened the gate to let the cows enter the field.

"By the way, you look nice in those jeans and top. Are they new?"

I smiled. Tim never gave me compliments nor did he notice when I bought a new outfit. "Yes, sort of."

He pointed his stick at Ruby, "Lie down!" he shouted.

"I'll take Ruby back if you like, will she come with me?"

"Yes, of course." He fumbled into the pocket of his overall. "Here take this, clip it to her collar, and thanks." He handed me a piece of thin rope. "You probably won't need it, but just in case a car comes along the lane, she likes to bite at the tyres." He squeezed my hand before he let go the rope. "Keep smiling," he said.

I'm sure my heart ruled my head at that point. I was never sure if Jonni was flirting with me or being kind; I began to wish he was flirting. I loved the way he always gave me a sideways glance. Those 'come to bed' eyes of his left me with an overwhelming desire for him to touch me one more time. Oh yes, he was real, all right, but it was me who wasn't being real. However, I decided it was okay to allow myself the occasional fantasy.

"I could take a longer walk with Ruby, is that okay with you?"

"Yes sure, she'd love that. Tuck her up on her bed when you get back, okay? Once you're away from here you can let her off the lead."

I left Jonni as he closed the gate behind him and disappeared into the field beyond.

After walking through the wood and following the path to the lake, I made my way in the twilight toward the house, with Ruby panting by my side. The aroma of new-mown grass filled my nostrils. The orange glow of sundown and the song of blackbirds on the lanes provided the perfect ambience. As I walked, I kept thinking about Jonni; he was never far from my thoughts these days.

It was important that I didn't arrive too early and bump into Connie and her guests. I strolled along and arrived at the house just after sundown.

The house was silent and a mountain of washing up and wasted food littered the worktop. The dishes were uncovered and a fly landed on the pâté. It seemed everyone had abandoned the place in a hurry leaving the washing up for someone else to do. I ignored the mess, and bedded Ruby down in the far corner of the kitchen, ensuring she couldn't reach the food on the work tops, and went to my room.

I heard Ewan's voice. He seemed to be encouraging Hans to sit down. "Come on mate, you'll be fine, just sit here."

"I've told you before, you heff to be careful," he slurred. "Why de fuck don't you ever listen to me."

"Not whilst you're in this mood, Hans."

"I'm not in any mood, I'm just trying to warn you off, that's all. That lot, they got under your skin. You're hooked."

"Don't worry about me, I can handle it. It's not a problem. It's not what you think."

"Oh yes?"

I must have slept for an hour when a door slammed so loud the house shook and I sat up in bed like a corpse after an electric shock. *What the heck...? What was that?*

With my heart racing, I got out of bed, and put my ear to the bathroom door. I heard Hans' voice and the sound of a chair being scraped across the floor, and a cupboard door slammed in anger. Some of the dirty pots crashed to the floor.

His low voice complained. "Bloody stoopid vench, what de fuck does she sink she's doing? I AM NOT HER BLOODY SLAVE!" His voice boomed through the house.

Oh my god. More pots being smashed.

I don't think I shall ever forget what happened next. The dreadful sound of loud yelping in agony. I'd never heard a dog make a noise like that before. The rapid beating of my heart took my breath away as Hans' dreadful threatening voice boomed across the kitchen, "Bastard dog. Get outa my way you stoopid animal," and then more screams coming from Ruby.

I ran down the stairs, scared of what he could do to me and what fate had befallen Ruby. I peeked into the kitchen from the hall and saw him. Ruby yelped loudly again and I couldn't stand it, I had to stop him as he drew back his foot for another kick.

I yelled at the top of my voice, "Stop—you'll kill her! Look what you did—Oh, my god. You've broken her leg. Stop! You've broken her leg." I picked up that all-important poker again and defended myself. My screams stopped him from giving Ruby another blow and I went to comfort her. Tears fell on my pyjamas as I watched her drag herself toward me for protection. She squealed. I was shaking. I thought for a moment Hans would kick me, too, but no, again he backed off and sneered, "You'd better get her to a vet then, hadn't you? And for your information, Miss High and Mighty, I didn't deliberately break her leg. I tripped over her. How dare you accuse me of being cruel to her, you idiot woman! There's no pleasing you, is there? Perhaps you prefer something else."

He stared right through me, his piercing eyes met mine, his drunkenness overtaking his right mind. I stopped and froze. I knew something terrible was about to happen. Then he came toward me wagging his finger. "Jessica Stamp, you're a bloody liar and a troublemaker. If you tell anyone about this, it's your word against mine, remember that."

Those words choked my throat and I saw Hans place his hand toward the zipper on his jeans.

I think my jaw dropped to my stomach. *Oh no not again, please.* I thought I was going to be sick, but he must have heard someone coming along the path. He smirked again. "Yeah, I thought not, you little cock teaser."

Seconds later Jonni walked through the door and saw my reaction. I stood there mouth agape unable to speak; I pointed at Ruby.

Hans staggered out of the kitchen into the darkness and pushed Jonni out of the way. I saw Jonni's confused look.

"Jess, are you all right? What the…oh Ruby, Ruby, look at her leg! I think it's…oh hell it's broken. Jess, what happened? Oh, poor Ruby, what on earth happened to you, old girl?" He went to touch her and she bared her teeth at him. "Did this happen on her walk?"

"No, I'm soddin' well not all right and no, it bloody well didn't happen on her walk!" I blurted out, my breath heavy, my face white and frozen with fear. I looked at Jonni, the blur of tears over-spilling to my cheeks. I shook as I told him what Hans had done to Ruby. My first concern went to the dog more than what Hans had done to me, and I felt utter shame at having to tell Jonni, yet again, about Hans' threatening behaviour. I decided to wait to tell him about Hans. Tomorrow morning, I would pack my bags and leave. I couldn't stay here anymore. My feelings veered between anger, sheer revenge, and utter confusion. Why did he do this to an innocent animal? As well as being a barefaced liar, he was crazy and needed locking up. Maybe he did have the most terrible psychological problems but there was no excuse for his extreme aggression. What came next—murder?

"No, he…he didn't kick me, but…look, let's get the dog sorted quickly, she's in agony and shock." I tried to be brave; ignoring my shortness of breath. Ruby needed help more than me.

"Oh, Jess, I'm so sorry. I'll get that bastard. He doesn't hate you—he hates everything in this world."

"I heard him threatening the dog and I came down to see what was going on."

"I'm sorry, so sorry." He rubbed his hand on my shoulder, torn between sympathising with me and listening to the yelping from Ruby.

"The vet won't be happy about coming out at this time of night, that's for sure. We can't possibly tell him what Hans did, it's more than our lives are worth. They'll call the RSPCA and all that palaver, we can't be doing with it and Hans will only deny what he did—your word against his, he always twists things. Whenever he's punched me, there's never been anyone else around to prove it."

Punched you? I felt my jaw drop.

"I believe you, Jess, but Connie and Hans are in cahoots with each other. He could easily lie to her. Hans is dangerous, believe me. You mustn't be involved—I can't let you. You don't know this village. I mean, you don't know who are your friends and who are your enemies. Even the vet. We need to be careful. I rarely see Hans in a good mood, he's one hell of an angry man and he hates my guts."

"I can't stay here, Jonni, it's getting dangerous with Hans in the house; he's mentally deranged. We must help Ruby, she can't be left like this. She'll go into shock and die," I sobbed, as she laid there whimpering in pain. All I could do was concentrate on Ruby's welfare. I kept telling myself as I sniffed back the tears to stay calm but the image of Hans stayed with me.

Jonni held me close and then he stroked Ruby. "Come on, Jess, love, you're going to be alright," he sympathised, not knowing what had happened before his arrival. "I'm here now." I saw the pained look on his face. It was the first time he'd called me 'love' but his comforting words were not going to change my mind.

I sat on the stone floor as he made the phone call and listened as Ruby whimpered.

I heard Jonni apologising for his late call. "Yes, I'm afraid Hans fell over her in the dark. She seems to have a broken leg," Jonni lied to the vet.

He returned and placed a blanket from the sofa around the dog.

"Jess, sorry to ask, but can you help me get her to the vet? We have to go there quickly."

"Of course, Jonni, we can't leave her until morning."

I was still in pyjamas, and with tears in my eyes, I ran upstairs to put my jeans on.

When I returned Jonni had wrapped Ruby more securely in the blanket and we were able to carry her to the car.

She looked at me as if to say 'What happened, why did he do this?' How would she ever trust anyone again? She panted the life out of her body and yelped with every move. It was the most horrible thing. I couldn't help shaking at the sounds she made and found myself in a swirl of anger and sheer despondency.

With Ruby in the back seat, Jonni offered to drive, but I suggested he sat with her. He cushioned her ride whilst providing directions to the surgery. I did my best to drive carefully over the bumps; each time the car went down a hole in the road Ruby squealed again.

"It's okay Ruby, it's okay, we'll be there soon," I said. My voice began to break.

How the hell we made it to the surgery, I shall never know—it was well after midnight and the lanes had no lights, my bleary eyes peered into the darkness as we drove along the road.

On arrival, I heard Jonni breathing heavily as we carried Ruby inside. He looked at me and I saw the fury in his eyes. We sat in the waiting room whilst the vet took her into care. I put my arms around Jonni to comfort him and we sat together, my hand on his.

I felt dreadful revulsion at the violation of my boundaries. I was too shocked and decided to tell him later about Hans when I felt more like talking about it.

"I love that dog. If anything happens to her, I'll...She's all I've got."

I felt like saying 'You've got me, too,' but no, he hadn't got me, I was like the proverbial ship about to pass in the night when I moved back to Yorkshire.

The vet beckoned us into the surgery. "And you're saying someone stood on her?" he asked, with a look of disbelief.

"Well, it was more like Hans fell on her in the dark." Jonni lied again. "I wasn't there at the time."

At least the last comment was true.

"Right, I see."

The vet looked at me and then at Jonni and then back to me again. "Hmm, is that what Hans told you?"

"Oh yes. We came home to find her in great distress, I'm not sure if Hans knew she was this injured."

"She's had quite a shock; she's in a lot of pain. I'll keep her in tonight and you can pick her up tomorrow lunch time. I'll X-ray the leg, set it, and give her a pain killing injection. It's very swollen now." He looked down his spectacles at Jonni and his expression seemed very unconvinced.

After an hour we left the surgery, Ruby panting in pain but bravely wagging her tail when we said goodbye.

Outside in the fresh air we both sighed together as we took in the reality of what Hans had done. Jonni hardly spoke as I drove along the road. At Tanglewood I stopped the car on the drive and turned off the lights.

"Are you okay?" he asked, and hugged me before walking toward the house. "I'm so sorry you were involved, believe me, I am *so* sorry. You're a lovely person, Jess. Thanks for everything tonight. My room being next to yours, I won't let anything happen to you. We'll sort it out in the morning. I couldn't have done this without you." He paused for a moment.

"...Jess?"

"What?"

"Oh, it's okay. Look, let's talk tomorrow, eh?" He passed me a kiss on the cheek. "Try to sleep, I'm here if you need me. Thanks, I appreciate your support." He gave a half-hearted smile.

I blew out my cheeks with relief. His tender moments, and the fact that we got away with a dirty big white lie, gave me mixed emotions. "I'm going to work in a few hours. I must get my sleep."

"Me too. I understand. I'm sorry you got in Hans' cross fire. He's dangerous and I must to speak to Connie about him. We can't have him behaving like this. Anyway, you're not alone. Things will work out. I am here, okay?"

"Good night then, Jonni." My sadness must have shown as we climbed the stairs together. I didn't want to be left alone, but I had no option. If he could have slept on the chaise longue, I would probably have felt safer. "See you tomorrow." I took a deep breath and opened the door of my room. He was as supportive as my dad had been and I felt comforted by his words.

He went to his room and we closed our respective doors. I locked mine tight; I think I heard Jonni do likewise. I wished I had been able to tell him the full story about Hans' threatening behaviour, but my insides churned with anger; I couldn't do it. Jonni's face stayed in my head until I fell asleep in sheer exhaustion.

Chapter Ten

"Morning, Jess. Sir Roland Samuels is coming in at eleven and while his car is being serviced, he needs a courtesy car for the day. Could you arrange it with George? Thanks," said Mark.

I couldn't concentrate that morning as the sight of Hans' behaviour kept haunting me.

"Are you all right, Jess?" he asked. "You look tired."

"I was up late last night, the sheep dog's got a broken leg. I had to help take her to the vet. I didn't get much sleep." I almost broke down in tears, but somehow managed to retain composure. I reminded myself that Mark and I were not *that* well acquainted. At this moment, I didn't want anyone to tell me 'I told you so,' nor did I need anything to affect my work.

"Would you like to join me for lunch again?" he asked with a sympathetic look on his face.

"If you don't mind, Mark, I promised to help Jonni collect the dog in the lunch hour. But thanks for asking." At this point my emotions had drained me to the core.

"Isn't that the Holbrook guy? I hear he's been in trouble in the past."

I felt my pulse race and tried to ignore the comment, pretending I wasn't shocked. Honestly, what did Mark know about Jonni?— pure gossip. He had no right to tell me this. Perhaps he was only trying to protect me. But goodness knows why.

"Don't worry, I'm all switched on," I assured him.

"As usual, it's gossip, but look after yourself, that's all." He walked back into his office to make a phone call and left me wondering what the hell he meant. Had Jonni been in trouble with the law? If this was the case, I was getting myself, yet again, into more hot water. I had to move on before it was too late, but where could I go? Who would I turn to, being so far away from home? I ran to the toilet to have a good cry. *Where are you, Dad, when I need you?*

On my lunch break I collected Jonni by the gate. He sat in the car and updated me on Ruby's care. I was dying to probe, but dismissed Mark's words as hearsay.

"I phoned the vet, she's doing fine. He's put a plaster on her hip. It wasn't as bad as we thought, but painful enough. She's bruised, as well as the fractured leg, poor old girl. Thanks, Jess, for everything. I'm sure the vet didn't believe me. We'll have to watch our step."

I went quiet, and couldn't make conversation.

"Jess, I hate myself sometimes for living here." He patted my hand on the steering wheel. "Thanks for being you, I couldn't have got through last night without you. Maybe…"

My eyes began to water as I drove along the road.

"Pull over, Jess, I'll drive if you like."

"The Fiesta's not insured for you."

I began to sob as I stopped the car. The shock of everything that happened last night had been too much. He listened as I finally managed to explain.

"Oh hell, Jess, not again. This is dreadful I'm so, so sorry." He put his arm around me. "Come here, love. Connie has to know about this."

"No don't." I sniffed through my tears. "I'll be alright. I'm disappointed 'cos I thought I had found a great place to live and I end up with the wrong kind of people." I sniffed into my paper tissue. "I need to find somewhere, another room."

"I hope *I'm* not the wrong kind of person and you'll change your mind?"

"No, Jonni, I didn't mean you, but…"

"I told you, he is screwed up about his own happiness. When he sees other people being happy he thinks they have no right to be that way. I believe Hans has nothing in his life other than himself. I think he is jealous of you being my friend. He hates my guts, and anything I do is wrong in his eyes."

"I don't have my dad anymore." I began to cry again.

He gave me a kiss on the forehead. How could such a kind person end up in this mess? I had to know more. I needed a friend; it was important to me right now, but Mark's comments left me feeling confused.

"Jess, at least you know I'm not like them. Let's stick together for now. We can get on with our lives and maybe go out to the pub a bit more. Get to know each other away from the farm. But please give it one more chance, Jess—please?"

"Exactly. Away from the farm," I echoed with disdain.

"Think carefully about it, I…I know I've said this before, but I really love having you around."

I wanted to say more, but everything got too complicated and I began to lose patience. It was important that I was back at work before Mark returned at two o'clock. He was never on time after a lunch at the pub and on this occasion, I felt glad I hadn't gone with him.

We arrived at the vets and helped Ruby walk with her back leg in plaster. I supported her belly with a large crepe bandage. She was still groggy from the sedative but was glad to see Jonni again. He talked to her and she licked his face and seemed more comfortable than the night before. She winced a few times, but from the delight on Jonni's face it was obvious Ruby meant a lot to him. If only I hadn't offered to take her home, we might not be in this mess.

"She'll need a lot of looking after. You can walk her a little in the next two days. You'll have to lift her outside to pee," the vet explained. "I'll send the bill to Connie, should I?"

"No. No…don't do that, send it to me—she's my dog. I'll have to use the Land Rover to round up the sheep. It's a good job the field is dry. Connie doesn't know anything about this yet. She was out last night."

"I'm helping to pay for this," I replied in a low voice. "Send the bill and we'll work it out together." Was I mad?

Jonni rolled his eyes, dismissing my comment, but I knew he couldn't afford it. Someone had to pay the bills and after all, she was Jonni's dog. Anyway, Ruby deserved better treatment after last night.

The vet looked at us as if to say 'are you two an item?' I wanted to explain, but it wasn't worth the effort.

"You're new to Connie's Cavalry, aren't you?" the vet asked.

"I suppose you could say that, except I don't feel part of The Cavalry, because I rent a room—my job's in town." I didn't mean to sound pompous and hoped Jonni hadn't taken my comments the wrong way.

I didn't like the expression on the face of the vet; I could read his thoughts. *She may think she doesn't belong to those hippy types at Tanglewood. That's how they all came to live there. Connie Dijkman always gets them in the end.*

I helped Jonni with the stretcher and Ruby lay on her side. I could have cried as her eyes showed how much trust she had in us. I knew she would never go near Hans again and, if possible, we had to help her get over it.

On the way home, Jonni told me he would take Ruby with him to the cowshed each day in the Viva. He asked me 'did I mind?' Of course not, she was a lovely dog and I would have done anything to ensure she wasn't suffering. The shocking scene from the night before would remain with me all my life. Perhaps I should go to the police, but couldn't—Jonni was right, more trouble. As long as we stayed out of Hans' way and minded our own business, everything would be fine. However, there were plans to leave if the situation didn't improve. If I found a place not too far away, perhaps Jonni could visit me, but did I want him to? Whatever he had or hadn't done I had to know. Was he really the gentle soul he made himself out to be?

We parted at the cowshed gate and on the return journey I stopped along the way to tidy my hair and a tear-stained face. I put on lipstick and squirted Nina Ricci perfume on the inside of my wrists. The perfume brought back memories of Tim. It had been a birthday gift and I wondered for a moment if I had been a bit of an idiot. Had I been running away from my life in Yorkshire?

On arrival at the office, Mark was late, and I entertained his afternoon appointment for a while, before he escorted his client into his office.

I was sitting at my desk drinking tea when the phone rang.

"Jess, is that you dear? It's Connie. Sorry to phone you at work, but what happened last night?"

"Look, Connie, I can't really talk about it here, can we meet later?"

"Of course, dear, I understand. Jonni tells me Ruby is so sick. I can't imagine how she broke her leg. I wanted to thank you for taking her to the vet's last night. I was with friends until late— I didn't know about all this until this afternoon."

Why she couldn't wait for me to get home I had no idea. I was in no mood for conversation and Ruby wasn't even her dog and, did she really not know the full story?

"I'll talk when I get home okay? Sorry, Connie, but we *are* busy."

"Oh…okay, Jess. See you later then, dear. Bye."

"Bye then," I said quietly. I could hear Mark coming out of the office.

He escorted his client to the door, they shook hands and departed. He grinned at me when the client had gone. "Yes," he hissed, showing a fist of triumph. "We sold another car!" He held the deposit cheque in his hand in triumph.

"Our sales figures seem to be up this month. It must be the

weather. How was lunch?" I enquired, wafting a leaflet in front of my face.

"Well…sitting on my own without my secretary wasn't…" He shrugged. "But I managed," he teased. "I hope the dog's okay?"

"Yes fine, she's resting now."

"Must get on, I'm going home early tonight so I'll see you tomorrow." Despite the sale, he seemed to trudge back into his office. If he had a problem he wasn't likely to discuss it with me.

Chapter Eleven

I arrived at Tanglewood after work and went to my room. I didn't stop to say hello to Rosie but acknowledged her. "Back soon," I called—I'm going to get changed. It's been a lovely day but the weather is stifling me. I don't remember it being this hot."

With the longer hours of daylight, I knew Rosie might ask me if I wanted to go riding with her. It was then that a faint voice came from the upper landing.

"Jessica, it's me. Come over to my room when you're ready, dear."

Connie had invited me into 'her space'. After the phone call I knew what she wanted, or at least I thought I did. "I'll be with you in five minutes," I called across the corridor. Moments later I knocked on the door and stepped into her room.

A sweet smoky perfume wafted to my nostrils. Joss sticks.

I opened the bedroom door to find Connie resting on her bed, dressed in her nightgown; it was almost six o'clock and the room felt stuffy despite the open window.

"Oh hello, how are you, Connie?" I surveyed the scene and wasn't sure what to say next, it felt awkward.

"Come and sit down." She patted the eiderdown.

I stepped across the wooden floor toward a beautiful carved oak four-poster bed. On her dresser were bottles of coloured—well, dare I say, potions? Placed in a line were glass pots with leaves and berries inside. I assumed it was all to make the room fragrant, like a potpourri. Light peeked through the gap in the closed curtains and a tape cassette played soft pan pipe music. She had wind chimes near an open window and a gold chalice and bell on what I can only describe as a kind of altar draped with a cloth of red velvet with gold tassels. The room was cluttered and the wardrobe bursting with clothes, but there was a certain charm about the décor. I had seen enough, and didn't want to believe what Mark had implied about witchcraft was true.

"Why are you in bed at this time?" Perhaps she had been out all night.

"Oh, I often get up very late. I expect Rosie will have told you; I'm a bit of a night owl, I can never sleep—just had a nap."

I knew that once someone got into this routine it was hard to get them out of it. At this moment, I didn't have much sympathy for her.

"What a lovely room, Connie." I was only trying to make conversation, but it was pleasant and peaceful enough with the birds singing outside and those chattering magpies again.

She lay in bed with a plethora of photograph albums over the eiderdown. Some of the photos were loose and I couldn't help admire the old Victorian pictures she had collected.

"Tell me about last night. I hear you did a very courageous thing," she said.

I didn't think it was 'courageous' but I wasn't going to put my foot in it and say something I shouldn't. I wanted to find out exactly what she knew. "How did you find out?" I asked her.

"Hansi told me. He such a caring person."

She smiled sweetly which made me angry. *Oh my god, the bastard got his foot in the door first, hmm…*

"What did he tell you?" I tried hard to smile. Hansi was her pet name and if she knew what he had done last night, would he still be her pet? I listened to her explanation.

"Y'know, how he'd tripped over Ruby in the dark and he broke her leg. What a dreadful accident, poor Ruby. He seems very upset about it."

All I could hear in my head was 'bastard, bastard, bastard'. That guy was unbelievable in all aspects. How could he have lied to Connie? But of course, he would, he was like that.

I started to tell the truth and then the words came out all wrong. "Well, it didn't quite…No, I mean I just did the right thing—I had the car and Jonni asked for my help. It was nothing really."

"Well dear, I'm glad you did and I wanted to thank you. We must take care of all the animals—they are very precious to me."

"Oh, absolutely."

"Well, as you can see, this is my special place in the house. I suppose it summarises the real me. I find my inner sanctum here. You're a good girl, Jess. I bet your father was proud of you." I saw her smile in empathy for my loss. "One day you will see the light after the grief. I am there if you want to talk. I will be there, for you, Jonni, Ewan, Hansi and, of course, Rosie. I sometimes feel I will *always* be at Tanglewood, in death, too."

I shuddered at the thought of seeing her ghost haunting the corridors at night. "Thank you, Connie, that's very kind of you, but…" I felt it was an odd thing to say, and what did she mean? A vision came to mind of Miss Havisham from the pages of the Dickens novel, *Great Expectations.*

She patted the eiderdown. Her grey-black wisps of hair seemed to lie on every part of the pillow. "Come, I want to show you something," she said.

I did as she asked, wondering, with a touch of anxiety, what was coming next.

"These are my family pictures. You remember I used to live on the Isle of Skye?"

"Yes, I do, and these are your childhood photos? How interesting, Connie, what a pleasure." All I wanted to do was leave the room for a shower, I didn't know how she could stand sleeping there in the summer heat.

I began to realise perhaps there really was some good in Connie. Most of the time, she seemed so caring and thoughtful. I began to doubt what Jonni had told me about her, although he never said anything bad, it was all curiosity for me and poking one's nose in where it probably wasn't wanted. I wished I had got to know her better. Perhaps now was my chance.

"This was my mother…and this one is somewhat…you could say he's the black sheep of the family. He was my cousin."

"Oh, I am sorry. When you say 'was' I gather you mean he passed away. He looks a charming young man."

"Well, we *think* he is dead, but I can't be sure. He disappeared you see. It was quite a few years ago now. They never found him," she explained with sadness in her voice.

Two and two suddenly began to make four or was it five? Lord Hannings. I couldn't be sure. I wasn't supposed to know anything about him, only what Jonni told me. I pretended this was the first I'd heard of it. So, he was her *cousin*? "May I ask what happened to him?"

"He was a wine connoisseur but I think more than likely he was a rich alcoholic in later years. He had vineyards in France. He's the chap whose ancestors are dotted around the house in the portraits. I inherited some of them. He loved his home in France more than here. Something dreadful happened to his wife—she was found in the lake. Despite the tragedy I never wanted to move, even after Theo left us."

I had to ask the next question. "What do *you* think happened to him, Connie?"

"I don't know; it was all a complete mystery to me. I mean he was such a polite child. We were very close and he adored Rosie. He never had children of his own, you see, and he used to tease and play with her and he taught her how to ride. He treated her like his own daughter. We often used to meet on Sundays for afternoon tea. I'll never understand it. Mary his wife, she…oh, you don't want to hear about our family troubles."

"No—it's all right, Connie I'm interested." I'd suddenly forgotten about the shower.

"Well, I always knew him as a kind chap. Something went wrong in his life. He seemed to lose all sense of himself. I can only assume that when his wife met with the accident—at least, we think it was an accident—he couldn't stand living anymore. I doubt we shall ever know. I hoped he would contact me, but he never did. No one seems to know what happened." Connie swallowed hard. "The verdict on Mary was death by drowning. Nothing was proven. But then why would he suddenly disappear like that after the tragedy and leave all his wealth behind at the great house? I mean it's a possibility that someone murdered him and his body was never found. The estate manager is looking after the old house. It's all very complicated and sad." She sighed with a sense of hopelessness.

Perhaps Connie needed someone to talk to and was pleased I'd spent time with her. I felt my understanding of her would improve.

"And this one was my sister; she had no family either, she died in a plane crash. It was terrible. Oh yes, our family has gone through quite a few tragedies in our time, believe me. It makes you wonder who is going to be the next victim."

"Oh, Connie, don't say that." I patted her hand.

She smiled. "Anyway, here he is again, in this photo. He was a bright boy, university education, such a great future...And this one is all of us together. I treasure these pictures as they remind me of happier times on Skye. We used to go up into the mountains with my father. We had a hunting lodge and staff. A wonderful atmosphere—especially at Christmas. I miss all those holidays."

"I can imagine. Christmas carols, a log fire, Hogmanay, eh? And haggis, too—yes?"

She leaned over, her spare hand sandwiching mine. "Oh yes, those were the days."

She wore a talisman around her neck, a gold Celtic cross with a small ruby in the centre.

"What a pretty cross you're wearing, Connie, is it a family heirloom?" I asked.

"No, someone gave it to me during the war. The ruby is supposed to represent a droplet of the blood of Christ. Glad you like it."

"Yes, I love it. I like wearing jewellery with a history. My grandmother left me a diamond ring when she died; it belonged to her mother. I reckon it goes back to about 1850. I must get it checked sometime."

"Rosie won't want the cross after my death, I expect she will sell it, she's not into pretty things as I am."

We shared experiences and I realised perhaps I had finally built a rapport with Connie Dijkman, but all this talk of death unnerved me. It seemed she had a warm heart after all and something was happening in this household, which hurt her and caused the whole family to drift apart. I reminded myself of the rules—don't get involved.

Connie took my hand. "Jess, I'm pleased you've taken an interest in Rosie, she has become a recluse in recent months. It's good that Ewan has come on the scene but if anything should happen to me in the future, please keep in touch with Rosie for me, will you? Her father left us and I can see how it has saddened her. I never forgave him for walking out on us like he did. Do you miss your father, Jess?"

"Oh yes, of course. It was like a knife in our soul when he died, but I think you'll still be here in a hundred years' time, Connie. You're a fighter in disguise. Why shouldn't you be here?" I nudged her in play. "Yes, I also hope that Rosie will stay in touch with me; she's a lovely girl."

"Jess, I see a lot of myself in you. Don't ask me why, but I do. You are so…so much the person I would like to have been: outgoing, free, and enjoying your life." She stared at the photos. "You know, it is predicted that I will not live to old age."

"What do you m—?"

I heard a voice. It was Rosie calling her mother from the bottom of the stairs. Time for me to leave. I stood and thanked Connie for allowing me into her past. As Rosie reached the top of the stairs, I left the room. She looked surprised as I closed her mother's bedroom door.

"Just had a nice chat with your mum. Are you going riding tonight?"

"Sorry, Jess, I'm not, but maybe before next weekend, eh? I know you want to get back on a horse again, but we've been so busy recently with the summer season and the drought. I did promise you a ride and we will do it soon."

"No problem, Rosie. Let's do that, eh?"

I went to my room and showered. The last twenty-four hours and Connie's surprise invitation had changed everything. What had I got myself into? Why had Hans lied to Connie about the dog and most of all what did she mean it was predicted she would have an untimely death? It was Rosie I felt sorry for, she'd had a raw deal throughout her life, always having to live with people that Connie had taken in. The relationship between the two of them blew hot and cold. I never understood how Rosie felt about her mother; perhaps one day she would explain it all.

I hadn't eaten since breakfast so I went down to the communal kitchen to find Jonni tucking into a beef burger and chips.

Thank God for frozen pizzas! Connie's chest freezer was full of all kinds of meats and cheeses. I never knew you could freeze Cheddar cheese. I closed the lid.

Jonni looked up at me from behind his copy of the *Daily Mirror*. "Pizza again, Jess? You don't want to spoil that pretty figure of yours. Anyway, how are you feeling today, are you okay?"

"Not really," I told him and lowered my voice, "but I've had an odd conversation with Connie. Perhaps I'll tell you later," I whispered.

"Come on, sit down—bring a cup, I've made a pot of tea."

I checked the oven temperature and put my pizza in to bake. Jonni poured the tea. We sat in silence for a while.

"Can we go out together again, Jess?" he asked. "How about this evening?"

I hesitated for a moment. It was obvious that Jonni was enjoying my company and this was my chance to get to know more about him.

*

It was eight o'clock when we arrived at the Duke of Wellington in the small village of Allansfield. We found a cosy corner and I ordered a sweet martini with lemonade; Jonni supped a local brew.

I asked about Ruby.

"She's doing well with her plaster cast. I've kept her down at the dairy to avoid the trauma of seeing Hans again. I still have to lift her in and out of your car, but she doesn't seem to be in pain anymore."

"I'd be glad if I didn't see Hans again too," I remarked.

I began with the story of the photos and Connie's chat with me.

"Have you seen her room?" I asked.

"Not for some time, why?"

"The stories about her being a white witch could be true. She also said something about not living into old age. Does she know something we don't?"

"Come on, Jess, your imagination is getting the better of you."

"No really, Jonni. She had all kinds of stuff in there and it looked like she worships some god or another."

"You're kidding?"

"You know, witchy-type things. There were bottles and potions and a book of spells. So yes, it made me think what Mark had said was true, although I didn't want to believe it."

"I wouldn't be taken in, by Mark, or anyone else. She's a dreamer, she lives in a world of her own. My gut feeling tells me her so-called witchcraft is also a flight of her imagination. She's not really a white witch, she only *thinks* she is. It's because she had no outside friends as a child. Even though I don't know much about it, it's important for Connie to live her life as she wants. I feel within the next six months, she is going to lose Tanglewood."

"My god, you mean she's in that much debt?"

"I'd hate to see her lose the farm, it's all very sad. If she lets things go much further into ruin, the value of the property will go down. Someone is bound to turn it into a nursing home or something." Jonnie screwed up his face. "I don't know why, but I feel a desperate need to help her to save the place."

"But, Jonni, that's not up to you surely?"

"I know, but I love Tanglewood and everything it stands for. You probably don't think I'm serious, but I wish this place was mine. I love it here. Ewan has already shown what we can do with free-range eggs, so why can't we do all free-range stuff with beef and cheese making, too? I've read so much about it. Connie is holding us back and, because she owns the place. Whatever we do has to go through her. Plus, I've got nowhere else to go these days. I always worry in case someone or something puts me in a backward spiral in my life. Since you came to the farm, Jess, I'm beginning to see through it all. You're an inspiration."

I gave an impatient sigh. Was there something Jonni wasn't telling me? I gave him a sideways glance. "Well at this point I think I had better inform you that I am becoming more serious about leaving Tanglewood; the whole situation here scares me. I want to live somewhere safe and after the incident with Hans, I feel quite the opposite."

"Oh, Jess, you're not, *surely?* I rather enjoy having you around me and, well, I know the place is somewhat insane but you and I, we kind of...you know..." He hesitated.

A man with a dog came into the pub and it distracted our attention for a moment as the dog sniffed my hand.

"Jess, can't you give it one more chance? I'd like to get to know you better."

I blushed. "Oh, I see. I may be going to London to meet my mum and my sister. When I come back, I'll need to think good and hard about it all."

There was a brief silence between us.

"Please think carefully about it. I shall miss you very much if you leave the farm."

"I'm confused at the moment, Jonni. I want to leave but I know I'll miss you, too." As soon as I'd said it, I wished I hadn't. "Let me think about it and when I get back from London, I'll be able to tell you how I feel."

I wasn't sure I could walk away again, although perhaps it was the sensible thing to do. I began to realise that I didn't do *sensible* anymore.

Before I became too involved in my own thoughts, I feebly changed the subject.

"How many cows have you got at the dairy?"

"Thirty-two and they must be milked day and night, holidays, weekends, you can't just leave them for a day." I caught the weary look on his face as he sighed. "You see, Jess, I want to help Connie build the farm. Ewan, Rosie and I have discussed it a lot in recent weeks and we know it can be done. I'd like to build the herd to 100 and more, and we've got the land. We can make silage and hay and that's the one thing Hans is good at, too, although I don't feel I should include him. Fergal does a good job with the few crops we grow. I know we can make it pay. Natural farming is the future; think of the products we can sell—ice cream, yoghurt, even cheeses, if we set it up properly. It's...well, Connie is dragging her heels at the moment. Even Rosie doesn't seem to grasp that if we don't do this we stand to lose the farm, it's that simple. This was my idea and when I put it to Ewan he said we should try and do it. I know he likes to do things as nature intended, but I'm not sure yet if it will be profitable."

"Mm, I see what you mean. Quite a responsibility, I suppose."

He shrugged. "I have to do something, because we can't go on like this. Connie spends money like she is rich. I know she has cash that never goes into the bank. God knows where it comes from. I'm sure the taxman will be on her tail soon. She spends money on Hans, I know she does, and I'm bloody sure there's something going on between them which allows Hans to have things he could never afford. No matter how much I think I shouldn't be involved, I am. I would love to know who the guy is that picks her up in the Bentley. I daren't ask her." Jonni grimaced. "I need to be paid real money, not as and when she can afford it."

"Jonni be careful." I touched his arm. "Don't poke your nose in where it isn't wanted; that's what you keep telling me, isn't it?"

"I know and I won't, Jess. But thanks for your concern."

Why couldn't Jonni just leave here? He could easily get another job.

"So…what does Rosie mean when she says her mother has another source of income?" I asked.

Jonni sighed. "I don't know. They keep that information to themselves. All Connie keeps saying is that she'll make it up to me soon. I suppose she's referring to the equipment I need for the herd. Promises, promises."

"I don't see any signs of wedding plans. They hardly talk about it. How will they afford it?" I asked.

"Oh, Connie will afford it all right. When she earns some money, she lavishes every penny on Rosie's stables and stuff she needs for the horses. It doesn't make sense. She can't pay my wages or have enough money to get the vet to Darcy and yet…I have no idea where the cash comes from. If I mention it to her, she always has an excuse. Notice how many expensive new leathers and blankets there are at the stables. She had a gymkhana last year which cost her thousands of pounds. Afterwards, there was nothing left and we were poor again. Mind you, Rosie somehow manages to earn a living in the summer through her riding lessons. Also, what about the BMW racer that Hans has in the old garage? He went to the Continent to pick it up a few months ago. He drove to the Netherlands and met someone he knew and collected the bike in Germany; brought it back on the ferry from the Hook of Holland."

"Jonni?—Holland? Isn't that where Theo Dijkman is living? There has to be a connection. I mean why wouldn't he buy the bike in England?"

"Mm…I don't know, Jess, maybe it's cheaper over there."

"No, hang on, you're not listening to me. Think about what you just said. Theo Dijkman is a rich guy, Connie's ex. You don't think Hans is running some kind of drugs deal with him, do you? I mean he's always stoned, where does he get it? Do I have to spell it out to you? There has to be a connection between him and Hans."

I knew I was jumping to conclusions—big time. But it had to be said.

"Yes, I understand, but Connie hasn't seen Theo Dijkman for about fifteen years, since Rosie was about eight. They used to have lavish parties up here with Hannings when he wasn't involved in affairs of the government. Hans only came here three years ago, so the chances of them knowing each other would be low."

"So? Why can't Theo Dijkman and Hans know each other?"

"It's highly unlikely, that's all. I mean Connie and her husband had parted long before Hans came on the scene. Come on, Jess, I think we are getting carried away."

I looked at my empty glass and then back at Jonni. "Would his lordship like another beer?"

I knew there was no point in getting excited about an assumption; it was all pie in the sky stuff. Jonni was right. He needed to sort his finances with Connie first.

By the time we left the pub, it was dusk, and I saw Jonni glance at me under the street lights. He smiled as if I was supposed to know what he was thinking.

"Yes?" I queried.

"Nothing," he said. "I sometimes wish you…" He glanced at his watch. "I need to change and be the person I used to be. I want people to like me again."

"Don't start all that nonsense, Jonni. I like you the way you are, and I am your friend as well, and why shouldn't they like you?" I shut up before I went too far. We laughed together and he ushered me toward the Fiesta.

I drove along the lanes with a warm and mutual understanding between us. Jonni was still trying to get his head around his life and I was looking for a new lifestyle. With a stab of recall, Mark's face came to mind. What *did* he mean about Jonni's brush with the law?

I hoped he might further his remark very soon.

I stopped to allow Jonni to check on Ruby before driving back to the farm. She was sleeping on an old cushion in the barn. We drove on toward the house and parked the car. I climbed the stairs ahead of Jonni. At the top of the landing I sensed a sickly-sweet aroma, like new mown hay, but I soon realised this was not an aroma I wanted to get involved in—weed.

The laughing and joking coming from Rosie and Ewan made me curious. I heard Hans' low voice as he gave a groan and then Ewan playing guitar. He made a good tune and I wanted to stop outside the door and listen to him singing the last line of *Forever Young*, sounding like Bob Dylan.

Jonni knocked twice and shouted, "Honey, I'm home."

Rosie called back, "Hiya, Jonni. Is that Jess you've got with you?"

Jonni opened the wooden latch door to reveal Hans stoned on a mattress on the floor. I could hardly bear to look at him. Ewan laid back, only in his underwear, and Rosie lay beside him with a pillow supporting her back.

"Come on, Jess, you may as well get out of that stuffy room of yours and live a bit," said Ewan. "Buggerlugs down there is out for the count, he won't bother us."

I stood by the door looking away from the sight of Ewan in baggy boxer shorts and trying to search for a sensible answer to my being there. Ewan handed me a joint, which I declined; he passed it on to Jonni. Seeing Hans lying on the floor, I dreaded him waking up to find me standing in the same room. I felt trapped between them and I wanted out of there.

Goodness knows why I stayed. They were still smoking, drinking Vodka, and getting wasted. Jonni darted me a glance and saw I was looking uncomfortable.

"Jonni, I'm tired. Will I see you in the morning?" Hans hadn't moved an inch and Ewan's voice seemed to get louder with songs from Neil Young and The Grateful Dead. If he hadn't been so stoned by now, the notes coming from his mouth may have sounded more in tune.

I retrieved my jacket from the chair and made toward the door. To my relief Jonni followed. "I'll come with you," he said.

Out of earshot from Rosie and Ewan, I asked, "What the heck do you think you're doing?" I bit my lip. The smoke was making me feel sick. "Come to my pad and I'll make you a coffee. I just bought one of those new-fangled coffee machines, I'm trying to make my room more self-contained," I explained. "You need to sober up too."

"Okay, Jess, I'll come, but you gotta behave yourself with me in the room—you understand what I'm saying." He laughed. "I'm very unaware of myself when I'm stoned, so don't you be taking advantage of me, do you hear?" He shoved his hands into his pockets.

I rolled my eyes again and tut-tutted at his comment; the number of times I had put Tim to bed in moments like these. Friday nights after work and a couple of hours at the pub. Always the same.

I made coffee. "Two sugars, isn't it? Honestly, Jonni, I really didn't feel comfortable in there."

"Okay, Jess, sorry. Give us a kiss and make up."

"Don't be daft. If I did that you'd regret it."

"Would I?"

I didn't know how to answer him. One thing I knew, he didn't mean it. Tomorrow would be another day and all would be forgotten.

It was after midnight as he lay on my eiderdown. I watched him close his eyes as he fell into a mindless sleep. I wanted to move him but I couldn't; it was late and I didn't have the strength. What if I left him there, doing no harm? After placing a blanket on top of him I slid between the sheets. I could hear him breathing and it was comforting having someone next to me again, although it was tempting to kiss him goodnight. Should I leave him there until the next morning pretending we'd made love and he couldn't remember? No, a stupid idea. I had to do the right thing, no tricks. Anything at all to stop him being involved with Ewan and Hans. I didn't own him, he could do what he liked; but sleeping on my bed, what was I thinking?

Jonni slept all through the night and so did I, until early the next morning he awoke with a groan. I knew he had to be up to milk the cows, so I prodded him, whispering in his ear, "The cows are mooing their little heads off to be milked."

He opened his eyes very wide and looked around my room. "God, my head hurts."

"You are no longer dreaming," I whispered, "and yes, you did sleep with a blonde woman last night, and in case you wonder, we are still good friends." I leaned on my elbow and grinned.

"What? Why am I in your bed, Jess?"

"You mean you don't remember?" I was desperate to make a juvenile joke.

"Fuck! No, I don't," he said sleepily.

"It's okay, and we didn't do that either. Your virginity is still intact. You have nothing to be afraid of." I giggled.

A cockerel crowed below my window.

Jonni sat up looking astounded. He realised he was on top of the bed and I was inside the sheets. "Oh yes, maybe I do remember now, whoops sorry I swore. What…?"

"Don't ask me about last night," I joked. "You make a nice house guest in my room, but don't make a habit of it, Jonni Holbrook, otherwise I'll have your guts for garters."

He grimaced. "Sorry, Jess, I really didn't mean to be such an idiot. I gave it all up last year, but sometimes I have to chill out with Rosie and Ewan, just to show them I'm still part of the team. I apologise, honest I do." He took my hand. "Sorry." He looked into my eyes. "I hope I behaved myself. Look, I must get to my room and then go to work. Will you forgive me?"

"Ar, them thur cows ain't gonna wait. Mooooo." I pouted my

lips in play. "Okay, just this once, I'll forgive you," I whispered.

He stood by the bed yawning and rubbing his head. Could there be a 'Jonni and me'? He was endearing, kind, and a good person but his confidence had been taken away, for a reason I couldn't explain. My heart began to rule my head, but it wasn't going to happen. He was unstable, no real job, he lived this reclusive lifestyle, and I didn't really know him. It all sounded bad, very bad. I mustn't get involved, but still... *Oh hell, I forgot to phone Mum.*

The following evening the phone rang.

"Hello, Rosie speaking, oh right, erm...yes, hello...well Jess isn't here at the moment. She'll be back...oh hang on, here she is. It's your mother, Jess."

I grabbed the phone from Rosie whilst at the same time dumping all my work stuff on the floor of the hallway.

"Hi, Mum, I just got in from work. Sorry I didn't phone you last night. No excuses, I got involved with the guys at the farm and then it was too late to phone. How are you?"

I listened to her usual chit-chat. "I'm looking forward to meeting you in London, pet," she said.

"When do you want to do it?" I asked. "Okay, 2nd July. Fine, that sounds a good plan, have you booked it?"

I acknowledged Rosie as she passed me in the hall.

"We could visit St Paul's Cathedral perhaps. I'd have to leave work early on the Friday to come up to London and take Monday off work. I'll speak to my boss. Will you be coming down on the train into King's Cross? It might take me about three hours to get there. You know what the trains are like."

Mum's idea to spend the weekend in London was a good one. I missed them both especially since my indecisions of the last few days. I needed Mum's support.

Chapter Twelve

I still hadn't really changed my mind about leaving Tanglewood. I wanted to discuss it with Jonni first. Part of me wanted to stay here and to my relief, for the time being, life had gone quiet again.

I'd heard there was a sale in Axminster at the shoe shop and I fancied a pair of platform-soled shoes but also the opportunity to browse the town, but then I heard Rosie calling my name.

"Jess, are you there? I'm down at the stables this morning and need a helping hand. We can go riding before lunch if you like?"

I opened the latch door and poked my head into the bathroom where Rosie stood on the other side of the adjoining door.

"Oh ok, I'll come down, what a good idea; that would be lovely. Give me a few minutes to get dressed." Ah well, there went my shopping trip. I wanted to show Rosie I was keen. Since my chat with Connie, I found myself being sisterly toward her and supposed I was missing Anna.

I hadn't been out riding since my arrival and Rosie had been too busy; I didn't like to ask, with her losing Darcy. I'd only helped with mucking out and brushing the horses in the yard and I knew my riding skills were rusty—but what the heck, it would be fun.

At the stables, I must have given Rosie's friend, Val, a nervous smile.

"Don't worry, Jess, we'll ease you back into riding. No cantering or jumping over fences, just a gentle ride out in the woods. I won't be coming; I have too much to do for the event tomorrow.

There's a point-to-point meeting. I've saddled Hope for you. You'll be fine, she's very quiet."

"Thanks, Val. When is Merry due to foal?" I asked.

"Another few more weeks, then we should have a new arrival."

We set off about eleven o'clock. Rosie rode Carlow along the wooded paths. "Tighten up your reins, Jess. That's it. Let her feel your hands."

She trotted beside me. We chatted along the way and the subject of Darcy passed through our lips.

"I miss him. I've had him since I was ten."

I could tell how it still upset her.

I asked her about the wedding as we rode through the dank woodland, the horses stepping over dead logs. Hope seemed to know what to do, she'd been this way many times before, and I allowed her to take me.

"What are you wearing for the wedding or is it a secret?" I grinned.

Rosie smiled. "I was hoping you weren't going to ask me, it *is* a bit of secret. You know Mum is into ancient history and all that stuff? Well, we're having lots of flowers and people dressed in mediaeval costume." She looked as if she was trying to appear passive and not make a big thing out of it.

"I bet you're looking forward to it," I said encouraging her to say more.

Instead, Rosie puffed out her cheeks. Her horse seemed on edge, "Come on, Carly behave yourself you silly animal." She stayed in front of me. I sensed a wariness in her tone, almost as if I had done something wrong.

The light from the sun glinted through the trees and my uneasiness relaxed as Rosie spoke again. "Val's Mum comes down here with the handicapped kids during the school holidays. They have a holiday club and we use the Tanglewood stables to let the children enjoy themselves with the horses." She paused. "You know, you should get out of those jeans, Jess, and into some smart riding gear. With that slim waist of yours and those legs in a pair of leather boots, you would turn every head in the countryside."

I laughed at her comment. "Honestly, Rosie, what a joker you are."

"No, I mean it, Jess, you'd look great in a hacking jacket and jodhpurs. If you're going to come out riding with us lot, we are the élite round here and jeans are not allowed." She glanced at me with that mischievous grin of hers and then retracted some of her comment. "Hm, I wish we were the élite. Ah, well such is life," she sighed.

Rosie stopped by the gate and waited for me. I sensed the decaying odour of the woodland floor. She leaned forward and opened it on horseback holding it back for me to go through. I patted Hope and noticed her ears prick when I encouraged her to walk on. The trees provided the shade we needed as we hadn't seen rain in four weeks.

"How about coming to the pub with Jonni and me tonight?"

She smiled and I felt relieved she hadn't taken my interest in her wedding to heart.

"You and Jonni seem rather close these days, Jess." She gave me a sideways glance.

"Not really, he's a nice guy, isn't he? When we took Ruby to the vets I think he was grateful I was there." I closed my eyes for a moment trying to erase the image of Hans reaching for the zip on his jeans. I was so glad that Jonni had walked in when it happened but I could hardly tell Rosie about it.

"What about the other night then?" Rosie asked.

"What about the other night?"

"Nothing gets missed around here." She grinned.

"I can assure you, Rosie, there's nothing between Jonni and myself. You could say I was saving him from getting even more stoned—he fell asleep; pissed as a newt! Anyway, you guys weren't much better either." I laughed. "Won't you come out with us tonight?"

"Ok, I'll come, it'll do me good." Rosie pushed Carlow in front of me again.

"I never see Ewan these days, he's always dashing here and

there, mending fences, feeding the animals. Will he come along as well?" I asked.

"I doubt it. He's not the social type, he prefers to hang around with Hans most of the day. I think he's the only mate Hans has, he seems to have a calming effect on him. It's this mentor...Oops." She stopped in mid-sentence as Carlow stumbled on a stone and shied away from the branch on the ground. She pulled him under control again and her sentence was never completed.

"I'll speak to Jonni when I get back, I'm sure he would love you to come." I said. "We should go out for a meal or something—soup in a basket?" I teased.

It was then I knew I had begun to gel with The Cavalry. I tried not to get involved, but each time I felt as if someone grabbed me around the ankles to pull me back. After all, it was only a temporary stop in my life and couldn't do any harm. I was glad to be back on a horse again after so many years. I liked Rosie, but with Connie, I still wasn't sure. I found her to be a sweet lady, but from what Jonni told me, she seemed easily led by her peers. She was kind and caring but ridiculously eccentric. Perhaps this financial crisis of hers was more serious than I realised. But what about me? I wish I knew what I was supposed to be doing. If only...

"You've gone all quiet, Jess," Rosie called to me.

"I was just thinking, you know how it is..."

Rosie hung her head and took a deep breath. "The way Mum's behaving now, I'm not sure we'll be living here for much longer."

"Isn't there anything that can be done?" I asked.

"She spends a fortune on the horses, but we can't afford it. Ewan has told her, repeatedly, she can't keep going like this, spending money on lavish stuff. She forgets she isn't wealthy any more, all the money is in the land. I'm trying to persuade her she should leave it to us to manage. We could at least look after her, but she won't hear of it."

"So where does she get her income if the farm isn't doing the job?" I felt I had gone too far.

"Best I don't say anything on that score, Jess, sorry. Mum has made me promise not to mention it and to be quite honest with you, I don't know; she won't discuss these things with me either. She's working with Richard Millington on some kind of project, I really don't like to get involved. She can be very deep at times."

Richard Millington?

I gathered up the reins and walked in line with Rosie on the wider path.

"Hum, that's Connie. I adore your mum but she does seem forgetful these days. Sorry, Rosie I didn't mean to offend, but you know what I mean."

Rosie was a sweet soul, but sometimes it was as if she was holding back, not brave enough to say what she really felt.

"Have you got many regulars going riding?" I put on my business hat.

"Yes, but the work doesn't bring in a vast income. Ewan's in charge of the finance for the chickens and the stables. He's also got a big contract in Somerset at the markets for free-range eggs, so we are making a small profit and saving up for our future. Jonni is helping us improve things, too. I sometimes wonder what we'd do without him."

We made our way back to the stables and home for lunch. On arrival in my room, I found a bunch of flowers in a vase on the low table and a note which read:

Thanks, Jess, for being you. Lots of love, Jonni x x x x

I knelt on the wooden floor and leaned across the low table. I gave an overwhelming gasp from the perfume. My lips tightened, my chest contracted, and after a wobbly lip moment, I recovered. Tim never bought me flowers. Through the fragrance I felt more of a connection with Jonni; what was he trying to do to me? Did he want me as his girlfriend, or was this him being thoughtful again? The flowers impacted on my feelings. I wished he would be more open with me.

I pulled myself together and considered my options. There were only two. Leave or stay. After my ride out with Rosie, I knew I would have an answer very soon.

After a well-earned shower, I took my planned trip into town and bought a new skirt. The platform soles were not as comfortable as I had hoped, and so instead, I considered what Rosie said and eyed the riding gear in the shop across the road. The boots were gorgeous. I could borrow a hat from Rosie, but yes 'joddies' were important if I wanted to look good on a horse. Ah well, next time. The hacking jacket was expensive too and would have to wait. Wellies would be fine for the time being and so I left town and came home.

I had another six months to go before leaving Tanglewood, so being part of The Cavalry may not be so bad after all. I liked Rosie, and Connie too, despite her unconventional ways. Ewan seemed to be more pleasant these days, although he kept out of the way most of the time and Jonni was another mystery to me. My head felt unable to make decisions anymore. What was keeping me here? Is this how it had been for Jonni, Ewan, and Hans? Was Connie putting a spell on us all?

Chapter Thirteen

I drove Jonni and Rosie down to the pub that evening. She seemed in a jolly mood and Jonni linked his arm in mine for a brief moment, then politely stepped back to let Rosie and me go first through the door.

"There's an empty table over there in the corner." Jonni pointed the way.

"This is great, eh? I'm so pleased you came, Rosie," I said. "Pity Ewan couldn't make it."

She pulled out a chair and hung her jacket on the back.

I wanted to tell her she had looked tired over the last few weeks. All those worries about the wedding and her mother's financial affairs would drive anyone crazy and, with the death of her horse, it had been a stressful time.

"Pity he's such an arsehole about coming out like this. I wish he would. I always thought Aussie people were sociable types, but all he wants to do these days is be with Hans. I wish I understood why. We love each other, I mean…he's very good to me. He came from Australia to work here and we kind of ended up being an item."

I looked at Jonni. "I suppose I'd better watch my step then, eh? I mean if being at Tanglewood does that to you, then I'll have to be careful." I noticed Jonni rolled his eyes at my comment. I was glad Rosie was looking the other way.

"Have you asked him why, Rosie?" Jonni enquired as he passed me the menu.

"Yes, but he says I worry too much. He likes Hans' motorbike and he hangs around with him in the hope he'll let him ride it one day. Ha. He'll be lucky. Hans guards that bike with his life. Mum…" She stopped in mid-sentence. We waited for the next word, but it never came. Jonni's eyes met mine. Rosie had a habit of evading questions. I assumed she learned it from her mother.

We ordered our bar food, the usual meal in the basket with chips. I had sausage, and Rosie chose the chicken. Jonni ordered curry. We didn't have to wait long before the bar staff called out our number and we put our hands up for them to bring the tray to our table.

As we ate, Rosie asked about my life in Yorkshire and the conversation rambled without any sign of her discussing anything significant. It wasn't long before we made a couple of references to marriage but as much as I hoped Rosie would open up to us, she diverted as if she had been trained to move the conversation elsewhere.

"What did your dad used to do, Jess, before he passed away?" Rosie asked.

"He was a sales manager with Hartings, the motor component company."

"Oh, I see." She looked away from me as if wishing she hadn't posed the question. "Will you excuse me both of you, I must visit the loo."

She stood and walked across the room. We finished our meal and stacked the cutlery with the baskets.

"What the heck is going on with Rosie?" My curiosity had returned.

"I expect she is having some concerns about getting married." Jonni took a swig of beer.

"I'll say she is. I mean what you told me is weird, it can't be true, surely? Look, before she comes back, I'd like to talk about it. To me the situation is getting out of hand. It's confusing. Each day I get the heebie-jeebies about living here and then suddenly everything's okay again. I've got mixed feelings, especially since that dreadful business with Hans and the dog and what he did to me. If it wasn't for you and Rubes, well…things…I probably wouldn't have stayed."

"What d'ye mean 'things', Jess?" He wrinkled his brow and gave me one of his sideways mischievous glances.

"Well, you know, your personal life and what's a nice guy like you doing here? You're a clever chap, Jonni. You went to university, studied, but that doesn't mean you have to stay here, does it?" I hoped I hadn't pushed him too far.

"Look, Jess, I will explain more soon, I promise." He placed his hand on mine with assurance. I had this sudden urge to reciprocate, but thought better of it.

Before I could answer Rosie returned. "Sorry, Jess I must get back now. I promised Ewan I'd be home before ten. We have to put two of the horses away and we always do it together. Carlow hates going in the stable at night without Dirk and Hope, he creates havoc. He's such an insecure animal, a bit of an oddball, he has to have routine."

Disappointed at not being able to stay longer, we left the pub. Rosie walked on alone to the car and Jonni squeezed my hand again. "See you back at the ranch, okay? Is your coffee machine still working?" he whispered. I nodded a yes.

Arriving home Rosie almost cantered down to the stables in those clogs of hers. I tried to imagine her in, high heels? Hell no.

"Thanks, Jess. It was good, I enjoyed it. See you in the morning." I gave her a hug. "Go on, off you go," I said.

She waved her hand in a half-hearted way, almost as if she was sad to be back.

I locked the car and, as usual, we let Ruby out of the house to pee on the grass. She was still walking around with her plaster wrapped in an old jumper sleeve to keep it clean. She wagged her tail and we helped her into the house. The extent of her psychological damage was yet to be discovered; she was fine with us, but I couldn't see her going anywhere near Hans ever again. As for myself, I felt the same.

"Can I come over to your pad, Jess, is it okay? We can talk there; we won't be overheard."

"Okay, I'm a bit tired but I always have time to talk to you though."

We crept up the stairs as Jonni carried Ruby in his arms to leave her in his room. It dawned on me that perhaps tonight Jonni had other motives about our friendship. Until now, he hadn't shown interest in anything other than having a friend when he needed one. I supposed, up to now, the feeling was mutual, but what if… what if tonight was different? I hadn't provided him with any false hopes except pure concern and he also with me. I passed his self-invitation to my room as nothing more than a friend needing his usual chat.

The coffee bubbled and within a few minutes I was pouring two drinks.

We spoke in whispers so not to disturb anyone. We knew Connie was out, but where, we didn't know, and neither did we care.

"Okay, so what do you want to talk about?" I asked.

"It's like this, at the moment I have to stay here, I love the old place. I feel I was born to live here, if you see what I mean."

"But there's no future for you here unless you're content to stay as you are?" I passed him the coffee in one of my blue mugs and sat on the chaise longue. He came to sit beside me, placing his mug on the small table with the vase of flowers.

"Thanks again for the flowers, by the way, they were lovely. You didn't have to…I didn't want to say much in front of Rosie, 'cos I didn't want her to…you know." I was going to say 'get the wrong idea' but thought better of it.

"That's okay, it was a pleasure."

I wasn't sure where this conversation was going. I was beginning to wish he would take it one step further than a lovely bunch of flowers.

I cradled the hot coffee in my hand and blew breath across the top, fighting the twist in my stomach. I wanted to know more, it was only natural I should worry. I had visions of me being homeless in a very short space of time.

"What do *you* think is going on with Connie and Rosie? I mean, I am living here and if the farm is going bankrupt, don't you I think I ought to be informed? I hope she isn't going to leave it until the last day to tell me."

"Yes, true. The thing is, Connie is never around when I want to speak to her. I need money to buy clothes and personal stuff. My pay is peanuts. She hides away in that room of hers." He turned his head away and sighed. "I know this sounds crazy, and don't laugh, promise? I love those cows—each one has a personality—and since my arrival here, I've built up a trust with them."

I wanted to laugh at his comment and had visions of him hugging cows, but thought better of it.

"But the truth is, I'm a bit down about it all. I wish I had the cash to make things better. I am sure I could do it and manage the farm with the Holsteins, build the breed up, and the milking. For me that would be a dream come true. I don't know if Rosie realises how bad the situation is. I think bankruptcy is something she hasn't thought about."

"Well, she did mention it to me when we went riding, but you could be right. Come on, kiddo," I said trying to cheer him up. "Something good will happen soon. You're a good person and a good manager, Jonni, I've seen that over the last couple of months. One day someone will recognise what you do here, I'm sure."

We both heard someone climbing the stairs. Jonni looked alarmed as Connie called out in her sweet voice. "Hello, dear, anyone at home?" She knocked on the bathroom door.

Jonni withdrew. "God, she mustn't find me here," he whispered.

"Why not?" I whispered back.

"She'll ask me what's going on," he mouthed.

He looked as if he wanted to hide in the wardrobe.

"Well, er…nothing is going on. For God's sake, hush up. I'll talk to her." I flapped my hands at him. "And what if there was something going on, it's nothing to do with her," I mouthed.

"Hello, Connie, I'm here," I called. "Come in." Again, I noticed how Jonni's face looked strained and anxious. What was it with him?

She walked through the bathroom and down the step into my room.

"Oh, hello both of you." She seemed to notice the cups of coffee and shot a glance at Jonni. "Having a tête-à-tête, are we? That's nice. I hope I'm not intruding."

"What can we do for you?" Jonni chipped in.

"I was hoping to find you at home, Jess. There's a party at the Millingtons' and I wondered if you would like to come; you seem to have fitted in with our family very well and I thought perhaps you may be a party girl."

"Er…yes, but I'm due to meet my mum and sister in London next week. When is it?"

"Two weeks on Friday."

"Oh, I should be back by then. That would be lovely, Connie, thanks. Can I bring a friend?"

Connie hesitated, as if cornered by her prey. I realised she had probably drawn the wrong conclusion about 'us' but I didn't wish to enlighten her further. In truth, I wasn't too happy about going to a party on my own to meet strangers. She nodded in approval.

"Wanna be my friend at this party, Jo-jo?" I stood beside Jonni and pressed my finger into his spine. "Please." I hoped he'd got the message.

Jonni gave a pained look. "Erm, yes er…that would be nice."

If the room could have exploded with awkward looks, now was the time. I should have declined the invitation.

"Okay, don't do anything I wouldn't do." Connie gave a cheeky smile which reminded me of Rosie. "Enjoy the rest of your evening. Oh, and here's the invitation card."

Jonni shook his head when Connie wasn't looking.

"Good night, dears, don't let me keep you any longer."

I closed the bathroom door behind her and returned to my room.

"Honestly, Jess, you're more devious than I had thought. A party at the Millingtons', you must be in favour with Connie. I've never been to the big house."

I looked down at the invitation card and the formal wording. *'Requests the pleasure of...'* "See, you didn't have to worry, she now thinks...you know."

"Jess, we aren't though, are we?" Jonni's eyes met mine.

"I don't know what we are to be honest. What do you think?" I asked.

"Listen, Jess, the reason I am not pushing things with you is... I don't feel I'm...well...your lifestyle is very different from mine and I'm not sure you would want to be burdened with someone like me."

"For goodness sake, Jonni, what on earth are you talking about?"

"It's difficult, that's all." He glanced at his watch.

"What's difficult? Is there something I should know?"

"Well yes, but please don't judge me, promise?"

"Promise. But don't you think you may be getting paranoid? I think it's good we support each other through this odd lifestyle we are both leading. I mean, we aren't all perfect, are we?"

Jonni smiled at me. "You're very sweet, Jess, but it's not that easy and I don't know if what I am going to say will allow you to support me any longer, and to be honest I'm afraid of chasing you away."

"Try me." I frowned. My heart felt it was shrinking.

Jonni walked across the floor toward the half-open window and looked down into the courtyard below. It was almost dark outside and a light shone from the wall of the house. He took a deep breath then turned to face me.

I thought, my god, what's he going to tell me?

"Some years ago, I was accused of a crime I didn't commit. I went through hell. Oh shit, this is hard." He drew in a deep breath and rubbed his fingers across his brow. "It happened at university.

I was half-way through my studies, you know the usual student way of life: late nights, discos, drinking and the occasional bit of weed. I'd been to the Glastonbury Music Festival and I met this girl. It was no more than a friendship." He took another breath. "Two days later, the police turned up at the halls of residence and came to my room. I'll never forget them, the way they had me sandwiched between them asking questions, churning through all my stuff, throwing my books on the floor in the hope they would find something sleazy in-between the pages. They kept on asking questions. 'Where was I on the night of such and such a date? Yes, I was at the festival, I knew of the girl in question, but we weren't close or anything. We'd only just met.' Those guys went through a thousand questions over and over again and finally I was arrested, all that stuff about 'anything you say may be taken down and used in evidence', that's bloody scary, believe me."

"Jonni, that's awful, but why did they want to speak to you? What had you done?"

"The innocent have no defences. I began to feel guilty for no reason. Then I got scared. The police came down heavy on me and I was on the point of confessing under pressure. I don't trust the police; they are a corrupt load of bastards. I see on the recent news they are talking about sacking about 400 of them for corruption."

"Confessing to what?" I pressed. "Why did they need to arrest *you*?"

He hesitated and put his head in his hands. "It was rape and they thought I'd killed her." He let out a pained sigh and watched the expression on my face.

With the sensation of things moving far too quickly for me to comprehend, I flinched at his words. In those few seconds, I swear my mind went from the sublime to the ridiculous, not knowing if I was supposed to be scared or sympathising. I opened my mouth but nothing came out.

Jonni stared at his own feet and carried on explaining. "Jess, what I am about to tell you, you have to believe me. I did nothing wrong, honest. I'm as innocent as you are."

I felt his anger, loud and clear, and stood, staring into his face. He turned away from me and sat on the edge of my bed.

"We were camping and my tent was close to hers. My mates left me behind. I was going to join them later." He took a breath. "As it happens, I had used the last match for the stove and I needed to borrow a box of matches for breakfast. She was sat outside in the evening sun. She told me she was with two other girls who had gone off with a couple of blokes for a walk. Someone said they saw me going into her tent. Yes, I did go in, she invited me, I stayed for a while, chatting, nothing more, and then I left. Later, I went to the other field to join in the music; I asked her to come but she told me she had things to do, so I gave her the halls' phone number and said, get in touch. When I returned in the early hours of the morning, I rolled into my sleeping bag and awoke around 7.30 the next day. I took a walk to the local dairy farm to get some milk and when I came back, the police had been and I wasn't allowed to go back to my tent until late afternoon, it was terrible. She was dead in her tent with my phone number and personal details on a bit of paper. The police asked me if I'd seen anything and naturally I said no. It must have happened when I left to join my friends. As far as I was concerned the police arrest made no sense. Corrupt lot they are."

"Oh my god." I felt my hand touch my lips.

"Apparently, she'd been strangled and raped and above the noise of the music no one could hear her screams. By the time the news got out, the press had made a meal out of the story and there were pictures of me on the news, being dragged to court only because my tent was next to hers and as I looked a bit of a hippy type then, I think they picked on me. Don't you remember the case, Jess, didn't you see it on the BBC? Perhaps not."

"Er…no." I shook my head trying to think, but nothing came to mind. My heart pounded. I had known something wasn't quite right. *But not this, no, not this—please.*

"All my close friends were there and then one of my mates gave evidence to say I was with him all night, but they didn't take that into account and then there was this matter of going to her tent. They asked me repeatedly, what we talked about, what frame of mind she was in, and did I touch her? Some of the questions were downright dirty and humiliating. It made me feel sick. The timing of her death and me leaving her tent, was very close. I feel someone had been watching me. My friends knew I wasn't involved with her, they testified in my favour when the case went to court but it didn't seem to matter, the barrister kept on hammering at me. They had no real evidence to prove my guilt."

"Oh my God, that's dreadful." I wanted to say more, but couldn't speak.

"Oh yes, I touched her all right, she asked me to put sun oil on her neck and shoulders, she was sunburnt. You know me by now, Jess, I will do anything to help anyone. She was fine when I left her, everyone else had gone to the festival. There were no witnesses."

I sat in silence for a moment with a heavy heart—my God, was this real? What with Hans behaving in the way he did, and now the only friend I had, accused of rape and murder. I sat there shaking my head in denial of his confession.

"See, I thought you would be shocked, Jess, and well…I hope you can understand why I didn't want to tell you before, I didn't want to lose your friendship. You had to get to know me first. It was a case of now or never to tell you about it to prove my innocence. Look I'm here now, which proves I didn't do it. I'm sorry."

"I'm not sure how to respond." I puffed out my cheeks. "It seems you went to hell and back."

"I promise you, Jess, I *am* innocent; eventually acquitted on the lack of evidence, they couldn't prove anything. The good news is two years ago they found the guy and he's in jail now. There is more to this, but I don't wish to go into the details—not nice stuff. The things they do to you to get their evidence makes me want to puke. It's just that…Oh God, I suppose I did fancy her, I mean she was beautiful, leggy with gorgeous red hair; any bloke would have. I still see her face, it kind of haunts me. She could easily have been my girlfriend and now—she's dead! And then you came along and I had to hide my feelings like a tormented cat."

I could tell he was shaking as he spoke and tears came to his eyes. I felt sheer panic wondering how I should deal with this dreadful news. Was he still in love with a dead woman he never really knew? All kinds of thoughts invaded my head.

He put his head in his hands. "I kept blaming myself, because if I'd stayed with her she would still be alive. You've no idea how that makes me feel." He looked up with watery eyes. "Okay," he sighed. "I've told you everything—can we put the whole wretched thing behind us? You have to believe me, please." He sniffed.

"Yes, of course, I can understand," I replied softly and put a caring arm around his shoulder.

"I've lain awake thinking about it too long, I have to move on. I absolutely promise you, Jess, I never did anything wrong, okay? I got myself into trouble because I cared and now I am afraid to… to care for someone else."

I sighed, my feelings for Jonni were still the same, but there was this nagging doubt. I really didn't know him, I mean, *really* know him, and now this…

"Do you have any parents, Jonni? You never talk about them."

"Well, yes and no. My real dad died toward the end of the war. Mum says he came home on leave; I was conceived but he never returned from Germany and I never knew him. Mum got a letter to say he was missing in action. She remarried when I was seven years old."

"So, what happened? Where are they?"

"I think they're in Scotland now."

"You *think* they are in Scotland, did you say? Don't you have *any* contact with them?"

"I had their address but I never got a reply. I suppose they were good to me, but after the situation with the police, I lost all faith in myself and I think they were unsure of what I had done. I also let them down by not continuing my studies. Quite a few years have passed since I last saw them. I don't think they got over it."

"Oh my, that's sad, but you haven't let them down. Don't you phone them or anything?"

"They retired and went to live on the Isle of Mull and the calls are expensive. I did try but I never got an answer."

"Why don't you write to them again? Something might have gone wrong at their end. I mean it's your mum, the person who brought you into this world, you ought to stay in touch."

Jonni hesitated at my question. "Look, can we leave it for now? It's still a sore point."

"Oh, okay. I didn't mean to pry, I was trying to understand, that's all."

Ever since my arrival I knew he needed to talk, he must have been tormented by all this. I recalled his face when Ruby's leg was broken, the tears in his eyes, the anger and hate at what Hans had done. The mutual respect we had built since I first arrived at Tanglewood seemed good for both of us. What I needed was not so much the financial security of a relationship as Mum and Dad might have wanted for me. I mean, would Jonni ever earn a good wage? It was more—much more. I needed emotional fulfilment and wanted a relationship where I could be one half of a beautiful and close friendship. Could Jonni be that person? My dad 'spoke' to me—*Jess be careful, take it slowly, don't rush into things*.

"Come on, let's leave it, there's no point in allowing the past to haunt you any longer," I assured him. "Let's live in the here and now."

Jonni gave me a hug. "Thanks, Jess. Perhaps later we can see how it goes. I love having you around me and it is hard for me to stay away from you, so I resigned myself to 'us' being best friends for now. To be honest the whole relationship thing scares me. I'm not one for jumping into bed with every woman I meet, especially after, you know…Anyway, Connie knows about most of my problems. We had a chat when I first started here and she was a sympathetic ear, which I needed at the time. I don't know if she believes me, but being in the room alone with you brought it all back when Connie found us chatting, I freaked out. Sorry. I have to be careful, I can't get into any trouble, in case it all starts again. I suppose that's one reason I hide away at Tanglewood, it suits me."

"Oh dear…You need to get your confidence back, don't you? You will come to the party? I don't think I could do this on my own, it's all a bit daunting, I'll need your moral support." I squeezed his hand. "It might do us both good."

"Yes of course, I'm interested, too, but as soon as I see any signs of…well I don't know what to expect—we are both out of there, is that a deal?"

"It's a deal. It could be fun to mix with the posh people."

I was glad to see him smile again.

"Okay, but I'm only doing this for you, mind." He nudged me in play.

I wanted to say I believed him, but right now it needed a lot of thinking about; it could take me a while.

Jonni's eyes met mine. "Jess, I hope this doesn't spoil things."

"Well, it's hardly an everyday occurrence. It's a shock for me, that's all."

"I wouldn't want to lose your friendship now." He stood to leave the room.

"I think you were very brave and I have to believe you." I gave him a reassuring smile. "It's okay."

"We'll talk again soon, eh? Sweet dreams and thanks. It's been a tough time and I want to forget it."

"It's good to talk. Brushing this under the carpet can't have been good for you."

He leaned to one side and kissed me on the cheek.

"Night, and thanks."

I closed my door.

Chapter Fourteen

It was Monday and I arrived early at the office. I tried to unlock the door to find it was open. At the side of the forecourt, I noticed Mark's car with his cherished number plate, *Parson 1*, parked in a bay.

I shouted, "Morning, Mark. You're in early today. It must be the good weather."

He came out of his office looking as though he had just rolled out of bed and it seemed that was the case. He was unshaven and his hair uncombed.

"What the...I mean are you alright?"

"I slept here last night, nowhere else to go, it was late and I couldn't face looking for a hotel." His straightened his shirt sleeves.

"Oh oh, what's up?"

"It's...the wife, we, er...we...split up. She wants a divorce."

"Oh—my—goodness, that's not what I expected." Another blow, and it seemed my world was falling down around me yet again. Why did this keep happening? When was it going to stop?

Mark sighed. "I'm sorry, Jess, that you had to find me in this state." His voice grew weaker.

"No, Mark, it's fine, I understand, honest I do. It wasn't long ago I had a similar situation. Look, you get tidied up and we'll talk. There isn't a lot to do until this afternoon except the appointment with Mr Starkey. I'll make coffee. Go on. I'd like to help keep your reputation intact." I smiled.

He gave a fake smile. "Thanks, Jess, I'm grateful for your discretion."

For a moment, I felt like his mother scolding a naughty child and had to stop myself from saying any more.

Since my first meeting with Mark, I'd discovered he was a good businessman with an excellent sales reputation, but off the scene, he was a private person, deep, I suspected. I realised why a 'personal assistant' was important to him. I mean, couldn't he just call me his secretary, because in fact, the PA title didn't mean a lot. He needed someone around him for support. Why had his wife chucked him out of the house? I'd never met her, I'd not heard him talk of her much either. I didn't even know if he had kids, he never even talked about them and there were no family pictures on his desk. I made coffee and within ten minutes Mark came out of the men's loo, looking tired but more respectable.

"You'll er…keep this between us won't you, Jess?"

"Of course," I replied with dignity. "Do you feel like talking?"

"Not really, but it's been on the cards for some time. She's taking the kids with her for a while and going back to Edinburgh to her mother. We had a dreadful argument about the children and I couldn't face it all again so I came here. I'm sorry you found me like this."

I went quiet at the mention of his children.

"Drink your coffee, you'll feel better with some caffeine down you. I didn't know you had kids, Mark."

"Yes, twin boys aged six."

"Twins? You never talk about them."

"I love my boys, but my wife rarely lets me get close enough to them. She is very possessive and a doting mother. I sometimes wish we'd not had twins. I only want to spend more time with them. It's been difficult recently when Tina left us and I had all the office work to do myself for a while and that's what the argument was about: I am always too busy with the garage. I'm glad I found someone from the Agency who is reliable and may I say very understanding. You don't want to hear about my problems, Jess. I'm sure we can sort it out soon. You caught me on the hop, that's all. I apologise.

I didn't expect you to arrive this early."

"No, fine, don't worry, I understand," I reassured.

Not wishing to get too involved, I couldn't help him, even if I wanted to. There were enough problems at the farm with Jonni's confession, without adding another one to my list.

"Look, Mark…a suggestion, mind you, but would it be better if you took a break? I can hold the fort here for you if you like and I know what to do with your client, I mean I am used to dealing with the customers. Anyway, George will do the sales, we can manage for today, honest."

"Mm, I might do that, if it's okay with you. I need time to think away from here. Do you mind? I will try to get back this afternoon."

"'Course not, see if there's anything more you can do."

"Thanks, Jess, you're a good worker. I sometimes wish you weren't temping. Perhaps I can find a permanent job for you soon."

I saw his collar was sticking over his jacket.

"Come here a minute, you can't go out like that."

"You remind me of my dear old Mum." He laughed.

"Don't start. I've had enough back home. I'll explain to Mr Starkey you're ill, should I? Don't worry, I'll think of something and tell you later how it went."

Within half an hour Mark left and I found myself alone waiting for the rest of the staff to come into work.

What on earth happened? I had no idea his marriage was on the rocks. All this was more than I bargained for. It seemed the whole world had gone mad. This time I wasn't going to delve deeper.

Chapter Fifteen

I met Mum and Anna in London before lunch on the hotel steps around the corner from the tube station. Another hot day and we'd not seen rain in many weeks. We were officially in a drought and water levels were at the lowest in many years, revealing lost villages before they built the reservoirs.

"Hello, love, how are you?" Mum kissed me on the cheek.

"Okay, Mum. Hi, Anna, give us a hug then, Sis." We all embraced. Anna's hair was much shorter than when I last saw her; it suited her.

"Anna, Mum, how are you both? Gosh, I missed you so much."

"Look, there's a cosy café over there, we can sit outside in this lovely weather. We'll come back in a short while. They say it'll get very hot by lunch time. I'll buy us all a cold drink," said Mum. "First let's check in and go to our rooms, get changed, and pop into Russell Square."

I couldn't help gazing at them both. They looked well from the warmth of summer. Anna in her mini-skirt and sandals and Mum wearing pale mauve cotton trousers and a white t-shirt. She looked well and young again. Her hair was tied back and she'd had a change of hair colour with blonde highlights in her mouse-brown hair.

After checking in and changing our clothes, we made our way to the café. I put my arm around Mum's waist as we walked across the road. I could smell her familiar perfume and it reminded me of how much I'd missed her. I opened the conversation.

"Well, how are you, Mum?"

"Bearing up, I suppose."

"How do you mean, you suppose?" I echoed, wondering if something more than Dad's loss was bothering her.

"It's getting easier, but some days I forget Bryan isn't with us anymore. I find I want to tell him things and phone him at work and then I wake up to reality and it takes me an hour or so to get going again. He was a good father to you two."

"Yes, I agree. I miss him a lot."

"Me too," said Anna.

We sat outside the café and Anna wore her sunglasses as we sipped cola through our straws. I felt as if we were back in our childhood again and Mum was about to tell us off for slurping.

"So how are things with you, Jess, love?"

"Well to be honest, Mum, I am considering moving from the farm. I really don't know what to do. The job is good, I like Mark and the staff in the garage, but the farm is another story."

"What's the problem?"

"Well I'm okay, but the family are an odd set of folks. I have tried to understand them. I'm an outsider, so I really can't say much. I would leave there except..." I turned down the corner of my mouth.

"I could tell something was worrying you, love, when we spoke on the phone."

"Well there's someone living at the farm who I like very much and I feel we kind of need each other."

"Ah, you've got a man in your life again." Mum smiled warmly.

"Well, not exactly, we're like best mates. It's different from my relationship with Tim. We're not dating or anything." I listened to my own words, was I really saying these things?

"You know I never interfere with your decisions, Jess, but take care, pet; make sure you know what you're doing. I know how involved you can get with other people's problems, you were always like that—willing to help, I suppose. Bryan, being your dad, was the same."

"Tell us about this new boyfriend then, go on, Jess," Anna enthused.

"He's not my boyfriend, he's a best friend, you might say—and has been most supportive."

"Well if you ask me, Jess, it sounds as if he likes you more than a best friend," said Anna.

"Honestly, Sis, you always jump to conclusions."

"That's a good thing, surely?" said Mum. "I mean, having a best friend."

I couldn't possibly tell her about Jonni's problems and I thought it best to skim over them. I needed someone to tell me everything was going to be fine, but giving Mum half the story wasn't going to help.

"Well...he's tall, good looking, and kind of rugged. I like him a lot, but he's got his own problems, and I'm not sure if I want to be part of them."

Anna discreetly slurped the last of her cola. "What's his problem?" she asked.

"We've been out together a few times, but he holds back on me. He doesn't have the confidence to take our friendship to the next level."

"Why is that?" Mum asked.

I felt cornered and wished I hadn't started the conversation and the last thing I needed was an interrogation from Mum.

"Well...let's just say he lost his confidence because of a woman he once knew."

"Ah I see, another break up, eh?" She nodded slowly and rolled her eyes. "Why don't you make the next move, pet? Test the waters, if you like him that much. I mean you both seem to have gone through a huge change. It could be a good thing to share it all."

"Well, it's all about the farm, there are some financial uncertainties, too. At the same time, the people at the farm tend to grow on you. It's hard for me at the moment. Connie Dijkman, in her own way, is a kind lady, but there is a side to her I have yet to

145

discover and then there's her daughter Rosie; we're good friends and have similar interests. The problem is, they live a totally different life from me. I want to encourage my friend, Jonni, to move on."

"What does he do now?" asked Anna.

"He's the...he's the herdsman. He has the responsibility for a large herd of Holstein cows. He is trying to be scientific about their welfare and improving milk yield. I suppose you could say he's a farmer." I tried to make it sound more important so that Mum wouldn't think Jonni was a cowhand without much of a future. Perhaps the way things were, he didn't have a future, but I was sure everything could change. He had once made it to university, I was sure he could do it again.

"Ah, like your grandparents eh? You know what goes around comes around," she joked. "Why don't you get to know him better? Take your time and things will turn out in a good way, it certainly sounds as if you more than just *like him*, Jess. Enjoy your time with him, he sounds really nice, pet."

"Is it that obvious?" I gave a coy smile.

"What's the house like?" Mum asked.

"Well, it's very old and rambling with mullion windows and roses growing up the walls. It's surrounded by woodland and lots of sheep and lovely green fields." I delved into my bag to show her a recent photo. I made sure the one I had of Jonni remained in my bag. He was dressed in his shabbiest of his working clothes and wouldn't have made a good impression with Mum. This photo didn't do him justice.

"Wow—that's lovely, pet, when can we visit?"

"I'm not sure. You may have to stay in a local hotel because all the rooms are taken at the farm. Perhaps you could come down soon and visit us. It depends on my job really."

After an early lunch we sat in the shade of the trees, and planned where to go sightseeing. The heat of the afternoon became intense and with the noise of the traffic, after living at the farm, I felt over-whelmed. The barometer in Russell Square read 85 Fahrenheit.

The hotel receptionist suggested that we take a trip to the British Museum and cool off inside the building. It was a ten-minute walk and on arrival we were glad of the respite from the searing heat. We wandered from room to room to include the Elgin marbles. I longed to find somewhere to sit for a while. I took off my sandals and placed my heat-swollen bare feet on the cold marble floor. I could tell Mum was tired after her journey to Kings Cross and we made the decision to return to the hotel for dinner. In all that heat, I needed to soak in the bath. On the way back, I could feel my feet throbbing to the beat coming from the sounds of the BeeGees at the local record shop.

One of the best features of the Hotel Russell was the late Victorian Renaissance architecture and terracotta marble staircase. Porters carried luggage to waiting taxis, and a never-ending buzz of hotel life prevailed. Anna and I shared a room, and Mum slept in the room next to ours.

The next day a trip to St Paul's Cathedral was on the agenda. None of us had visited it before. With a personal guide and a leaflet to follow the history of the cathedral, we made our way up to the Whispering Gallery and walked around the perimeter. The height made me feel unsafe and I stayed close to the wall.

"Can—you—hear—me—Anna?" I whispered.

"Yes—I—hear—you."

"Do you like sausages?" I said.

"What—did—you—say?"

We waved at Mum below us. Her phobia of heights was far worse than mine.

"Come on then, Sis, let's go down those horrible narrow steps again. Mind how you go 'old girl'," said Anna.

"Cheeky," I replied.

It had been fun, and the trials of life at Tanglewood seemed far away. I was happy to see my small family again; it made me feel secure. It was only at night, in my bed, I thought about Jonni and wondered if he had missed me. I could hear Anna breathing as I used to listen to her when we were kids. It all came flooding back; the riding lessons, the time when she jumped in the water after the ball and Dad giving me my first driving lesson when he took me out on the moor. That night tears fell on the pillow. I shut my eyes and drifted into a deep sleep.

Mum and Anna enjoyed their trip to London and early on the Tuesday, after the Bank Holiday, I returned to Axminster. I'd taken an extra day's holiday so I could spend more time with them. We'd talked about Jonni again and Anna actively encouraged me to stick with him. Jonni hadn't even asked me to be part of his life, so what was I thinking?

"Bye, Mum, love you. Bye, Anna, love you, too."

We hugged and kissed and parted with mixed feelings.

I was glad to see Mum again and perhaps she was right; I ought to lead the way, put Jonni's past behind me, and move on. I knew it wouldn't be easy. The train journey gave me time to think. I still had difficult decisions to make. To be part of Jonni or not, that was surely the question.

Chapter Sixteen

It was the day of the party at the mansion house. I put the final touches to my make-up and tested various smiles in the mirror. I heard a knock.

"Can I come in, Jess?"

My hair needed a brush, but I held back a few more seconds until I finished fastening the buttons on my blouse.

"Hi, Jonni, yes…come in. Oh my, you look great. Love the tie," I said as I scraped the brush over my scalp.

"I do have *some* nice clothes, you know." He wore grey trousers with a blue shirt and multi-coloured tie. He smiled at me.

"You look a treat," I said. "One day you'll find someone who really believes in you."

"I think I already did."

He gazed into my eyes, his face beaming at my compliment. "Are you ready? You look lovely, Jess. I missed you when you were away."

"Aw, that's sweet of you. I had a lovely time with Mum and my sister. I was sad to leave them at the station. In a way I wish it were possible for Mum to come and live down here, I know she would love it."

For a moment I caught his pensive expression and wondered if he had been listening to me. "Do you still plan on leaving Tanglewood?" He turned his gaze away from me.

"Well, with all this stuff going on, I haven't yet made up my mind."

"I hope what I told you about me hasn't changed things—us being friends, I mean."

"No, of course not. The job will finish in a few months and it will be a case of going home for Christmas to see everyone again. It's just…the only people I know these days are those around me at the farm and at work. All my friends are in Yorkshire."

It was then that I realised most of them had got married or divorced and moved away, and after a few years, as a single person, there didn't seem to be time for me anymore. What was the point of it all? I would go back to Cresswell's and spend time with Verity again, drinking coffee in her office. There was nothing left for me up north except Mum and Anna. I know they were the best reason for me to stay up there. Perhaps with time Mum might also find a friend as I had done with Jonni. She was too young to be alone.

"What about us?" Jonni asked.

"Well yes, but there is no 'us' is there?" I wasn't sure if I should have said it in that way and swept past him to pick up my jacket.

"Mm…your perfume smells nice."

"Nina Ricci. Come on, let's go," I replied, trying to move the conversation toward the party.

He turned to me and gently took hold of my arm. "Forgive me," he said. "I have to do this."

An air of change seemed to have swept over him. He was no longer the herdsman at Tanglewood, but a good-looking guy and with those lovely David Essex eyes and bubbled curls. He made me want to melt in his gaze. The next thing I knew, he took me in his arms, brushed his hand across my cheek and kissed me full on. I squeezed my eyelids together and took a breath as my lips pressed against his. I felt his hand caressing my hair and it all felt so warm and loving and all the things I had been missing. I stood in the doorway unable to move as he released his grip but held me close. Then he caressed my face and kissed me again but this time I responded knowing what to expect. As he drew away I could feel his breath on my ears and around my neck and by now, giddy with excitement, I had already lost myself to his soft and caring kisses.

"Mm, well…that was a nice surprise," I said.

"Jess," he whispered. "I've been thinking, in fact, I've thought a lot about you during your absence, and you look so lovely tonight." He placed his hand against my face and stroked my cheek. "You're wonderful Jess—prepared for anything. I've been doing a *lot* of thinking lately."

"I…I don't know what to say." I felt the blood rushing to my cheeks and patted them together.

He gave a loving smile and took me by the hand. "Come on then, let's talk about it when we come back—okay? Shall we go?"

Inside me, I grinned my socks off. I felt the warm feelings of sun-drenched beaches and touching each other in places we shouldn't. I had to behave myself even though perhaps the kiss had now changed everything. Like the whipped cream advert on the TV, it was naughty, but oh, so nice.

Jonni descended the stairs and stopped at the bottom to wait for me. He squeezed my hand. "You *do* look lovely, I mean it."

I followed him to the car, avoiding my heels getting stuck between the stone slabs. I was still lost for words and although I secretly wanted him to kiss me, I'd kept thinking *not yet*. We got into the car and our eyes met. "Look," he said. "I've been in denial. I needed to know how you feel about me, that's all. I got a lot off my chest last week and have you to thank for that."

"I was thinking the same, Jonni, all the time I was in London with Mum. I wondered if you'd miss me. You make your kiss sound like a routine enquiry," I chuckled. "You startled me that's all… where do I begin? Yes, you can do that again any time."

"Like this?"

So, he did—and we sat in the car kissing, lots of kissing, deep and meaningful. "My God, I didn't expect you…"

He put a finger to my lips. "Only you and I know about this," he whispered. "Let's keep a low profile in the house for a while. Come on, we'll be late if we keep this up. I adore you, Jess."

At last I got the message and I reckoned we had a lot of talking to do. Tonight, with his kisses photographed in my head, we were suddenly much closer and without a doubt, love lingered.

Ten minutes down the road, with Jonni providing directions, we arrived at a mediaeval manor house, a building of battlements and towers. I read the sign; *Avoca House*. A large iron gate with a crest on the top barred our entrance. Jonni pressed the bell and a muffled voice said through the speaker, "Please state your business."

My heart pounded and I replied, "We have an invitation. Jessica Stamp and Jonni Holbrook."

"One moment please." The speaker clicked.

"Bloody hell," I exclaimed. "What the…?"

The gate opened as if by Sesame in the Ali Baba story. I must have looked cynical as I glanced at Jonni. He shrugged his shoulders as if to say 'nothing surprises me anymore'.

"God, look at all these posh cars!"

Aston Martin, Bentley, Jaguar and my little Ford cleaned that morning by my personal valet, George. Okay, I was being ironic, but we did feel like the odd couple arriving at the country estate of 'Lord and Lady Muck'. I saw Jonni cringe.

"Come on, Jonni, you'll be all right," I assured him.

We got out of the car and rang the doorbell and I assumed, from the sounds emanating from within, that the party was in full swing. A man in a penguin suit answered the door.

Jonni handed him the invitations provided by Connie, who had gone to the party ahead of us.

We stepped through the grand oak doors and someone took my jacket and and gave me a raffle ticket to retrieve them.

The butler announced us. "Mr Holbrook and Miss Stamp."

I knew Jonni wasn't comfortable with the gentry of Axminster. It was that look on his face and the way he turned his head away from me, standing rigidly as he searched the room. I had, after all, persuaded him to come; it would be my fault if he didn't enjoy it.

In the grand hall, a black-and-white marble floor led to a wide staircase with carved oak banisters. Priceless paintings of lords, dukes, and landscapes hung on the walls. At the entrance to the ballroom an orchestral balcony hung above the door. Marble statues adorned the niches and more oak doors led to various other palatial rooms. I was used to being shown around by the National Trust, but this was someone's grand house and they lived here full time. The grand hall buzzed with conversation and as the music began, people waltzed to the live orchestra playing Strauss above me.

A dark-haired young waitress carried fluted champagne glasses on a tray. We declined her offer as I was driving and I knew Jonni was a 'real ale' man.

The men wore floral or paisley shirts and the women long floating gowns and skirts. "Nothing formal, just smart casual," Connie had said. A woman with a cigarette holder in her hand blew smoke to the ceiling. I heard her say, "Darling, I told him how frightful he looked last Friday. Do we always have to take him with us, it's humiliating?"

Jonni glanced at me and with his hand across his lips he stifled a snicker.

I glanced at a door, guarded by what looked like a security man. His back, flat against the wall with his hands behind him. He wore a dark formal suit, and stood as though he owned the place. Well maybe he did.

"Who's that?" I asked Jonni.

"Dunno, Jess. No idea."

"Come on, shall we go over to the food, it's always best to meet people where there's a few canapés and sausages on sticks," I suggested.

We moved closer to the buffet table when we saw Connie. She waved at us in the crowd. "Hello, darlings, so glad you could make it. Make yourselves at home—we do."

You call this home? I thought.

Before she got closer a man with silver hair, wearing black-watch tartan trousers and a pale blue shirt, approached her. "You're on, Connie, your ticket was picked out."

"Oh, must dash, see you soon, darlings, have a lovely time." And she disappeared through the door where the security man stood.

"Jess, would you like a sandwich? I think this one's smoked salmon."

I nodded. "What was all that about?"

"No idea—here's your sandwich." He handed me a china plate and kept looking over his shoulder, glancing toward the front entrance. I could feel him wanting to run away with no destination in mind.

"Come on, it's okay, you're doing great. I think they are gambling in that room—hence the security guard on the huge door over there," I explained.

"I bloody well hope not, Connie has gone in there with a ticket. She mustn't gamble, no wonder she's broke."

"You don't think she has a gambling habit, do you?" I asked.

"I dunno, but I intend to find out." Jonni lowered his voice. "She pleaded she was unable to pay my wages last week."

"Ah, you must be Jessica Stamp?" a voice came from behind me. "Connie has told me a lot about you. She said I should come over and introduce myself. I am the party host." The man held out his hand. "Richard Millington. Nice to meet you."

I shook his large hand and introduced Jonni. "Ah yes, we've met once at Tanglewood, I believe." He looked down his nose from behind his spectacles as if searching the whole of my curves.

Jonni looked up with an air of reluctance and nodded. "Yes, I believe we have."

"I hope you'll be joining in with us soon," Richard invited. "It's nice to see so many lovely ladies here tonight. I hope you are enjoying yourself. Perhaps we can meet again soon."

I felt uncomfortable and wondered what he meant, then I supposed he was unlikely to say there were lovely men here, too— unless?

The butler called out, "Mr Millington, sir, your ticket and by the way, Mrs Lucinda Morton wants to talk to you before you go in there." He approached Richard more closely and lowered his voice. "She's not happy about something, thought I'd warn you. You know how it is with her at the moment."

"Thanks, Barrington, good man." He looked at Jonni and then at me, and the way he looked, I thought I'd arrived naked to the party. He grinned. "Excuse me. I have to go." He winked at me before he made his way through the crowd. There was something about him that made me want to squirm.

Jonni squeezed my hand and with a sandwich in the other, he smiled. "We won't stay long. We'll make our excuses and leave soon. I'd rather be with you on my own than with this lot," he said. "I don't know why I agreed to come to be honest, I'm not very brave in these circumstances, but I didn't want to disappoint you. Sorry, Jess, I have to go and find the bog, will you be okay by yourself for five minutes?"

I didn't really want to leave so soon, I had only just arrived, but I admitted to myself I would rather be kissing Jonni again. I felt disappointed that maybe I had dragged him along under duress. I heard a voice I knew, and looked across the room. Oh my God! It was Mark. What the bleedin' heck was he doing here? He hadn't noticed me. Should I acknowledge him or pretend I hadn't seen him? It never crossed my mind that Richard Millington was one of his contacts. I stood by the table, wondering if I should walk across to him and ask why he hadn't said he was going to Avoca House that night. What would I say? *How come you are here as well?* Or—*My goodness I didn't think I would see you here* or...Oh, never mind. I turned my back and pretended discretion was the better option in case I embarrassed him. He hadn't mentioned any parties, but there again why should he?

I waited for Jonni and tried to avoid Mark, but it was too late; he tapped me on the shoulder.

"Jess. My God! I had no idea you were into this kind of thing?

How embarrassing, you didn't mention you had an invitation as well, I would have told you I was coming, too."

I wanted to say *what d'you mean 'this kind of thing?'* I pulled myself together and stood with an arm holding the other at the elbow.

"Er yes, I was invited by Connie but she's disappeared into that room over there."

Mark gave an unconcerned reply. "Oh, has she?"

"Er...I think she's got a raffle ticket and then she left." I darted a glance at the entrance to the room.

"I thought I could cheer myself up after, you know...and it's good networking for the business," Mark said. "So, who are *you* with, then?" he asked. "I'm on my own here, it's not really my thing." He wrinkled his nose.

"Jonni from the farm, he knows one or two people here. Connie said we should mingle with the crowd. Oddly enough, I've just spotted the vet, Chris something or another; he fixed the dog. I wonder if he's networking, too." I laughed.

"Oh yes, I believe there are lots of professional people here but they tell me you'll have to join in with the activities in order to become initiated, you know. I've been told they play party games, whatever that means." Mark seemed to mock his own words. "I gather it's your first time here, too, I had no idea you were..."

Jonni returned and Mark nodded at him in recognition. He had taken his car to the garage for repair some months before. Despite his remarks about Jonni's past, he was extremely polite toward him. "How's things at the farm?" Mark enquired.

"Fine thanks. Sorry, look would you excuse us, Mark? I must talk to Jess, it's important." Jonni hurried his words.

"Okay, see you at work," I said.

Jonni took hold of my arm and guided me away to a place on the other side of the room. "We're going home and PDQ." He shook his head then carved his hands through his hair. His expression changed as he lowered his voice. "I've just seen what goes on behind that door.

Get your jacket and we'll sneak out, no one will notice."

"Jonni, you're kidding? What's up? Aren't you being paranoid?"

"No, I'm bloody well not. Please, Jess, let's go home. Sorry, I can't do this. There's something about this place you ought to know. Connie won't miss us, she's too busy doing things she shouldn't. I'm so angry with her."

His words alarmed me. We reached the front entrance and the cloakroom.

"My friend isn't feeling well, we have to leave," Jonni spoke sharply.

"Fine, sir."

I stood there like a lemon with knobs on. Curious and unsure how I should take to being bossed around. I couldn't believe what he was doing.

"What's up?" I whispered.

"Trust me. I'll tell you when we get back."

"What?"

Within a couple of minutes, I had started the engine of the car and was driving toward the main gates making our way into the open countryside. There was a silence between us and I felt sure he was annoyed with me for accepting the invitation. I was about to apologise.

"I need time to think this over," he said. It was as if he'd had a panic attack. "Wait till we get back and I'll explain."

He hardly spoke another word and I prayed it hadn't been my fault.

We arrived at Tanglewood to find Hans asleep on the sofa in the lounge and the TV still on. We crept upstairs to my room and Jonni sat on the bed whilst I boiled the kettle.

"Come on, Jonni, tell me what's this all about," I whispered. "What happened?"

"I know what I saw, and you're never ever going to believe it. It's not a casino or gambling it's…Oh God! I think I am going to throw up." He shook his head and sighed a very deep sigh.

"A sex dive—you know where they all put their tickets into a box and you get a partner or someone's wife for the evening. I heard a bloke talking whilst I was in the bog. The thing is, I don't see the connection with Connie on this—I mean she is getting on in years, I find it hard to understand if she is…doing that kind of thing. It's a sort of brothel or whatever you want to call it. I saw them, through a gap in that huge door, the one that Connie went through. They were all stark naked, cavorting, flirting, and kissing. Do I need to say more? It wasn't exactly what a young person of my age wants to see—old people strutting their bare bottoms to the wind."

"What? You're having me on. Oh hell, what has Connie got herself into? And Mark was there and our vet, I noticed he was there, too, did you see him? This is what they meant by party games."

"What?"

"Mark mentioned it. Oh, my giddy aunt! No wonder Connie doesn't come home until the darkest hours. She must have something to do with it because she was in that room. I watched her go in. I think I recognise some of these people from Connie's party. I watched them coming down the lane. You don't think you got it wrong do you?" I suggested.

"Oh, come on, Jess, I know what I saw. I'm not sure how they can believe in all that cult stuff, it's an excuse to 'have it off' with whoever is gullible enough. Where money is involved and people are being drawn in, then I think Millington is taking advantage. He has the house and the safety of his little kingdom. It's a bloody excuse to romp around and have sex with whoever wants to take part. And I'm not being stuffy. I'm annoyed that Connie is involved. Poor Rosie. I doubt she knows about it. Do you know what I think?"

I took a breath, anticipating his next piece of evidence.

"…There's more to this than we realise. Connie gets paid. Yes? To keep her bloody mouth shut, that's what! This business with Ewan and his cultural lessons to prepare them for marriage, it all sounds like brainwashing to me. Absolutely nothing makes sense. They're a load of leering pornographic monsters up at Avoca House, that's what they are. We need to prove it. I'm convinced she doesn't fully realise what Ewan has in mind for the wedding. We have to find a way of checking it out before we all make fools of ourselves. I mean, what if it's all a bit of fun and it's you and me exaggerating the evidence. We have to know more before we can be sure."

I stood gazing at the pained expression on Jonni's face.

"I like Connie, but do you think *she* really understands what's going on? There's a certain naivety in her personality which makes me think she doesn't 'get it', if you see what I mean. We'll do nothing, that's what we'll do, sit back and see what happens. I'll pretend I didn't know anything about it. Mark is putty in my hands at the moment, his wife has, let's say…'gone away' for a while, and he's also relying on me to help in the showroom. When I get back to work, perhaps I can find out more. You don't think he's one of them too, do you? Which reminds me, there's something spooky about Richard Millington. I felt it at the party when we met. Didn't you? His eyes were all over me, reading my curves like a book."

"Yes, I agree, he's a smarmy character." Jonni lowered his head and sighed. "Come here, Jess, I promised we'd talk about us. That is, if there's still some of 'us' left at the end of this evening? I'm sorry it had to turn out like this."

We sat, our legs touching as he pulled me gently toward him and folded his arms around my waist. I felt warm in his embrace and we kissed.

"Mm, you're so good to me," I said, glad he wasn't upset with me for accepting the invitation. "I have to tell you that I've waited for this moment for quite some time."

Jonni smiled. "Sorry you had to wait; it's all my fault."

He took my hand and kissed it.

"I shouldn't have dragged you along to the party. I'm sorry too. I can't help thinking about all this with Connie. What do we do?" I asked.

"I've suspected something odd was going on with Connie's disappearing acts late at night and tonight's party was one step too far."

I sat on the bed to remove my high heels. Jonni sat beside me and reached his arm around my waist.

"Bloody hell, it's shocking stuff," I whispered. "Mark told me he'd heard rumours about Connie. All those innuendoes, local gossip, I paid no heed and then I went into her room, I found it hard to believe what I saw. I also read that white witches are good people and Connie is very keen to take care of the animals." With that comment, I realised Jonni had had enough. "Sorry, I didn't mean to..."

He shook his head. "Nothing surprises me. I don't know, but you're right, let's leave it for now. Tomorrow is another day. Look, Jess, I wouldn't want to push our relationship too far, but may I sleep on your bed tonight, you know, like we did last time? I would like to...you know...but it's a bit too soon. We need to get to know each other in a more meaningful way and take each day at a time. I want to be beside you. I'm feeling uncomfortable after that party and I need to comfort you too, without, well... going too far."

Jonni leaned forward and we embraced. His kisses were not his usual supportive 'it's going to be okay, Jess' kind of kisses. They were long and meaningful and I wanted them last forever, but I had to say more about how I felt when he pulled away.

"Yes, I agree, it would be taking our relationship to a higher level a bit soon. After this evening's experience, it's great to have you close to me. You're right, I'd feel safer. You're a good person, Jonni, but I think we have to allow this friendship of ours to develop as adults and not teenagers, if you see what I mean. We live on this farm together, but being an item here is something else."

"Well, your bed is so much bigger than mine and more comfortable." He tilted his head with a smile. "Gosh, I hope I don't sound like a wimp, but I'm only trying to be sensible after all this carry on. I promise to be good and wait for our special moment."

"Yes, I know you will."

I still had those feelings of 'he shouldn't be here at all', but he was here and to my secret delight my friendship with Jonni seemed to be blossoming; but how would it end when I left the farm at Christmas? I must hold back but the kissing had made some rather big and not so surprising jumps in our relationship.

"Okay, I agree."

I went to the bathroom and put on my pyjamas. *What the heck was I doing?* I hoped he would stick to his word. When I returned he had stripped to his boxer shorts and t-shirt and was getting into bed. I smiled at the way he looked at me.

"Come here, my gorgeous girl."

I snuggled into his arms feeling warm and wanted. All he was doing was showing me I could trust him.

I lay awake for a while with Connie's antics in my head and it wasn't long before I could hear Jonni breathing heavily and assumed he was asleep. After all the events of the last few days, I knew he was exhausted and felt glad he was beside me now. He was true to his word and that's what I needed.

When I awoke the next morning, Jonni had gone to the dairy. His body clock must have woken him. There was so much going on; I had still not appreciated that we were now an item. At least, I *think* we were.

I lay there wondering if my comments to Mum could become a reality. Perhaps I should encourage Jonni back to study to finish his course. Okay, a few years had passed, but maybe the Open University could help. I'd suggest it to him soon.

As I lay in bed, I stared into the rising daylight, controlling each breath, visualising Jonni's face. I felt a warm and caring love, but how realistic was I? I knew I'd have to make difficult decisions and would Jonni be open to my ideas? I was constantly afraid of bitter disappointment; it all seemed so challenging. Dad always said how much I loved a challenge but I was now in this up to my neck. From today I would have to confront my fears.

Chapter Seventeen

I opened a new packet of Weetabix. The sound of Rosie's clogs told me that she was now in the kitchen standing behind me.

"Had a nice evening with Mum, did you?"

"Oh, I left early and your mum disappeared with her friends. That house is so big, you can get lost in it. There was an orchestra playing on the balcony in the great hall—an amazing place. All those antiques must be worth a fortune."

I sat down to breakfast when Rosie glanced at me. She peeled a banana to spread on her toast. We didn't say much; my mind was on too many other things. We smiled at each other across the table and I poured the milk on my cereal and ate it quickly.

"Look...I must dash, otherwise I'll be late for work," I explained. "I'm not sure if Mark is coming in this morning, I may have to take over the office and meet clients for him."

Rosie sat with her head in a copy of *Horse and Hound* and I left. "Bye, see you later," I called and closed the door behind me.

As I drove along the road I turned my thoughts to the party. Surely, when I got to work, Mark and I would have the inevitable chat. He seemed to know more than I did. I turned into the garage forecourt, and noticed Mark's car parked outside.

"Morning, George," I said.

Pete, the young apprentice mechanic, rolled a tyre toward a car. "Boss wants to see you," he announced. "He's bin asking if you were in yet, only five minutes ago—you're not late or enufin'," he assured with an innocent smile.

I scoffed. "Okay, thanks."

"Morning, Mark. I hear you wanted to see me."

"Come in, Jess, shut the door. Nothing special. Can you spare five minutes to share a coffee with me?"

I nodded and watched as he poured the drinks. What I had I done wrong?

"I forget, do you take sugar?"

"No thanks."

"Tell me about the party last night? I didn't see you after we parted." He wasted no time in asking the inevitable question. It was as if he *needed* to know.

"Jonni had a problem and we had to leave early."

"I got an invitation, like you, see. I was also there for the first time and just curious that's all. One of our clients invited me. I felt rather odd, did you get that sense, too?"

"Aw, come on, Mark, you knew all about it surely?"

Mark paused at my comment. "What?" he frowned. "You know who owns the house, don't you? He doesn't live there anymore; his brother-in-law is the caretaker."

"Go on surprise me—whose house is it then?" I felt maybe I was being too flippant.

Mark smiled at me. "You mean you really don't know?"

"No, I don't. Isn't it Richard Millington's?" I tried to smile to cover my feelings.

"Lord—Augustus—Hannings. Connie's relation!"

"Oh my God! Really? Avoca House? But he's dead, isn't he?"

"It's not confirmed. He disappeared at the same time his wife was found at Tanglewood Lake. You knew about that, obviously."

I nodded.

"...Don't get me wrong here, Connie is a nice lady and I'm not sure if the rumours about her are true. I was only at that party because I was invited and I admit, a trifle curious. I left not long after you. Someone was handing out tickets for a raffle or something, and to be honest with you, I got bored and went home,

163

it wasn't really my cup of tea. I only knew a few people through them coming into the showroom."

I tried to hide my feelings and changed the subject. "Oh, I see. And how are things at home now?"

"My wife's gone up north and I'm pleased to say is coming back soon with the boys. We're trying to make things right for our sons."

"I'm really pleased for you, that's lovely. So...you didn't see what they were doing behind that guarded door?" I tried to laugh it off. "That security guard looked like a gangster out of a movie, don't you think?"

I had this awful vision of Connie running around naked in a circle of nymphs and fake fairies; things I didn't understand. How could we possibly say anything to Rosie; what if we had just been nosey parkers and everything was kosher, then what? No, that wasn't possible.

"I assumed they were playing black jack or craps, but someone asked me if I'd been initiated so I said yes. I had no idea what they meant. So, what were *you* doing there?"

I didn't want to push the issue. I felt sure he knew there was more than gambling and sex parties going on at the big house.

"Connie invited Jonni and me, but we made our excuses too. It wasn't our scene either. We didn't know anyone, so we left."

Mark gave a small laugh. "By the way, Jess, thanks for being so discreet the other day, I appreciate it. I hope things will improve. Jacqui and me, we had a long talk on the phone and I think it's going to be fine."

"Glad to hear it." I felt relief. With all these things going around in my head, how the hell could I concentrate on my job? Perhaps I had been wrong about Mark. Maybe all he wanted was to do his job and take care of a valued staff member. I wasn't going to tell him what I knew. I'd found out more than enough information for now and Mark was inclined to be over-curious about me. I suppose in that respect, we were a bit alike. I had to work with him and discretion was the better option. He'd gone to the party for the same reasons we were there; an invite and nothing more.

"Well, anyway, I'm glad you're back at work safe and sound this morning, Mark." I smiled at my own comment. "Mr Foster from Ax Foods is coming at eleven, he wants to discuss corporate leasing with you."

"Oh good, he's a local client and his custom can only be to our advantage."

"Mark, do you mind if I go home a bit early this afternoon? I have some things I want to do at the farm?"

"I owe you one, Jess; by all means, go when you want."

Later that day, I was driving back to Tanglewood when I changed my mind—I would go to the dairy, maybe Jonni was out there finishing up. Further down the lane, I parked the car outside the sheds, and could hear the generator being switched off and the noise dying away.

"Where's Ruby? How is she doing?" I asked as Jonni came out of dairy.

"She's in my room resting. I took her to the vets for a check-up. She can have her plaster taken off at the end of this week."

He gave me a kiss on the lips and offered not to hug me; he stank of disinfectant.

"I missed you," he said. "How was your day?"

I sighed and explained I had come home earlier than usual.

"Do you know who owns Avoca House?" I asked.

"Yeah of course I do, Richard Millington, the guy who introduced himself to us. He's some kind of relative of Connie's, I think. I don't ask really. He was living there when I first arrived at Tanglewood."

"Ah no, that's where you got it wrong—It's Lord Hannings' house. Mark told me. The thing is, Mark isn't involved, at least, that's what he claims. He got an invite like us. I reckon our invitation was some kind of test to see if we were good enough or rather interested enough, to be part of their little clan. I think they are recruiting new members."

"Really? Mind you nothing around here surprises me anymore."

We spent some time trying to work out who was doing what and to whom. Did Connie get her money from sex parties? Then there was Lord Hannings' disappearance. Maybe Hannings was dead and Millington was paying Connie not to tell how he was murdered. Perhaps Millington did it? There were too many scenarios going on in our heads and we seemed to be running away with ourselves as usual. None of it made any sense and I decided we should stop supposing.

"Hang on a minute, Jonni," I said. "I've been thinking. Do we really need to get our knickers in a twist over all this stuff? I mean we have *us* to think about now, and I know we keep saying this, but each time we don't want to get involved, we seem to get sucked back in again. Why don't we concentrate on enjoying each other and forget about them? As long as Connie pays your wages and I earn my salary, we'll be fine."

"Ha. That's a laugh. I think I told you that I didn't get paid this month *again*." He fondled his right earlobe, something I'd discovered he often did when he was troubled. "She's promised to pay me this week. I noticed that Ewan is getting a bit loud-mouthed with Connie recently. He told her to 'piss off' today. I've never heard him talk to her in that way before, he's usually more patient."

"Oh dear, you're going to have to be more forceful with Connie I think. I hope you get some money out of her; it's not good enough, is it? By the way, I was thinking about the party, I don't think the vet saw us, Jonni, do you?"

"No, we weren't there long enough. Which reminds me, Connie talked to me today about Alvin, he's got a cyst on his leg."

"Oh yes? I wonder who's paying for that? My dog had the same problem, it can be an expensive operation—and fatal if she leaves it too long. Oh heck, it's like the whole world has gone mad. I despair."

"No, don't give up, Jess, it's going to be okay, and you've got me now."

"If it wasn't for you, I'd be feeling very lost. You make everything seem right. I want to support you to help put your life back on track, at least that's my plan."

"Sounds all good, I look forward to it." He beamed. "I'm not used to being cared for."

"There's the Open University courses, maybe you should talk to them, see if you can finish your studies. I can work and help you, maybe stay down here after the contract is finished. I can easily go to Monk's and get another contract. We don't need Connie and the farm. Let's do this together."

"Oh, Jess…if only. It costs a fortune to do all that. I can't afford to study. I used to feel safe here, but it seems you are the only person who understands right now."

"Yes, sweetie, and you have to realise this could be your last chance to move on. Come on, let's go back to the farm, we can discuss this later. You can follow me in the Viva and maybe I can get fish and chips—the mobile van is on the bypass tonight—or we can retire to my room and let the coffee machine do its job; we can talk there."

Jonni stroked his hand over my shoulder. "Sometimes, Jessica Stamp, I wonder which angel sent you to me."

He kissed me briefly on the lips. "Must get a bath and then I'll join you later."

We drove in convoy along Five Acres Lane. Once again, I had been drawn to stay at Tanglewood Farm a while longer but somehow it didn't seem to matter anymore.

The weekend crept up and we were now nearing the end of July. The weather became stifling. There was always something that needed doing; Jonni could never take a rest. I had just cleared the breakfast dishes and finished washing up when I saw the milk tanker passing on the lane. Jonni came in from milking, so I made a pot of tea.

"I've been training Fergal to milk the cows," he announced. "He knows what to do, but there are things I like done my way, if you get my drift."

"Do you think you could take some time out to go to the beach this afternoon at Lyme Regis?" I asked. "I mean, if Fergal is going to help you in the future, you have to learn to delegate, you know."

"Yayss, I do know," he drolled. "I don't see why not, that would be lovely. I'll ask him."

"Well you deserve it, surely, and this weather is incredible; they say it's the hottest since records began. I certainly don't remember it being like this before. The beach will be crowded, but if we're lucky we can hire a couple of deck chairs and take a swim in the sea and cool off."

Jonni laughed. "Come here, Jess, no one is around—give us a kiss!"

I sat on his knee and he cushioned his lips against mine. "Mm nice, you're lovely."

"You'll need your bikini," I teased.

"I'll borrow yours; you wear the bottoms and I'll wear the top."

"Ha, that would be a laugh. I hear there are naturist beaches along the south coast. I don't fancy that, though."

"I didn't think you were shy, Jess?"

"Quick—Rosie's coming—good job she wears clogs." I stood and pretended I was reading *Woman's Realm*, which Rosie had left on the worktop.

"You two seem to be getting along swimmingly together," she said as she walked through the door.

"Well, talking of swimming we are planning on going to the beach; it's so bloomin' hot."

"Wish I could go with you, but Carly is playing up again. He had a touch of colic last night and I need to make sure there are no more disasters at the stables, especially with the water shortages. I have to keep Merry cool whilst she's pregnant."

"I'm going to ask Fergal to do the milking for me. I need a day off, Rosie, so if your mum asks, tell her I've gone to the beach with Jess."

"I will and you two have a nice time, do you hear?"

Rosie sounded like my Mum.

Jonni stood to leave. "Back soon, Jess. I'll check with Fergal and let you know."

Rosie wore cut-off denim shorts and a grey strappy top. "Phew, it is hot, I'm stifled. Yes, I reckon Jonni needs a friend; he's a good bloke. I was afraid he was becoming a recluse," she said.

"Yes, I know what you mean."

"You're a very caring person, Jess. I do hope you'll stay with us a bit longer, we've all enjoyed your company. Mum likes you a lot, too."

"How are the wedding plans going, Rosie?"

"I got my dress yesterday. Mum bought it for me. We went to Axminster together. There's a wedding shop; they opened it last year. I had a fitting a few weeks ago."

"Really? Oh wow, how lovely, and so exciting, eh?"

"It was expensive, but nothing flash, just plain and simple. There was a row about it, of course, but in the end, I got what I wanted. I didn't want to go to the altar wearing a meringue, if you see what I mean."

"I bet. I'm sure you'll look wonderful."

I tried not to show my true feelings. Poor Rosie, did she grasp what her mother was doing at Avoca House? There were times when she seemed so childlike and innocent.

"Will some of the guests from the party be there? Your mum seems to know such a lot of people."

"Oh yeah sure, the usual crowd will be coming. Ewan is making the altar. We are putting up a marquee in the park this weekend. I shall be riding side-saddle on Daisy; you've seen how lovely she is when we brush her up."

"Oh yes, a white horse and a bride, you'll have me in tears. I tend to cry at weddings," I said. I hoped the look on my face wasn't one of horror. The visions of the cliché white horse with its tail catching the sunlight seemed perfect and I hoped, for Rosie's sake, she would have the day she desired.

Rosie smiled at me. "I think I will be more nervous than tearful," she said. "All this handfasting stuff, it's not my scene really. I'm only doing it because Ewan is such a romantic; I want to please him."

"What will you be expected to do? I mean this is your day, Rosie, you should have some say in it, surely?"

"Yes, I do but…Oh, you'll have to wait and see—I'm not sure myself yet until the rehearsal; there's too much to be done here now with this summer drought and we have all the invitations to send out."

Behind her smile I detected anxiety. Did she really have no idea about what she was doing? I couldn't help but feel her reluctance; it had been with me since I first arrived at Tanglewood. She was too young to be doing all this stuff. I wanted to say, 'Whoa, Rosie, don't rush it, make *sure* this is what you want.' I wish I could have said it, but realised that the chemistry between Rosie and Ewan seemed fine. In his own way he idolised her. He was always happy when she was around and I couldn't help admire their resolve with trying to build a business of their own.

I rushed off to the local store and bought Oxo flavoured crisps, Ski yogurts, ham, buns, and a packet of Jammie Dodgers for our lunch. A spare plastic bottle lay in the crockery cupboard and I filled it with diluted orange Quosh. I put some ice cubes in a plastic bag.

"Ready?" Jonni asked.

"Yep. Come on, let's go."

We drove to Lyme Regis. "See that house up there?" I pointed up the hill. "That's where I stayed the first night I arrived here." The empty beach I had seen was now crowded with people. I parked the car with difficulty after driving around for a while but managed to find a parking space as someone vacated it and we walked down the hill to the beach.

"They're selling ice creams over there; would you like one?" Jonni asked.

"Yeah, lovely, thanks."

We stood in a queue as the sound of herring gulls mewed overhead, and then made our way down the hill to find a space on the beach. "Do you want to hire a deck chair?" I asked licking the fast-melting ice cream.

"No, I think we'll lie on our towels on the sand."

I had my bikini on under my shorts and after I'd eaten the pointy-bit of the ice cream cone I stripped off to sunbathe. I was shyly aware that Jonni was watching me and I turned around and smiled.

He unzipped his jeans and stripped off to reveal a pair of black, rather sexy, swimming trunks. I had never seen him *that way* before. I hoped that my eyes didn't reveal where I was looking. His dark chest-hair tangled around his nipples and my thoughts subconsciously and rapidly turned to sex. Oh boy, if only I could wrap myself around him, here and now.

"Did you bring any sun cream?" he asked.

"Yep, got that." I delved into the bag to pull out the Nivea. "I burn easily."

We laid our towels side by side on the sand.

"Should I do you first?" he asked.

"What?"

"The sun cream."

"Oh yes, of course, please."

Jonni laughed. "What did you think I meant?"

I lay on my front and Jonni poured the cream on to his fingers. "I'll do your shoulders, okay?"

He began soothing the Nivea across my shoulder blades. I swear I was in heaven and then he stopped and took a deep breath, looking away across the distant blueness of the sea.

"Sorry, Jess, I can't do this."

"Why not?"

"I can't, it's too painful."

"Well, shall I sit up then?"

171

"No, I didn't mean that sort of painful, I meant…"

"Oh, Jonni, yes of course, I forgot, I'm sorry I hadn't realised. You still haven't got over it, have you? Poor you. It's going to take time." I paused to think about what to say next. "I think you have to confront your worst fears. Here, finish what you started and I promise nothing will happen to me. Come on, it will be fine, honest. I was loving it, you've got really caring hands. Be brave, think how much pleasure you are giving me."

"Okay, Jess. Sorry, but sometimes things like that keep coming back. It kind of hits you without realising it."

"Yes, my dad used to say that about his time in the war, but once you have done it you'll feel proud of yourself. Come on, sweetie have a go, to prove to yourself it's okay."

So, he did and it felt sublime.

"There, see? Done! That was wonderful, thanks. Well done." I kissed him. "That was very brave of you and I loved it. Now let me put cream on you."

I splattered the cream down his back.

"Ah, ah, oh," he flinched.

"Was it cold?"

"No, I didn't expect it on that spot," he replied, laughing.

I swirled the cream around his back and massaged his shoulders. His skin felt soft and his body fit and brown. I kept wishing, for a moment, we weren't on the beach. He put his face toward the sun and gave a deep sigh. "Mm, that's so nice. If we weren't on a beach full of people I'd…"

"Well, let's be glad we are." I laughed.

We lay side by side on our fronts, holding hands. He turned his head toward me and was about to kiss me full on.

"Oh oh, don't get carried away," I jested and then responded.

"You know, Jess, since you came here you have become a rock for me."

"Yes, I think I do know. Isn't this nice?"

"Mm, it's wonderful. If only every day was a beach day," he said.

"You mean a 'Connie free' day."

Jonni laughed. "Yes, a 'Connie free' day. Lovely," he said lazily.

"Jonni?" I said slowly. "Do you mind if I ask you something?"

"What's that, love?"

"What makes you think you let your parents down? I never understood what you meant."

"This whole accusation thing. You have no idea how it feels, Jess."

"But...didn't your parents try to protect you after the incident?"

"Yes, they did and my stepdad was very helpful, but it was me. I couldn't take it anymore. I felt so drained and eventually I couldn't cope. I realise now I was traumatised by it all. The police were awful to me. I began to wonder about my real father and why he had to die, and in my head, it was all so confusing. I was very alone. I walked out on everything and I knew I'd let them down with university. I needed the time at Tanglewood to sort out my mind. You don't know how that feels. Now I've got you, Jess, I have never felt so good."

I smiled at his comment. "Yes, I do sort of know what you mean, remember I lost my dad, too. So...do you have any other relatives in your family?"

"I have an aunt somewhere. I don't think they want me to get in touch with them. It's all been so...difficult. I've been a failure."

I still didn't fully understand the rift with his parents, perhaps with time I would. I was sure it was all Jonni's problem and not theirs. Anything could have gone wrong and it didn't have to be so bad.

I heard a dog bark and the owner calling for it to come back.

"Come here, Dora. Dora! Do as you're told, get back here— Dora!"

The next thing I knew, Dora was next to us digging a hole and showering us with sand.

I sat up to see a young mixed-breed scruffy pup digging and then poking her nose into our picnic.

"I'm so sorry," the breathless owner apologised.

"Aw, she's lovely," Jonni said. "How old is she?"

"Five months and she's a little terror."

Jonni held her down by the scruff of her neck so the man could put Dora on the lead again.

We glanced at each other and laughed.

"Well, you know what we have to do now? Come on let's take a dip in the sea." I giggled. "I'm covered in sand."

"Race you," he said.

We ran toward the water and Jonni waded out and then dived in. "Come on, Jess, get in. It's lovely."

"Oh no, it's not, I bet it's freezing."

Step by step I made it up to my knees and then my buttocks and finally up to my waist. It wasn't so cold after all; the hot days had raised the temperature more than I realised. After a few minutes I found I enjoyed it, but then Jonni picked me up in his arms and dropped me in the sea. I squealed and he planted a delicious kiss on my lips, his wet hair dripping over my face. I held onto him and he carried me back to our spot on the beach. It felt as if my world had turned into something more beautiful than I could have imagined.

We ate our picnic and as the afternoon progressed the beach cleared and in the warm evening air the wind blew across the sand and we entwined in meaningful kissing and touching. I wanted to lie on top of him, but I had to restrain myself. I kept saying in my head 'not yet, not yet,' but when would be the right time? Not here on the beach that was for sure.

"When the time is right, Jess, we will know. It will be a very beautiful moment, I promise you," he said. The sound of the sea and his caring made me feel that today was a day I wanted to last forever but the story of his parents saddened me. Maybe…just maybe I could…no, that would be ridiculous.

Chapter Eighteen

At breakfast Ewan opened the conversation and for a change Connie had come downstairs in her dressing gown.

"Jess is right about the leg, Connie, you really ought to get Alvin seen to."

I nodded in agreement. "I believe it can be dangerous to have a cyst of that size. I think it can stop the blood flow."

"You're right, Jess," said Ewan. "If you put the animals first as you say you do, Connie, it's not fair that you're holding back with Alvin. That dog relies on you for his health."

It was the first time I had seen Ewan being so outspoken. He always seemed so quiet and relenting. There was something about him I couldn't quite understand. I was left guessing why he always said 'yes' to everything and Rosie wasn't exactly the dominating type. In recent weeks he seemed to have become a recluse, almost like a lost member of The Cavalry. Where was he going in the evenings and why? He never seemed to take Rosie out for a drink or a meal as Jonni had done for me.

There was a silence before Connie replied. "I don't have time to take him today, Jess. I have to meet Jonni."

Ewan rolled his eyes and sighed and looked at me. "Connie, we have to do this. I can't understand your reluctance; you are always so caring, what's going on?"

"I'll take him, Connie," I offered, "but it will have to be when I get home from work." I looked at Ewan when I said it. "It depends on what time the vet has an appointment."

She turned to me. "I can't bear to think Chris will say we have to put him down. You know what he's like, he's very stern. Also…" Ewan interrupted.

"I'll come with you, Jess, if you like; we don't need an appointment, he'll see us without one."

I wasn't very keen to see the vet again after the incident with Hans, but with Ewan, I felt it wouldn't be a problem.

"Chris will see you, if he knows it's Alvin. The poor dog is fourteen now, and I'm not sure if he will be up to an operation," Connie whispered, clearing her throat.

"Connie, we have to do this, I *know* it costs money, but you can't leave it," replied Ewan. "We learned our lessons from Darcy—if you remember!"

"I don't know, Ewan dear, it's all so difficult at the moment and Jess you are a good person; I'm sure you mean well but I worry in case he doesn't come back."

"Think of the dog," I said, eyeing Ewan for support.

Connie looked at Alvin. "I feel I have let you down, old boy," she sighed. "Okay, take him, Jess; a small operation can't do any harm, can it? I'm worried his heart won't stand it."

"Connie, it's okay, once we get him back, a few stitches, and he'll be fine again. Our dog had the same problem. We'll take care of him."

"Thanks, Jess." Connie smiled and gave me a brief hug.

"You mean Jess is the only person who doesn't shout at you, Connie," Ewan jested.

Connie shrugged her shoulders and gave me a wry smile. I guessed this was her way of feeling defeated.

After arriving home from work, we encouraged Alvin to sit on a blanket on the back seat of the Fiesta and I drove down the road with Ewan in the passenger seat. I opened all the car windows and he stuck his head out enjoying the air as I drove along the country lanes.

"Thanks for backing me up, Ewan. I have been wanting to say something about Alvin to Connie for ages, but yesterday I saw how much pain he seemed to be in; he was licking the lump on his leg and making it red raw."

Ewan turned down one corner of his mouth. "Hm…things are not good at the farm. I know why she was putting off taking the dog to the vet's. The bill is sure to be high, there's not a Buckley's chance she would have done this herself."

The next few words I might regret. "What does she do at Avoca House? She's always up there."

"Well, Rosie and I, we don't ask. She is…well let's say, she loves to socialise and that's not our thing, as you've probably gathered.'

I tend to keep out of the way and as long as Rosie and I have a nice life together, that's all that matters to me right now. I'd do anything for Rosie; she's my best mate as well as…you know what I mean? When the wedding's over we'll shoot through for a few days."

"You sound as if the ceremony is something you have to do rather than a special occasion that will change your lives. Rosie tells me you're a romantic at heart."

"Well…I'd like to think so. I suppose I want to make her happy; she's everything to me. You see, I've had a difficult home life. I came here to get away from it all and Rosie, she's been great."

Ah, now I got it. So…Ewan, too? What was it with Connie? Why did she need to adopt us all? I felt she was about to 'adopt' me as well.

"I love the wildlife and peace and quiet, like in the bush back home. I can't wait to have Rosie to myself and manage the farm. Perhaps then we can make some real money in the future and let Connie see she should retire and leave it to us."

"Ah, that's your plan, eh?" I wanted to say more but I knew that if I did, it may be a step too far. I smiled at him, knowing Connie wasn't going to give up the farm that easily. "So…how's it all going? The wedding plans, I mean."

Ewan paused. "Gud, gud, as far as I know. Rosie is arranging the flowers and the guests—and God help us—Connie wants to do the catering with that bloke from the village. A few snacks on sticks and a barbie would do me, but, as usual, we had to spend hundreds on it."

"From what I see he's pretty good. I saw the food Connie had prepared at one of her meetings, it looked great."

We turned off the B-road into Axminster.

"Is there anything I should know before you undertake your plans?" I felt I would squeeze at least *some* information out of him.

"No, just be there to enjoy yourself and wish us well."

I drove into the car park. Both Rosie and Ewan seemed determined to keep their plans to themselves. I felt I had to know if they really were going to perform this crazy ritual on the day. Surely not?

"Come on, Alvin, out you come," I said. He followed Ewan, paused outside the door, and sat stubbornly on the ground.

"Come on, you old bludger, get inside," Ewan encouraged, and pushed him through the door.

Alvin's ears rested over his head.

"Here's his lead. We may have to drag him," I explained to the receptionist through a half-open door. She laughed at the two of us dragging Alvin across the slippery floor, his claws digging into tiles and growling in protest.

"G'day, g'day. Can Chris see Alvin? He's got this enormous lump on his leg." Ewan blurted out in the room full of people.

"Yes, so I see." The receptionist looked at the diary. "You may have to wait half an hour, but I'll tell him you're here."

We sat in silence again with me giving Alvin the occasional pat on his head. Ewan kept looking at his watch and sighing.

"I'm sure we've done the right thing." I said.

"I hope the vet doesn't tell us Alvin has to be given the chop. I'd never live it down."

"I doubt it, Ewan; he's got plenty of life in him yet."

"Hope so, otherwise Connie will kill me."

"Don't worry; it'll be fine, honest." I nudged him in play, hoping he would calm down.

Ewan's leg began to shake from the ball of his foot to his knee. I had never seen him so nervous.

After waiting for a while, it was now our turn in the queue. "Evening, Chris. I brought Alvin for you," said Ewan.

Chris looked at me strangely. "Oh, hello again. Do you always do the 'vet run'?"

"I *finally* persuaded Connie to allow us to bring the dog in for you look at the lump on his leg." I smiled, hoping he would understand what I meant. "Sorry, but we couldn't persuade her to do it earlier."

Alvin cowered and the nurse gave him a biscuit. "You hold him, Ewan," said Chris.

The vet held Alvin's front paw. "Mm. This could be worse in a couple of weeks. We have to operate, I'm afraid. I make no guarantees because of his age, but he should pull through; he's a tough old devil, aren't yer, boy?" He patted him before washing his hands.

"How's Ruby doing?" Chris asked.

"Fine. She's still limping but less and less each week."

Not wishing to discuss Ruby I pushed the conversation one step further. "Okay we'll leave Alvin with you and come back—when?" I enquired.

"Tomorrow around three o'clock; it will give him time to recover. I'd like to keep him a bit longer to see how he copes. Okay?"

I turned to Ewan. "Oh, I can't make it at that time I will be at work. Perhaps you could ask Jonni to help."

"I'll see you, all being well," said Ewan. "I'll phone you if there's a problem."

"Ewan, er…please give my regards to Richard on your next visit."

Ewan seemed to go into shock and gave a hasty reply. "Oh, I don't know when that will be."

The vet gazed at Ewan. "Oh, er yeah, erm, yes, I see…okay we'll talk soon, eh?"

I have never seen anyone try to remove themselves from a situation in such a hurry. Ewan was out of the door before I could say goodbye to the dog.

All the way home Ewan's silence unnerved me. What was he thinking? I could tell he was worried about Alvin, or was it something else? Why would he give the vet such alien looks when he mentioned Richard? And what had Ewan got to do with Richard? Did he mean Richard *Millington*?

"Will you tell Connie, or should I?" We stopped outside the house and I got out of the car and pushed the door closed.

Ewan shrugged. "Maybe I should tell her," he said. "Forty pounds is a heck of a lot for a small operation."

This time I was certainly not paying the vet bill.

"Thanks for coming with me, Jess. I feel you ought to stick around here. Things are going to be different once Rosie and I get married. Anyway, must go feed the chooks. See you later." He walked off in the direction of the hen house. There was obviously something on his mind; I wished he would be more open with me.

I looked up the lane to find Jonni walking in my direction and waved. I was dying to tell him about my strange encounter with Ewan and to warn him about the arrangements to pick up the dog the next day.

Chapter Nineteen

Ewan and Jonni collected Alvin from the vets, and although still unsteady he was doing fine.

As it was my day off, and there was nothing better to occupy me, I drove to Axminster library. I felt it might be cooler in there and it would be good to borrow a book or two. I filled out the form to become a library member and looked through the crime shelf. It struck me that I may find more information if I found a section on paganism as Jonni had suggested. When I asked about it, the librarian looked at me in an odd way. I knew it was all hearsay about Connie, but then she found me a book on handfasting. I told her I was doing some research.

I opened the page.

Handfasting—the binding of couples symbolised by the use of cords wrapped around the partners' wrists. The modern-day term of 'tying the knot' originates from this ancient ceremony.

It all sounded fairly normal to me, at least, harmless, and Rosie had mentioned it when I asked her. Then I read *the vows don't have to be binding—after a year, they can be renewed or rendered invalid.*

Ah, so that's what this is about. So…she wasn't getting married in the sense of a civil ceremony at the register office or church. I was somewhat taken aback. This wasn't a real wedding? Or was it? I had no idea. I smiled to myself and began to understand… well I thought I did. If it was good enough for Tim and me to live together, then it was fine for Rosie, too. Were they simply finalising a loving partnership? I must stop being judgemental. How foolish of me, but I still couldn't get my head around the 'wedding'. It all seemed so false: had I got it wrong?

I skimmed through the pages. *Page 30. Chapter 4—The Vows. They will be written down or ritually rendered invalid as in a divorce after one year.* So, she can leave him if it doesn't work out. Perhaps it was more sensible than I had imagined.

I skipped a few lines further down the page as my eyes drew me to the text.

In ancient times their binding was similar to pagan rites. To consecrate a marriage, the couple consummated their union in public. Marriage in the good old days became quite shamelessly and brazenly liberal.

I'm sure my heart missed a beat. No, they wouldn't, would they? Surely Rosie and Ewan wouldn't actually 'do it' in front of an audience? But yes, this was 1976 and anything was possible. Flower power, sex, drugs, rock n roll—and knowing The Cavalry as I did, I wouldn't put anything past them to behave in this way. Maybe this was the part that Rosie was reluctant to discuss.

None of this made sense. I felt strange, *very strange,* to the point of wanting to get out into the fresh air before I threw up. I had the urge the laugh my socks off, but it wasn't funny at all, just hideous.

Driving home, I tried to convince myself that everything was going be all right. I had become far too absorbed in *everything.* Whatever Rosie and Ewan were doing was their choice. Only a few nagging questions stayed with me. Were Rosie and Ewan really going to consummate their marriage as the book had said? Where was Lord Hannings in all this? Hans had a new motorbike, Connie supposedly had no money, so perhaps her orgies were her earnings and Rosie knew nothing about it. I kept losing concentration over the sheer number of unanswered questions. It was a relief when I finally turned down the familiar lane to see Jonni in the Viva behind me, flashing the lights. I waved before we reached the bend in the road to turn toward Tanglewood and stopped on the drive, reminding me of the day I waited for Connie to arrive.

"Hi, Jess. You're home early." He opened the door of the Viva and came toward me and gave me a hug.

"Day off, remember?" I felt the need to cling onto him a while longer. "Thanks, I needed that."

"Are you okay, Jess? You seem a bit…"

"I've been to the library and…" I gathered my thoughts.

"And?" he said, looking puzzled.

I proceeded to explain my discovery.

"Yes, of course, I knew something of the pagan ways, but I don't think it's going to happen in Rosie's case."

"I hope not. I have a nasty feeling about this."

Jonni frowned. "This isn't the Dark Ages, let's not run away with ourselves." He mused at the expression on my face.

"That's what I kept telling myself, but now I'm not so sure with all that carry on at Avoca House. I mean what if something illicit is going on and Rosie doesn't realise?"

"I know what you mean, but it doesn't bear thinking about and we promised, remember? Not to get involved in other people's lives. Also, Rosie does have her wits about her, she isn't as quiet as you might think."

"Sometimes she's too quiet."

"Let's think more about *us*," he said.

I looked up to hear Hans riding toward us on his motorbike. He was loaded up for a journey. Rucksack on his back, leathers tightly fastened and a smart crash helmet covering his pirate beard and menacing facial expression. His cheeks were squashed inside the helmet, which made him look even more menacing than usual. All I could see were his eyes. God, how I hated that man. I moved away to the car to let Jonni talk to him.

"You off somewhere then?" Jonni asked.

"Ya, I am catching the ferry tonight to Holland and then going across to Germany for a break. Getting away from this godforsaken place."

"You didn't tell us."

"Do I have to tell you bastards everything I do?" He glared.

"I gather Connie knows."

Hans pulled the visor down on his helmet and said nothing. He never said goodbye, but instead revved up his bike, and sped down the lane.

Jonni and I looked at each other. "Well…" he said showing dismay, "I hope Connie *does* realise he's gone off like that. I shall have to check. I mean we need all the help we can get right now—it seems so unfair."

"Good riddance, that's what I say. You've got Fergal's help now."

"I've been thinking about what you said. You know, about going back to uni and continuing my studies. I need money. If only I could get a proper job. The trouble is they usually ask for police records, and I have no work history—they are the two most important things and thirdly, it's me; I've lost my confidence. What if they find some more lies about me and the whole problem starts over again?"

"Mm, I am sure you can get a better job with proper pay. You only need one employer to see good in you, and you're made."

"Connie did that—and see where it got me?" Jonni lowered his eyes and sighed. "Milking bloody cows, for God's sake. Oh yes, I like doing it, but the pay is peanuts."

I sighed. "Being a herdsman is an important job—I couldn't have my breakfast cereal without the likes of you."

Jonni smiled and paused in his conversation. "Jess?"

"Yes, that's me." I grinned.

"Do you really want me or are you only being nice to me?"

"Oh, Jonni, what a daft question. I do it because I find you to be honest and kind and all the good things. I want security, too, you know. It's human nature. You're a lovely person, and I must say I do miss you when we aren't together. I may be…well…closer to you than you think."

184

"That's nice. I realise there is no future here for me, and I'd rather be with you," he whispered. "You seem to understand me more than anyone. Look, I promise I will try and get another job, and as soon as I do, we can move out."

"Okay, I think we both have to be realistic. I'm also glad Hans has left us. Do you think he had a row with Connie and left the farm?"

"Na, don't think so; he'll be back. He often goes over to Europe to visit a girlfriend and disappears for days on end then comes back as though nothing has happened here."

I sighed. "I'm surprised he's got friends."

"As far as I'm concerned, the feeling's mutual," he said. "We should take a walk in the woods tonight, clear our heads."

"Okay, good idea, yes I'll come." I smiled at his comment.

Chapter Twenty

It was late evening and Jonni had finished the milking when we took our walk. We followed the paths laid down through ancient woodland.

So much had happened in the last few weeks it was a pleasure for us to walk alone, hand in hand, listening to the birds, and taking in the earthy aroma of the wood. The ground was so dry, and the paths, usually muddy, were now caked with the impression of horses' hooves and hiking boots.

With the dry season, there had been many changes and I still had this nagging doubt about where I was going in my life. Did we really want to be together? I must have more confidence about our relationship. It was all the things I had endured since Dad passed away; they still haunted me.

As we strolled deeper into the wood, the fading sun cast eerie shadows through the canopy floor. I stopped a moment to remove a twig from my sandals. I kept wishing I'd worn my trainers.

"Do you like working with Mark?" Jonni asked me.

"Yeah, he's a good bloke and very fair. He has a few problems at home; he and his wife are…well he isn't spending so much time at work these days. I hope he can sort it soon, 'cos I'm doing quite a few sales on his behalf. Marriage presents many challenges. Most of my friends are married or divorced. I think I'm a lost cause and they've given up on me. Since Tim and I split up, I haven't really wanted to get married; it's all been a bit of a damp squib since Dad passed away. I'm trying not to think too much about it."

"Do you still have feelings for Tim?"

"Well no, but…I have to confess, I do feel guilty. You see, I walked out and left him. They say you don't know someone until you live with them and it's true. I like a man with independence and he relied on me too much. Feelings, you say? No. I don't have those any more, well, not the kind you mean. It seems such a long time ago, so much has happened in our family. I would have to say, truthfully, I don't miss him, he was kind to me but things got a bit…well, awkward between us."

"How do you see me, Jess? Am I a failure, too? Do *I* rely on you too much?"

"Oh god no, Jonni. Listen, you have taken care of me from the moment I arrived. What can I say? I love being with you. You'll only be a failure as long as you stay on here and continue doubting yourself. Together we could enjoy life without Tanglewood. I know how much you like it here, but there are two of us now and I feel sure we could do great things together. Don't you feel that, too? I mean you do consider we are together, don't you?"

"'Course I do, love. I keep telling you. We *are* together now, okay? You're smart, Jess, and it seems to me you let nothing stand in your way. I admire you for that."

Those words were like the opening of a flower bud. I needed to hear him say it.

We stopped, and I settled myself against a tree to look above me into the canopy. It was getting quite late and Jonni came to me and kissed my neck and shoulders. His kisses were not as I had felt before. They were meaningful kisses, arousing my deep feelings of love and emotion.

"Jess?" he whispered as he held my hand.

"What?"

"I think I'm a little bit in love with you." He pressed against my thigh.

My heart thumped as he placed his hand around my waist and slotted his fingers into the waistband of my jeans against bare skin.

I felt his warm hands sliding up and down my spine.

"A little bit?" I asked.

"Okay, a lot then."

"Jonni, darling, I think I love you, too. It's just…"

"You don't trust me, do you, after what I told you?"

"Of course, I do, but I'll feel much better once we get this stuff sorted, or at least find a rock to build on. I'm scared we could both get into something we may regret." I stroked his hair and kissed him on the lips. "I'm not entirely stable myself just yet. Coming down here to live after a tragedy, walking out on Tim, and where will I go next when I leave Mark? There are too many uncertainties."

"Let's forget about other people. We are the important ones right now."

"You're right. Let's walk on," I encouraged. "It's quite dark now and we don't want to get lost. I didn't bring a torch."

"Don't worry I'll find my way back."

We strolled on a little further.

"Let's sit on this bench for a while, eh?" He pointed to an old secluded seat almost hidden in the undergrowth, and took hold of my hands. As he gazed into my eyes he said, "Jess, when I tell you I love you, I mean it."

I lay in his arms searching his face and feeling wanted. "I know you do."

"I have a vision that one day I will feel as free as a bird, and not so inadequate. Do you think it will ever happen?" He shook his head in despair.

"I don't know, but for your sake, Jonni, I hope it does. I want you to be happy and more confident about yourself, too. Anyway, you've got me now."

We kissed and Jonni traced the line of my cleavage with his finger. He began to undo the buttons on my blouse. I didn't stop him as I felt his hand reach inside.

"Do you…?" he whispered in my ear. "May I?"

I couldn't stop myself or deny him. I had been waiting for this moment from the day we first met. He pulled gently down on the straps on my bra and reached inside to bare both breasts.

"They're lovely, Jess. Oh God, they're lovely. Oh my, you're one hell of a gorgeous woman."

I felt the incredible pleasure of having my nipples stroked.

"God! I've waited a long time for this, longer than you could ever imagine," he said.

We kissed and he held me closer. All I could do was listen to his soft voice in my ear, willing me to love him. Pinning it all down in words became impossible. I became aware of darkness falling, the silence of the wood, and the birds had stopped singing. He placed his jacket around my shoulder and began to remove my blouse and bra.

"You are so beautiful, Jess. Wow, so beautiful, let me look at you."

"There's more of that," I encouraged, not caring a damned thing about what was going to happen next.

"It's okay, let's take it slowly," he said, fondling me and whispering in my ear. "Do you want to hear a fantasy of mine?"

I nodded like an innocent child listening to an enchanting story.

He stared into the void. "Well, I've had these feelings—and promise me you won't laugh—but I dream of running naked in the wood with you and making love to you under the moon."

"God, you're such a romantic," I whispered and we kissed again. I gazed into his eyes. "Well…that's probably my fantasy as well."

He placed his jacket in a niche on the ground and led me by the hand to sit on it.

I felt the strength in his arms as he gently lowered me to the ground. The warm summer air and the freedom from baring my body to the warm night sky, was like no other.

I helped him with his t-shirt, kissing him as we stripped each other naked and threw our clothes away. We lay there, skin to skin, in the darkness; the faint and eerie light of the rising moon caught our shadow. Oh, how much I needed Jonni to love me.

"Oh boy, I feel that wonderful freedom," I said.

"Let's walk that freedom; let's walk naked up the path together," he suggested. "We can fulfil our dreams."

I stood as he slipped his sandals on his feet and hand in hand we saw each other completely naked and beautiful. Half of me wanted to look away in case it was wrong, but I didn't, and stroked my hand over his bare skin in the darkness. He took my hand and pressed it against his thigh, guiding me to the right spot. We didn't care anymore. This was love. He paused for moment.

"Stand there," he said and stood to walk on in front of me. "I want to watch you come to me from out of the darkness."

I did as he asked and as I came closer, I had this surreal feeling of what it would be like to be Eve, and Jonni as Adam. We walked toward each other in the moonlight and embraced, me touching his nakedness, him touching me with a closeness and warmth I hadn't felt before.

"I love you, Jess, can we...? What I mean is, I want us do all the lovely things that couples enjoy. I want to make love to you."

"Yes, I want that, too," I whispered, realising my libido had raced over the top of the scale.

With the warm air and still night on our skin, we belonged to the wood as we stood on a soft bed of ferns and moss. We lingered on the path, feeling for each other in the darkness. I held him and caressed him, kneeling down to kiss him, working my way up to his lips.

He paused, seemingly holding back, and I heard a rustling sound as he felt on the ground for the pocket of his jacket and knew he had come prepared.

"You mean you planned this tonight?" I asked with a smile.

"Sort of, I wanted to be sure I had one with me. God, it's so bloody dark in here now." He fumbled with the packet.

"Isn't this amazing?" I whispered.

The surreal perfume of earthy woodland and a sense of rubber wafted to my nostrils and he led me to a tree and as I opened my thighs he carefully pushed himself into me. I wrapped my legs around his waist as he rocked me into delicious and sensuous lovemaking. We sank to the floor, him on top and I encouraged him to hold back. This had to last forever. His slow, gentle thrusts made me feel secure, entwined in his arms.

"Love me now, my love," he whispered.

The darkness gave me the assurance we were alone and my calling out in sheer pleasure must have echoed through the wood like a crying animal. We carried on and on with calm and meaningful feelings, breathing deeply, telling each other how much we were in love. He made it last for a long time until neither of us could hold back.

"Jesus, this is incredible. Oh God! I think I'm..." he choked.

"Oh me, too!" I shouted.

Together we cried out in overwhelming tenderness.

"Oh, I love you, Jess, I love you so much. Oh yes, I do." He gave a last push and then it was over. I swear that if God had sent down a thunderbolt we wouldn't have noticed.

"Oh, Jess, my lovely Jess," he whispered.

"I love you, Jonni, I know I do."

We lay on our backs on the ground looking into the moonlight through the tree canopy, without a care in the world.

"Shh, what's that noise?" I whispered and drew myself together.

We heard the sound of footsteps and sat stiffly, listening.

A snuffling noise came through the darkness and along the footpath; the low thud of footsteps seemed to vibrate through the dank woodland floor.

Jonni whispered in my ear. "I think it's a deer."

We kept still and perceived the ghostly shape of a majestic stag passing us close on the path. It sniffed the air then trotted on its way. The moon had risen and ahead the shadows of the trees probed deep into the void.

"I think it heard us," he whispered.

He puffed out his cheeks and sat up with bent knees then he leaned toward me as I lay on my back. "Wow that was amazing... No regrets?" he asked.

"No, none, you were just...mm...lovely." I squeezed his hand.

"Are you cold?"

"No, it's okay. After all that, I'm very warm. Can we do without our clothes a bit longer?" I asked, feeling tired but not wanting it to end.

Jonni laughed. "I hadn't realised you liked to flaunt yourself, Jess. I thought public nudism wasn't for you," he teased.

"On this occasion I don't bloody care, you were so..."

He kissed me before I could finish what I wanted to say. "Oh, Jess. You know, I want to fall asleep every night with you in my arms and tell you wonderful things and share my life with you. I want to let myself go, and be the person I always wanted to be with the most beautiful woman by my side."

I looked into his eyes. "In a strange way, I think we were made for each other."

After recovering from our delicious lovemaking, we stood to pick up our clothes and walked along the path without putting them on.

"God, this is the freedom I have always wanted." Jonni held his arm around my shoulder and his fingers around my breast as we walked. It was like the sex you always wanted and could never dream of doing in the open. We had fulfilled our fantasies and fallen in love.

"I know, it's marvellous isn't it? And so naughty of us." I chuckled.

'Come here, Jess, I want to kiss you all over. It's that perfume of yours, it's very moreish."

I dropped my clothes to the floor. "You'll have to come and get me." I teased.

Jonni dropped his, too, and chased me up the path. He caught me and as I landed with a thump, the smell of crushed grass and wild garlic hit my nostrils.

"Gotcha," he said in play. "Can we do it again?"

"So soon, I didn't think you…"

"No, I'm not bloody Superman, but you know what I mean. Anyway, I only brought one with me; I didn't dream it was going to be this good. Wow, Jess. I won't be able to keep away from you." He hugged me close to him.

It must be very late. "What the hell's the time?" I asked, still calming myself and breathing deeply after the feelings of extreme passion.

"Dunno, can't see." He pushed the light button on his watch. "It's almost eleven thirty."

I swear I could have gone on all night but for the sound of a fox barking in the distance; the sound unnerved me as it came closer.

"We'd better get dressed, you never know who might be lurking around here after closing time at the pub," he said.

"Where are our clothes?" I hoped I could remember where I had dropped them. "I've got mine here, near this tree," he called.

"Where's mine?" I panicked.

Jonni put on his jeans.

"Jonni, where've my clothes gone?" I couldn't help but think what a crazy madness I had got myself into.

"Hang on, I'll help you look." He laughed.

I ran up and down the path searching without any inhibitions about my nakedness.

The moon had risen and I heard Jonni's voice, but couldn't see him.

"If you want your clothes back, Jess, you'll have to kiss me first."

"You devil, you've got my clothes?"

"I may have."

"Where are you?"

"I am here, come and get me," he sang from behind a tree.

"Come on, Jonni, don't be daft."

"Boo."

I jumped as he came up behind me and turned around to see

the shape of this semi-naked man standing in front of me, with the moon shining through the trees behind him.

"Let me dress you. I got some practice taking your clothes off and now I want to practise putting them on again. One kiss for each."

I felt like a child, but enjoyed the adult version of the game and I couldn't stop laughing. By the time I owed him four kisses, I was dressed, and he patted my bum.

"Come here, you gorgeous woman. That was incredible. Mm... love you."

"Did we fulfil your fantasy, Jonni?"

He kissed me. "What do *you* think? This first time with you was everything; you were so good, my darling."

"Whose bed are you sleeping in tonight? God, I'm knackered." I yawned.

"Yours—mine stinks of cow shit," he joked. "That is, if you'll have me?"

"Of course!"

We ambled back to the farm to sleep soundly and cradled each other in my bed. My life was about to a take a new turn.

Chapter Twenty-one

The following day I heard Jonni discussing with Ewan about the best safety measures they could take against the drought. In the distance, we frequently heard the sound of sirens from the fire brigade racing to emergency calls.

Connie returned earlier than usual that night from the Millington's and before I retired for bed I sat with her on the sofa, chatting about her evening. She looked harassed in the heat of the summer night and poured herself a whisky and soda. The temperature had soared and at work, that day, everyone seemed to get on each other's nerves. Mark gave Pete, the mechanic, a severe ticking off for being late. "Apprentices are supposed to keep up a standard," he'd said. A customer had disappointed George on the sale of a car. I'd kept my head down and stayed out of the way. I had never seen Mark so upset. I hoped the weekend would calm it all down.

"We had a wonderful time tonight, full of London businessmen," Connie remarked.

"Oh good. Connie?" I hesitated. "Can I ask you what's so important about Avoca House? It's seemed like a club or something. I mean why did they need tickets to enter a room? Did I miss out on something at the party, we left early, see?"

Connie swallowed hard at my pointed question and her eyes turned away from me as she spoke. She gave a silly affected laugh. "Oh, it's a game we play and I help with the catering."

"And the guard on the door, who is he?"

"Ah, that's the games room, roulette, big money." She smiled.

"We must have the security. You have to get an invitation to go in there. I'm playing hostess."

I knew her comment was a white lie.

"So why do you need a ticket to enter the room?"

She paused. "Oh...everyone has a ticket, it's the rules."

I wanted to say '*Do you take part in those things?*' I couldn't— no, mustn't go that far. She had gone into that room and if what Jonni told me was correct, I found it hard to believe her version of events. I could tell something bothered her, but what she had described made it all sound perfectly natural.

"The main thing is you are enjoying yourself, eh?" I tried to change the subject. "I meant to ask you, why has Hans left us in such a hurry?" I frowned.

"I have no idea, he just took off. On this occasion, I'm annoyed—I need him right now. I wish he hadn't done that. Fergal helps us sometimes, but I regularly have to go down to the old house and drag him out of bed; he drinks too much. How Sandy puts up with him I shall never know. I have to say I do have my reservations about Jonni's idea to let Fergal do the cows, but Jonni says he's very good at it, and he needs a responsible job." She yawned. "I have an appointment with the accountant on Monday. And tomorrow we are rowing up the hay."

"Okay, I'll leave you in peace. Goodnight then, Connie, I must get some rest, too."

In the early hours I awoke for a visit to the bathroom. I had all the windows open and slept with only a sheet on top of me. Jonni had gone to a meeting with the local farmers' association and told me he wouldn't disturb me when he came home as he would be late. He would sleep in his own room.

I heard Connie slapping around the kitchen floor in her pink mules talking to the cat and giving Alvin a biscuit. If only she could sleep. All this anxiety was getting on top of her and the rest of us, too. She made her way toward the lounge. I listened from the top of the stairs and had learned which of the treads creaked the most.

Why was Connie still awake long after I had gone to bed? I thought she wanted to sleep early that night.

"Damned Millington," she whispered. I managed to find the floorboard where I could see between the gap. She was counting out twenty-pound notes. Over the weeks she had lost weight and although Jonni told me she was fifty-eight, these days she seemed a lot older. Her hair was tied back in the usual 'Connie style', her make-up thickly spread around her face. Her eyes bore the greenest of eye shadow—and those false eye lashes didn't really suit her and she looked tired.

She counted two hundred pounds into a box in the dresser and more into another box marked *Wedding Funds* and locked the drawer with a large key.

What I saw next left me astounded.

She began to speak in a foreign language, which meant nothing to me. There were no similarities to any language I had heard before. She held a gilded chalice above her head then placed it on the table beside her, chanting in whispers. Her chanting held a strange melodic flow and on the table, she opened the pages of an old leather-bound book and read it aloud.

Hurog, hurog, aybe ran
Quetre hurog kanbe skram.
Peace be with me, all around me, below me, and above me.
Thank you to all those who love me and care for me.

She lit a candle and offered it to Alvin who was sitting on the rug beside her. "Your leg will get better now."

I watched her fingers stretching toward the dog and my heart missed a beat at the pained look on her face as she appeared to release invisible energy.

Hail Mother Earth, hail to the fire and water. Fire will prevail, water will soothe. My time here is short, you were my life and my soul. I will be with you soon.

She began to talk to herself in a whispered voice and repeated her strange rhyme. I noted she had placed a circle of artificial flowers around the dog and I watched as she gazed intently at a photo of someone I couldn't see. She turned to Alvin. "We will show them. I've had enough of being harangued for my beliefs. If only I can prove through what I do, I am happy. I know I will always face rejection but I don't understand their anger. I shall come back to this earth and show them—it's all true." She looked at the photo again and sniffed back tears.

I wasn't going to sit there any longer; I'd had enough. At any moment, I expected electric sparks to fly from the end of her fingers; most unsettling—and who or what was she looking at in the photo? As quietly as I could, I turned away and crept to my room.

I took a glass from the coffee table and filled it with water from the kettle. What the hell was that all about? Mark was right, she really did practice witchcraft and now I'd seen it with my own eyes. Was it a spell she was putting on Alvin? How ridiculous. Of course, the dog was getting better after his operation and his improvement had nothing to do with witchcraft. In all the time I had lived at the farm, it was only in her room that I saw evidence of Connie's spells and the old book on her dressing table. White witches are supposed to be good people, harmless. If I told Jonni, he would laugh and think I was joking, but he knew her better than that and maybe he'd seen this, too. It was best to leave her alone in her strange world. If it made her happy, I couldn't see any harm in it. I shook my head in disbelief, rolled back into bed, and pulled the covers over my head. I shut my eyes. *Good night Mum, Dad, and Anna.*

On Monday morning I woke to the sound of petty arguing across the landing.

"For gawd's sake, Mum, get up. You have to be at the accountants for ten o'clock. I'm not putting up with this any longer. You've let me down, *again.* Why do you always do this to me?"

I heard what I assumed was Rosie stomping down the stairs. Later, I met her in the kitchen and she hardly spoke. I could see her face about to burst with anger and it was best I said nothing.

It seemed Connie's life was in deep trouble. As the days progressed, we would all discover the outcome of her visit to the accountant.

When Jonni told me Connie gave Hans money, I suspected the reason—to pay for his drug habit and his unplanned trips to Germany. However, Hans returned to Tanglewood for a short while and had seemed less stressed. He even smiled at me instead of sneering. Needless to say, I didn't smile back.

"Look, Jess, if you understood my life, you may see it's not easy," he'd remarked.

If I'd replied as I felt, the words would have come out all wrong. Instead I opted for a more positive approach. "Well, try being more pleasant to people and stop sucking in so much weed." To which he'd sighed and went on his way. It struck me as being odd. This wasn't the insufferable Hans I had known. What had changed his dreadful moods? His demeanour had softened.

He didn't stay at Tanglewood long and the following week, disappeared again without telling anyone. I hoped he wasn't coming back. Perhaps he'd fallen out with Connie.

Chapter Twenty-two

Rosie finished her mug of tea as a red post-office van drew up in the stable yard. I was grooming Briony for Val; she was on holiday. I acknowledged the driver.

"Thanks, Tom, much appreciated," Rosie called as the postman drove away. She stared at the postage stamp on a letter, and then proceeded to open the envelope.

"Oh gawd, it's...it's from my dad," she said with a momentary ounce of delight.

"Really?"

"Yeah...it says..." She paused to read it to herself. "I wrote to him, you know, about the wedding. I've only recently got his address."

Rosie went quiet as she continued reading.

I grabbed a broom to sweep the yard and left her alone to peruse her father's words. I heard her suck in a breath and minutes later she burst forth with horror in her tone. "Oh God! This is..."

"Well?" I asked.

"Oh hell, this is all a bloody mess, isn't it?"

"What's a mess?"

"Here, read this." She passed me the letter with some disdain and promptly sat down on a bale of hay with a look of sheer horror in her eyes. Reluctantly, I took the letter from her hand and read it as she chewed the end of her thumb. She gazed at my expression, eager to see my reaction.

Dear Rosie,

I was delighted to hear from you.

I met Hans yesterday in The Netherlands (long story) and he told me some very disturbing facts. I am worried about you, the farm, and what your mother is doing to you. We really must talk. I think Ewan may need help, too, I feel sure he is mixed up in something he can't handle. Did you know about Millington's plans for your wedding? Hans felt the need to tell me about it because he knew you wouldn't listen to him.

Bloody hell, I was right, Hans does know Theo Dijkman, but how?

Your mother always was a character, but from what I hear, things are not what they seem. I am confused about your wedding plans. I want to help and need to talk with you. Can you phone me? I will pay for the call and phone you back. Please do this before your wedding; it could save you a lot of embarrassment. I've discovered something underhand and illegal going on with Richard Millington, which we have to stop. I have important information for you which could affect your future and Ewan's, too.

Please call me as soon as you get this. Don't phone from the house, I don't want your mum to know about it yet. Try to find a friend's house, no-one must know. Please phone me, Rosie; it's for your benefit. I care about you, I want to explain everything and why your mum and I don't live together anymore. It is not what you think. It's a tragedy you never knew about. Your mum is in deep trouble and we have to help her out of it for all your sakes. What Hans told me could change everything and I want you to keep what's rightfully yours.

Your mum will squander away the farm no matter where she is. She has no control over her finances and never will. This isn't your fault, but we have to talk so I can help you. You must promise me that you won't discuss this with Ewan until we

*have spoken, it could be detrimental to your future. You have
to trust me, I mean—really trust me. Please wait until we talk
about it. Looking forward to hearing your voice again.
Much love from Dad. X X*

Rosie was in the middle of a dreadful and stupid crisis. I could
hardly believe Theo's words, although I think I already knew what
he was going to tell her.

She clutched the letter as I handed it back to her. "How can
I phone him without Mum knowing or anyone hearing me? Val's
gone to the Canary Islands on holiday, and I don't know anyone
with a private phone I can use. It's a call to Holland, no one is
going to let me use their phone." The note of panic in her voice
became louder and high-pitched. I could feel her emotions clawing
for help. "I can hardly make a call from the bloody phone box
down the road, can I? Anyway, that phone box has been pissed in
more times than I care to mention. It stinks."

"Heck, Rosie, this *is* unbelievable, but stay calm. I'm sure I can
help you. Let me think—maybe…" I heard footsteps.

"Jess, hi. Oh, sorry, am I disturbing you? I didn't realise…Hey,
what's up, girls?"

"Rosie?" I turned toward her.

She nodded and sniffed. "Yes, I have something to tell you as
long as you can keep a secret, Jonni. Mum mustn't know about this
or Ewan, for now. Promise?"

"Of course."

"I contacted my dad some weeks ago and we have been corre-
sponding."

Jonni raised his eyebrows. "Really?"

"Something has happened and Dad wants me to call him, but
please, Jonni, don't tell anyone, will you?"

"Of course not," Jonni replied. "Cross my heart."

Rosie sighed, "I shouldn't be showing you this, but I trust you.
I can't do this alone." She gave him the letter to read. "I thought it

202

may be a good idea to invite him to the wedding. I discovered he's been sending me a card every year on my birthday and Mum didn't give it to me. It was only one day, when the post was delivered to the stables by mistake, did I find out that Dad had been sending me letters. I haven't told her. Mum always said my father didn't want anything to do with either of us, which wasn't true. I am so angry with her."

I shot a glance at Rosie as she searched both our faces for a reaction.

"What do I do?" she asked. "I can't phone from the house and must do this from another phone because Mum can listen in on the extension. She mustn't know." She flapped her hands.

"Well…maybe I can help on Monday but you'll have to come to work with me and I will ask Mark. He owes me a favour, I suppose. We'll explain to him that we need to give an important message to someone who is coming to the wedding and they'll phone us back as soon as they have the number. I am sure he will understand if I say our phone is broken."

I saw Rosie's face light up. "Oh, Jess, I'm so grateful to you. Sorry to be such a pain. Do you think Mark will mind? I mean it's your place of work."

"Rosie, you are not a pain, Jonni and I…we *want* to help you and anyway Mark kind of knows your mum, he'll understand, I'm sure. Don't worry about it, that's *my* problem. Monday, it is then— we are on your side, okay?"

Jonni asked Fergal to attend the cows for the evening milking and I met with Rosie and Jonni outside my office. Jonni offered to take her home in the Viva before I left work.

"Mark, I have something I'd like to ask you—a very special favour. I wouldn't normally ask, but it is urgent. The phone at the farm is broken." I hated myself for lying. "Rosie is getting married and we need to make an urgent call to her father in Holland, but he has promised to call us back. It's all a bit awkward, sorry."

"No problem, Jess."

I sighed with relief. "Okay, it'll only take a few minutes."

"It's okay, I owe you." Mark shot me a corner-of-the-eye glance. He seemed happier and I was sure this was the weekend his wife had returned with his sons. He walked into his office, closing the door behind him and I dialled the number on the letter. A brief silence followed then a long tone and I passed the receiver to Rosie.

The situation got me wondering how Ewan would react to all this. We'd left him at home doing his usual chores at the stables. Rosie hadn't told him anything and I assumed it may not be long before he was due for a big shock.

"Hello, Dad, it's Rosie, can you call me back? Here's the number."

After a few minutes her father returned the call. I answered it in case it wasn't him and then passed the receiver once again to Rosie.

"Hello, Dad, when are you coming over to see me? ...You are? Oh good. That's excellent news."

After listening to his words for a few moments, I heard her say, "Oh my God! It can't be true," and, "How did *you* know about this?"

I watched the expression change on Rosie's face. She nodded as he spoke then sighed. I heard her exclaim, "This is all too much for me to take in."

She listened again. "Can't you stay here at the farm with us?" Her voice wavered. "Oh yes, of course...Yes, yes, I understand. I've been worried for a long time, and what you told me confirms my thoughts. I'm in shock and I know Ewan will be, too. He's such an angel, but there are times when I despair of him. I don't know how I am going to deal with this. I'll explain when I see you."

Theo seemed to be reassuring her. "Yes, I thought it wasn't your fault. I know a bit about what Mum has been doing."

She listened again to her father's voice.

"You will? That would be fantastic if you could. Why can't I ever have a normal life like most people? Mum is in deep trouble and you're in Holland. I only have Ewan, and the way things are I'm not sure after today if I'll have him as well. My God, what you told me, I never…" She cleared her throat.

After a few more minutes of listening and agreeing and saying goodbye, Rosie replaced the receiver with a huge sigh. She blew out her cheeks and then came the flood of emotion, the one that had been bottled up for many months, the helpless crying.

Jonni took charge. "Go on, Jess, I'll deal with this. See you back at home soon, love. Come on, Rosie, let's take you home, but first we'll stop somewhere and have a chat before you go mouthing off to Ewan." He hugged her, realising he needed to take her out of the office before Mark saw her distress.

"It's going to be all right, Rosie. Your dad seems a good man," I assured her.

Jonni smiled at me. "I'll take care of her, see you later." He screwed up his nose in sympathy and squeezed my hand.

Chapter Twenty-three

I left the office a few minutes after Rosie and Jonni. When I got back to Tanglewood, I discovered they hadn't arrived. I realised that Jonni must have been consoling Rosie before she came home.

I went to the stables first to see if I could find Ewan. He was sitting on the sofa holding a cup of tea in one hand and reading a newspaper.

"Where's Rosie?" he asked.

"She's on her way back with Jonni. She won't be long; they've been out somewhere."

"Where's she been?" he puzzled.

I changed the subject.

"God, it's so hot in here. Shall I open the big doors?"

"I'll do it," Ewan offered.

I knew it would be difficult to hold out on information and I must have given a deep sigh, as one of the horses seemed to copy me. I tried not to mention Rosie.

"Tell me about Australia, what's it like?" I asked.

"Huh! It wasn't a good place for me."

I hoped he would share his experiences. Perhaps now was the time to probe deeper.

"I was at school there," he said, "...and growing up became a nightmare with my father being the way he was. Having been exposed to many contradictory ideas, he was deeply religious and I couldn't take it. I no longer believed in anything anymore, so I chose to come here."

"But what was so bad about it?"

He took in a deep breath. "It's a long story, but my dad was a controlling bastard. I couldn't live with him. He treated my mother like a dog and when she left me, I never forgave her. He was also a sour racist, and did nothing but complain about the ways of 'those bladdy savages'. The aboriginal people were my friends and they were good people." Ewan curled his lips. "When I needed support, they were always there for me. So, there was me and the old man trying to make a mere dollar or two with the farm, but to no avail."

"It sounds a bit like Connie's situation," I reminded him.

"I'm not going to let it happen to Connie, over my dead body; she's been very good to me." He settled back into the sofa.

"You must have been quite young when you came over here?" I asked.

"I found work in the local bar in Oz when I was seventeen. I pinched and scraped for every dollar I could lay my hands on. I got a passport and went up to Sydney to the cruise ships and got a job on board and worked my passage to Southampton."

"Ah that's how you got here, I see. So where did you meet Connie?"

"I was working in Axminster in a café and she used to come in for a coffee. We got talking one day and she told me of her powers in witchcraft."

That didn't surprise me.

"…With time, she taught me how to have more confidence in myself and I learned how to be at one with nature. For me, nature's way is best. Connie gave me the inner peace I needed." He shrugged his shoulders.

"I bet you were glad you met Rosie then?"

"Oh yes, I'm so much looking forward to the wedding. She's given me my happiness back."

"Ewan, I wanted to ask you what you know about Richard Millington?"

"Richard? Why?"

"Let's just say it was something he said at that party I went to?" I lied.

"Oh yes?"

"What do you know about the priesthood? Am I right in assuming you are a member? Richard seemed very keen to have me as part of the clan. He invited me to the initiation ceremony." I knew that very soon my white lies would get me in trouble and I longed for Rosie to hurry back.

Ewan's eyes opened wider.

"Why do you want to know, Jess?" Ewan furrowed his brow with justified suspicion.

"I'm wondering what he meant. What would I have to do?" He hesitated and I encouraged him to carry on. "Go on tell me. It's okay, I understand it's a bit of a sensitive area." I tried smiling and playing it down.

"If you promise not to say anything to Connie or anyone else."

I nodded in agreement. "I understand. You can trust me Ewan, it's okay."

"When Richard asked me to join the priesthood, I was obliged to show I wanted change and enrichment. The money he offered, it's going to help Connie to improve the farm—that's what this is all about, *but* on the proviso, that on our wedding day, we would go back to the ancient pagan wedding rites and consummate the marriage as they did in ancient times. I'm only trying to help Connie save the farm, that's all."

"I know all about that stuff, I read a book on it once, and I spoke to Richard about it, but I gather Rosie has given her consent too?" I was compelled to keep him talking before Rosie turned up.

"Oh really? Well yes, sort of." He took a gulp of his tea. "Richard said we wouldn't be the first to undertake the initiation ceremony. Every couple has a duty to prove their love to the gods of the earth by consummating the marriage in their presence. A failure may result in deep unhappiness and bad luck—even early death."

"You can't believe that, surely?" I said, attempting to stay calm.
"I think I do to a point, but Richard is such a good bloke.
He told me the chosen ones have absolute privileges. The money
we receive and need to keep the farm, would help us experience
a complete and wonderful change of lifestyle." He paused for breath.
"Although, each time I go to the mentoring sessions, Richard's
intensity has grown with his insistence about our agreement and he
is always asking me if I am learning the Holy text. Oh hell, which
reminds me, I need to practise it. He said the text must be word
perfect. 'Learn it,' he said. 'Believe it, and your life together will
always flourish. It has to make the perfect marriage'."

"Yes, for sure," I nodded and pretended that everything he told
me was normal. All the while I kept wishing that Jonni would get
back here quickly. I glanced at my watch.

"Listen Jess, you have no idea what it's liked to be whipped. I was
abused by my father, it was terrible. Look, sorry I'm telling you all
this, but sometimes it's good to talk to someone outside the family."

"Yes, I understand the importance of having support."

"Hans has had his bad times too, and underneath all that
mean and brutal image he portrays is a man in torment. He's going
through a bad time, that's all. I think that's why we we've been able
to talk to each other. We shared a common ground. Then there's
you, Jess, a stranger who walks into our lives and seems to understand everything we do here. You've been very tolerant of us." Ewan
gave a gentle smile. "Rosie likes you very much and only yesterday
she said she wished you had been her sister."

"Oh, Ewan, that's really sweet of you to say so. I don't think
I can forgive Hans though, he was truly horrible to me—hold on,
is that a car door I can hear?"

He listened. "No, I don't think so. So where is Rosie?"

"Ewan…I think you had better be prepared for when Rosie
gets back. All I know is that she wants to talk to you. I'm sorry. It's
not my place to say anything more."

"What's going on?"

"Oh, nothing you can't sort out." I said with a smile. *Hurry up you two.*

"You know, Jess, she's the one person who really understands me. This wedding is going to be the best moment of my life." He paused to think. "She's not going to call it off, is she? I'm scared I might mess it all up on the day with…you know…the consummation part. I mean she's so open with our sex life, I know she doesn't mind."

"No, no, don't worry." I tried to hold out as Ewan's explanations were making me feel out of my depth and I certainly didn't want to know about his sex life. He seemed so child-like at times and unable to make his own decisions. I supposed it was understandable having a father who controlled everything he did.

"So where is Rosie?"

"I think this is her now, you can find out for yourself."

Rosie stood in the doorway of the stable block with a tear-stained face. I gazed at Jonni standing behind her.

"Where the hell have you been? Jess tells me you need to talk to me."

Behind Ewan's back I shrugged my shoulders and opened the palms of my hands.

Jonni encouraged Rosie to speak. "Tell him Rosie, don't hold back."

My heart raced as I waited for Rosie to speak.

"Rosie, what's going on?" Ewan tried to kiss her but she had tears in her eyes and took a handkerchief from her pocket to blow her nose.

"Get off me. How could you, Ewan?"

"What do you mean, love?"

"Did you know about Richard Millington's plans?"

"What plans? Rosie, what are you saying?"

Merry whinnied in the stable and kicked the door with a loud bang.

"Rosie, tell him," Jonni urged.

"Did you realise Millington is paying you to have sex with me in public on our wedding day? Did you ask me about it?"

"Waddye mean? It's…"

"Ewan, stop! I don't want a full-blown row with you, but really, this is the end and just before our wedding, too. I couldn't believe it was for *real.*"

"Rosie, what the hell…"

"It's all voyeurism. Those mentoring classes you went to—it means nothing—they are conning us. It's a big joke, it's *not* real, understand—*not real!*" she shouted.

"What? Eh? Rosie, this isn't what it's all about, you know that."

"Yeah? You don't think we have to consummate the marriage at the altar, do you? A complete farce," she screamed, then laughed in his face.

I had never seen her as bad as this. I glanced at Jonni, his lips in a tight seal.

"How could you be so stupid? Millington was grooming you for his own greed. He was in trouble some years ago for allegedly having sex with underage girls. It means nothing to him to get someone to follow his instructions. He's conniving and manipulative and dabbles in hypnosis. Just think what could have happened. What if I had refused?" Rosie's faced burned bright pink with anger and the heat of the day.

"Well…yes, we had the mentoring; They told us it was for real and why not? Everyone at the wedding understands. They are the elders. You wouldn't refuse, surely, if it means saving Tanglewood?" He paused for breath to think about her words. "Well, we could have faked it, I suppose; no one would know!"

I watched as Rosie banged her fist on the sofa. He was about to finish speaking when she cut him down.

"Ewan, for GOD'S SAKE! Fucking elders? You're living in bloody cloud-cuckoo land. I know different. I'll bloody kill Mum; she doesn't realise what she's doing. These so called 'elders' are a false cult thriving on sexual favours. The guests at our wedding are paying him to watch us! It's out of control! You didn't think I would consent, did you? It's disgusting and as for you...you're disgraceful, Ewan—unbelievable!" She grabbed his jumper and it seemed we were about to have a full-blown fight on our hands. She pushed him down with brute force on the sofa. I looked at Jonni with alarm. I had never seen her being violent before.

"You don't have to do this. I explained it all to you at the beginning, when we had that first meeting with Richard, didn't you listen?" he snapped.

"But, Ewan, you went ahead with the plans anyway, I hardly got a say in the matter. You're the biggest fool ever and I don't want to marry someone who is stupid and gullible. All those people who think they have a following, oh my God, it doesn't bear thinking about."

It was time I left the stables, but for Rosie's sake I decided to stay and support both of them. "Calm down, you two. We're here to help you sort out this whole sordid affair. Shouting at each other isn't going to help."

Ewan looked away from her, sweating. "But, Rosie, you had the option to simulate or do it for real. Richard told me to inform you that we'd be offered more money if we followed ancient traditions, you obviously didn't listen to me! We could have enough to set us up for the rest of our days and keep the farm and it's not like we haven't had sex before, is it?"

"Ewan, you are unbelievable! When you said ancient traditions, I didn't think you meant...You still don't get it, do you? Richard has been psychologically blackmailing you, and as for Mum, she hasn't been helping, she's been..." Rosie swallowed hard. "Oh, I give up. I can't marry you under these circumstances; it's the biggest farcical lie I've ever heard of. If I didn't laugh about it..."

I'd never seen Rosie this angry and she scared me. Jonni moved forward and put his hand on Ewan's shoulder. "I'm afraid, Ewan, we found out that Richard Millington is a fraud. He is a con man. The nights at Avoca House involve innocent people, groomed for sexual favours by a non-existent cult."

Rosie chipped in. "When Gus Hannings disappeared, Millington used the house for that reason. He has always had permission from Gus; after all he is the Estate Manager. Until Gus is found or considered legally dead, then he is entitled to use it to stop the estate becoming derelict. It was thought that Gus' wife committed suicide, but it could have been something else. You remember Mary Hannings was Richard Millington's sister and, of course, Millington is Gus Hannings' brother-in-law. They couldn't have kids of their own apparently. There was no real heir to the Hannings estate. He probably murdered his wife after an argument and disappeared, I don't know. Mum never tells me anything. All I remember is the police coming around here and we weren't allowed into our own house for many weeks."

"How do you know all this?"

I noted her reluctance to answer him.

"Ewan, I can't marry you if you continue to believe all this stuff."

"But, Rosie, love, we have to do it this way to save the farm. It's our future as well as our commitment to each other. I told Richard it would be fine."

"What? Bloody hell, Ewan, I can't believe you said that. You still don't get it, do you?"

"I'll ask you again, who told you all this?" Ewan frowned.

"My father did and right now don't call me 'love'. I almost got sucked into this, too."

"Your father? But…how? What does *he* know?"

"I was out riding at the end of last year, when I began to think something wasn't quite right with Mum and her friends. That morning, I found one of my letters that *she* had opened. When I confronted her, she said it was a mistake, but I didn't believe her. She always handed me my mail after she picked up hers. So now you know why I requested all post, in my name, be delivered to the stables, see? It was then that Dad sent me a birthday card in January, and I never understood why. I mean, why now after all this time?

It was then I realised that Mum's been opening my mail. I now know she has kept me away from my dad and all his cards which I've never had. I am so angry right now. What was she thinking? Selfishness, sheer selfishness!"

"So...? What did he tell you?"

"A lot more than I bargained for, but he wants to help us. He's done some detective work, because Hans told him about it. He knows a hell of a lot more than we do about Millington and his clan."

"Yes, I know all that, but Rosie, what has Hans got to do with this?"

"He warned my father when he was in Holland on his way to Germany. He made enquiries about Millington's background. Did you know Millington's been in prison? You spent more time with Hans, who got suspicious when you told him about what you were studying up at Avoca House. He felt it was time to contact Dad."

"What? But how does he know your Dad?"

"I haven't the foggiest idea, but I suppose it's through Mum somehow, I mean..."

Rosie kept on talking, hardly taking a breath until Jonni spoke.

"Ewan, I think you've been brainwashed and Connie too. This is not the way to save the farm, think about it. Rosie has lost most of her inheritance anyway. The farm will be gone within a couple of weeks if Connie can't find the money."

"Oh my God, if this is true then...oh bloody hell. Rosie, I... I thought I was doing this for us. Are you sure? I'm still new to life in England. I thought it was the way of things, you know how I hate to say no to people who have been kind to me." His gaze lingered on her face as she scoffed at his remark.

"Ewan, sometimes I wonder why I ever consented to marry you. You are incredibly naïve, when will you ever grow up?"

Jonni felt it was time to say a word or two. "Rosie, I don't believe Ewan knew what he was getting himself into. I know he loves you and..."

"What do we do?" Rosie wailed. "The wedding..."

"Rosie, I do love you, I do. I don't want us to part. I really thought I was helping you—us, the farm. We can still get married but…"

Rosie looked at Jonni for assurance.

"It's up to you, Rosie…and Ewan, this is your life and your future and I can't advise you. You have to make your own decisions—be strong."

"I'm going in the house to think about it," Rosie sniffed and stormed off.

"Leave her Ewan," said Jonni. "She needs time to think and talk to Connie. That is, if Connie will listen. She is too stressed about selling the farm. Connie blurted out to me yesterday that she needs a five hundred grand investment to get out of the bloody mire. Now do you see, the few thousand pounds Millington said he was giving you would never have covered the costs? If you love Rosie, you don't need to prove it, for God's sake. I also want to explain that Connie has been less than pure in this. She's a desperate woman. Rosie doesn't know everything, but I believe Connie hasn't been honest with what she does late at night—and it isn't knitting. I saw it with my own eyes."

"You mean…?"

Jonni screwed up his nose and continued to speak. "Yes, I mean…You do know what goes on at those parties of theirs?"

"Not really, it's a kind of…" He paused for thought.

"I'm afraid that Connie has been lured into, let's say…the darker side of life, it's all about drugs and lots of rockin' and rollin', if you get my drift. All she wants is for you and Rosie to be happy and not be left with all her debts. She is very stressed right now."

"What…? Connie? At her age? Don't be so bladdy stupid."

"Sorry, Ewan, but I don't think you have a right to say that. Older people do have sex, you know! I saw it with my own eyes the night I went to Avoca House. Connie went into that guarded room at Avoca House but it doesn't mean to say she does that kind of thing, but draw your own conclusions or better still—ask her. They pay lots of money to participate in wife-swapping parties. All those people Millington has conned into believing it is precious to share their bodies and souls to the pagan gods. Connie included. It's total rot—they're a lost cause! Most of them are as high as a kite on far worse stuff than we've ever used. Millington is a drugs dealer, I'm sure of it."

Ewan stood with his mouth open in shock. "Oh hell, yes, now I see…" Ewan sighed, "…it's all beginning to make sense now. I remember the night I found Connie inebriated on the doorstep, cold and having wet her knickers. I had to put her to bed. It was my own worst nightmare. She was unconscious and I couldn't let her lie there. I did my best. I didn't want Rosie to see her like that. Then there was the incident with the money she'd given me. 'Take this, Ewan, you and Rosie go out and have a nice time together.' She'd squeezed two hundred pounds into the palm of my hand. I thought it was a 'thank you' for not telling Rosie about being wasted. I tried to give it back to her and eventually I stuffed it in a box she had on the dressing table, in the hope she might forget she gave it to me. There were other incidents, too, but I never considered Connie had been 'used', like me. My God, I've been such a fool. What do I do?"

When Jonni shook his head, I answered the question. "If I were you, I would leave it until the morning. We ought to inform the police, but there's nothing to stop you going on with the handfasting as you wanted, but without that stupid lot out there. If you really love Rosie, it makes sense to carry on. I'll talk to her, if you like. We can tell the guests you are postponing the wedding date. It will give us a chance to sort this out and for you two to decide your future. We can do this without making a fuss. I know you've been taken in by all this cult stuff and Connie, too, but Rosie is a forgiving soul. Tell her what an idiot you've been and apologise."

"Yeah, I know, but I'm…" I saw the tears in his eyes and he squeezed his eyelids together to make them go away. "I'm going to see Rosie and put everything straight."

We followed Ewan up to the house to find Rosie rolling a cigarette and sniffing away her tears.

"What do I do, Rosie? Where do we go next, love?"

"I don't know and don't keep calling me love," Rosie sobbed. "Mum's been up to all kinds of weird goings on at Avoca House, I dread to think what she's been doing. I'm doubly ashamed of her and you, too, now. I would never have arranged that kind of wedding if I'd realised what was really going on."

"Jonni has just told me what he learned at the party. Unfortunately, I didn't pick up on it. I'm sorry."

"Why didn't you say something, Ewan?" Rosie's eyes narrowed.

"I don't know, it was Richard's idea. All those months of mentoring; they promised me the world. I know how much you wanted to run the farm, but I knew we couldn't do it without the money. Richard said that if I went through the Rites of Love in the marriage ceremony, he would see that Tanglewood was ours and you could have your new riding stables. I did it for you and Connie. I now realise it was all lies and deceit; utter trash. I'm in shock. My God, Richard's made a dreadful fool out of me. All that reading, persuading me this was normal and done with dignity. I thought it was a beautiful thing to do. I feel such an idiot, taken in by persuasion, lies, and a promise of wealth. How stupid could I be?" He banged his fist on the worktop.

Rosie gave a deep sigh in her anger. "Oh, Ewan, bloody hell. Yes, how stupid are you? When I had been to two of those so-called sessions at Avoca House, and Millington mentioned giving myself to the pagan gods, I didn't think of it as having sex in public! I didn't go back because I don't like him; I didn't understand why you did, either. In the last few weeks you seem to have spent more time at Avoca House than here with me."

"Hm…each time I went over there, I felt so much at ease with myself. He talked so calmly to us all. We were led by the High Priest into meditation and were told to visualise our aspirations for the future. Then we acted them out and each time I came home, I felt renewed and full of inspiration to want to do those things. It was as if I was compelled to believe in it."

"There you go, see. You've been induced into a robotic state of mind," said Rosie. "It's totally disgusting," she snapped. "I think he's brainwashed you."

"Yes, but Richard made it sound so normal and he told me that I would be with like-minded people, who understood the ritual and it was nothing out of the ordinary for them. All I had to do was show you the way."

"Oh my God, Ewan, what are you like? You talk in riddles. Don't you have a mind of your own?"

"Ho hum...it seems not! I wonder if he was hypnotising us all? It wasn't just me at the mentoring sessions, there were three other young people. When my father told me to do something, I did it without question, he used to beat me if I didn't. Now do you understand?"

Rosie didn't speak, she sat there and stared into the void. "I'm not sure about getting married now, especially to someone who can't think for himself."

"Oh don't, Rosie, please don't. What are we going to do?"

"I dunno, I just don't know." She shook her head and blew her nose on the paper tissue she extracted from her pocket.

"I love you, Rosie. I wouldn't swap the world for you. Please forgive me."

Rosie turned her face. "Yes, I know, Ewan, that's my problem. And I do understand how you got into this mess."

"Come on, love, it's not all doom and gloom. If your dad comes here, he may be able to support you."

"Dad *is* coming here and Mum mustn't know yet. Please don't tell her. She is about to lose the farm, then what? We'll all have to live in a slummy council house up north," she retaliated and stood up in defiance.

"It's good we found all this out before it was too late," I said.

"If you promise to grow up, take some control over your life, then fine. Okay, okay." Rosie stomped off to the bathroom to wash her face and Ewan followed to the bedroom. On the way up the stairs I heard him say, "How stupid have I been, Rosie? I'm so sorry."

Chapter Twenty-four

I arrived home from work at the usual time.

"Hello, love. I always look for you when I hear a car engine." Jonni hugged me and we kissed.

Ruby tried to squeeze in between us at the table and it was a delight to see how she had improved. I stroked her and she licked my hand.

"How are things?" I asked.

"Well, as expected. Ewan's really cut up. I found myself being piggy in the middle yesterday—it was awful. I saw Rosie earlier, and she told me Ewan's been in tears most of the day—I never thought...well you know what he's like; he acts macho, but I know inside he's as gentle as Ruby, and now he's heartbroken." Jonni sighed. "In a way he's still a kid and I'm seriously worried about him. We've all had a talk this afternoon and I think Rosie is beginning to make some plans and possibly see sense, at last. They love each other—I know they do. He knows what a fool he's been. He's the kind of guy who needs something to believe in. His father was very religious and he wanted more than that, in fact, sometimes I wonder what he really wants out of life, he is always a follower and never a leader. Anyway...Rosie wants to talk to you."

"To me? Why me?"

"Oh, I think it's the 'girly thing' you know...and she trusts you. She needs a friend, like an older sister, you know what I mean?"

I smiled. "I've been the older sister most of my life."

"I bet you do it well. Go and talk to her, Jess. I feel very sorry for her. Love you," said Jonni. "See you later."

I went to my room. For the first time I had found someone I really cared about. I loved him—no, idolised him—and understood the meaning of real love, perhaps for the first time. Part of me was on a high, but today it was Rosie who needed me.

I had changed into my jeans and finished pulling up the zip when I heard a knock.

Rosie entered the room and flopped onto my bed.

"Come here, love. I know it's all gone wrong and if there's anything I can do to help, tell me, yeah?"

She began to talk under sobbing breath explaining the phone conversation she'd had with Theo. "I'm not sure whether or not to cancel this wedding." She sniffed. "I mean, I've got the dress and everything."

"Rosie there are only two things you can do. Cancel the wedding and leave Ewan or show him you love him and get married as *you* wanted. You've got all the time in the world. So much can change in such a short time. That way, you can still be together and…"

"Do a proper wedding later on?—yes, Jonni said the same thing. You're both right, I do want to marry Ewan. I know it's not his fault, he's that way inclined. He's a lovely person and I know he loves me. If we postpone everything, it may take the pressure off us both. I realise now how stupid we have been, I mean, how easy it is to get sucked into something because of an offer of money. I saw through Millington, but had no idea how much Ewan was up to his neck in it."

"It's important to communicate well when you are a couple, believe me I know about those things." I gave her a sympathetic smile. "I mean look at *me*, I'm almost thirty and not married, there's no rush to get married at your age you know." I felt some déjà vu from my mother. "Come on, love, let's go and have a cup of tea. I've just got in from work and haven't had a drink yet." I pulled gently on her arm and she followed me downstairs.

As we passed the phone, it rang and Rosie answered.

"Oh, hello there. I didn't expect you to phone here so soon. No, Mum's not here at the moment."

She listened.

"Well, I am going to talk to Ewan and maybe postpone the wedding. We'll cancel most of the guests despite having sent out invites. They weren't my invites anyway, Mum sent them and she said I could have up to twenty of my friends. As she was paying for it, she said she ought to be able to invite who she wanted. It's one big farce, don't you think?"

She listened harder as I filled the kettle for the tea.

"Sod him." I heard her say. "You will? Oh…okay then…that's really good. I'm very upset; it's a tragedy, but we have to do this." She sniffed.

As I sat, drinking my tea, I realised I hadn't seen Connie. Perhaps the reality of losing the farm had set in.

"Oh yes, that'll be wonderful, Dad, thanks so much. When? So soon? Where shall we meet? Okay, see you soon, bye."

Rosie replaced the receiver and blew out her cheeks in sheer relief.

"I gather that was your dad?" I asked, hoping she had good news.

For the first time in a couple of days she had a smile on her face.

"I'm thrilled to bits. Dad's coming over; he arrives on Friday night. Mum will be horrified! Sod Mum, this is Ewan's affair and mine. We will get married and Dad will give me away, like in a proper wedding, but not yet."

I knew how confused she had been about the whole affair, but hoped it would soon all work out. "Oh, Rosie, that's marvellous. Have you told your mum about Millington?"

"Not yet, Dad said to wait until he comes. He wants more time to discuss it with *me* first. In a way it's a good job she isn't around during the day, but I wish she would stop all this weird stuff, it's breaking my heart to see what she is doing to herself. We can't say much until we go to the police. Dad is going to come with me, he asked me not to tell her just yet."

"The police? Oh goodness me." *Jonni will freak out.*

*

It was Saturday morning. Rosie had arranged to meet her father in Axminster at a local hotel and asked me to go with her. Jonni drove into town and we parked behind a Gateway supermarket.

"I'm feeling very nervous," said Rosie. "He seemed so caring on the phone and for him to help me, I have to find out what he wants to do." She turned down one corner of her mouth.

As we walked into the hotel, Theo Dijkman awaited us.

Within minutes I realised she need not have worried. Theo was a good-looking Dutchman in his late fifties with greying hair and a warm smile. He was tall and wore a smart tweed jacket and open neck shirt. His demeanour came across as well educated, charming, with an aura of wealth about him. His shoes shone to perfection, his hair cut very neat and his polite mannerisms and confidence gave me the impression he was an influential business man. He gave Rosie the warmest of smiles.

"Hallo my sweet, how are you?" He held out his arms to his daughter and I listened to his refined English-Dutch accent.

I saw Rosie bite her lip and then she raced into his arms.

"Dad, how lovely to see you. You look great."

He kissed her three times bobbing from cheek to cheek.

"It's been too long. Look at you now, huh?" He stood back, holding both of Rosie's arms out to her side. "All grown up and looking lovely. I'm really proud of you, but we have to get this awful business sorted and we need to act very quickly."

He made every word sound positive and welcoming. I felt sure I saw tears in his eyes when he greeted Rosie, and found it hard to believe he had once been married to Connie.

"Dad, this is Jess and Jonni: they are my best friends, and they live with us. They're on our side. I feel there is a lot of explaining to be done here."

We shook hands with Theo.

"Do you mind, Rosie, if I don't come with you this morning," said Jonni. "I have something to do in town."

I knew the real reason for his not coming to the police station and I kept quiet. Rosie looked at me and I knew she must have understood.

"Dad, Jess and Jonni know all about the problems with our wedding and why we have to go to the police. I didn't bring Ewan, it's market day, although I'm sure he'll need to talk to them soon. At the moment we're barely speaking, but..."

Jonni nodded. "I'm so glad you came, Theo. It's quite a story isn't it? Thank you."

We lowered our voices as Theo spoke and sat on the armchair. "We're all feeling nervous, but don't worry, Richard Millington deserves what's coming to him. Did you tell your mother? I don't want Millington to know we did this, do you understand, it could be dangerous. I hope they arrest him. I will need to talk with Ewan, okay? Let's get some advice first. They'll need a statement from him."

"Yes sure, Dad, I did as you said, I didn't say anything yet, but to be honest with you I'm worried what to tell her—and about us involving the police, what if they arrest her?"

"It's okay, my dear, let me sort it for you. I'll explain everything and yes, they will interview your mum, but she is innocent I am sure. I know her well enough to understand how her mind works. I'm here to help, don't forget that."

"So soon, Dad?"

"Yes, the sooner the better," Theo remarked. "We'll do it after we've had our coffee."

We all looked at each other, amazed at Theo's eagerness to sort out Millington.

The waiter came over to take our order for drinks.

"Jess, will you come with me to the police station? I might say something I shouldn't."

"You've got your dad now, Rosie; I am sure he will say the right things."

"Yes but..."

I could tell she meant that she didn't know her dad these days as much as she knew me and needed my moral support. "Okay, I'll come."

"You'll have to introduce me to Ewan. I bet he is very upset," Theo said.

"Ewan isn't a happy soul at the moment; he finds himself in the middle of all this and is wondering what to do about it, so if you could talk to him, that would be great," said Rosie.

"Of course, my dear."

After we finished our coffee, I arranged to meet Jonni later. I squeezed his hand and whispered, "Are you sure you don't want to come with us?"

"Jess, darling, there are still some things in my life I want to avoid and this happens to be one of them."

"Okay, I understand. I didn't want to go either, but Rosie needs me."

Rosie walked through the door of the police station admitting to her father she was scared stiff. She almost turned around and walked back out again until I persuaded her she was doing the right thing. What did the future hold? How would Ewan take all this when they got back to the farm? Would her father come with her and meet her mother again? On the way to reception, she asked me lots of questions but I realised there were very few comforting answers.

Theo approached the police officer on duty. "I want to report what we feel is a crime," he said. "The incident is of a sexual nature and this is my daughter and we both need to talk to someone, it's urgent."

The officer on the desk looked hard at Rosie. "Don't I know you, young lady?" he asked. "You're Rosie Dijkman who owns the stables at Tanglewood, aren't you?"

Rosie looked away from the officer. "Yes, that's right. My mother owns the farm."

"Would you prefer to talk alone to a woman police officer?" he asked her.

"Oh no, my dad and my friend are here to help. We need to talk to someone as soon as possible, it's all a bit difficult. I'm fine, nothing dreadful has happened to me, well sort of…"

"You must be Theo Dijkman the artist who used to live at Tanglewood? You live in Holland, don't you? If you hold on, I'll make a call and then I'll ask Detective Sergeant Hicks to come down and take details. Hang on a minute."

Two hours dragged by with lots of questions and we were provided with cups of tea. Rosie gave a statement explaining the so-called 'Rites' and she talked about the way Ewan had been 'groomed' over the last twelve months. Rosie broke down trying to explain how foolish she had been and how Ewan believed in all the ritual nonsense. Theo told them that Connie was naïve and misled. It seemed they already knew; she was well known to the locals for her outlandish ways and flamboyant personality. He explained his relationship with Connie and how his ex-wife had no caring for the family fortune. She'd had the castle in Scotland, the swimming pool and all the servants. All she wanted was to live her life around local people and love her animals and the land. Richard Millington had taken advantage of her. Perhaps he knew something about Connie and he was blackmailing her. It was all speculation.

"Well…to help you here…" the officer replied, "we've had our eyes on Richard Millington for some time. This so-called 'cult religion' became known to us in recent weeks and we are already dealing with it, your young man isn't the only one involved here. We are very glad you came in to report this."

"Yes, but Mum is easily led and Ewan, too; they're alike." Rosie rolled her eyes. "I believe she didn't really know what she was doing. She thinks she's done nothing wrong. I only hope Ewan can recover from all this."

"Don't worry, we'll investigate further into your statement. Mrs Dijkman always seems to have been an honest and harmless lady, but we have to speak with her. I'm sure you understand. I feel you could be right, she has been misled, but we'll get to the bottom of this before it goes too far." He turned to Rosie. "We'll need to interview Ewan, perhaps when you get home you can ask him to come down to the police station as soon as possible so he can make a statement."

Rosie turned down her mouth. "He'll love doing that, I'm sure."

I smiled at her comment; *poor Ewan.*

"Now, Mr Dijkman, where can we find you?" The police officer sat with a pen in his hand twisting it between his fingers.

"Oh, you can call the Wild Ox Hotel, or at Tanglewood with my daughter. Connie doesn't know I'm here, but I have to tell her today. She is in such a mess with her money. Something has to be done. Tanglewood is too precious to allow someone else to take it on. I'm doing this for you, Rosie." He looked at her. "Don't look so scared, sweetheart, I'll break it to her gently, I promise. I hope to have some good news soon, anyway."

I made lunch. The Cavalry was now minus Hans and we seemed to have our own place to sit and respected the space each of us had allocated for ourselves. I was about to start eating when the phone rang.

"Who is this?" I heard Connie shouting down the phone, something she often did when she didn't know who was speaking.

"Theo? Theo? Oh right, Theo, what on earth…Why are *you* phoning me?" She placed a hand on her brow.

Oh gosh, he's done it, he's on the phone. Now the shit is really going to hit the fan, as Dad used to say.

"Why, what's happened?" Connie snapped.

I knew she was on her way to the cowshed to speak with Jonni about the hay she couldn't afford and what she would do with the cows if she sold the house.

"Sorry, I can't meet you, we have a crisis." Connie listened hard to the voice on the other end of the line. "There's no need to be like that, Theo. If you want to come over you can, but I'm very busy," she said with defiance in her tone. "You talked to *Rosie*? How

could you do that? God, Theo, I don't need *your* help." Connie's
faced changed to a look of sheer defeat. "All right then, but I can't
see why you need to speak to me after all this time, I mean…But
Theo, I don't need…Why? What the hell is going on?" She gave
a deep sigh. "Okay, I'll see you at five."
She put the receiver down hard. "I need a drink," she exclaimed.
I lowered my head, attempting to remain neutral.

That same evening, I returned to the house after helping at the
stables and saw a Volvo parked outside. I realised it was Theo's
voice I heard in the lounge. I said a brief 'hello' and then rushed
upstairs to soak in the bath. Later, I came down to make dinner,
and although Jonni helped me, the silence between us made me
feel uncomfortable. If anything was going to change our lives, it
would be today. Theo had plans and we would soon learn the fate
of Tanglewood and The Cavalry.

I'll never forget the look on the face of Connie. It was one
of shock, guilt—everything; but I heard her say, "Oh God, I've
been such a fool. Rosie mustn't know, I'm so ashamed." She looked
ashen and I assumed every bit of bad news possible was out in the
open.

"Look, Connie, I have to tell you that Rosie already knows,
she's not stupid you know, but Millington mustn't find out okay?
You *must* hold back, the police are going to take him into custody
for questioning—no phone calls, do you hear? They will search
Avoca House for evidence and I gather there will be plenty of that."

"I can't take much more," Connie replied. "The whole of my
life has fallen apart. You being here, the house, I owe so much
money. Why did you have to come here, Theo? Why?"

"Listen, Connie, I have to do this for Rosie; she's *our* daughter.
Remember? I met Ewan, he seems to be a pleasant young man. He's
very upset and his life has turned into something on the verge of
a disaster."

"Yes but, oh I don't know what to think. All my life I've had to fight for what I believe in. I never once gave up until today. I've always faced rejection and I could never understand why I have been misunderstood by everyone, including my own mother. I only wanted to prove to you all we could be fine again if I worked hard for all of us. Please, Theo, you have to…"

Theo butted in. "Connie, I want you to accept the situation now I'm here. Yes, I'm angry with you and only you know why. Yes?" He stared hard at her. "I think you owe it to all of us to sort this out. I won't let Tanglewood be sold to the highest bidder; we have to look at making some changes. I am here to help you and if you don't want my help then fine, but I am doing this for Rosie, okay? You have been very selfish, keeping her away from me. Why, Connie? Why? To spite me for leaving you? Huh?"

That evening Jonni and I spent time in my room talking. We were lying on top of the bed, with pillows propped against the bed head, his arm around my shoulder.

"I wanted…" Our conversation collided.

"No, no, you go first," he said. "Go on."

"My contract doesn't end for a while, but time passes so quickly. It looks like now we might have to find somewhere else to live and not by choice anymore. I mean this could leave us in a bit of a mess. I know Theo has good intentions, but it won't include us surely?"

"Yes, love, I agree, it's dreadful. We've both been through so many highs and lows in recent months. We just seem to soldier on trying to sort out other people's problems."

I sighed one very big sigh. "This is really difficult for me. It's all to do with my dad, when he passed away he made me promise I would see the world and do wonderful things and so far, I've got myself in a bloody mess."

"Oh thanks, Jess!"

"No, no I didn't mean…Oh, Jonni, I'm sorry. It's like this see. I should have gone backpacking around the world by now but I wanted one more job to make sure I didn't leave Mum and Anna too soon. At least I could get home easily if things didn't turn out, it was a kind of trial run coming here. I don't suppose we could… well I mean, do it together could we?"

Jonni smiled at my suggestion, but I knew it was impossible for him, he had no money to do these things.

"It's just that everything here has been so awkward and with my dad…I need security and I miss my mum and my sister, they miss me, too. I have to go back home and see them, explain everything; it's been on my mind for weeks. We could go together. I keep phoning her and she seems to understand how busy I've been, bless her. But…"

"Okay. Thanks for the invite and we will do it."

"You talked about being 'together'. What exactly did you mean?" I asked.

"Marriage, kids, all that kind of stuff."

"Marriage? Oh, heck I hadn't thought…"

"Well, look at our age; we don't want to leave these things much longer, do we? I would rather hope that within a short time we can consider all that."

"Jonni, love, we've been so casual and relaxed about our relationship and suddenly we find ourselves discussing marriage. I mean how long have we known each other—a few months? You need a proper job and I need to find work, especially now, thinking about life after Tanglewood. I feel another disaster coming on. I really don't want to lose you now."

"What do we do? Any ideas? I think we ought to see what Theo has to say first." He paused. "Do you need a few more months to be sure about me?"

"Oh no, love, I'm feeling confused not knowing which direction I should be going. Sorry, I didn't mean it that way." I sighed.

"Come here, my darling, let me hug you. I don't want to lose you now."

He kissed me deeply and caressed my cheeks. "A kiss always makes it better," he said.

Chapter Twenty-five

Despite the balmy summer nights, everyone's mood had changed to deep gloom. Theo had returned to Holland to attend his work, but was due back soon. I walked up the path after parking the car and heard the familiar sound of a BMW bike coming up the drive; I glanced over my shoulder. I could hardly believe Hans had actually come back as I had begun to think he'd gone forever. No such luck so it seemed.

I was about to ignore him when he stopped and spoke to me. "Hey, Jess, is Connie around? I need to see her urgently. I'm not staying long."

"Er yes, she's a bit upset. Hardly been out of her room for days."

"Why's that then?"

"I'm not sure I should tell you."

"It's okay, I need to see her. I gather things may have changed since I left."

"Humph!—you can say that again. You saw Theo Dijkman then?"

His eyes widened at my comment.

At that point I supposed I should have been grateful to Hans for his warning to Theo. He paused for what seemed too long and before he could answer, I explained further. "He's been here in England and all hell's broken loose. Rosie went to the police with him."

"Shit!" Hans exclaimed in a gruff tone from the depths of his helmet.

"She told us the house will be up for sale soon. The money's almost run out. All of us will have to find somewhere else to live. The horses will be sold, the stables…everything."

"More bloody trouble; I have to see her and sort this out," he muffled.

What did he mean by 'sort this out'? Who was he to think he was the saviour of Tanglewood?

"Enjoyed yourself whilst you've been away then?" I asked.

"Yeah, I suppose so."

"Look Hans, perhaps you and I can agree to disagree." I decided to be bold. I realised at this point he could either punch me in the face or be a little more understanding. I got ready for the punching moment and glanced to check the quickest exit.

"What do ye mean?" he asked, removing his helmet. He'd had his hair cut shorter and his beard was no longer thick, but styled and short. Dare I say he looked clean and smart for a change with a sense of the good-looking man. At last I could see the real Hans.

"You haven't exactly been very nice to me since I arrived here—I'm an innocent party and your behaviour toward me has been appalling."

"Look, Jess, if you'd had a life like mine, you may have killed yourself by now."

His comment took my breath away and knew this was my chance to say how I felt. "I can see you have problems, but there's no need to take it out on me—or the dog."

"You may not need to put up with me much longer." He sniffed.

"Oh, and why's that?" I asked. "I think I need an apology."

"Give it time, and with Connie's situation it looks like I was going, anyway. I've come back to pick up a few things and…I don't do apologies."

I felt an air of change in Hans but inside me I still had the deepest reservations about his actions. An apology would have helped.

"Hans?"

"Yeah."

"Why don't you find it easy to be nice to me?"

"Well, you've got everything you want, haven't you? A mother, a family, and money."

"But money isn't everything, you know. I don't have a father anymore."

"Look, Jess, listen to me, girl. Your father was good to you and you'll never begin to understand the pain I suffered. I can't live with the niceties of life. It's been a struggle of the worst kind."

"I'm sorry to hear it, but I haven't done anything wrong. You can be so threatening, it doesn't do you any good. What happened to *your* father?"

"Please don't ask me that, it's still too painful; there are things I can't talk about. Let's say that Ewan and I share the same kind of pain. Anyway, life is about to change for me; I'm leaving after today and you might not hear from me again." He rolled his eyes and frowned as he slung his rucksack over a shoulder and strode inside the house.

I felt glad of his imminent departure and a moment of relief came over me but if what he told me was true, then perhaps I should stand back for a while. After his trip to Germany, I guessed there was a woman in his life. My female instinct told me it was true; he had smartened himself up and looked like a human being for a change. I never really understood Hans' reason for being at Tanglewood. It seemed there was a missing link in his life story. Why was he here? What had brought him to the farm other than a job and Connie taking him under her wing? Perhaps with time I would find out.

It was late afternoon as I leaned against the stone wall in the garden, and closed my eyes against the sun. The sound of bees and the cooing of wood pigeons gave the afternoon a sense of peace and relaxation, but the temperature kept on rising. Forest fires raged throughout the country, and I heard that the burning heather on the North Yorkshire Moors had been devastating. It could take years to extinguish the peat underground.

Despite the sounds and fragrances of summer, I also felt a moment of sadness.

I had Jonni in my life now and it concerned me that all this could be snatched away. Then, I began to think about my time with him and how much I loved him. His confidence had been ruined by his arrest, but with my support I was sure he was improving. Our evening in the wood had been amazing. We were in love and I never wanted it to change.

I strolled along the path and into the house. Alvin, looking more arthritic than usual, was locked out and whimpering. "Come on then, old boy. I'll let you in."

Upstairs, I heard the sound of a man's voice. It sounded like Hans talking to Connie, so I listened. Then I heard Connie's voice becoming louder. "Oh, my goodness."

"Hells bells, Connie. You can't keep going with your so-called 'friends' anymore, I keep telling you, but you never listen—they are bad for you. Be warned. They are not true pagans, they are voyeurs; you've been tricked. All the payments were for sex and don't tell me you were making friggin' cakes at Avoca House!"

"What right have you to tell me that, Hans?"

"Because you know what I am talking about. I *repeat,* these people are not your friends, do you hear me? If you continue in this way, you'll end up in prison and please don't think I've gone all soft all of a sudden, but I never had a proper mother and you know you've been very good to me in view of what I've been through. It seems your cousin was mixed up in all this, too, there was a lot of corruption and in my opinion, he's either killed himself or he's still alive and Richard Millington knows where he is. It's Millington who is in the driving seat. You've been tricked and Tanglewood could easily have belonged to Millington if he'd had his way."

I sat on the stairs hoping Hans wouldn't see I'd been eavesdropping. I was ashamed of myself, but I had to know. The last thing I heard was Connie 'shushing' Hans—"Shut that door, dear."

Chapter Twenty-six

It seemed over the last day or so our lives had taken a direction to the extreme left instead of an easy right. I hardly slept a wink. I went to work and must have looked like hell.

"Morning, Jess, are you okay?"

I didn't wish to explain it all to Mark. He'd been kind enough to me already. I was annoyed how things had turned out. This business with Connie and Rosie was stressing me out. "I didn't sleep too well," I said.

"If you don't feel okay, do you want to slip home?"

"Oh no, Mark, I only just got here. Also, I must finish the job I was doing on Friday. You've got loads of appointments today."

"That's good of you, Jess, thanks," he said. "There'll be plenty of work in view of the new season, everyone wants a car for the summer holidays." He smiled, seemingly grateful I was staying.

"Sorry I didn't mean to…"

"No, it's okay. I sometimes see you looking rather worried these days. I hope everything at the farm is going well."

"Well, things are changing, but anyway…would you like a coffee before we start?"

It was my lunch break and yet another hot day. I took a short ride in the car with a packed lunch and a couple of sausage rolls I had bought from the local bakery. At a viewpoint on the edge of town I sat, with all the windows open, wallowing in my own sadness. Where was I going in my life? With Dad's wishes in my head, I felt sad that he would never know how it turned out for me. Right now, I needed him for guidance—'*Jessica, you must follow your heart,*' he would always say. I considered my options. I could stay here and get another job, go home and see my family, or move on with Jonni and forget all that had happened at Tanglewood. Where was my heart beating now?

I saw Jonni's face in my head, the kindness he had shown, the problems he'd encountered, and I realised he still had some pride left after his broken lifestyle. For me it was different, I could move out and find another place to live, but like Jonni, Tanglewood had grown on me too and now we were going to lose it.

With tears in my eyes I knew the decision had already been made. I would stay at Tanglewood and see it through. I wiped away my tears and tried to pull myself together. I put the last of my sandwich back in the paper bag, I couldn't eat it; it was time to get back to work and concentrate on Mark's appointments.

Later that day, I found Jonni walking down the lane wearing his familiar hat. I felt overwhelmed with love for him; I really was the other half of a delicious peach. I waited at the gate with a smile on my face, trying to be brave and hold back the tears. His curly hair and smile made me want to rush into his arms and love him to bits.

"Hey hey, what's all this?" he asked.

I put my arms around him in floods of tears. "I really do love you," I sobbed.

"Oh, Jess, come here. I love you, too. What's up?"

"I realised this afternoon how much I care about you and couldn't wait to get back to tell you."

"Oh…that's wonderful, love. I've been thinking, too and what we need is a better plan. I'll start this week, but not until we speak to Theo. He told me today not to be too hasty about leaving the farm just yet. He wants our help during this crisis. It looks like I'm going to get paid, too. He's a real nice guy. Come on, love, chin up; it's going to be all right." He hugged me again and looked into my eyes. "We were meant to be together," he said and kissed me.

This was one of the wonderful things about Jonni, I knew he would always be there for me.

Chapter Twenty-seven

I passed Rosie standing in the hall, her ear almost glued to the telephone receiver.

"Hi, Dad, glad you could make it back here." She listened to his news. "Look...can we go riding together, give us chance to talk things through? Ewan's in Somerset today with the egg orders. He seems to be making a living now, thank goodness. The police have been here and he went to the station to make a statement." There was a moment's silence before Rosie spoke again. "Hang on a minute, she's here, I'll ask her."

She turned her head toward me. "Jess, Dad wants to know if you would you like to come riding with us? He wants to spend time talking things over with the two of us."

I looked at Rosie querying her invitation, wondering why I was included in what should have been a private moment between Rosie and her Dad. I mouthed, "Do you really want *me* to come?"

"Yes, it's okay, he's got something he wants to ask us both."

I shrugged my shoulders and gave her a smile. "Yes...why not? Okay, that would be nice." I had never envisaged Theo, Rosie, and myself riding out together.

We took sandwiches in our rucksacks and a bottle of wine and rode with Carlow and Hope. Theo borrowed Briony from Val, who had returned from her holiday. The horse was a good sixteen hands and able to carry him well. We rode deep into the wood and found a spot to sit for a while and allow the horses to relax. I turned around to look for the seat near where Jonni and I made love. The dank odour of the woodland floor brought memories of my night without clothes. I smiled to myself.

Theo and Rosie found a clearing. We tied the horses to a tree and sat for a while on an old log, munching ham and cheese rolls and drinking the Cabernet Sauvignon in plastic cups.

"It's been quite a week, eh?" Theo said. "They took Millington into custody. As long as he stays out of our way we are fine. The police suspected what he was up to, his previous custody didn't do him any favours. He's been under suspicion for a while. They searched Avoca House and found all kinds of dubious items. There were traces of 'stuff' in his room. I told them all I knew about Hannings and they said they would get in touch. It's bound to be in the press but I think we are safe for the time being."

Rosie looked at her father but, at the mention of the press, she frowned.

I listened to Theo and felt it was the right time to drop a hint of our plans. "I had a serious talk with Jonni last night and we are thinking of moving out. I didn't want to tell you yet, Rosie, but that's the plan. We'll help you get sorted and then we hope to move on."

Rosie's face fell. "You mean *both* of you intend to move out of Tanglewood for good?"

"If your mum's selling the farm, we have no option, do we? I mean we can still find somewhere to live and come and see you."

"Where will Ewan and I live? I'm heartbroken. It's all Mum's doing; how could she be so stupid? Everything we wanted to do has now been destroyed."

Theo listened and then spoke. "Millington is a very powerful man and can be dreadfully persuasive. I know. I remember him from the old days. There is a saying in Dutch, 'Als je hem een vinger geeft, neemt hij de hele hand.' It means if you give him a finger he will take a whole hand."

"Ah yes, give him an inch and he will take a mile," I offered.

"Yes, right, Jess, and he's very self-obsessed."

"Dad, what do you want to do about all this?" Rosie screwed up her face.

"There is something I want to discuss with you ladies. I know you have plans, Jess, Jonni mentioned it, but I am going to put a proposal to Connie in the next few hours. I don't have many days left in England. I must get back to work in Holland, I have an important client over there; I can't walk away from him. But I'll return soon."

I watched as Rosie's face fell. "But, Dad what about...?"

"Hold on, my dear, there is more. I am considering buying Tanglewood to get your mother out of this dreadful mess." He raised his eyebrows. "That way, the deal will go through quickly and we can get on with our lives."

Rosie and I looked at each other and gasped. "Dad. Are you sure?"

Theo continued. "The impression I get is that your mum has had enough of the stress of coping with the farm, and wants to live somewhere else. She is very ashamed of herself and local gossip. I am so sorry you had to find out about this, Rosie, but perhaps it's best for us all to start a new life. I would like to retire soon and pursue art in a more personal way. Mary Hannings and myself used to paint the landscape here. I remember her well. She was a good watercolour artist. I think one of her paintings is here at the house. She always signed her work as Conor Perkins, I seem to remember. At the moment, I don't get the chance to visit a beach or walk along the cliffs and I want to enjoy all those things when I retire. Where I live is so flat and although we have woods in Apeldoorn; it's not the same as all those lovely English hills. I can take a walk with my easel and paints and enjoy a new life."

I smiled at what Theo had said about the picture, I had no idea it was Mary Hannings work.

"Really, Dad? That's amazing but..." Rosie smiled and then her expression weakened. "I hate Mum for what she did to me and the shame of her behaviour; it's been a big shock. But there is a side to her which makes me feel very sad. There's always been something about her which I could never put my finger on."

"Your mum, I have to say, is a very lonely woman. Yes, there are things which she never wanted to talk to me about; her childhood, the war years and her life after Scotland."

"Yes, I know what you mean. We've been thinking what we should do now that we've decided to postpone the wedding—but, Dad—buying Tanglewood? What will happen to all of us if you're buying the house?"

"I have some good ideas which include you," Theo replied with steely confidence. "And it needs investment and renovations. I could re-build some of the old cottages as holiday homes; that would bring in an income and furthermore I have another idea. What if you and Ewan stay at the farm to manage it, with Jonni and Jess? The four of you get on so well together, it would be perfect. I mean this is all for you in later life, my dear. Having met you all, I know Jess is good at her job." He nodded at me. "I went to see Mark Parson yesterday—sorry Jess, but I was in the garage enquiring about cars and he told me you worked for him. I really didn't know you worked there, honest I didn't. I wasn't being nosey; he has a car I like. Anyway, he told me you had done an excellent job and would be sorry to see you go at the end of the year. You and Jonni wouldn't care to reconsider your plans, would you? It's just…I'd like to ask you to stay on at the farm and work with me?"

I felt my chin drop at his last remark.

"I need someone with secretarial skills and managerial experience if we are to make a successful business out of Tanglewood Farm. I won't be able to stick around here until I retire next year. It's important I have a team of people managing the work in advance of my leaving Holland."

I blew out my cheeks. "Did you explain all this to Jonni?" I asked. "And Ewan?"

"No, just you girls, at the moment. We'll have a family meeting.

As I said, I won't be able to spend time on the project until I retire. I'll supply the finance, no doubt Rosie told you I'm not short of cash, and you guys can oversee the work. You'll all get a proper wage each month and you no longer have to worry about the future. From time to time, I'll come back and see how you are getting along. You can phone me every week and I will advise. Delegating is my forte," he grinned, "and besides I love England. I'm doing this for you, my dear. One day all this will be yours and more, but now it's time for me to apologise."

"Apologise? What for? You've done so much already," I said.

Theo smiled and I couldn't help feeling he was the favourite uncle I never had. He turned to face Rosie. "You see, my dear, I couldn't bear living with your mother anymore. I didn't leave you or abandon you. Your mother told me quite sternly that she didn't love me. I wrote to you often and it seems your mother kept you away from me. I tried so many times, but then I thought maybe as you got into your teens you didn't really want me to be involved in your life. When you wrote to me it all came to light, all those letters, she must have destroyed them."

Rose chipped in. "Yes, I know, I found it really spiteful. I suspected she was opening my mail and so I got my letters delivered to the stables. It was only then that I found your card. I am so angry with her. I suspected things were not as Mum had said. Oh God! I keep asking, why? Why did she want to do that? I've not had a nice life with her, either. She has totally humiliated me through the years. My friends at boarding school used to laugh when she turned up at my school concerts wearing a sari and carrying a large fan. It was so embarrassing. She didn't know how ridiculous she looked."

"Yes, she always was the theatrical type," said Theo. "At first, I loved her for her artistic ways, but over time I realised this was nothing to do with art, but being self-centred, she couldn't help herself. I suspect it was because she had very little socialising with children of her age and she wanted attention."

"Poor Connie," I said. "She can be such a sweet person, but yes, Rosie, I can understand how confusing it must have been."

"Look, Rosie, I'm sorry for not being able to see you over the years, but your mum seemed to go out of her way to stop me. I did try, honest I did. Perhaps now, we can make up for lost time. Now, we should be on our way, I have an appointment with her. Wait until later on. Don't tell anyone yet; your mum needs to know first and then we shall see what she says. If she agrees I will go to the notaris, er…I mean, solicitor, tomorrow, and get their advice."

We mounted our horses and rode back to Tanglewood feeling very overwhelmed by Theo's idea. I kept looking at Rosie and smiling and I could tell she was not sure whether to laugh or cry. She looked back at me from behind Theo, who had trotted on ahead.

"Dad's done very well for himself over the years, he told me about the paintings he sells. Some of the most famous artists in the world have gone through his catalogues; he sold an Andy Warhol recently."

"Well, let's see what he can make out of Tanglewood. His idea sounds great."

We caught up with Theo.

"You know, Theo, I never say yes to anything first time, except the day when I came down here to live, but I'll have to discuss it with Jonni." I felt hot and cold all at the same time.

"Yes, that's fine, Jess, I understand."

We unsaddled the horses and Theo left us to make his business calls. Rosie and I couldn't stop talking—we laughed and made jokes about the things we could do. After a dark past, I could tell things were about to change, and I suspected Rosie had begun to feel that way too. She smiled when Jonni came down the path, Ruby by his side with a slight limp to her gait.

"Hi, Jess, Rosie. You two look happy, what's up?"

I let Rosie do the talking. "Oh…we've been riding in the woods. We took Dad with us; he's a good rider, he's got a racing and trotting track in Holland. We had a lovely picnic. It was good fun."

"Oh great, glad you could show him around the place. I bet he saw a difference, eh? I hope he wasn't too disappointed."

"He's going back to Holland soon."

"Did he say what he wanted to do? I mean—what Connie will do when she sells the house?"

"He's talking to Mum tonight and maybe we will hear some news this evening."

"Oh okay," he replied with a puzzled look on his face.

He turned to me. "And how's my lovely girl?"

"Who's that?" I joked looking around the stables. "Oh, you mean, Merry?"

I tried to steer the conversation away from Theo and hoped that our happiness levels didn't arouse too much suspicion of the good news. I so much wanted to tell him, but I had to do as Theo had requested and keep it to myself for now.

"Come here, you naughty woman," he teased.

Jonni chased me around the yard with a broom in his hand. Rosie laughed out loud when Jonni caught up with me and threatened to tickle me to death. I had never seen us all so happy.

Merry exhaled. Jonni looked into her stall at her swollen belly. "It won't be long now, old girl; your baby is on the way."

Chapter Twenty-eight

Theo invited Jonni, Ewan, and me to the family meeting. Theo sat next to Rosie and Connie and they sipped a glass of wine with the rest of us.

"...And so, this means that I will need help from you guys to make it all work. I will provide the finance and I think it will also be a great opening for me when I retire. So, everyone, what do you think?" Theo checked the reaction of each of us in turn.

Jonni didn't wish to be the centre of attention, I could tell, but I knew what he was thinking. He shook his head in sheer amazement.

"I was shocked, when Theo told me earlier," said Connie "but we can't go on like this; he's right. But what about me, where will I live?" Connie asked.

"I think I can help you there, Connie. Although goodness knows why, but I think it's only fair that I do." Theo sighed through his words. "I will find you somewhere to live, anywhere you want, and help you to move on. Look, I know we haven't seen eye to eye for many years, but, Connie, you can't deny Rosie her rightful inheritance. You made a mess of your life here, I'm sorry to say, and you kept Rosie away from me, I find that hard to forgive. Tanglewood is such a wonderful place and it can't be lost in time, we have to rescue it and keep it in the family."

"I'm not worried about the money so much, Dad, it's the humiliation of being taken in by Millington," Rosie said.

Ewan seemed to slink into the depths of the sofa and said nothing but I knew he was listening with guilt in his heart.

"Me, too, Rosie," said Connie. "Me, too."

"But, Mum, you had control of this; you *could* have said no. You *could* have walked away. I feel ashamed you sold yourself in that way. It's disgusting, you may as well have been a—dare I say it—a prostitute! Did you know about the wedding rites, too?"

"Oh, Rosie, don't." Connie looked highly embarrassed in front of the others. "I never did anything you know, it was always so, so…the circle gave me hope to carry on. I thought what I was doing was right. Richard kept telling me I had certain powers and I know I have; this is why he took me on, you haven't seen what—"

"Mum, bloody well shut up. Don't even go there, do you hear?" Rosie snapped and raised her hands in defeat as Connie bowed her head.

Theo spoke. "Now, now, everyone let's stay calm. There are questions I would like to ask, but I feel it doesn't matter now. The main thing is to move forward."

"Millington could be out on bail. I hope not, but we shall have to see how it all goes. He will go to court and then we let the law do its job."

"Mum, what do you think of Dad's idea? I think it's bloody great. Ewan and me, along with Jonni and Jess, can manage the farm and the stables and you can do whatever you wish—all your debts paid and Tanglewood remains in the family forever. All Dad wants us to do is make a proper business out of it and he will pay us a good wage to be project managers for him whilst he is in Holland. I know we can do it, it's a dream come true for Ewan and me. I reckon Jess and Jonni are pleased too."

Jonni nodded in agreement.

Connie sat with her fingers sliding across her lips. She was about to burst into tears, but I knew Connie's pride wouldn't allow her to show her true feelings.

Jonni spoke first. "We haven't had a chance to discuss this yet and we need to do that as soon as we can. When do you want an answer, Theo?"

"Sorry to ask, but I need to know as soon as possible. I'm leaving soon and will be contacting the solicitor and so on." He turned to Connie.

"I don't know about all this, maybe…" Connie hesitated whilst we waited for an answer.

Rosie piped up. "For God's sake, Mum, do something worthwhile in your life—Dad listen—she'll do it!"

"No no, hang on it's all too quick," Connie protested. "And what about Hans?"

Ewan joined in. "Connie, I despair of you, you have to give Rosie the life you denied her for so long. I'm up for it and as for Hans I hear he is going out with this woman in Germany. We'll never see him again."

"You don't have to worry about Hans; he's in love at the moment." Theo rolled his eyes and smiled. "He's gone to live with Helga, his old schoolfriend. Ewan's right, I doubt you'll see him again. I saw him before he left he's making some changes in his life."

I hadn't known this news, but I could never forgive him for his actions. I hoped that this Helga person would have the strength to sort him out and she wouldn't be murdered in the process.

"Well, if Jess is agreed, I'd love to stay here, but we have to talk," said Jonni.

"I don't know what to think; Tanglewood is my life too," Connie protested.

"Not anymore, Connie," said Ewan with a regretful expression. "Go now, whilst you have the chance—follow your dreams. You told me to follow mine; maybe you should listen to yourself."

At this point, Connie realised we were all voting for Theo's plan and she was defeated.

"Look," said Theo. I'll buy you a little house wherever you want. You'll make new friends and do something different. I'll work something out with you soon, okay? I have everything I want these days, if I can't do good things for my daughter, then there's something wrong."

"She'll do it, won't you, *Mum*?" Rosie stared into her mother's eyes with an expression of 'if looks could kill'.

"Just think, you can start living again. No worries," said Ewan. Connie gave a deep sigh. "I don't know what to think...I don't want charity, but I'll be back, that's for sure." She sighed again. "I don't want to leave Tanglewood, but...okay I agree, I *must* agree, I've got no other options, have I? I don't know what to say." Her bottom lip trembled at the shame of it all.

Rosie gave a terse reply. "You could thank Dad for getting us out of this crappy hole."

"I suppose we have Hans to thank as well. I mean, Theo wouldn't have been here if Hans hadn't gone to see you," said Ewan, nodding toward Theo.

"Well," said Connie reluctantly, "I'm not sure what to say except..."

"I think you've said enough, Mum. I'll say it for her, thanks Dad—for *everything*." Rosie stood to hug Theo.

Jonni shook hands with Theo and Ewan took his turn in the queue.

Theo came to me last of all. "Jess, I do hope you will think carefully about my offer. Mark said some good things about you."

I smiled. "I will, Theo, and thanks."

Theo squeezed Rosie's hand. "You're a lovely young lady. I'm so proud of you."

Chapter Twenty-nine

That same evening, after Theo left our company, Jonni called me to the stables. "I have some news, I think Merry is about to give birth. Would you like to come and see?"

"Oh yes, love to. Is she okay?"

"Yes, I think so. It's a waiting game now. She may not drop until the early hours of the morning."

I took tea bags and a jug of milk to the stables. We opened the coach doors to let in the fresh air and the sweet smell of camomile came drifting through the stables as if we had just sprayed air freshener.

"Mm, that's better," I announced.

I gazed at Jonni; his expression seemed miles away in thought.

"You mean a lot to me, Jess."

I smiled, unable to speak, the moment felt right and my mood seemed to detach from life beyond the tack-room door. Merry gave another sigh and became restless, walking around her stall and banging her hooves with some impatience against the wooden door.

Another bang on the door from Merry, and Jonni calmed her. "It won't be long," he said. "Another hour, I reckon."

"What do you…?"

Our conversation collided. "I was going to ask you…" he said.

"You first," I insisted.

"Well…the thing is, Jess, I wanted to know how serious you are about Theo's offer? I know we more or less accepted his idea, but we have to be sure."

"Are you having doubts?" I said.

"No, not doubts. I'm just mulling it over. It's all happened so very quickly, in fact, too quickly in many ways, but yes it's a step in the right direction," said Jonni.

"I like Theo," I said. "I hope we can trust him. He seems very positive about everything; I wish I could be like that. Perhaps we can attribute his success to his personality. What it means to have real money and be wealthy is beyond my imagination."

"I suppose money isn't everything, love. I have you and that's more important to me right now, you're my brick in the wall, as they say." Jonni smiled and gave me hug.

"I suppose in a few days' time I'll get used to Theo's idea. I hope the decisions we make will be the right ones."

Bang! Merry needed our attention. Jonni made his way toward the stable door speaking quietly and stroking his hands around her bulging belly. Her neck steamed with sweat.

"Okay, let's leave her another hour, it could be a while. Horses are like the animals in the wild, they will birth in the dark. Her udders are quite swollen now. I'm getting in her way, let's go."

The retreating sun peeked through the cracks in the tack-room wall. We felt the warmth of summer radiating from the wooden walls of the stable block. Dirk being the 'old man' in the team, hardly stirred in the stall next door. Then we heard a crash of hooves from Merry, which caused Dirk to make a sound like a train exhaling steam.

"We need to talk in whispers. She's quite a nervous animal."

Merry gave a half-hearted whinny and more thrashing about in her stall.

"She'll be fine. I've padded out her stall with hay for when she drops the foal."

He turned to me and we kissed.

"Mm, this is so cosy. Someone makes me want to stay here forever," I smiled.

"See, I told you how this place gets you hooked. It's not about

Connie, or Rosie and Ewan, it's the atmosphere, the ambience of the whole place. At this time of year, Tanglewood is paradise. How can we leave it, Jess? And now you and me here, waiting on the birth of new life in Merry."

I had to admit he was right. "It's sometimes very hard to keep up with it all."

Darkness fell as we heard the faint and distant chimes of church bells. We counted them and at the precise stroke of eleven, we heard a thud in Merry's stall.

"This is it, Jess, she's about to give birth. I'll take a peek. Come behind me and I'll show her it's me. I don't want to go in yet, anything can alarm her."

He looked through the latch in the stable door. "Gosh I can see the feet and the nose of the foal. Go on have a look," he whispered.

"Oh my God, it's coming. Look…"

"Be prepared to make a phone call to the vet, just in case we have a problem. So far so good. I'll leave her a bit longer."

I gave a shiver outside in the yard. Jonni held me close. He glanced again through the hole in the door to see that Merry was biting her sides and breathing heavily.

"I'm going in," he announced.

He quietly opened the latch on the door and without a word I walked behind him then stood back to watch. I wasn't sure if my shivering was due to the chill in the air or because I was nervous. Jonni knew his stuff when it came to animals. He was so calm about it all.

"It's okay, Merry, I'm here. Come on, girl, you're okay. Where's that baby of yours? Come on baby, come on out—Daddy's waiting," he whispered jovially.

I had to smile at his caring and wondered if one day he might be stood by my bedside encouraging me to push like hell. Oh my God! What a thought.

I watched the foal as Merry, with each contraction, pushed it further into the world. Within a few minutes the foal was almost out.

Rosie came breathless to the stable and quietly opened the door.

"Sorry I'm late. I was up at Val's house, and I just heard about it. We were in the woods for a walk. Anything I can do, Jonni?"

"No, I think Merry has done all the work, she's fine."

"You're in time, Rosie. Look it's coming," I whispered.

Wrapped in the amniotic sac, the foal dropped into the hay and the sac ruptured, revealing a brown and steaming foal with a white blaze. Jonni wiped it down with straw and stood back to allow Merry to bond with her newborn. Rosie and I stood there with tears in our eyes.

"I can't help it. I cry every time we have a birth, no matter how many times I've seen it," Rosie admitted.

Within a few moments Ewan poked his head around the door.

"Oh, hi, Ewan. Merry has had her foal." I wiped away my tears as he entered the stable.

Ewan sighed and I sensed his relief. He seemed unusually cheery. Things were definitely changing at Tanglewood.

"I'll cut the cord, Jonni," said Ewan. "Have you got the iodine in there?"

"Yes, on the side table."

"We have a young filly," he said. "It's a girl."

I stood in awe as the foal tried to stand for the first time. At two in the morning, we made it to our bed and left Merry to enjoy her newborn in peace.

Jonni and I walked hand in hand up the driveway to the house. "It's okay, I don't have to be up this morning—Fergal is doing the cows for me."

"We need a name for the foal," I said.

"How about…Jessie?" Rosie suggested as she followed behind us.

"Aw, Rosie, that's sweet of you."

"Well, it's seems to fit her and you are my new best friend."

Jonni put his arm around the two of us. "Jessie it is."

Chapter Thirty

After two weeks, we awaited further news from Theo. We had a full day to ourselves and began with a discussion about what we were going to do once Theo began the proceedings for purchasing the house. I wanted to go back to Yorkshire and take Jonni with me, but we had been drawn into this situation and now it was a case of patience until we heard from Theo again. He'd been on the phone a few times with snippets of news about the legal proceedings.

I sat looking in the mirror in my room with Jonni behind me, his hand on my shoulder, kissing my neck and glancing at our reflection. I tried to brush my hair when he took the brush from me.

"Let *me* do that, love."

I watched as he brushed with gentle strokes down my back and placed the tresses in a casual style. "You're so lovely, Jess. I look forward to having you in my life forever. This job sounds perfect. Theo is a good man; he's making up to Rosie for lost time. I know we could help him and now we've got each other it makes sense, don't you think?"

Jonni worked hard through the months I had known him and I saw how his confidence had returned. I felt sure we were right for each other. Together we could make a difference.

Connie seemed happier and was already making plans as to where she would live, although she kept talking about not being long for this world and each time Rosie glared at her she went quiet.

Jonni placed the brush on the table and came to me, his eyes meeting mine. I watched through the mirror as he kissed my hand and then the inside of my wrists.

"I'm not very good with romantic words," he said tucking a strand of my hair behind my ear.

"Oh, I think you are."

"I'm hoping we can take our relationship up a notch once we are settled. Theo is going to start on the house purchase as soon as possible. He phoned Rosie again yesterday and things are moving along well, which should make it so you almost finish working at the garage at the same time the house changes hands. He said it could be November before it all goes through."

"What 'up a notch' is that, love?" I asked with a coy smile.

"Well, as I've said, marriage, kids, you know. We're both mature enough to know what we want now and…"

"Hold it there, young man," I replied and put my fingers to his lips. "I have a better idea. Why don't you get yourself back to university part time and get your degree? I can support you once Theo has employed me. You have brains, Jonni—use them. You could go to agricultural college. Let's look it up at the library."

"That sounds far too sensible. Okay, I promise to look into it. I hope we'll get a chance to have a holiday together soon. Although, for now I want to kiss you. Come here, my darling."

His hands searched under my t-shirt, stroking my spine and moving around the front to caress me. Oh boy! I was in heaven. I helped him remove his shirt and pulled myself toward him. Together we stood and locked ourselves together, lips to lips.

"Come on relax. It's going to be fine. I know we'll be happy together." He lay on the bed and pulled me beside him. "Jess, love me, my darling."

When we finally untangled ourselves from one another, I could hear people outside, shouting, but it took time to digest who was saying what and to whom. "It's the police," I said when I heard a siren. "Get dressed quick—what's going on?"

"I can smell smoke, Jonni. Oh my God! It's not the police—it's the friggin' fire brigade. What the heck are they doing here? Someone must have dialled 999. Where's Rosie? Come on, Jonni let's get down there. This bloody drought is causing more fires than we bargained for."

He stared out of the window as the smoke drifted in the direction of the house. "Oh hell, yes you're right, what on earth...?"

We put on our jeans and t-shirts at lightning speed and leapt downstairs. Outside the house we ran toward the stables.

"Oh my God! Jonni, it's the bloody stables, they're on fire."

Breathless, we arrived to see flames coming from behind the tack room which quickly shifted to the wooden walls of an empty stable block where a bale of hay had caught fire.

"Oh, bloody hell, we have to get the horses out before the fire catches hold," said Jonni.

We ran as fast as we could and found Rosie taking Carlow out of the stall. She was carrying a wet towel around her head, and draped another towel over his head and mouth. She jerked him out of the stall. Jonni ran to the other side of the yard for Hope, and Merry with her foal, and managed to rescue them. Then I watched Connie go in to the main stable where the fire had taken a hold, carrying a wet blanket and a bucket of water to rescue a small pony in Rosie's care. Jonni took out three more horses, including Briony.

With the whites of their eyes showing terror. Hope whinnied as the smoke came too close. Jonni ran into the stall and chased her out with a stick in his hand.

Ewan yelled, "Shit! This is like the fire we had in Oz. Stand back everyone, let the guys do their job." For the first time I saw him taking control of a situation. He ran back and forth, yelling instructions.

The sofa in the tack room, had ignited in seconds. I gazed in horror at the flames coming out of the roof.

We looked around and then at each other in dismay as the firemen set up the hoses. All those expensive saddles in the tack room and the hay and straw going up in flames.

Ewan and Jonni ran around the yard attempting to corral the horses into the field beyond. Rosie pushed away a bale of hay and Jonni rushed to help her. The remaining horses were whinnying to be rescued, unable to get out of their locked stables. The fireman unlatched the doors and guided them toward the parkland.

Ewan shouted, "Where's Connie? Oh my God! Where's Connie?"

"Connie?" I screamed over the noise of the hoses and the fire engine. "I think Connie's in there, you have to get her!" I was frantic by this time. We heard dreadful screams and whinnying coming from within the stable. Then silence…

The small pony emerged alone, trotting out of the building, its eyes wide with fear and panic, coughing on the smoke and at the same time barging into a fireman who tried to get to Connie. The sheer pandemonium begged belief.

Rosie yelled, "Where's Mum, where is she?"

"Get her out!" I screamed at the fireman and pointed toward the inferno. "Connie's in the small stable. Oh my God! Somebody help her. Quick!"

What I saw next would remain with me forever. The firemen in breathing apparatus beat the flames and with the fire hose they entered through the main stable door. A few moments later they emerged, dragging a blackened figure. It was Connie. They carried her across the yard and tried to revive her with help from the ambulance crew. Her burns looked severe, her black hair frizzled on one side of her scalp. The smell of burnt flesh and singed hair was more than Rosie and I could take. Rosie collapsed in the yard and I couldn't bear to take a second look. I had an overwhelming desire to escape and felt the breath sucked from my lungs.

Ewan helped Rosie, and on the instructions of the fire brigade, we all sat close together on a garden bench along the path. My stomach clenched tight and a strange acrid taste came into my mouth. I'd had that same taste when my father died.

Jonni held me close and I can't remember much except the sandwich I ate earlier came back at me on the path. A member of the ambulance crew whom Rosie knew, ran toward us and gave us both a whiff of oxygen. His face said it all.

"I'm sorry," he said. "Your mother, Rosie…it's too late, she passed away in the ambulance before we set off for the hospital. We tried to revive her, but it was no use." He paused to see the reaction on Rosie's face. "I knew Connie, I don't think she would have coped with the injuries she sustained. She always seemed a proud lady. I am very, very sorry, Rosie."

Once again, I threw up.

"Oh no, no, no, I didn't want it to be this way, it's cruel," Rosie wailed with her hand over her mouth trying not to be sick as well. Closing her eyes, she rocked back and forth and sucked the end of her thumb. "How did this all happen? Mum, I didn't mean…Oh God! Why did she have to go in there?"

Jonni turned to Rosie and tried to give comforting words. "She went in there because she loved the horses, it was her life…and now it seems…What I mean is without your mum's love for the animals, Tanglewood Farm would never have happened and…oh hells bells, I can't say anymore." Jonni closed his eyes, took a deep breath and moved his head toward the sky, tears streaking down his cheeks. "Are you okay, Jess? I feel sick as well, now."

With eyes closed Ewan and Rose held each other. We did the same, not letting go, even for a second.

"It should never have happened. Why? How?" I asked, knowing I was about to throw up again.

We sat together in silence and horrendous shock for what seemed like hours.

"You can go back to the house in a few minutes," said the ambulance crew. "Catch your breath and leave it to us, you are all in deep trauma and I want you all to go inside and rest. I'll come up soon and see how you are doing. We have to finish tidying up here."

Moments later we trudged back to the house, Rosie coughed a few times from the effects of the smoke and my sickness began to diminish. Jonni's white face regained colour and on arrival we made strong tea with lots of sugar and sat around the table staring at each other in disbelief.

"How the hell will we cope with all that?" said Jonni. "Rosie, are you okay? No, that's a stupid question, sorry."

Ewan held Rosie close to him and shrugged his shoulders; there were no more words.

It was with aching sadness that we realised none of us would see Connie again. Rosie went to her room with Ewan and left Jonni and me staring into the void.

Jonni spoke first. "Connie was such an inspiration when I first came here, but in recent years she seems to have gone into hiding. I have no idea why. She was lonely, but I think it was somewhat self-inflicted. You know, Jess, she was the founder of Tanglewood and no matter how misguided her management skills, I remember when she used to have vision. Only recently did it all change and she began to lose control. I know we were her waifs and strays, especially when Ewan, Hans and I came on the scene. The Connie you knew was not the woman I remember. I shall miss her. We know she wasn't perfect and I'm sure we all loved her in our own way, despite her strange beliefs." Jonni sighed in deep sorrow.

"Yes, I know what you mean. She kind of took me under her wing, too. I won't forget her." I sobbed. "This is all so shocking, I doubt we'll survive it."

In our distress, I phoned Theo in Holland. Jonnie took the call and gave the sad news.

"I'm sorry, Theo, we are in dreadful shock; it only happened a short while ago."

There was a brief silence.

"Yes, we are *reasonably* okay. The doctor on call has given Rosie a sedative." He listened to Theo's words. "Yes, sure...and the horses are fine, thank goodness. I hope you will excuse me if I'm not making myself clear enough. The firemen are down there tidying up. It's a dreadful mess. We've no idea what caused it."

Theo continued his conversation until he couldn't say anymore and Jonni replaced the receiver.

The next day Theo caught a plane to Gatwick and drove the rest of the way in a hire car. On arrival, he took control of the situation by providing us all with a stiff whisky and soda. I don't think I have ever needed a whisky so much in all my life. Even when Dad passed away, we had a few days to realise he wasn't going to recover. But this…the shock and horror of seeing Connie in that way—I did my best not to think about it. We soldiered on in dreadful disbelief and the house took on the air of a place in ghastly mourning. I felt I was back to square one again. Was tragedy always going to strike Tanglewood? Would this be the final warning to me? Eventually I plucked up the courage to phone Mum and Anna and tell them the dreadful news. I had been hoping Mum would meet Connie, but it was never going to happen. I didn't wish to spend too much time talking about it, so I chose my words carefully and then I couldn't say any more.

"Bye, Mum. I hope you are okay. I miss you."

It was four weeks before we could set a date for a funeral; it seemed to take forever. Rosie had decided on a graveside ceremony only. Her mother hadn't left instructions about her funeral arrangements and she knew Connie would want to be returned to Mother Earth. Rosie thought that a cremation may seem, to her mother, like shaking hands with the devil.

We arranged the funeral on a Tuesday morning as the sun rose over the Axminster countryside. I recalled what Connie had said about her impending premature death. My goodness, did she know this would happen, had she predicted it? I was struck by her words and wondered if she really did have powers which none of us believed in. She put her trust in me to take care of Rosie. But why me? Perhaps it was because I happened to be there at the time or something else? I shivered for a moment, thinking about it. Upon reflection, I knew she had a warm place for me in her heart. Was it because I was the only person who didn't chastise her for her beliefs?

"What a lovely day for a funeral," Rosie remarked with some irony in her tone. "I'm not going to cry. Mum wouldn't have wanted me to wail over her."

I knew from experience she would miss her mother; the little moments when she would want to tell her things and Connie was no longer there. I held on to Jonni's arm as we walked to the graveside. I cried, not just for Connie but because I missed my dad, too. It was the first time I'd had the chance to let go and it all came flooding back. I sobbed my heart out.

"It's all right, Jess. I am here for you, my darling." Jonni held me close.

I counted twenty-two people at the graveside. I knew some of the mourners, but couldn't put names to all their faces. It was pleasing to learn that the people from the parties at Avoca House had stayed away. Rosie made it clear that the funeral was to be invitation only. She told me that having Connie's posh friends by the graveside, weeping their hearts out, was so false. She couldn't bear it. If anyone wanted to put flowers on the grave they were welcome.

Theo and Rosie dropped two red roses over the coffin as it was lowered in the ground and a flat monotone voice came from Rosie.

"Mum, as we lay you to rest in your Mother Earth for the last time, may you be in peace."

It was at this moment I heard her voice crack, but still she didn't cry. I turned to Jonni and felt another sob coming on. I squeezed my lips together, swallowed, and tried to be brave.

The local vicar stood to offer prayers for those who needed them. Rosie didn't want a religious ceremony, but we persuaded her that others may feel it was important to invite the vicar as a goodwill gesture. He seemed to understand. He had known Connie for a long time, so it was good that he came as a friend. I felt Connie had *some* religious convictions and we should honour them. I mean, Jonni mentioned there was a point where paganism and Christianity crossed paths. So, we all felt this way was best.

Theo made a short low-key speech. "Connie was a good person in many ways; her heart was always with the land and her animals. She cared deeply for Tanglewood Farm. Could I ask you all for a one-minute silence to help us remember Connie as your good friend and mother of Rosie? Thank you."

Ewan stood forward and placed a rose on the lid of the coffin, and as they left, each person threw a flower into the grave. It had been a very simple and moving occasion.

We walked toward Theo who took a deep breath as Jonni and I approached him.

"Very sad," he remarked, his arms hanging loosely by his side. "To think I once loved her with all my heart." He pulled out a white handkerchief and blew his nose.

"I am sure you still had a soft spot for her somewhere, Theo."

"Well, she was once a very beautiful woman, but unfortunately, I soon discovered things about her, and I didn't feel comfortable, but I won't go into all that here."

"No, of course not."

We stopped for a moment to allow Rosie and Ewan to catch up with us and made our way home, leaving the other mourners behind. I looked over my shoulder as I left the graveyard. A young woman in a long black coat and with a small dog by her side, stood by the mortuary chapel. There was something familiar about her, but when I looked again, she was gone.

Chapter Thirty-one

After Connie's funeral, the mood became sombre. Jonni and I had to tread carefully with Rosie and Ewan. I was still working at the garage, but part-time, and this enabled me to stay at the farm to help Rosie clear up. Tina was doing fine and her son's operation was successful, so I was happy to share the work.

After a while, Rosie became depressed and Ewan still struggled with Richard Millington's deception. Theo kept suggesting he should move on because it wasn't his fault. He'd had a fatherly talk with Ewan and assured him that no one blamed him. Over the weeks that followed, Ewan seemed to take more control, with guidance from Theo. I knew this is what he had needed all along, someone other than Rosie—a father figure.

I was doing a crossword whilst Rosie read a copy of *Woman's Own*. I managed to get her to open up to me.

"How's Ewan feeling now?" I asked her.

"We talked yesterday. After all this stuff we've been through, the future seems brighter now that Dad is holding the fort for us. I suppose I've forgiven him, he's a good person really. He and Dad have become friends."

"It will take time and I'm glad it's all working out. Jonni and I are looking forward to helping you as my time at the garage is coming to a close."

Rosie turned to face me. "You know, Jess, I couldn't have had the confidence to make all these decisions without you and Jonni. It's comforting to know I can talk to you both when I need to."

"Aw, Rosie, that's sweet of you. Let me give you a big hug."

I moved to put my arms around her and she responded with a smile.

"Dad is going to give Ewan some projects to be getting on with. He knows how depressed he's been. Sorting the probate on the house could take ages. We don't have the money to keep it running without his help."

"What did the fire brigade say about the hay when they phoned last night, I didn't quite understand? Was it all to do with the drought, did the hay catch fire?" I asked.

"Well no, not at all, more of a freak accident. It seems that one of us must have left the tap dripping behind the stables. The Coroner said it was accidental death—poor Mum."

"Yes, well I never thought it was arson. But how...?"

"The police told me that, earlier in the year, at the start of the drought, water must have leaked into the barn from a dripping tap, see? Unfortunately, we think it was Hans who had put a few spare bales of hay behind the tack room. None of us did it. They told me that over a period of a few weeks, the lower stacks got composted, and of course, when moist hay is mixed with oxygen, it produces carbon dioxide and heat. The heat intensified and it caught fire. None of us could have foreseen this disaster and with the weather as it was, everything became a fire hazard. It's a miracle the whole farm and the woodland didn't catch fire. You know, that was my worst fear—losing the farm because of the drought."

"Oh my God! But how come we never knew it was there?"

"The stack was stored behind the stables. We don't go behind there usually. When the hay steams, we all kind of get used to it but on this occasion, we didn't see it or we hadn't realised it was smoke rising, I haven't a clue. With all the smokiness around us just now, we didn't really consider it was on our property. It must have caught alight very quickly. We had all been through so much recently. I can't imagine why Hans left it there, maybe he forgot about it, his mind was never in the right place. I'm sure he didn't mean to. He did all kinds of stupid things when he was stoned."

Hans was in Germany and there was nothing more we could do. We could never tell him; he'd left no forwarding address. Rosie decided as everything in their lives had changed, it was better he didn't know. Perhaps, one day soon, he would contact Theo who would surely tell him that Connie had passed away and it was an accident.

Several weeks later, Jonni and I, Ewan and Rosie, made our way to the pub to drown our sorrows. The September day became grey as the afternoon unfolded. The still air and humidity overwhelmed us as we sat drinking our cider and it looked as if the heavens would open. I wished I had put a raincoat in the car. I hseard the most enormous clap of thunder overhead which caused me to duck in case something was about to fall on my head.

The rain didn't trickle, it happened all at once and the road couldn't cope with the deluge of water. A new river ran past the pub and over the step. The landlord rushed from the barn with a wooden board to place over the entrance and Jonni helped him. We felt we were about to be swept away. Everyone in the car park began dancing up and down with their arms in the air and getting soaked. "It's raining," they all shouted, "it's raining. Whoopee!"

Ewan stood with his head toward the sky and his eyes closed. "Oh, this is wonderful and the rainwater is so warm. It's like a shower."

Rosie called to me after a large thunderclap drowned our voices. "This is it, Jess. All our sorrows, we are washing them away," she shouted joyfully.

I laughed, Rosie laughed, Jonni stood with his arms in the air and his tongue out, lapping up the rainwater that fell on his lips. Ewan jumped up and down in the flood like a child in a paddling pool and Rosie and I joined in. We all held hands splashing in the puddles under the claps of thunder.

"You're right, Rosie. This is our new life together—all of us," Ewan shouted above the sound of the rain.

"Ewan's drunk too much cider," Rosie tittered.

"And me, too," I called, "but oh, this is so refreshing. It's lovely."

We wore only our shorts and t-shirts and somehow it didn't matter anymore that we were soaked to the skin as the thunder and lightning clattered above our heads. It seemed that now happiness prevailed.

"Well, I've never seen anything like this," I called out.

Jonni kissed me and our hair hung limp around our ears as water dripped from our eyelids and the ends of our noses.

"My God! It's lovely, lovely, warm rain. Oh, how I love you, Jess."

"I love you, too and right this minute I love everyone in the world," I said.

Everyone began to sing 'Raindrops Keep Fallin' on My Head'. And they kept on singing whilst the rain poured around our feet.

If I was to look back, despite our sorrows, it had been one of the most rewarding days of my life.

Chapter Thirty-two

We had an inevitable job to perform. We put off cleaning Connie's room for as long as we could and on our way upstairs, Rosie chatted half-heartedly about her plans for the future.

"I know this sounds odd, and please don't think ill of me, but I don't feel I shall miss Mum for a long time. You see, she was never a mother to me. I often felt I was in her way—unwanted, if you see what I mean. It was as if she said she wanted me, but she didn't, I could never feel close to her."

"Really? I always considered her to be rather motherly toward me. I got on well with her, but, naturally, you knew her far better than me."

"I don't know. She never once told me she loved me, you know. She was very controlling, and all I could do was sit back and let her get on with it. I only managed the stables because Mum got too tangled with Millington. There was a time when we used to work together as a team, but as I got older I told her not to bother, I would manage—she got in the way. I had Ewan to help me, too. It was almost as if she was glad."

"That's sad, Rosie. When I lost my dad, I felt I had lost a friend as well. But it can take a while, I suppose. I wake up to find I need to talk and he isn't there anymore. I feel sad you never experienced love as I have. I phoned my mum the other day. She and my sister are thinking of coming down this way for a holiday next year. You will meet her, I think." We reached the top of the landing. "I hope to go back up that way with Jonni soon. With

all the problems it's been impossible. Now where shall we begin?"
I sighed.

We trudged toward Connie's room and paused by the door, then glanced at each other. Rosie gave a pained look and turned her head away with a sigh.

Everything was as Connie had left it, untouched. The unmade bed, the altar with its potions and perfumes, the ash from the josh sticks and melted candles. She was virtually still there, I could almost feel her presence. A patchwork quilt lay crumpled on the unmade bed, the impression of where she had lain on the sheets and the book she had been reading before the fire; it was as if she was about to return from the bathroom and get back into bed again. I began to shrug off those eerie sensations and get on with the task. My 'Miss Havisham' had gone and left us to sort the muddle of her past.

The dank and stale odour in the room caused me to open the window. "Come on, Rosie. We have to do this, love." I felt guilty that the plan was more or less to trash the place and throw everything out. "Let's start on the bed and get the sheets in the wash. Ready? You take this end of the sheet and I'll help you fold the blankets and the eiderdown," I suggested.

To keep Rosie on track I kept talking to her and when the bed was clear, we moved on to the wardrobe and dressing table, piling everything on to the bare mattress.

"You do the drawers, Rosie, and I will sort her clothes. Is that okay with you?" I knew the drawers may hold Connie's personal trinkets. The clothes I could deal with, and I could ask Rosie about them as we went along.

"You know I'm sure your mum loved you, Rosie, she asked me to look out for you."

"Did she really? Hm, now I am confused." She gazed around the room. "I don't know where to begin." She sighed in despair.

"Look, let's be methodical about it, shall we? Okay? Clothes in this pile, the dresses you could send to the charity shop, and the small trinkets you may want to keep." A familiar feeling came over me. It wasn't that long since I'd helped Mum with Dad's personal possessions. I could feel Rosie's sadness as if it were mine, and I suppose it was mine. I liked Connie and she seemed to like me, but her motives, I would never understand; our lives were very different. I was also aware that a part of her was detached and wandering around aimlessly. Perhaps it was that side of her she saw in me, too.

I saw Rosie's pained look again. "I'm worried as to what we may find up here. I never came into this room for more than a couple of minutes. It hasn't been cleaned in months, there could be dead rats in here for all I know."

"We'll cross that barrier when we come to it, but in the meantime, we have to try and sort out the rubbish. Are you okay, Rosie?"

I was definitely acting the big sister again, which reminded me to phone Anna.

"Yes fine, I suppose; it has to be done."

I started in the wardrobe whilst Rosie searched through the drawers. "Say 'yes' if you want to keep it or 'no' if you don't, okay?"

We began with loads of 'no' answers. Many of the dresses seemed to date back to the late 40s and 50s. Why had Connie bothered to keep them? I swear if she'd tried to close the wardrobe, the doors would have burst.

"Gosh, Jess, there are clothes in this pile I've never seen her wearing." Rosie stared at me in despair. "There's so much *stuff*, it will take us weeks to sort all this out."

"Well…if you wish, I'll make a phone call to Oxfam; I think they'll come and collect it for us, if not we'll have to drive to Axminster and take it there ourselves."

I thought about Mum again, and how we had taken my dad's things way out of town.

Rosie searched the drawers and found jewellery. She held up a charm bracelet. "I gave Mum this for her birthday, about ten years ago."

I could tell she wasn't getting on with the job, just reminiscing.

"And this little brooch belonged to my grandmother, look—it's got her name on it and a lock of her hair. *Agnes McPherson.*"

"Why don't we put all the jewellery in this other box and sort it out later?" I suggested.

"Okay, I'll come and help you with the clothes."

After an hour, we had most of the clothes out of the wardrobe and into an appropriate filing system.

"What the heck is this?" Rosie exclaimed as she pulled out a hat from a box at the back of the wardrobe. It was a green beret with the letters WLA written on a gilt badge. Further down the pile she found a green moth-eaten jumper, a khaki shirt and green tie and a pair of old fashioned baggy jodhpurs.

"Let me see," I said. "Good heavens that's *really* old."

"I suspect it's some fancy-dress stuff," Rosie replied.

"Hang on, WLA, isn't that the Women's Land Army?" Mum had been in the ATS during the war in Catterick. She had talked about the land army. "Was your mum a Land Army girl, Rosie?"

"I don't know, she never said."

"It was a very important job; those girls helped keep agriculture on its feet during the war. I can imagine your mum doing that kind of work, can't you?"

Rosie smiled at my comment and she put the uniform to one side in case we had a home for it.

"Let's look in these drawers inside the wardrobe. It's the little things that are fiddly to get rid of," she explained. "I never know if they may be of value or not."

We spent the next hour with more 'yes' and 'no' answers, until Rosie came across a shoebox with the initials GK on the lid.

She opened it. "Oh gosh, all these photos. I've never seen these. Look, they are pictures of Mum when she was much younger."

"Oh yes, so they are. I wonder who the bloke is; they look like they belong to each other, I mean the way Connie is holding on to him."

Rosie stared at the man in the photo. "That's not Dad," she retorted.

"Here's another one. Look, she's wearing that uniform. Oh my God! I never knew that, it looks like you were right, Jess. She was a Land Girl, well, well...They are grooming the horses in this photo."

"I can't believe she never told you about it. It was such a big thing in those days."

Rosie stared further at the picture of her mother hanging on to the arm of her suitor. I leaned over. He looked very handsome in his RAF uniform; Connie seemed young, lovely, and very happy and I could see the likeness to Rosie.

Was this the same picture I had seen her worshipping the night I found her chanting in the lounge?

"Do you think she was the same age as I am now on that picture?"

"No, I think she may have been younger," I replied. "Look at the dates, July 1942. She looks only about nineteen or twenty."

"I wonder who the guy is in the photo."

I took it from her and turned it over to read the words on the back: *My darling Gerald.*

"Here's your answer." I handed her the photo.

"Oh yes—Oh my god! Who is that?"

Further down the pile we discovered a letter in an envelope. It was tied with a faded pale blue ribbon and labelled, GK.

"Oh, Rosie, this is amazing. They must be his letters to your mum. They say every picture tells a story, but here we have your mum, during the war, with some connection to a guy name Gerald whom you've never heard of."

"I think I'll save all this for when we have more time. I wonder why she never told me about him? Hey, Jess, you don't think that he's my real father, do you?" She gave an ironic smile.

"No, silly you." I paused to think. "Anyway, the timing is all wrong and you look so much like Theo, there's no doubt he's your dad."

"I found this as well," she said and handed me a diary dated 1944.

"Gosh, this room is a treasure trove."

"I've just read something. Here, the last entry in the book." She sniffed.

I could see the emotion in her eyes. "Rosie, what is it?"

"It's sad. I think Mum may have been engaged to Gerald and he never came back from the war. This page here says *I feel my life has ended, they told me today he wasn't coming home—The words 'killed in action' will be ingrained on my mind forever.*"

"Oh no—goodness, that's shocking."

"I know. Knowing Mum, she probably never got over it and then to die in the way she did. It's horrible."

Rosie burst into tears and I held her close. It was the first time she'd been able to openly grieve. I felt like crying with her; we shared our pain and after feeling cramped from sitting on the floor, we decided not to do any more that day; it had been too exhausting.

"Come on, Rosie, let's take a walk and get some fresh air. We can deal with your mum's more personal stuff later, you know what I mean; her more spiritual things." I knew how sensitive she was about her mother's beliefs. "We'll come back tomorrow, eh?"

Chapter Thirty-three

The following day Theo arrived at Tanglewood. "I've come for a social." He grinned. "How is everyone?"

Rosie sighed. "Okay, I suppose. It's been hard."

She hugged her father and then Theo gave me a 'Dutch hug' kissing me three times on alternate cheeks. I miscalculated by pulling away too soon. "Hello, Jess, how are you, my dear?"

"I'm fine, thanks."

I made coffee and we sat there, all three of us, with not much to say to each other.

"Tell us about your work in Apeldoorn," I said. "Is that how you say it?"

Theo grinned. "I'll teach you some Dutch whilst I am here. Okay, you really want to know about my work?"

He picked up his cup of coffee and took a sip. "Next time I'll bring you some Douwe Egberts coffee, it's better than your instant." He laughed. "Okay, so you want to know what I do? Some weeks I have exhibitions and auctions to organise, I meet with clients, often going to some very prestigious homes. You'll be surprised at what people have in their zolders er…lofts, I mean. I enjoy my work, but I need a change. I've had my time. Helping you guys has been great and despite our sad loss, I want us to look forward to happier times."

"I wish I could snap out of this gloom and doom, it's been far too traumatic," said Rosie.

Moments later, I caught Rosie's eye. It seemed she knew what I was thinking.

"Dad…can I ask you something?"

"Of course." Theo smiled.

"Yesterday, Jess and I were clearing out Mum's room…"

"Oh, well done; it can't have been an easy task."

I nodded. "No, it wasn't and we're still not finished." I turned down one corner of my mouth.

"We found some photos and letters," said Rosie.

Theo took a deep breath. "What kind of letters?" He frowned.

"Did you know anyone called Gerald who was in the RAF?"

Theo tightened his expression, then turned his head away. "Mm…sort of."

I had the feeling he was holding back.

"Well, I think he and Mum were, you know…an item," said Rosie.

"As far as I know, he was killed toward the end of the war."

"Oh, so you knew about that then? Did you know that Mum was in the Women's Land Army—I didn't, she never told me about it. It seems much of her past she never mentioned. She was always very elusive and secretive."

"Well, I suspected there was something about your mum none of us knew about. Can you show me those pictures and letters, Rosie, would you mind? It may help to tie up a few loose ends for me, too. I've often wondered about Gerald and his connection with Connie. I think he broke her heart. I didn't know much as she never spoke about him."

Rosie dashed up the stairs to collect the box we had found. She came down again to sit on the stool and placed it on the worktop.

Theo opened it. "Do you mind if I look at this stuff on my own in the lounge?"

He made his way toward the sofa where it was more comfortable and I placed his coffee cup on the table beside him. He pulled out his spectacle case and pushed the specs on to his nose.

"I hope we aren't opening Pandora's box here, Dad?"

"We may be, Rosie. I have been searching for answers for a very long time."

I looked at Rosie—she took my hint and we both went back to the kitchen to drink our coffee.

"I'd be interested to hear what he says," she whispered deflecting her voice with the back of her hand.

After about fifteen minutes I peeked into the lounge. "All right, Theo?"

"Yes, yes, I'm…" He looked at me over the top of his specs and seemed in his own world of past events, so I left him on his own a bit longer.

"What's he doing?" Rosie whispered.

"Still looking."

I heard footsteps coming up the path. It was Jonni for his mid-morning break.

"Hello, love, are you okay?" He kissed me on the cheek.

I whispered and pointed at the lounge. "Theo is here. He's looking at the photos and letters we found yesterday."

Jonni spooned the Nescafé into a cup. "Oh, that's nice. I'm pleased with Ruby now, she's not limping like she used to. All that exercise with the sheep has been good for her. As for Alvin, I'm not so sure he'll be around much longer, although you did a good job of taking him to the vet for his leg."

Rosie began to fidget. She got down from the chair and walked into the lounge. "Okay, Dad?"

"Yes, I'm fine, but I've been thinking about all this. Perhaps I'd better explain."

I passed by the lounge before I went upstairs and was collared by Theo. "Come in, my dear, you may as well listen to this, too, seeing you are part of our family now."

I smiled at Theo's kind words.

"When I met your Mum, Rosie, she was a beautiful woman, as you can see from these photos. Anyway, it seems Gerald Knudsen came from a wealthy Swedish family living in Scotland. Her mother approved of him because of the Scottish connection. His family later moved down here to Dorset; it was connected with the war. Since looking at these pictures, I think I have now put two and two together. Your mum was to be married to Gerald. When he was killed, she didn't come out of her room for months until her mother bought her a King Charles spaniel puppy which she thought may get her out of the house. After the war, I was working in London. I met her out walking in Green Park and I patted the dog."

My heart missed a beat. *Could it be? The funeral, the woman in black with the dog? No surely not.* I pushed my paranormal thoughts back to the real world as Theo continued speaking.

"As the weeks went by, I met her several times more and got to know her better. Her parents had a house in the city. She always looked sad, and one day on one of the walks, I met her mother who suggested that I ask her on a date to bring her out of herself. We went to dances and I thought she was enjoying her time with me. I later asked her to marry me." Theo sighed a very heavy sigh. "At first, she refused, then a few days later, after she had spoken with her mother, something changed. She agreed to get married. I asked her why she had refused me and she told me she needed time to think about it. Looking back now, if you love someone, you don't hesitate to say yes, do you? I felt her mother saw pound notes in me and pushed her into marriage, but who knows?"

I took a gulp of my coffee and Theo did the same.

"…However, your grandmother seemed to approve and all went well. Until we…you know, went on our honeymoon. Connie went all depressed on me and refused me. This went on for months after our marriage and I needed her to be a wife. I wanted her so much. We stayed together and she eventually relented, but in the times when she would let me near her, it was more like, we were 'together' because it was the right thing to do, rather than because she wanted to. It was such a reluctant relationship, I could never understand why."

Rosie looked at me and raised her eyebrows.

"After you were born, I'd had enough, but did my best to stay with her because of you. Then the time came for me to say enough was enough. I could do better in my own country and put my mind into my work. I stayed at Tanglewood as long I could but she made it impossible for me and I was very unhappy. She must have loved Gerald so much that she never got over it. It was the rejection, you see. I found it hard to live with her anymore."

I wondered if Richard Millington knew about Connie's past and the reason she didn't really love Theo. He must have remembered all this, it was around that time they all met and Gus Hannings married his wife Mary. I remember Theo had mentioned the 'old days' when we had our picnic.

Theo turned to Rosie and held both her hands. "Rosie love, I didn't abandon you, honestly I didn't. Now I've seen these photos, I see a different Connie." He pulled out one of the pictures of Gerald and Connie together. "Look how happy she is, look at that smile. She never smiled like that for me. I am so angry; I could cry."

"Oh, Dad, that's awful," Rosie sympathised.

Theo bowed his head for a moment. "I wrote to you lots of times, but you never replied and now we know why. After a while, I heard your mother had started to follow witchcraft and got involved with Richard Millington. I felt alarm bells at this point, because Richard had just been released from prison, at least, that's what I heard. We divorced and it wasn't until all this trouble stirred up that I found out through Hans what was going on; I had to do something for you."

"How come you knew Hans?" I asked.

"Well, I met him some years ago, when he was on the street. We got chatting and he said he was looking for somewhere to put his head down and have a bath. I learned later he was one hell of an angry young man. He told me he had left Austria to get away from his father, same as Ewan, I suppose. However, he then told me he had killed him."

"Oh my God!" Rosie and I chorused together.

"That was my reaction, too at the time. Naturally, I was shocked and thought I may be harbouring a murderer. He was staying with me. At that time, he must have been about twenty-three years old. That night he broke down in tears and told me the truth. His drunken father had tried to kill him with a knife and, in self-defence, Hans had hit him with a chair and his father never regained consciousness. Hans was arrested. It was only after a couple of years, at the trial, it was concluded Hans was innocent and free…I was the only person in the world he had at that time. I had taken care of him and discovered there is another side to Hans; believe it or not, he's very caring, all this anger is the result of a dreadful trauma."

"Well, I hate to say this, but he was abusive and threatening to me from the first day I came here. I find that very hard to believe, Theo. I'm shocked." I glanced at Rosie who seemed bewildered. "What was it with Connie that she always felt she had to rescue abused people?" I asked.

"I'll explain," said Theo. "You see, where Hans is concerned, I discovered when he came to me he had this mental breakdown. I saw him through it."

It was at that moment that Jonni's brush with law came to mind. It seemed Hans had his share of problems too.

"It was the abuse he had suffered and I suggested he find his way in the UK. I sent him to Tanglewood with the promise he would never tell Connie it was my idea. I knew she would care for him. I bought him the BMW bike for his journey; I could afford it and he needed someone to believe in him again. It would be a chance for him to recuperate. He is a good chap, really, and I couldn't blame him. He seemed to calm down when he came back to Apeldoorn and we had a long talk. I suppose it was because I was living alone in a big house and had no one else except my own company. I helped Hans build his confidence and in turn I was able to keep in the background with Connie, but it seems when he got to Tanglewood all his bitterness came back with a vengeance. He could see what she was doing to herself and it made him angry."

Rosie and I looked at each other in dismay.

"We always thought Mum bought him the bike; no wonder he kept quiet about it. I kept asking her, but she always told me it was none of my business. Maybe she didn't know either?"

"When I heard about the fire and the verdict, I felt it best not to tell Hans. He'd had enough tragedy in his life and now he's met Helga, I hear things are changing. He sent me a postcard from Italy a few weeks ago."

"So, what you are saying, is that Mum never got over Gerald Nudden…whatever his name?"

"Yes, they pronounce it Ker-nud-sen, that's right and the worst thing is, she ruined my life. I could have been married to someone who loved me. Even now when I think about it, I feel angry and, today, seeing these photos has caused my heart to bleed again." Theo sighed heavily.

"Oh, Dad, I'm so glad you told me all this. It's so tragic." Rosie moved to sit next to her father on the sofa. She hugged him. "I'm glad Gerald thingy wasn't my Dad, I love *you*."

"She's right, she does and we all do too; and we hope your new life will start soon, Theo."

Theo put the box of photos on the coffee table and looked at Rosie. "You know why your mum took in all these people with problems, don't you?"

"Well, she just did," Rosie replied.

"No, it was more than that; she felt she should give a home to people who had been lonely like her. She felt she understood what it was like. She wanted them to be happy and thought that Tanglewood could help them find happiness again. It was that simple."

I pouted a lip and caught Rosie's sad expression.

"New start now, eh?" Theo smiled.

Rosie nodded. "New start, Dad," she echoed with her infectious smile.

*

Later in the day I relayed all of this to Jonni who seemed equally shocked at Hans' life.

"And to think I had it bad...Hans must have suffered mentally *and* physically. My God, it hardly bears thinking about."

I hoped all the tragedies of Tanglewood had now come to an end.

I phoned Mum and Anna and this time I told them the whole story.

We chatted about our plans with Theo and I hoped once we got the place spruced up she would soon come down to Tanglewood.

Chapter Thirty-four

December 1976

"Well I think my dad's been great." Rosie smiled. "He's phoning us tonight. By the way, they've finished cleaning up the mess down at the stable site. Nothing left. It looks odd, there's an empty space. We aren't going to put the new stables in the same place, because Mum died there. I think it's best we re-site them on the other side of the house. I like to be close to the horses at night in case of problems. The old cow barn has proved useful in the last few weeks now that winter is upon us."

"Yes. Good idea. I saw the JCB leaving this morning."

The evenings had drawn in and Ewan brought logs into the house to stack in the open hearth. It all felt very cosy with the Christmas decorations and a tree. Ewan and Rosie were curled up together on the sofa like two cats and Jonni stretched out watching the TV. I was doing the cross-stitch I hadn't picked up in months.

With the warmth of the fire, the perfume of pine crackling in the hearth, we all felt the ambience of winter nights. I smiled at Rosie. I'm sure she knew what I was thinking. We had finally achieved our goals. She remarked how sad it was that her mum didn't see us all like this.

Connie had collected a lot of clutter. The bottles and potions, Rosie destroyed, and I noted the aggressive way she chucked them in the refuse sacks. She found a witch's wand and destroyed that, too. I felt we should have kept it in Connie's memory, but any talk of witchcraft, good or evil, would have to be put behind us.

I honestly couldn't see it did any harm, and it wasn't as if her items were a threat, but I could tell Rosie's anger remained. Over the days we had spent time cleaning and making life pleasant again. We found all kinds of oddments; the book of spells made by Connie, and many different kinds of herbal remedies. Rosie insisted that everything must be thrown out. I rescued the book in Connie's memory. The drawings inside were a treasure, perhaps they held clues as to who she really was. Maybe I could learn something from it. Rosie didn't seem to mind when I told her. I felt I was meant to have it and I couldn't explain why.

Ruby rested beside me with her head on my knee.

"I've asked Dad if we can make some changes to the kitchen and he told me that as soon as the contracts are signed, we are going to go ahead and improve the farmhouse. We may have to get planning permission but I am sure it will be okay, after all we are only replacing what we lost."

At this point, I realised that Rosie, Ewan, Jonni and I, were about to become 'Team Tanglewood' and not 'The Cavalry' anymore.

Christmas was finally the season to be merry, and soon we were celebrating New Year. Theo brought us bottles of Gluhwein from Holland and he invited Mum to come and stay for the whole of the festive season. Anna couldn't make it, she and Neil had decided to spend Christmas abroad. I welcomed Mum being with us and after the celebrations were over, she seemed a much happier person than I'd seen her in a while. Theo made sure she had a family atmosphere around her.

At the end of the holiday period, I escorted her to the station. She had been thinking she should move down here with me. She loved the area and a few days before, we had taken a drive to the coast.

"I feel bad about not coming up north, since summer," I told her.

"Well, we did miss you a lot, but I understood when I heard about Connie and the problems you all had. Why you got involved so much astounded me, Jess, but now I've met everyone I think I understand why."

"What do you think of Theo and Jonni?" I dared to ask her.

"They're both lovely, and Theo is such a gentleman."

"I know, isn't he?"

"He's invited me back soon," she said. "Jonni is good for you, too."

I kissed her on the cheek. "Let me know if you decide to put the house up for sale," I said. She stepped onto the train, we waved, and she was gone. I couldn't help but smile, perhaps we had both found happiness again.

Jonni and Ewan had fallen asleep by the fire at the end of a hard day. The snow came down in flurries and as they sat in front of the television the BBC news blurted out its signature tune. I wasn't listening—but suddenly I was.

...has been found...It is thought that after all these years, the pressure of living a lie turned on him, due to health problems. Lord Hannings' home was Avoca House on the Devon border, recently raided by police due to the illicit drug and cult activities of his brother-in-law, Richard Millington. Millington was recently imprisoned after a trial in Dorchester Crown Court. In 1966 Lady Hannings was discovered in the lake at Tanglewood Farm near Axminster. Her husband disappeared and was never found, until this week, when local people found a body, now identified as that of Lord Augustus Hannings, near the small town of Maroa in Venezuela. It is believed the cause of death was a diabetic coma, connected to alcoholism. He never regained consciousness.

"Jonni, Ewan wake up. They've found Gus Hannings. Shhh."

Rosie put down her glass of wine and suddenly we were all talking at once.

"Oh—my—flippin'—God," she exclaimed and stood to peer closer at the TV. "Shut up, everyone, and listen!"

We sat, glued to the TV screen. I prayed that we weren't about to get involved in yet another pickle with the Dijkman family.

"Rosie, are you all right?"

"I don't know." She sighed. "I don't think I can take much more of this."

"Come on, it'll be okay. Speak to your Dad, he'll know what to do," said Ewan.

Rosie turned off the TV and waited for us all to speak again but we had nothing much to say. We hoped it was all over now.

"Well, what *do* we do?"

"We do nothing." Jonni remarked. "I mean, you'll hear more about it in due course. You are the closest relative, I guess."

"It's all a bit of shock," she said.

"Jonni's right," said Ewan. "Don't worry about it."

The phone rang. She rushed to answer it as though she knew who was phoning her. "Hello, Dad, you've heard the news just now?" Rosie asked. "No, of course you haven't, silly me. They've found Gus Hannings. It's been on the telly." She began to relate what she'd heard.

"Can't believe it, can you?" Rosie listened, nodded, and kept on listening for some time.

"Yes, South America. He was there all the time. Obviously in hiding. Called himself Marcus Dawson. I'm sure now that he must have done something terrible to his wife, otherwise he would have come back, don't you think? Of course…yes it makes sense. Now I remember. He had a friend over there who owned property, someone who he owed his life to during the war. I heard Gus was a brave man, fighting in the desert in Africa. He had a medal for saving lives and almost lost his own life. That's what Mum told me."

She continued to listen to Theo for a while longer. "Okay Dad, I'll go now, see you soon, yes I'm fine thanks. Love you, bye."

I turned to Jonni and Ewan. "I wonder, you know, if he went

off the rails. My dad was a soldier and he told me how hard it was coming home after the war. No one to talk to, only Mum, but he never talked about the war to me or anyone else," I said.

"Could be," said Rosie, and Jonni agreed.

They chatted with excitement and then Rosie seemed to have an afterthought.

"Let's hope we don't get a queue of bloody press on our doorstep again." She turned to me. "They did the last time, when they found Mary Hannings in the lake. I couldn't go out riding without someone sticking a bloody microphone in my face."

Jonni puffed out his cheeks and looked at me in sheer exasperation. "Yeah, I also got stopped by the press after Connie died."

We sat together again in amazement at how we had all had gone through tragedy…and now this.

Ewan turned to me. "We've got Jess now, she'll chase them away." He teased.

I laughed at Ewan's remark.

"Let's hope it's all over now and we can get on with our lives," said Rosie.

"Hear, hear," I said.

I nudged Jonni. "Come on, love, there's a cosy bed upstairs and not down here on the sofa. You have to be up for work in the morning. You must delegate more with Fergal, work a shift system. Theo agrees with me, it's time we got him working for real," I said.

"Yes, boss." Jonni grinned. "As Rosie said, 'Let's just get on with it.' I've mentioned to Theo about selling organic stuff. He thinks it's great idea, and he wants me to increase the herd. He's promised to talk it over with me." Jonni smiled at me. I could tell, at last, his enthusiasm had returned. "What do you think if we make ice cream?" he said.

Jonni and I now shared the upper part of the house in three rooms. I used his old bedroom as an office and Rosie and Ewan now slept in her mother's room. She and Ewan had a new bed and were living in more comfort than they'd ever done in their young lives. Theo provided the funds to decorate and hire a local contractor. Everything that had once belonged to Connie was now gone, although Rosie had kept a few personal things. I suggested she keep the photo albums and the letters from Gerald; it was a family secret to relate for future generations. All she wanted now was to save enough money and with the insurance she could build new stables and have a real state-of-the-art riding centre. Theo had promised he would look into that for her. Val had gone to university and sold Briony; it broke her heart, but she said it was for the best. The riding school didn't exist for a while and the horses were only ridden by Rosie and me. We spent time riding out whenever we could and discovered it gave both of us time to reflect.

The following day I wrote to Verity Cresswell and updated her on the situation explaining it was unlikely I would return to Middlesbrough and thanked her for changing my life. I looked back at my crazy decision to come to Tanglewood; what had I been thinking? I then realised that if it hadn't been for Verity, life would have been very different. I wouldn't have met Jonni and would still be wandering around looking for love. I wrote: *I am very grateful for all your support. You changed my life more than you will ever know. Best wishes, Jess Stamp.*

Chapter Thirty-five

Early Spring 1980

Life at Tanglewood had seen many changes since Connie's death. Rosie and Ewan married and Rosie gave birth to a son; they named him Simon Theodore Hey. They spent a holiday in the Netherlands at Theo's mansion, before he sold it for five million guilders. He had built an extension to Tanglewood for his own private apartment which Rosie nicknamed the 'Grandad pad'.

Jonni and I still hadn't tied the knot but all that was about to change as we had finally got engaged. We hadn't put off the marriage, we were busy with the farm and Jonni's coursework. Theo gave us a fantastic party for which we were most grateful.

Our love for each other never waned. Jonni got his degree in agriculture and I continued to manage the accounts. It seemed, at last, he'd fulfilled his dream of staying at Tanglewood. The house came alive with the sounds of the country and warm summer days.

Richard Millington, charged with being in possession of drugs and exercising illicit sexual activities, was still in prison. "I hope he hates his time in jail and gets so depressed he kills himself"— Rosie's quote, not mine. In the weeks and months that followed, everything seemed to be on track. A year before she died, Connie had made a will, leaving everything to Rosie. Unfortunately, all she had left in reality was a large debt and lots of hate mail. But I did wonder if that will had been made knowing, through her 'powers', she was going to die. I supposed I would always wonder at her prediction. I still thought about the woman I saw with the dog at the cemetery—perhaps a story for my own family one day.

"Isn't it wonderful; Dad is incredible. We've got sixty cows now; in fact we are due some more soon," said Rosie. "I love the new milking parlour."

"Yes, Jonni is thrilled."

I smiled at Rosie's happiness and knew how much Jonni appreciated the investment.

"Yes, it's amazing." Rosie remarked. "Ewan makes a good manager, he's doing a fantastic job."

"I see Fergal has changed a lot, too. Theo has really knocked him into shape. I can hardly believe how much our lives have improved. I never thought we'd make it, did you? I wish you could have seen Jonni's face when they finished installing the tanks and vats for making the cheese. He was like a cow with two tails," I joked and apologised for the dreadful pun.

Rosie chuckled at my comment.

With Hannings gone and Millington in jail, everything had quietened down. It had been intrusive with all the press hanging around at the bottom of the drive. The number of times Jonni had put off going down the drive to face a barrage of questions. He had tried so many times to avoid driving down there, and on one occasion stuck his head out of the window and told a woman journalist to 'sod off'. I had to smile, as it wasn't like Jonni to be so aggressive. I think after a while the press realised they weren't going to obtain more information and after a couple of weeks, the interest died away.

We managed the farm between the six of us with Theo at the helm. I organised Sandy to sell eggs and butter on the farmers' market stall and she also babysat for Rosie. We now had pigs and prided ourselves on the quality of our bacon. My role was to answer the phone, organise the marketing and ensure the accounts were up to date. I popped in occasionally to see Tina and Mark at the garage. Mum and my sister had been to visit and they loved what Theo had done to the house. We kept our promise to go north and visit Mum and spent two weeks exploring the North Yorkshire Moors. The farm looked wonderful with the flowers, the newly acquired antique furniture, and brand-new carpets throughout. We even had a new bathroom fitted and I hired someone to come and do the housework for us. We were living the dream. Alvin had been put to sleep the previous year and the feral cat simply disappeared after Connie died. We had stepped into a routine in the real world again, but I still had a mission to complete and I wasn't going to stand by and forget about it.

"Hello, Jess—how's it going?" Theo poked his head around the kitchen door.

"Oh, hi, Theo."

"I have to see Rosie, it's urgent."

"Ah, she's feeding Simon at the moment—I'll call her."

Theo looked anxious, or so I thought; perhaps he was tired.

"Hang on…" I called up the stairs, "Rosie, your dad's here."

I could hear her familiar footsteps cross the landing.

"Hi, Dad. What's up?" Rosie was beginning to sound more like me every day.

I knew I had become the sister she never had, as well as her friend.

"We have an appointment at the solicitor's office in an hour. There is something very important he wants to tell you. Don't worry, it's good news, I believe. That's all I'm saying for now."

"Aw, Dad, now what have you done?"

"This time it has nothing to do with me." Theo laughed.

"I'll baby-sit for you, Rosie. Go on, off you pop."

"Ewan, are you coming with me, love?"

"Okay, I live here, too," he said with a smile and rolled his eyes.

Rosie trotted off with Ewan and Theo to the appointment. I say 'trotted' because she still wore those clogs which reminded me of the sounds from the old stable yard and the stone kitchen floor.

"See you. Bye." I held Simon in my arms thinking it would

be lovely to have a child of my own. He cried when she left, but I switched on the TV to watch *Playschool*.

After playing with Simon for two hours, there was no word from Rosie, Ewan and Theo. I had put Simon down to sleep when Jonni poked his head around the door. "Hi, Jess. Where's Rosie?"

"Well, it's a bit strange, they all went off with Theo into town, and haven't come back yet."

"Really? I wonder where they went? Good heavens, are we alone together?" he joked.

"They went to the solicitor's office—and don't ask why, because Theo was in a hurry and I didn't ask. You know what he's like, always springing surprises on us all. He promised to have some good news for us when they got back."

"Bit odd, don't you think?"

I laughed. "Well nothing's normal around here, you should know that by now. Theo seemed happy enough. To be honest with you I'm dying to know what it's about—nosey, aren't I?"

"Yes, you are nosey. Always have been." He laughed. "I've been helping with the new pigs. The piglets are great; I'll hate it when we have to send them to market."

"Who would have thought it, eh? Us with *pigs*. Well, that's farming for you, I suppose. With all the problems we've had and Theo coming in to help us like this, the changes have been incredible—goes to show what a bit of extra money can do, eh?"

Jonni nodded. "Yes, sure and it's a heck of an investment, but Theo is seriously wealthy and has no one but us to spend it on. At least we are making profits now."

"I was thinking, you know…"

"Careful, you might explode." Jonni laughed.

"No listen…I'm glad in a way that Hans changed his ways, but Hans has never contacted us or anyone, you know, since he left. I don't even know if he knows about Connie. I suppose it's best if he doesn't know."

Jonni smiled. "I think maybe Theo would have told us if he'd seen Hans. He'd really had enough of his life here. Connie was patient with him and he leaned on her because of his past life, but I hope he found happiness."

I heard Theo's car coming up the drive. The old holes in the track were now pebbled and a new beech hedge lined the driveway. We had a gardener. I looked out of the window and saw Rosie waving and smiling.

She rushed into the hallway with Ewan ushering her forward. "Family meeting—family meeting everyone—in the lounge, *now*. Where's Jonni? Jess, you as well."

I looked at Theo with a 'yeah?' look on my face and Rosie strode around the house with an air of 'I'm in charge today'.

"We have some incredibly good news," Theo said.

"Simon's asleep, he's a really good baby," I told Rosie.

"Oh good. I'll go up to him when he wakes."

Rosie had been keen to organise a gymkhana on the parkland next year and I wondered if that was what we were about to discuss; why did they need a solicitor? I had never seen her so excited.

"Sit down everyone. Hurry up, Jonni, you sit there."

Theo chimed in. "What we are about to tell you is amazing—mind blowing! I received a call this morning, asking us to drop in at the solicitor's office."

"Well…" said Rosie bursting with excitement and taking over the story. "We were summoned to discuss Avoca House; the heirs have been informed and it's already got an interested buyer."

"Avoca House?" queried Jonni.

"Hannings had no family. They couldn't have kids," said Theo looking at Rosie. "No heir to his family fortune."

"Go on, Dad, you tell the story; I'm still shaking."

Theo smiled. "It seems that when the house was sold, there were only two beneficiaries. One is Rosie's cousin in Scotland and the other is Rosie. She's in line to inherit and they wanted to be sure both heirs were consulted first before they could proceed. Richard Millington thought the house would be his one day, but what he didn't know was that Gus Hannings had already made his will before he disappeared. When Hannings wrote a will he put Rosie in it. What we didn't expect is that Rosie would be in line to inherit but thinking about it now, it makes sense. He was always very fond of her. Then this dreadful incident with losing Mary. He must have gone off the rails."

We all sat looking at each other. I swear the clock stopped ticking and my heart might have jumped out at any moment.

"It's true," Rosie exclaimed with bewilderment. "I'm going to be super rich."

I felt the anxiety rise within me when she said those words. Connie was once rich and squandered the lot. I hoped that Rosie had learned her lesson and able to handle her inheritance. Then I realised she had Theo beside her now. He would guide her as he had done since Connie died. Everything would be fine.

"Oh, Rosie, that's…I'm lost for words! …amazing, *totally* and *utterly* amazing," I said.

Ewan, in his own world, was scratching his head, probably wondering what to make of it all.

"Yes, Ewan and I, we'll never have to want for much ever again and…"

Theo interrupted. "Now you can have your state-of-the-art riding centre. We can do this together, my dear, and design it like the stables I had in Holland. When you came over to visit, I know how impressed you were with the facilities. You can now have a pool for the horses to swim at Tanglewood and all the things you dreamed of."

"Oh, Dad, it's like winning the football pools a thousand times over. Yes, you're right, Gus Hannings was good to me when I was a kid; he not only taught me how to ride but he used to give me such lovely birthday parties at Avoca House when I was small. It's very sad that everything went belly up for him. I hope what happened to his wife was an accident he couldn't face; perhaps we will never know the truth."

Jonni stood and embraced Ewan standing next to him. "Congrats mate and...Rosie, come here let me give you a hug."

Theo went to the fridge and returned with a bottle of champagne. He filled five fluted glasses and we raised a toast.

"To all of us," said Rosie.

"Well, this is to you, Rosie," I said. "Congratulations. My dad always used to say 'good things come to those who wait'."

Rosie, cheeks now red from champagne and excitement, almost forgot she had Simon upstairs until she heard a small cry and her mothering instinct clicked in; she rushed to fetch her son.

Chapter Thirty-six

When I recalled the day I first drove to Tanglewood I had no plans and expected to carry on in the way I had always done; go to work, enjoy socialising and earn money to save for travelling. A few weeks from now I would be married and become Mrs Holbrook. We still had Dad's car, we knew it was overdue for the scrap heap, but Jonni had been in conversation with Theo, who had paid for it to be restored to use on our wedding day. That man was so amazing.

"Jess, I'd like to ask you something," said Theo. "May I support you on the day? I know your father is missing from this. I'm sad for you, can I help?"

"Oh, Theo you are so kind. What a lovely idea. The answer is yes. I was going to suggest it anyway I'm glad you got there first."

"I hope your mother will approve, she is such a lovely lady. When I see her we will take her for dinner."

I paused for thought. "I also want to talk to you about Jonni's parents. You know he lost contact with them? Well I have this idea I want to discuss with you."

I spent time chatting about if it would be possible get in touch with his mum and stepfather. Every time I had tried to seek them out, I came to a dead end. There was nothing in Jonni's address book, except a telephone number. I know I shouldn't have looked, but I did. I found a number in Scotland, written in scrubby pencil, with the letters M & D. I tried phoning but the line was dead. I wanted our day to be special and not only a union of a man and a woman who were crazy about each other, but also a reunion for Jonni and closure.

I was at an impasse. I didn't want to ask Jonni; I knew it might upset him. All I knew was his parents' last-known location on the Island of Mull. I feared I had left it too late but needed to find out more, so I discussed the matter with Theo. Would Jonni be angry with me for trying to find his family?

"Leave it with me, Jess, I'll see what I can do. I have a few friends up that way through the art world and maybe…I'll give them a ring tonight for you."

"Oh Theo, everything is easy for you. I still have a lot to learn. Sometimes it seems you are my second dad, you have been so good to us."

Theo patted the top of my head. "You kids are great, I am proud of what we've all achieved. We will talk tonight."

We had planned a wedding at the Register Office in Axminster, with a reception at Tanglewood in a marquee. I wanted it all to be so perfect. If only I could find Jonni's parents.

Almost a week later, Theo came to me with a piece of paper. "Here you are, my dear girl, I think this is what you are looking for. There are two numbers. The top phone number on the list, is the sister of Peter Holbrook, the adopted father of Jonni, so try phoning that first."

"Oh, Theo, you are wonderful—no, not wonderful—amazing! Thank you."

I couldn't wait to make the call, but had to wait until Jonni had gone to milk the cows.

Nervously, I called the number and a woman with a strong highlands accent, answered, "Fiona McLeish."

"Oh hello, I hope I have the right phone number. My name is Jess Stamp. I am looking for the parents of Jonni Holbrook and I got your number through a friend."

There was a brief silence. "Ah well, we are not his parents, you know, but Peter is my brother."

I listened intently to her accent. "Oh, yes of course," I replied.

"Can you tell me what it is you wanted to know?"

"Well, I'm Jonni's fiancée and I was rather hoping I could find his parents to explain a few things. I need to clarify how close they are to Jonni and if they would..."

"It's been difficult for them, as Jonni doesn't contact them anymore."

"Yes, I know. I was rather hoping I could bring about a reconciliation. Jonni is very sensitive about issues from the past and is also very upset. He has been through quite a traumatic time and has no idea I am phoning you. We are planning on getting married very soon and I would like to meet his mum and dad."

"Well that's understandable, Jess. Is there any chance you can leave me your phone number and I will get them to call you?"

"Oh, would you? That would be wonderful if you could. I would like to invite them to the wedding. I know Jonni would like to see them, but at one point, he'd lost all sense of who he is. I know he is sorry for losing contact, but he did try and got nowhere. It was my idea that perhaps he should try again. I keep telling him that his mother will be concerned."

"Yes, I agree; I mean, he is our adopted nephew and we miss him, too."

"So where do his parents live? I am in the south of England."

Fiona sneezed. "Oh dear, excuse me I must be coming down with hay fever. The wee medges are driving us mad this year, too. I have to keep wearing a medge hood to hang out the washing." She sneezed again.

I had to assume she referred to a midge hood and I remember the last visit to Scotland with my dad and how the local shop sold t-shirts bearing comic pictures of flying midges with teeth. The little blighters were bad that year, too.

"Er...Well, they moved about four years ago and are now living in France. It was probably the darned medges that drove them away." She laughed as she said it. "We tried to find Jonni and he'd disappeared after..." She stopped in mid-sentence and I realised she didn't wish to say any more in case she had said too much.

"Don't worry, Fiona. I know everything. He told me about the accusations from the police and it's hurt him badly. I think the fact he left university had a very negative effect on his life. He felt he let his parents down. He's got his degree this year in agriculture. I have been doing my best to convince him that he should contact them. Jonni wrote to them when he thought they were in Scotland and he tells me the letter was returned, which hurt him even more. He now thinks they don't want anything to do with him. I now understand why. I couldn't believe it was true and this is why I made further enquiries. Parents don't move house without telling their son, so I could only think there had been some misunderstanding."

"Well look, Jess…they tried to find Jonni, but when Madge fell ill, it was na easy. They had to move, she's been quite depressed in recent years. I think it's best I try to contact them for you and explain everything. Where are you getting married?"

"Axminster Register Office 30 August at 11am. You must come as well. I do hope you can find…is it…Madge and Peter?"

"Aye that's right and of course it's a very long way for me to come and not so easy to get there. We would have to fly from Glasgow I think. It's a long journey. I live on a very remote part of Mull, but I will phone them tomorrow for you."

"Please give them my best wishes and I hope we shall come to an arrangement about meeting up very soon."

"I have to tell you that Madge's illness was the result of an accident; she fell out of a tree picking apples in the garden and broke her leg quite severely. She almost had to have it amputated and then her best friend died and everything seemed to go wrong. This year she has been able to do without her crutches and is doing really well."

"Oh, how awful. I'm glad she is improving."

"I know; it's been a dreadful time for them both, but give me your details, Jess."

"Here is my phone number." I dictated the Axminster number

and asked her to speak only to me and no one else. "I am so happy I found you, Fiona. It's been lovely talking to you and maybe we could surprise Jonni very soon."

"I am sure my brother will understand; he is a lovely man. Madge will be in tears when I tell her. You sound such a kind young lady."

"Thank you, Fiona, that's really sweet of you."

I proceeded to tell her about the farm and that the owner had died and how Jonni and I had met there. I told her he was enjoying his job and everything was turning out for the better with a secure future. I mentioned Theo and, through him, I had found Fiona's telephone number.

"Well it all sounds most interesting. I will call you as soon as I hear anything."

"That's wonderful. Thanks so much, it means a lot to me; there isn't a lot of time now."

We said our goodbyes and after replacing the receiver, I began to worry in case Jonni didn't see things the way I had planned. By not telling him, would it be deceitful? I hoped he would forgive me and understand my well-meaning intentions. I assured myself it would be all right and Theo seemed to support the idea too.

I hadn't heard anything from Madge and Peter Holbrook and time was catching up with only six weeks to go before the wedding. I was in two minds whether or not I should phone Fiona. That same evening, I had a phone call.

"Hello, Jess, it's Fiona McLeish. I wanted to let you know that I haven't heard from Madge and Peter. I've kept on trying the number, and then I got through to discover they are away on an extended holiday. They always go to the same camp site, so let's hope I find them. I'll call you tomorrow."

"Oh, Fiona that's so kind of you. I was beginning to lose confidence. I hope I've done the right thing and you can make it, too."

"Believe me, Jess, we are thrilled about it and you might meet us sooner than you think. Andrew and I have discussed it and if Madge and Peter are agreeable, we will do our very best to come to the wedding."

I sniffed the tears back into my throat. "You don't know how much this means to me," I said. "I know Jonni will be shocked, but it's for his happiness and his closure more than anything."

"Keep your chin up and let's hope I can persuade Madge and Peter to come to England for the wedding."

Chapter Thirty-seven

On the day of our wedding, Theo escorted me in the Rolls Royce and I gave him a kiss on the cheek.

"Thanks, none of this could have happened without you," I said.

"Jess, you and Jonni are wonderful together. Success my dear, success." Theo congratulated us.

I met Mum and Anna at the entrance to the Register Office and Rosie stood with Anna in her long dress.

"Anna, Rosie, you both look lovely," I said.

"And you, too, Sis."

Anna hugged me. Mum straightened my wedding gown and ensured my hair wasn't out of place.

"I'm so proud of you, my lovely girls," said Mum. "You look great, Rosie."

I wore a fabulous oyster-coloured slim-line gown, with a row of cream embroidered roses down the back. My hair was tied in a swirl and my bouquet was full of fragrant autumn colour. I felt special, enchanted by everything going on around me.

I ordered four extra places for lunch and only Theo knew about Madge and Peter Holbrook's visit. I had mentioned to Jonni it was a pity he had lost touch with his parents. His answer was always the same. "They were ashamed of me, I am sure. Maybe one day things might change."

Before I entered the hallway, I caught a glimpse of four people walking together toward the entrance. When I heard Fiona's voice,

I smiled. "It really is you, Fiona? Oh my, I'm terrified this isn't going to work."

"Wow, Jess, you look fabulous. This is Madge and Peter." I shook hands and kissed Madge on both cheeks. "I'm so thrilled you came. Can we talk later, I have a man to marry?" I smiled. "I am dying to get to know you; thanks so much for coming." Madge looked windswept as she came limping through the door in her pale blue suit and large hat. Andrew stepped aside to allow Peter to go first.

Fiona laughed, "Aye of course, we'll follow you."

Across the hallway I saw Jonni waiting for me. We kissed and he turned around to face Ewan. "We're a bit early and have a few minutes before we can go in. It gives us a chance to say hello to everyone." We began to line everyone up for the ceremony.

"Hi, Ewan, you look great," I said.

Rosie held Simon's hand and stood back.

This was my moment. "Jonni, love, there's some people here I want you to meet, but don't be too long we have a wedding to get to."

It was then I quite expected Jonni to turn around and walk out of the door. Left in the lurch at the Register Office. What had I done?

Jonni searched the crowd. "Oh…Oh my…you didn't…Mum, Dad, Aunt Fiona, Uncle Andrew. How on earth did you know?"

Peter looked Jonni in the eyes. "Aye, well. That future wife of yours is an absolute miracle maker. Now go on say 'I do' to that wee girl of yours."

I smiled at the way he spoke and gave a deep sigh. "Oh no, we've got Theo to thank for all this. He is the one who makes the miracles around here."

I knew Jonni wanted to say something but underneath all the pressure of an imminent wedding, he couldn't find the words. He kissed his mother and hugged Peter. "Thank you, Mum and Dad, for coming," he said.

"Come on, son, this is your day not ours and we have loads to talk about afterwards. We didn't quite get it right, that's all. Jess seems fantastic; she and your aunt have hit it off talking on the phone together and trying to find us on the caravan site in Germany, would you believe? We had to come, we have a lot of making up to do," said Peter.

Jonni hugged his mother. "I missed you all so much," he said. "I didn't know your new address, Aunt Fiona, and my letter was returned. We lost touch. Oh, thanks so much all of you. We certainly do have a lot of talking to do. This is amazing!"

"Don't cry, Jonni," Rosie blurted out, "you'll ruin your mascara."

We all laughed and I knew Jonni wanted to say more. He looked at me with a smile.

"Honestly, Jess, whose idea was this?"

"Guess!" I replied with a grin.

The Registrar called our names. "Attention, please! Can we assemble now for the wedding of Jessica Stamp and Jonathan Holbrook. Thank you, ladies and gentlemen, follow me into the marriage room."

Jonathan? I mused. I'd never thought of him as a Jonathan.

Jonni squeezed my hand. "Let's get married and thanks for finding my parents, you little devil, you never told me." He laughed. "This is beyond my wildest dreams. What a fantastic surprise. I'm really overcome. I need a hanky, hang on." He blew his nose. "Ready? May we go to wonderful places in our lives, as your dad once said—'do wonderful things', but this time together."

Those words had always haunted me. "Good things come to those who wait." I replied, *Yes, Dad, I see you. Thanks for coming.* I gave a little wave to Mum and imagined Dad by her side. I looked away in case I cried.

When I gazed into Jonni's eyes that morning, I realised he had changed so much; he seemed more handsome than ever. He had a beard and his hair was shorter; his curls had always made him look younger. Today he seemed so mature; a father any future child would be proud of. He wore a grey suit and white tie and Ewan, as best man, wore the same. They looked a dandy pair; I felt proud of them both.

I hugged Mum and Anna before they moved forward to the marriage room to take their places. Jonni followed and I came last on Theo's arm.

Rosie and Anna stood together in their gorgeous pale blue dresses and I had never seen them looking so pretty, with flowers in their hair. Rosie wore gold slippers and thankfully had left her clogs at home, although Theo had bought her a new pair from Holland.

The Registrar read the vows and we held hands with a moment of rapid heartbeats and overwhelming happy thoughts.

"I do," I said.

"I do," responded Jonni.

We kissed and with the sound of the clapping from the guests, I glanced at Mark and his wife sitting together with Tina and her husband. We had all been through so much. Tina was expecting her second child. Perhaps, whilst she was on maternity leave, yet another 'Jessica Stamp' would come on the scene and eventually find happiness at Parson's garage.

Jonni kissed me. "Jess, my darling, you're the best thing to happen in the whole of my life. I love you so much."

"I think I'm going to enjoy being Jessica Holbrook, it sounds a bit posh."

Jonni laughed. "Come on then, Mrs Holbrook, let's go for the photos."

Our driver took us back to Tanglewood where Theo had arranged a traditional Ceilidh. Andrew McLeish was in his best highland dancing mood; he wore his kilt, and led the way, showing us the steps.

We spent time explaining to Madge how much Jonni had missed her. She seemed a kind woman and Peter danced with me because Madge's leg was still not up for tripping the light fantastic.

We chatted about their holiday in Germany and how they got the news from Fiona about the wedding and hadn't hesitated to pack up for the trip to England. They had tried to find Jonni before moving to their cottage on the Brittany coast but failed. Mull was too remote for Madge and they moved to warmer climates. They left their address with Fiona but she had a change of phone number and none of them had realised the difference it made. Fiona was lovely. She seemed so interested in what Jonni was trying to achieve with the cows; she had highland cattle and wanted to know more about what Jonni intended to do with his herd in the future. I introduced Mum to Madge and Peter and they seemed to hit it off. Mum told them about Dad and how Theo had kindly stepped in to give me away. We had the most fantastic day. Mum remarked how Dad was watching us. My life had changed and, at last, happiness prevailed.

It didn't escape my notice how Mum had enjoyed sitting next to Theo. He danced with her all evening. Mum was still attractive for mid-fifties; she'd had me and Anna early in her years. Theo, on the other hand, had been so tied up in his business he'd put all his life into his job. Despite his retirement he was still very much involved and happy in a pair of overalls and a bucket in his hand and I often found him taking a walk with an easel and paints.

Mum cried when she saw us in the car and I watched her waving until we turned the bend. It reminded me of the day I left Great Ayton to drive to Tanglewood.

I was happy for Mum, and in a way, I hoped she and Theo might become more than just good friends; somehow it seemed so right. I knew she couldn't live alone after Anna had gone and I knew she would soon move south to be nearer to me and Jonni. I couldn't see her wanting anyone else but Dad, he had been our rock. Theo had become a good friend to all of us and I felt Mum needed that too.

*

The following morning after staying the night at the airport hotel, we caught a plane to Rome. On arrival, we had a swimming pool and I couldn't wait to jump in and cool off after all the fun of the previous day.

Jonni unlocked the door of our honeymoon suite which overlooked the pool and the view of the mountains behind the city. He took me in his arms and we were so in love; those feelings, I wanted to last forever.

He kissed me and his caring never failed to make me feel like a real woman.

I undressed and came to him on a soft bed of white sheets and a flimsy cream curtain blowing in the warm breeze.

"Jess Holbrook, I love you with all my heart."

"We did it; we escaped," I whispered.

"We did, and isn't it wonderful?"

After the long honeymoon we returned to Tanglewood, sun-tanned and feeling refreshed. Theo had insisted this was his wedding gift, and the most wonderful surprise of all was that he had given us the cottage up the lane. It was going to be ours; our own house, no rent, no mortgage, just a legal document transferring the cottage to us. I could hardly believe our luck. Theo welcomed us back and I was ready to begin work once again.

We drove along the familiar track and down the well-remembered lanes. It seemed, on our return, Rosie and Ewan had missed us but I also saw how they had successfully managed on their own. Fergal had a new position in the business as Deputy Farm Manager and well...the rest is history, I suppose. Now was our chance to move on in life and be a proper married couple.

Mum had sold the house in Great Ayton and Theo had offered a room at Tanglewood whilst her new house was being built just outside of Axminster. Anna was about to go and live in Somerset with Neil. The whole family was once again within easy reach and now, at last, we had all moved south.

A couple of weeks later, we hadn't yet moved from the farm; our new home would be ready in a few more days but I wasn't feeling too bright, I had a headache. As I came through the door of our bedroom at Tanglewood I needed to lie down for a while; perhaps all this had been too much. I found a small box with a tartan lid on the bedside table. I opened it and inside was Connie's silver arcane cross. Why had we not found it when we cleared out her room? Perhaps Rosie had given it to me as a leaving gift. I placed my hand across my stomach. My feelings of sickness had returned, but this time I hoped it was all good news as I felt for the early life growing within me. A honeymoon baby? Well, why not? I smiled to myself hoping that was the reason. Time for these things was never going to be right and it didn't seem to matter.

Downstairs, I mentioned the gift to Rosie. "Thanks for the present." I was sure she knew what I meant.

"What present?" She furrowed her brow.

"It wasn't you then?" I asked. "Someone put a small gift on my bed."

"No, it wasn't me. What is it?"

"*Not* you then?" I repeated. "Hang on, I'll go look again."

I went upstairs to check. I mean, the gift may not have been for me, surely this belonged to Rosie. On the inside of the box lid, I read the words: *To Jess. Thank you. I'm never far away if you need me. Love C x*

"Huh?" A brush of cold air passed across my ear and I heard a whisper—*for you*; someone seemed to touch my shoulder. Yes, really! I almost fell off the bed as I jumped aside and sucked in a breath. Perhaps the ghosts of yesteryear were still here after all. Any moment now, I expected to find Connie's pink fluffy slippers outside our bedroom door.

The End

Acknowledgements

A book would not be a book without the help of those who have published before me. My thanks go to Helen Hart, Sarah Newman and Anna Loo at SilverWood Books for their wonderful support. A writer needs a good publisher and their help was invaluable. I am also grateful to my colleagues and members of the Exeter Chapter of the Romantic Novelists' Association and especially to Author, Sophie Duffy, who gave me the confidence to keep going. My thanks also go to friend and historian, Nicholas Mann and to my dear friend Ros, both of whom inspired me to write this book after rekindling a long-lost friendship. Above all, thanks go to my readers for their support when I wrote *Goodbye Henrietta Street*. There are plenty more books to follow.

Lightning Source UK Ltd.
Milton Keynes UK
UKHW041202060119
335045UK00001B/7/P

9 781781 327845